DEFEATING THE DEMON LORD'S A CINCH

IF YOU'VE GOT A RINGER

VOLUME

2

TSUKIKAGE

Illustration by **bob**

YEN ON

New York

Defeating
the Demon
Lord's a Cinch
(If You've Got
a Ringer), Vol. 2

TSUKIKAGE

Translation by Caleb DeMarais
Cover art by bob

This book is a work of fiction. Names, characters,
places, and incidents are the product of the
author's imagination or are used fictitiously. Any
resemblance to actual events, locales, or persons,
living or dead, is coincidental.

DARENIDEMO DEKIRU KAGE KARA TASUKERU
MAO TOBATSU
Vol. 2
© Tsukikage 2017
First published in Japan in 2017 by KADOKAWA
CORPORATION, Tokyo.
English translation rights arranged with
KADOKAWA CORPORATION, Tokyo, through
Tuttle-Mori Agency, Inc., Tokyo.

English translation © 2018 by Yen Press, LLC

Yen On
1290 Avenue of the Americas
New York, NY 10104

Visit us at yenpress.com
facebook.com/yenpress
twitter.com/yenpress
yenpress.tumblr.com
instagram.com/yenpress

First Yen On Edition: November 2018

Yen On is an imprint of Yen Press, LLC.
The Yen On name and logo are trademarks of Yen Press, LLC.

The publisher is not responsible for websites (or their content) that are not owned by the
publisher.

Library of Congress Cataloging-in-Publication Data
Names: Tsukikage, author. | Bob (Illustrator), illustrator. | Kerwin, Alex, translator. |
    DeMarais, Caleb, translator.
Title: Defeating the demon lord's a cinch (if you've got a ringer) / Tsukikage ;
    illustration by bob ; translation by Alex Kerwin ; translation by Caleb DeMarais.
Other titles: Darenidemo Dekiru Kage Kara Tasukeru Mao Tobatsu. English
Description: First Yen On edition. | New York : Yen On, 2018–
Identifiers: LCCN 2018023883 | ISBN 9781975327354 (v. 1 : pbk.) |
    ISBN 9781975327378 (v. 2 : pbk.)
Subjects: LCSH: Fantasy fiction.
Classification: LCC PL876.S853 D3713 2018 | DDC 895.63/6—dc23
LC record available at https://lccn.loc.gov/2018023883

ISBNs: 978-1-9753-2737-8 (paperback)
        978-1-9753-2738-5 (ebook)

10 9 8 7 6 5 4 3 2 1

LSC-C

Printed in the United States of America

CONTENTS

Defeating the Demon Lord's a Cinch
(If You've Got a Ringer)

Part Two

Let's Begin

Yutith's Tomb.

The Great Tomb is mammoth and lies underground in a deserted plain sprawling to the southeast of the Kingdom of Ruxe.

No one knows how or why it was built. Its internal structure remains a mystery as well. These days, the tomb is overrun with particularly troublesome undead creatures—such as the living dead—making it the perfect location for priests to level up.

The undead are not the most popular monsters to hunt.

Many need to be killed in order to gain levels, and because they use particularly irksome status ailment attacks such as poison or paralysis, even experienced warriors hate fighting them.

Truthfully, there are better places to level up, and the majority of demon hunters and mercenaries head elsewhere. However, the Holy Warrior's party is not so easily deterred.

One month has passed since the Holy Warrior Naotsugu Toudou was summoned to slay the Demon Lord. Toudou possesses divine protection from a number of gods and spirits, and as a Holy Warrior, he will not hesitate to lay down his life for the sake of justice.

*   *   *

Freely able to control one of the most powerful fire spirits is the elementalist Limis Al Friedia.

Aria Rizas, a swordmaster wielding a magical sword handed down from the Kingdom itself, is capable of battling ferocious monsters relying solely on her distinguished swordsmanship abilities.

Added to the party in the Great Forest of the Vale is the glacial-plant-turned-dragon-girl named Glacia. Through their combined transcendent levels of intelligence and bravery, the group chose to proceed directly into the dark clouds gathered before them—certainly unfathomable for the average party.

Stopping at the forest church to gather necessary items, including a map, Toudou and the others delve into the Great Tomb.

Inside, they are met with darkness and miasma, filled with vile undead eager to grab hold of even a single living soul. Despite this being their first campaign into the Great Tomb, nothing deters the party from moving forward.

Prior to being summoned just one month ago, Toudou lived a peaceful life, without a single day's battle experience. However, the Kingdom of Ruxe bestowed him with a holy sword capable of cleaving through everything on heaven and earth—one passed down through generations of Holy Warriors—and a set of holy armor able to withstand dragon flame. With these items, Toudou quickly displays a prowess reminiscent of the Holy Warriors of old.

Truth be told, even without such divine equipment, Toudou would not have hesitated for a second.

Why? Because to so boldly press onward in the face of terror is the defining characteristic of a Holy Warrior.

"The overdone sense of justice is a crime."

Prologue
The Heroes Stumble

What the hell am I being asked to do here?

Feeling despondent, I urge Toudou's party's enchanted carriage forward with abandon. Toudou, Limis, and Aria are all completely unconscious, and Glacia is shaking like a leaf, nearly in tears.

I doubt anyone would be able to recognize this pitiful bunch as the legendary Holy Warrior and his party.

It was just a few days ago that I received word that Toudou's next destination had changed from Golem Valley, my original suggestion, to Yutith's Tomb.

The reason? To recruit a high-level priest. Apparently, losing consciousness during battle with Zarpahn in the Great Forest of the Vale had done the trick, and my subsequent message relayed to the party via Helios had been...well, *permissible*. At any rate, regardless of feasibility, the importance of adding a priest to the party wasn't off the mark.

Yutith's Tomb is inhabited by a trove of different undead monsters.

The undead are notoriously troublesome foes and possess many status ailment attacks. These include poison and paralysis, and a direct attack can result in life-threatening physical ailments in addition to psychological ones such as panic. Despite this, the undead have extremely low life force and drop hardly any gold or items. Taking them on requires a priest who can restore status ailments as well as make the kinds of elaborate preparations needed for curative items.

Long story short—currently, the lack of a priest is putting Toudou

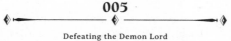

and his party between a rock and a hard place. That was the main reason why I chose Golem Valley in the first place.

But when I think about it, in the end...this isn't such a bad idea.

Dealing with status ailment attacks is a big hurdle for anyone fighting monsters. Yet status ailment resistance improves as you level up, and one experience with the ailment isn't usually an issue. Toudou is still low level, but I've shown him how to use the holy technique for status ailment recovery and passed along some curative items through the Church, so there shouldn't be any major problems.

Speaking of their low life force, despite their troublesome status ailment attacks, the undead in Yutith's Tomb aren't particularly strong, and killing enough of them will guarantee level ups. For Toudou's party, this is undeniably a rather tedious way of going about it, but their goal is the Demon Lord. A certain dose of psychological agony is necessary.

That's what I thought. Indeed, I did.

Toudou's group is still low level, but the upper levels of Yutith's Tomb contain weaker monsters than those in the Great Forest of the Vale. The party can handle them. They *should* be able to handle them, that is, as long as they put up as much fight as usual.

Who could have predicted that the Holy Warrior summoned to defeat the Demon Lord would have such a hard time with the undead?

§ § §

Located one kilometer from Yutith's Tomb is a single dilapidated village called Purif.

It's a medium-size village surrounded by a stone wall, originally built as a base for the Kingdom Survey Corps responsible for investigating the Great Tomb. However, the Kingdom disbanded the Survey Corps for a number of reasons, and the long-standing village now holds but a very sparse local population.

Outsiders seldom visit Purif, so there are very few inns. There are, however, three churches, and the barriers posted around the outer wall

"The overdone sense of justice is a crime."

are constantly rebuilt, allowing any undead that attack the village to be easily repelled.

There's only one shop selling weaponry and equipment, but it's well stocked, and anything you need for battle in Yutith's Tomb can be found within this village's walls.

We pass through the main gate and enter Purif. The sky is still bright, and villagers dot the road.

Seeing Toudou's collapsed figure in the dark tomb as a result of having taken mental damage from a wraith attack was an absolute nightmare. Of course, I did have prior knowledge that some monster hunters have a particularly hard time with undead foes.

The undead always look extremely unpleasant. As "living dead" monsters, they reek of death and decay, their bodies undulating and pulsing. Wraiths float in midair and are transparent, not to mention being unaffected by physical attacks—nobody loves fighting them. But in the end, it's just a matter of personal preference...and up to then, Toudou had sliced through foes with ease. For example, the dead tree sprites in the Great Forest of the Vale aren't exactly appealing, either, and pretty much every sort of beast-type monster—such as wolves and monkeys—gives off a noxious stench. In truth, all the monsters Toudou had encountered had been horrifying and odious, but he sliced through them just the same, spraying blood in his wake, the expression on his face remaining stoic and fearless.

So why is Toudou, whose combat skills should be more than adequate by now...why is he so terrified of the living-dead monsters? Why did he lose consciousness from the wraith's attack? The holy armor he's equipped with should greatly reduce any form of mental damage...

After delivering the miserable group of brave warriors to the church, I drag my heavy body toward the inn.

The scene of Toudou and the others being knocked unconscious flashes in and out of my mind. I must be traumatized.

The room I reserved at the inn is empty. Amelia and I always travel separately. I managed to convince her to ask the Church yet again if a female priest is available to join Toudou's party.

Good. Thank God Amelia isn't here. If she saw the look on my face right now, she'd be worried sick.

I hang my mace (which I never ended up using) on the wall. Trying to settle down, I go to pour myself some water from the pitcher…and that's when I realize.

My hands are shaking.

Ridiculous… I'm calm and collected even in the face of demons of the highest order… Why am I shaken up now?! I try to steady my hand, but it's no use.

This is unacceptable. I can't stay like this. If there's anyone who needs to regain their composure, it's me.

I head for the washroom and take a shower. I empty my mind and cool my head with the cold water.

I prepared a hefty dose of sleeping medicine for the unconscious Toudou and his party members. They'll sleep for an entire day, I'm sure. I wish this were all a dream, but it's absolutely stark reality.

All of them—well, at least Aria and Toudou—are *completely terrified* of the undead.

Pale-faced. Trembling. Teeth chattering, their wails echoing throughout the tomb. I shadowed them extremely carefully, and each of these symptoms proved the situation was worse than I thought.

The Holy Warrior is the one person who can return light to this world.

His fear of facing an undead follower of darkness would be deemed completely inexcusable.

Toudou is our only hope. In which case, that means all faith in the Holy Warrior has been unequivocally lost.

They need a plan.

It's been a month since I was forced out of the party and began assisting them from the shadows. My support mission is already facing its second trial.

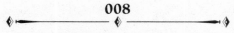

"The overdone sense of justice is a crime."

§ § §

Spica Royle's daily routine rarely changed.

Spica is an orphan. By the time she was old enough to be aware of her surroundings, she was already a part of the church in Purif.

She doesn't remember her parents' faces, but according to the head priest, they were mercenaries who dared to enter Yutith's Tomb.

Spica was born in Purif and fell ill soon after. Her parents, who continually journeyed to increase their level and prowess, left Spica behind in Purif before she could even talk and then disappeared.

The already dilapidated Purif certainly didn't have an orphanage. After being abandoned, Spica was placed with other children from similar circumstances into the custody of the church, where she was raised.

Regardless, Spica has never considered herself unfortunate. A few times, she found a fellow child abandoned by their parents crying in a corner, but Spica doesn't even remember her parents' faces and didn't understand the feeling. The other children looked down on her for not empathizing with their pain, but they lived together only by circumstance and didn't even play together anyway.

The church wasn't wealthy by any means, but it guaranteed the bare minimum for the children's upbringing: tattered used clothing and strictly austere meals. However, the church building itself was huge, a relic from when the Kingdom Survey Corps were still sent into the Great Tomb. There were plenty of rooms available, and the sisters and head priest taught the children how to read and write when they had time. Mercenaries and monster hunters visited the church regularly, so the children quickly learned how to keep their wits about them in the face of rough characters.

In order to pay for their upbringing, the children did chores and took care of miscellaneous responsibilities at the church. Spica was weak, and the jobs given to her were the simple kind an adult would finish in no time. Some of the orphans absolutely hated such tasks, but Spica didn't think anything of them.

There was no prospect of a future, but there was also little worry.

A knack for magic could qualify you as a mage, which paid very well. Befriending mercenaries who visited the village also provided a chance to learn how to fight—if you asked.

A few of her friends actually became mercenaries and left the church, but Spica didn't want to become like the faceless parents who'd left her behind. Neither did she want to become a priest, like many of her other fellow orphans.

Spica is only twelve years old—plenty of time before she has to choose. There's nothing she wants to do, but she has a vague sense that she'll spend the rest of her life in Purif.

And that is precisely why no one expected Spica Royle to get caught up in a tale like this.

Spica's fellow orphans are all lined up in the church's reception hall, which is seldom used.

While they were doing their laundry, the head priest instructed them to gather there. It is unusual enough for the children to be addressed by him directly but even more unusual for them to be asked to set aside their chores. Assuming something bad has happened, the kids all exchange anxious looks.

This is Spica's first time in the reception hall.

Two adults stand in front of the noisy, worried children. Of course, they know their head priest, the most distinguished in Purif, but they have never seen the other person, a woman.

It is a young sister with blue hair and eyes and a cold demeanor. Standing side by side, the pair looks like a father and daughter, but the head priest, who is a god in the children's eyes, speaks to the sister nervously.

The sister's lips move. She asks a question with the same emotionless stare.

"Is this everyone, then?"

"Yes… This is all of them. But why did you want the children to assemble here?"

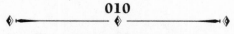

"The overdone sense of justice is a crime."

"By order from God. It's a top-secret mission, and I can't divulge the details."

An order from God. Spica's eyes go round as saucers upon hearing this rare turn of phrase.

The sister gives each child a serious look—a cold stare, as if appraising the quality of a product.

"We have no need for boys."

"What?!"

"I'm afraid I neglected to tell you. We have no need for boys."

The head priest is absolutely floored by this revelation, but at the sister's behest, he ushers all the boys out of the room.

The sister continues her questioning.

"Do any of the children have mental or physical abnormalities?"

"N-no... I believe they are all healthy."

"Is that so?"

The sister relaxes her shoulders slightly and peers into the eyes of each orphaned young girl left in the room. The oldest is fifteen, while the youngest is not yet ten. Each of them stiffens anxiously when she looks at them with her frigid, expressionless eyes.

It is Spica's turn. The sister studies her face for a few seconds and then speaks up, seemingly interested.

"What is your name, young lady?"

"Spi...Spica Royle."

Spica's body is frozen stiff, most likely from nerves. She is the only girl in front of whom the sister stopped and demanded a name.

The sister reaches out her hand and touches Spica's cheek with her fingertips. Naturally, Spica trembles in surprise, but she purses her lips tightly and keeps silent. She remains that way for a few moments, but the sister seems to lose interest before long and moves on to the next girl.

Spica finally relaxes, and the sister nods heavily after having examined each child's face.

"I choose her."

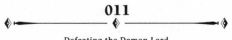

Her assertive tone leaves zero room for argument. She is pointing directly at Spica.

Her pointed finger is screaming out, almost in condemnation. From the corner of her eye, Spica can see her fellow orphans sighing with relief.

The shock is palpable; Spica feels as if she has been punched in the face.

Completely at sea, a flustered Spica opens her mouth to speak as the head priest looks at her worriedly.

"U-um… What is…? What is this… all about?"

She can't remember having done anything. She did nothing wrong, and among her peers, Spica is one of the most obedient of the bunch.

The sister takes a long look at Spica and nods again in satisfaction.

"We will be making you into a priest."

A priest…? But why?

Spica has zero training, and many of her peers already want to become priests.

"…Huh? But… Why me?"

"Because you're the cutest one here."

As a response to a question asked only out of sheer confusion, the sister's response makes no sense.

"The overdone sense of justice is a crime."

On the Hero Conquering His Weakness

I've just showered and stepped out of the washroom when Amelia returns. She looks the same as always, indigo hair tied in the back, equally dark eyes. Yet she appears puzzled to see me emerging from the shower in the middle of the day.

I sigh deeply and rub my eyes. Cooling my head worked for now—I managed to stop my fingertips from shaking.

Oh well. Can't be helped. Malfunctions happen—that's fine. What's important is how you resolve them.

"Amelia, we have to…rethink our strategy."

"…Y-yes."

Amelia is unusually stiff as her shoulders twitch at the sound of my voice.

We sit at the table in the middle of the room and face each other. Amelia remains silent, waiting for me to speak.

I'm not sure where I should begin… For starters, I'll open with a simple question.

"Amelia, can you handle the undead?"

"…? And if I say yes?"

"…You're not afraid?"

Amelia blinks two or three times and replies in amazement.

"Ares, what are you talking about?"

She's right. What sort of priest is afraid of the undead? Not to mention, most mercenaries don't even balk at them. Anyone who does definitely lacks the heart of a warrior.

Defeating the Demon Lord

For a priest who can conduct exorcisms, the undead are a piece of cake. Okay, enough digression for now… I put on my calmest voice and get straight to the point.

"The party has been completely annihilated. It seems that…Toudou and Aria…don't fare well with the undead."

"…?"

Amelia looks incredulous as she tilts her head to one side, staring into my face as if her response is written on it.

"They lost consciousness after being hit by a *Scream of Sorrow* from a low-level wraith, at which point, I brought them to the church. Of course, their condition isn't critical."

"Um… Who are you talking about?"

"…Toudou's party."

"???"

In truth, Limis and Glacia are less concerning in this regard, but those two have their own mountains of problems.

Amelia is still wide-eyed and shaking her head. This is no joke. She genuinely doesn't understand. If it makes her feel any better—neither do I, really.

"Toudou and Aria are pretty much incapable of fighting undead right now."

"…And why is that?"

"…Probably because they're afraid."

"…Who's afraid?"

"…Toudou and Aria."

We're stuck in a loop! We're stuck in a loop!

Amelia goes completely silent. She traces her lips with an elegant, graceful stroke of her pointer finger in deep contemplation.

Suddenly, she speaks softly, nearly in a whisper.

"Toudou is trash, but he is the Holy Warrior, no?"

…*So* that's *what you really think of Toudou?*

I simply nod. Amelia stays quiet and shakes her head again. Then

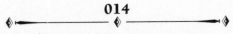

she glances around the room wildly, suddenly unable to relax, and finally looks me in the eyes before standing up.

"…Sorry, do you mind if I take a shower?"

"…Go ahead."

Cool your damn head off. Once you finally understand what's going on, we'll discuss strategy.

"So I take it…this is a bad thing."

Amelia finally understands the gravity of the situation and lurches toward me as she asks. She just got out of the shower. Perhaps she forgot to even dry off, because her dark indigo hair is stuck to her forehead—somehow still sexy.

Yeah… This is way more than bad.

"A warrior afraid of the undead? That wouldn't even make a good joke."

"So this isn't a joke?"

"I'll kick Toudou's ass if it is."

There's no joking about this kind of thing. This isn't a matter of being uncomfortable with monsters in general or being scared of fighting.

The undead and demons are explicitly different from other breeds of monsters. They are defined as "enemies of God" according to the dogma of Ahz Gried, the God of Order. Eradicating them is one of our primary roles as believers in the God of Order, and it is said that performing exorcisms was initially created for this purpose.

For a priest, fearing the enemies of God is a bastardization of the faith. For this reason, though we priests may fear dragons or beasts, we do not fear demons or the undead.

"Aria will… She'll power through somehow. The problem is Toudou."

Aria Rizas is an average human being.

She's a believer of Ahz Gried, but as someone whose faith is quite weak, she feels that the dogma doesn't resonate heavily with her, and the

Church knows it. Thus, it doesn't matter. It's not an issue if she's terrified of the undead.

However, when it comes to Toudou—the Holy Warrior—there is absolutely no excuse.

The Holy Warrior is an envoy of the God of Order. Can he, as a manifestation of that creed, possibly be excused for being terrified of the enemy?

The Church is not a singular entity. It has sects, each with their own motives and desires.

A Holy Warrior afraid of an enemy of God. That's an opportunity for someone to take advantage. If Toudou's fear of the undead was found out, it would be a huge mess for everyone—that's for certain.

"Worst-case scenario, he could be exposed as a fake and excommunicated..."

"Is that the responsibility of the kingdom that summoned him?"

Ostensibly, the procedure for summoning heroes is predicated on the faith of the kingdom that requested them. It is a strategic move to avoid responsibility falling on the Church if and when a warrior with personality or prowess issues emerges.

In this case, the burden would fall on the Kingdom of Ruxe, which bears responsibility for ordering Toudou's summoning.

"What should we do?"

"...Only one choice. We have to get him used to the undead before this goes public."

This could divide the entire kingdom.

There's no reason to worry that Limis or Aria will divulge the secret. They're from the Kingdom, and leaking the information would just cause trouble for them. Even if they screwed up and something got out, any information they leaked would be scratched from the record.

I rest my elbows on the table and hold my head in my hands. The headache I thought I'd quelled rears its ugly head again.

"Dammit, I'm not a therapist..."

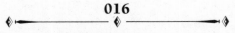

"The overdone sense of justice is a crime."

Fear is deeply rooted in our psychology.

Resistance to poison and paralysis can be boosted simply by gaining levels, but resistance to spiritual attacks can't. The fact that Limis was fine at a low level while Aria and Toudou, who are above her in both level and physical strength, completely lost consciousness is proof of this.

Thought and psychology are largely dependent on the environment in which someone is raised. Correcting Aria's and Toudou's weaknesses after the fact is a backbreaking uphill climb.

...In any case, I can't do it. I'd have no idea where to start. I am not a trained counselor.

"Maybe they'd be cured if we hit them over the head...?"

"Should we try?"

I genuinely can't tell if Amelia is kidding as her expression as she proposes it is dead serious.

That simply isn't an option. Toudou's the one tasked with defeating the Demon Lord.

This isn't the time for me to be sitting here with my head in my hands. No matter how daunting the task, I've got to face it head-on. I get out of my chair, slap myself on the cheek, and psych myself up.

"What about submitting a report?"

"Of course I'm gonna."

We have no other choice. For the moment, Cardinal Creio Amen is still on our side.

Toudou's failings would also reflect on the cardinal, who is partially responsible for the summoning of heroes. As the youngest cardinal in history, he has ties of obligation that are already immeasurable. He'll support us. There's no point hiding anything from him.

"Let's stay positive. We're lucky we were the first to find out."

The weakest of the undead are located on the uppermost floor of Yutith's Tomb.

Even if the group withdraws from battle, they should have no problem defeating them. With the holy armor Fried that Toudou possesses, the undead shouldn't even be able to damage him, and Aria and Limis also have fairly top-notch equipment. I have no idea about Glacia. That's irrelevant.

I'm just glad we didn't discover this disaster *after* they leveled up.

There's a steep gap between high-level and low-level undead. High-level undead are dangerous even for those who perform exorcisms. Zarpahn, the vampire we battled recently, was indeed high level, but even further advanced beings exist as well.

If a person was to faint in front of their likes, they'd be finished. Things could be worse. Yeah, they could be a lot worse.

Amelia suddenly speaks up, as if impressed.

"You sure are tough, Ares..."

"..."

I remain silent and take a map out of my bag. It's the same one Toudou has. Rather, I gave Toudou that map myself after getting ahold of it through the Church.

Everything we know about Yutith's Tomb is inscribed here.

This includes the layout, the traps and monsters present, and strategies for dealing with them; which rooms are the best to set up camp; which areas are best for leveling up; and points of caution for deeper exploration.

"Amelia, is there anything here you can't defeat?"

"I'm...strong enough."

I ask Amelia as she sneaks a peek at the map, and she replies somewhat proudly, puffing out her chest.

I've got a good handle on things now. I look away from Amelia and trace a line on the map with my finger. Naturally, there aren't any monsters I can't defeat in here. But what to do when it comes to facing one's fears...?

Amelia lightly taps me as I gaze at the map with a stymied look on my face.

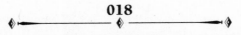

"The overdone sense of justice is a crime."

"I have a good idea."

"...A good idea?"

"I actually used to be a bit freaked out by the undead, a long time ago. But I overcame my fear."

"You don't say."

My spiritual abilities have always been quite strong, ever since I was a child—long before I became a priest. I've never been afraid of any followers of darkness.

As I stare at Amelia, she puckers her lips and smiles faintly. For some reason, I remember the time she told me she can handle her liquor and then got wasted off one sip.

She doesn't look like someone who'd be afraid of the undead, but... can I believe her?

Amelia is a serious person in general, but she has a tendency to say strange things with a serious look on her face.

She catches me staring doubtfully at her and makes a declaration:

"We'll make them fight a huge group of undead. Their fear will dissipate before the fight's over."

...That's a pretty heavy-handed solution, don't you think?!

§   §   §

"Actually, I... I'm not really into horror..."

Toudou speaks softly. Even though the party left the Great Tomb hours ago, her face is still haggard. Her black eyes, usually full of vigor, are listless, her dark hair dull.

Limis sighs and looks at the green-haired swordmaster next to her—Aria.

"It's just... Anything I can't cut with a sword...I'm not too fond of..."

Aria is having a really tough time admitting it, too.

"...But you *can* use a sword to kill wraiths and, certainly, the living dead, right?"

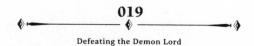

019

Defeating the Demon Lord

"…I'm ashamed."

How can these two, a warrior and a swordmaster, talk so pitifully after having shown such mighty prowess in battle in the Great Forest of the Vale? Limis shakes her head. This feels like a horrible nightmare.

Toudou's party reached Purif just one day ago. They sent word of their arrival to the church and, just a few hours prior, decided to enter the Great Tomb for a test run.

The group had been personally supplied by the church with many necessary items and a map, along with a room for lodging. Aside from the fact that they couldn't find a priest, everything else was coming together nicely… At least, it seemed that way.

"Unbelievable! …What's the matter with you two?!"

Limis's voice echoes throughout the church room serving as their accommodation for the night. She raps on the corner of a table with her staff and stares directly at Aria and Toudou, who exchange pitiful glances.

"What on earth do you mean…you're scared of the undead?"

"I mean… But—"

"No buts!"

"…Yes, ma'am."

The pair are dejected. Glacia, the little girl with dark-green hair and eyes, sits unbothered on a chair by herself, hugging her knees as she munches on a hunk of stale bread. Limis is irritated by her but quickly cools off. Now isn't the time to scold the girl. If anything, it's a chance to applaud her rationality.

Limis turns back to the pathetic pair of vanguards, staring daggers.

She slaps the wooden table with all her might, nearly toppling a water glass.

"If Glacia hadn't carried you all the way into town, you could have been completely annihilated; do you realize that?!"

"Y-yeah, I do!"

Toudou sighs heavily.

She still has some memory from before she collapsed: a vision of eyes rife with enmity and a bloodcurdling scream that froze her body

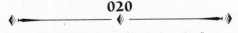

stiff. Even though Toudou had heard of the Scream of Sorrow before, she was completely unprepared for it.

"But, Limis, you also lost consci— U-um... Never mind."

Toudou decides to keep her mouth shut as Limis lords over them. Mages are used to having a frontline vanguard to survive in battle. She and Aria were that vanguard for Limis when the skirmish occurred—what else can she say?

Aria takes a sip of water to wet her lips, something that should calm her nerves, and sighs.

"The issue is how we move forward from here."

At the time, they had been searching for a priest. Unable to find one, they'd decided to venture into the dungeon, which led to the discovery of yet another of their weaknesses.

Toudou holds her head in her hands as Limis stares reproachfully, then begins mumbling excuses.

"In the world I'm from...there's no such thing as undead, y'know?"

"...And just what's so scary about them?"

"...Everything."

"...'Everything'? Listen up, you..."

The memory of the incident itself is too much. Toudou heaves a sigh so heavy her soul seems to escape from her body.

As she presses her cheek to the table, Toudou pounds her fists and begins insisting.

"Their looks and color and stench and sounds... I can't stand them... They're awful!"

"Well, they *are* monsters..."

"But I don't get why they don't bother you, Limis... It doesn't make any sense!"

"Myself included... Anything I can't cut with my sword, I just..."

Aria echoes Toudou's comment with her own woeful remark. How can this be the daughter of a legendary swordmaster?

Limis is awash with a genuine sense of dread from the pitiful duo. This isn't just a matter of being uncomfortable. This is a serious condition.

Limis's response to Aria is stiff—after all, it was Aria who changed the party's destination to the Great Tomb in the first place.

"That's why you need magic."

"...Then you should fight them yourself!"

Taken aback to hear Toudou—the Holy Warrior—suddenly stoop so low, Aria blurts out:

"Nao, the holy sword Ex that you possess is capable of damaging spectral beings, including wraiths."

"Wha—?!"

Toudou looks like Aria shot her in the back.

Limis stares up at Aria reproachfully.

"Aria, your sword can also kill wraiths, right?"

"..."

A direct hit. Aria shuts her mouth and averts her gaze.

Aria's sword is a national treasure of the Kingdom of Ruxe. In reality, weapons that can kill wraiths and other spectral beings are not particularly rare.

Limis furrows her brow as Aria and Toudou purposefully avoid eye contact. Then, she sighs and cuts to the chase.

"So now that we know you're scared of them... What are you gonna do about it?"

"What am I gonna do...?"

Truthfully, Limis didn't care either way. Sure, it's less than ideal for the Holy Warrior to have such a weakness, but Limis isn't scared of the undead. Neither is she particularly fond of the idea of leveling up in the Great Tomb. For her, a fire-based elementalist, fighting outdoors is largely preferable.

Waiting for their leader to speak again, Limis opens and closes her palm a few times and confirms it's empty.

During their quest into the Great Tomb, the undead should have had some presence, but she didn't feel like they were more powerful than before.

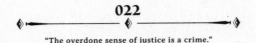

"The overdone sense of justice is a crime."

Rather, the undead are famous for having pitiful life force. In particular, low-level undead—the type that are essentially brain waves taking on physical form—are largely useless, given how many you have to kill to level up.

A drove of undead, with their status ailment attacks, surging forward... Limis doesn't doubt her own abilities, but proceeding through the dungeon carrying these two pathetic sacks of flesh is altogether too risky. Not to mention, elemental spells can't be used limitlessly. Limis was down there only once, but the Great Tomb did hold an element of menace that she, too, felt.

Toudou purses her lips, perplexed. In response, Limis sighs for the umpteenth time.

In Limis's experience, the Holy Warrior Naotsugu Toudou has always acted of her own accord.

Yet the hero before her hesitates for such a pathetic, trifling reason.

"Nao, you said before that you want to learn how to perform exorcisms... Would doing that help you face the undead?"

"Well..."

"What if we had a priest? Would that help?"

"..."

At the end of the day, exorcism is just a combat skill, a means to an end. Priests are the same. Limis doesn't believe Toudou and Aria can fight the undead in their current state.

Toudou, racked with fear, deflects the question to Limis—someone an entire head shorter than her.

"Limis... Which do you prefer?"

"I'll go with your choice, Nao. Either way...I can fight them."

She responds flatly, without batting an eyelash.

Glacia blinks suddenly as she gnaws her bread, letting her gaze wander between Toudou and Limis.

"...And you, Aria?"

"I, too...will defer to Nao. But I think we should start leveling up right away."

The Church estimated that news of the Holy Warrior would reach the Demon Lord within one month of being summoned. That month had passed just a few days ago. In actuality, word of the Holy Warrior's presence had leaked to the demons via the Church, it was reported. No damage had been done yet, but each party member agreed on the importance of leveling up in a timely fashion.

Toudou closes her eyes as she listens to Aria speak.

She stays that way, pondering, for some time. Then, after heaving a deep sigh, she slowly opens them.

She exchanges glances with Limis and Aria, a dry smile on her face.

"…Let's leave tomorrow morning and head for Golem Valley."

"And give up on overcoming your fear of the undead?"

"…N-no, I just think we need to level up a bit first, is all."

Toudou laughs as if to skirt the question.

Exasperated, Limis expels her deepest sigh yet.

The role assigned to them is to defeat the Demon Lord—there's nothing mentioned about killing undead. Whether that attitude suits the legendary Holy Warrior remains to be seen. However, Limis has known that Naotsugu Toudou is far from perfect ever since they met a month ago.

Aria exhales in relief at Toudou's words. Limis nods slightly, too.

Even if this is an escape maneuver, no matter how pathetic a decision it is, Limis intends to accompany Toudou, just as she asserted earlier.

That is precisely Limis's role. And the fate of the entire world rests on her leader's shoulders.

§　§　§

After finishing my report to Creio, I let out a sigh.

His reaction to hearing Toudou's weakness, which should have proven fatal, was surprisingly calm.

My superior, Cardinal Creio Amen, survived the Machiavellian trickery pervading the upper echelons of the Church. Perhaps he's acting

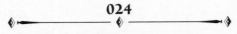

"The overdone sense of justice is a crime."

subdued because it's before breakfast, but when his reaction is this paltry, I get a little worried.

I've said it before, but maybe Toudou isn't such a high priority for Creio.

A Holy Warrior hasn't been summoned for many years, or so I've heard. Toudou isn't some sort of test case...is he?

Amelia, having changed from her loungewear into a bright-blue mage robe, asks me, "What did the cardinal say?"

"...That he'd leave it up to us."

Amelia is wearing black gloves. She previously lost her mask in the Vale, but she purchased another. She slips it into the folds of her robe against her chest.

The Great Tomb is different from the Vale; you can't source any food from within. Highly portable and nutritious food that doesn't take up space is a must. Water can be gathered through magical means, but in the end, going into the Great Tomb requires far more supplies than the Great Forest of the Vale.

I still haven't replaced the knives I lost fighting Zarpahn. I applied through the Church for replacements, but mythril is a precious material. I could raise the priority and have one made for me, but it seems like it will take a bit longer.

"How are they doing?"

When I ask, Amelia closes her eyes softly. Her lips move imperceptibly; she's murmuring a detection spell.

Toudou's party asked the church to let them stay there. It's the safest place to be if any undead hordes do appear.

We have a long way to go, but Amelia is reputedly a highly skilled detection caster. After a few seconds, she opens her eyes.

"He seems to have come to. However, he still remains within the church walls—"

Amelia shuts her mouth unnaturally. She furrows her brow slightly, then pauses.

Is something happening again…? Now what?

Amelia shoots me a pitiful look as I wait silently for her to continue.

I don't care anymore. No matter what happens, I won't be surprised. Just spit it out.

"…It's Toudou."

"Yeah?"

Amelia falters—a rarity. When I urge her on with a glance, she reluctantly continues.

"He's…thinking of leaving here…and heading to Golem Valley."

"…What?"

That wasn't the answer I anticipated. I do a double take.

Just what exactly did you come here to do, Toudou?

Normally, he'd charge right back into the Great Tomb after reviving, drunk on valor… He's reckless, after all.

That would have been acceptable if we were talking about *before* he'd entered the Great Tomb. However, now that we're all aware of his fear of the undead, there's no way we can let him leave this place.

"Why the sudden change of heart?"

"Probably…because he's afraid?"

Afraid? He's had a change of heart because he's afraid?

The word *hero* entails an inherent sense of bravery. Show me a hero who runs away because they're scared.

"He's the hero, though."

"But he's also human."

Amelia answers without changing her expression.

Where's your useless bravery now, Naotsugu Toudou?!

For better or for worse, the Toudou I've watched up until now has something transcendent about him. At the very least, he's far removed from a normal human. So why are we suddenly focusing on his humanity?

"We're not on the same wavelength here… Dammit."

I lower myself into a chair, put my entire weight on it, and cradle my head in my hands. If Toudou doesn't return to the Great Tomb, we can't deal with him using the method Amelia proposed earlier.

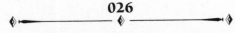

"The overdone sense of justice is a crime."

"We can't let this stand. This sort of problem only grows more onerous if you ignore it."

The undead appear in places other than the Great Tomb. The corpses of humans or beasts can also be taken over by undead spirits. In this world, if you're going to make your livelihood by waging battle, the undead are a type of monster you simply have to confront.

The majority of the Demon Lord Kranos's underlings are undead or demons. Being able to dispatch them is the first step in vanquishing the Demon Lord.

Aria's flaw is her complete lack of magical ability. She'll more than likely drop out halfway through because of it, so that's largely a nonissue. But Toudou absolutely has to find a way to persevere, no matter what it takes.

The clock on the wall softly ticks the seconds away.

There's no time. It's already early evening, so while we can't leave immediately, we need to hurry up and figure out a plan.

A method of getting Toudou to go back into the Great Tomb of his own free will...

Making Glacia call out "Go to Yutith's Tomb!" repeatedly would only fall on deaf ears.

"Toudou lives for justice. This tends to complicate matters, but it's also a fact we cannot ignore."

Let's forget about the time he nearly slaughtered a bunch of mercenaries in Vale Village. Let's also forget about his lustful streak and the time he snuck into Limis and Aria's bedroom the first day we all met.

Toudou readily accepted defeating the Demon Lord with few complaints. He also agreed immediately when asked to slay the glacial plant and never ran from the battle with Zarpahn—and he threw me my mace. The more I think about that incident, the angrier I become at how much of a pain in the ass he was. But he simply didn't know his place—he wasn't malevolent.

We'll use that lack of maliciousness against him. It'll be easy to get him into the Great Tomb again. Yes, I've got it—

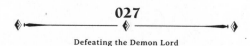

Defeating the Demon Lord

"—A child has gone missing in Yutith's Tomb."

Toudou would more than likely quell his fear of the undead and reenter Yutith's Tomb in such a scenario.

Realistically, there's no way any of the children from this village—who have all been endlessly warned about the Great Tomb—would ever set foot in it alone. But Toudou wouldn't analyze it that deeply.

If he doesn't go in and save the child...we'll just have to think of another plan...

Amelia responds without batting an eye.

"Are you going to abduct a child and take them into the Great Tomb?"

"...What sort of person do you think I am? It's simply a hypothetical."

A follower of the God of Order would never do a thing like that.

We don't even need to actually take a child, as long as we can get Toudou in the tomb. Then again...if there isn't an actual child involved, Toudou might stay in there looking and never come out...

Surely there are a few children available through the church. Let's ask for their help.

"In that case, I have a great idea."

Amelia claps her hands together. I'm a bit worried but glad to get her opinion.

"Yes?"

"Let's discuss it over drinks."

"Not a chance. Tell me right now."

Amelia looks a little bit hurt but quickly regains her composure and responds.

"I should have told you earlier, but actually, I found a female priest who should be suitable for Toudou's party."

"..."

I blink a few times and stare at her. She's straight-faced, not showing an ounce of pride.

She found a female priest? But Cardinal Creio said he wouldn't dispatch one. Does that mean Amelia convinced him? And she actually succeeded?

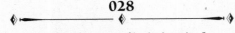

"The overdone sense of justice is a crime."

I did ask her to visit the cardinal, for what it was worth. Ordinarily, a female priest would never want to join a group of one male and three females (including Glacia). It was like Amelia had...denied my request.

"You're not lying, are you?"

"The faithful of Ahz Gried do not tell lies."

"...Count me in for that drink soon."

This is the first good news in a while. Maybe it could offset the exposure of Toudou's weakness?

If the priest who Amelia supposedly found can carry her weight, the remainder of our journey will be a breeze.

"Let's lure this female priest out with some bait. If all the cards are lined up, that piece of trash Toudou and his party will come to the tomb as well."

"...Do you hate Toudou or something?"

"No... Not particularly...?"

Amelia shakes her head with a puzzled look on her face.

"...And? What's the meaning of this?"

Amelia left the room, and after a while, she returned with a young girl. She's clean enough but wears tattered clothes.

"A sister."

She has dark-gray hair and eyes, like so many of the people in this area. She must only have access to the bare minimum nutritionally—her arms and legs look so thin they could snap, and her cheeks are slightly sunken. She's probably twelve or thirteen years old. Yet the most surprising thing about her is that she isn't wearing earrings, the sign of a priest, and her left ring finger is also bare. She can't be a priest.

The girl is obviously nervous as she shuffles toward me and glances up, but I look to Amelia instead.

"There's no way this is a sister."

Literally anyone would say the same. Above all else, she has none of a priest's requisite features.

Amelia responds, unshaken by my gaze.

029

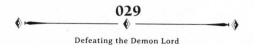

"Officially speaking...she will be a sister soon."

"...Where did you find her?"

The girl looks around observantly, trying to ascertain our expressions through her fawning eyes. An old memory revisits me, and I grimace.

An orphan. The Demon Lord's appearance incited hordes of his monster followers, and the number of orphans rose dramatically as a result. These children were typically taken to orphanages run by the Church or the Kingdom.

Amelia looks down at the girl and gives her a pat on the head, continuing calmly.

"I brought the cutest orphan in the church's care. I have their permission."

Astonishingly, ability hadn't factored into her criteria. How irresponsible is that?

"We're talking about taking down the Demon Lord. Am I wrong?"

"It's better than nothing. Not to mention, it was a lot easier than finding a sister who's already in the Church. Faith is best tested in moments of life and death... That's when she'll really shine."

Indeed. I don't understand why the Church wouldn't assign a priest for us, but the decision was Cardinal Creio's.

In that case, we'll make a new one. I get it in theory, but in practice?

However, Amelia does have a point. Compared with magic, holy techniques depend less on heritage and prowess and more on experience and intelligence. The fact that faith deepens in life-and-death situations is also common knowledge.

That said, holy techniques aren't something that can be learned overnight. That's what separates Toudou from the rest.

Annoyed, I cast my gaze on the girl. As she looks back at me, her face twitches, and her shoulders shake.

...What exactly am I supposed to do with her?

"I'm reluctant. Nine times out of ten, she dies midway."

Forget nine times out of ten—there's a 99.9 percent chance she'll be killed in battle.

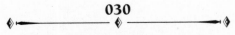

"The overdone sense of justice is a crime."

Most warriors who fought the Demon Lord didn't even have the chance to run.

"If she succeeds, she'll be a hero. There's going to be a few risks here and there."

"Do you really intend to put a child who doesn't know any holy techniques on Toudou's team?"

"Let's consider her a talented understudy. Toudou will take her in, that much I'm sure of."

She must have been prepared for this level of questioning. Her responses come easily but are contradictory... She's right, though—Toudou probably will let this girl into his party.

As an orphan, her clothes are a mess. Yet despite her frail appearance, on the whole, she seems somehow put together. If she had some more meat on her bones, she could certainly be quite pretty.

But—is that a good thing?

"Toudou's party is still low level. If she joins now, she can catch up."

"Level and strength of holy techniques have little to do with this. Divine protection and faith are the most important factors related to holy techniques."

They aren't totally unimportant, but it's not completely unheard of for a low-level priest to possess stronger holy techniques than a high-level one.

Toudou's holy techniques, blessed by the divine protection of Ahz Gried, manifest from a kind of power beyond comprehension. It wouldn't matter if the girl's level caught up.

Amelia blinks repeatedly, looking somewhat shocked.

"It's quite rare for someone so efficiency-minded as yourself to vacillate."

"Just who the hell do you think I am?"

Even I have a modicum of common decency. It's a given that I would never send this naive girl into battle to die.

"...In that case, should we send her back to the church?"

"Yeah, we probably should."

Do it, for all I care. As I open my mouth to say the words, the source of this ordeal, who until now had remained silent, lifts her head.

Her gray hair is lackluster, but her pupils are shining brightly. Her voice is withered.

"Um... I..."

"...What is it?"

She gulps lightly. Her cheeks stiffen at my tone; she looks about ready to cry.

I'm not even trying to glare at her... When I look away, she hangs her head and speaks.

"I...I will do my best."

"This isn't a joke—you could die."

"I will do my best."

Living under the care of the Church or an orphanage isn't such a bad thing. You might lead an impoverished life and others may look down on you, but your life isn't at risk.

You're afforded a listing in a family register, and if you grow up and get lucky, you could end up with a better lifestyle than most. Between that and setting off on a mission to defeat the Demon Lord that most heroes have failed, I'm not sure which would make her happier.

"Amelia, how did you convince the cardinal?"

"I told him that it's a dangerous journey, but if she pulls it off, she'll have a better life than now."

That's not exactly inaccurate, but...

A dangerous journey. A journey full of danger. One where demons have their sights on Toudou and his group. The level of danger involved is vastly greater than your average monster-hunting party. The chances of biting the dust in the middle of your life's work aren't exactly low.

Above all else, there's not much at stake for this girl. Limis and Aria are prominent daughters of the Kingdom of Ruxe, and Toudou goes without saying.

I'm not plunging headfirst into any danger... Then again, from my

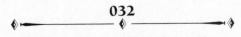

perspective, everything works in my favor. It's no skin off my back if she dies, and if she fails to make any substantial growth, we can replace her along the way.

Should we take the humane route or not? If this girl, whose name I still don't know, refuses our offer, we're obligated to accept that. However, from the looks of it, she's not opposed to the situation at all. Of course, you could also say she doesn't understand the reality, but... maybe...

As I waver, Amelia makes a proposal.

"Let's forget whether or not she'll make it into the party. For now, how do you feel about using her to lure Toudou and the others into the tomb? Whether or not she joins the party is a decision to be made after she has actual battle experience anyway."

...I see. I hate to use the word *bait*, but we'll need someone regardless.

There's nothing stopping us from using this girl Amelia brought into the fold, and what's more, we're running out of time. We have to take action before Toudou runs off.

The girl looks at me as if awaiting my decision. It certainly doesn't seem like she'll object.

Why not give it a try? If it's undead we're dealing with in the Great Tomb, providing backup won't be a problem.

"What's your name?"

"Um... Y-yes, my name is...S-Spica. Spica Royle."

Spica, is it? Her timidity shows she's clearly unfit for battle. This will be a short acquaintance.

Spica is still peering up at me nervously, and Amelia interjects with an over-the-top comment.

"Don't worry, Spica. Ares may look like a murderer, but he is undoubtedly a priest. He won't eat you...probably."

...*Is she comforting her, or is she making fun of me?*

Spica continues cowering before me in spite of Amelia's quip.

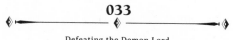

"Okay, let's get started on trapping Toudou!"

"Yes!"

"…O-okay… I will do my best."

Just before daybreak, the Great Tomb feels completely different than it does in the afternoon. The sky-high behemoth of a structure bathed in darkness is monstrous. I sense the presence of powerful followers of darkness coming up from deep underground and furrow my brow.

In general, the farther underground you travel in the tomb, the stronger the undead you encounter. Nobody knows what's buried here, but it can't be anything good.

The sky is still pale twilight, and the cold air grazes my face.

Our plan is to lure Toudou here just before he leaves the village. I want all our preparations complete by noon.

Yutith's Tomb is an underground labyrinth, but the aboveground areas comprise the ruins of a desolated sanctuary.

Countless broken sections of thick pillars and walls litter the ruins. They are gigantic, signifying the power of the beings that once ruled this place.

Even if you lived in Purif, there would be no reason to ever come here. I brought along Spica, who is drinking in the grandiose surroundings. We pass through a crumbled gate and set foot into the rubble-strewn interior.

Crunching pebbles underfoot, in the center of this large room, I notice a massive hole surrounding the partially destroyed statue of *something*.

Once, a massive stone coffin had closed them off—steps into the lower levels. The hole is approximately three meters wide. At the base of these stairs, which seem to descend straight into hell, is a labyrinth incalculable in its total area, even with modern technology.

It makes no difference to me what numerous archaeologists have unearthed in the Great Tomb or its origins.

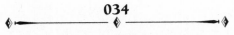

"The overdone sense of justice is a crime."

All that matters are the countless undead, the enemies of God, that exist in these depths. That's it.

The rubble around the stairwell has been cleared away, and while there are signs of a camp, no other human beings are present.

Spica follows close behind me, fearfully peeking around the area.

She no longer wears the disheveled clothing she had on when Amelia introduced her earlier.

She's dressed in a brand-new, pure-white robe and hood, part of the equipment provided to priests by the Church. It's temporary peace of mind, but it carries the effect of warding off followers of darkness. The short staff in her hand is also largely for show, but it does buff her holy techniques.

For now, she's still a blank slate, but we made her look the part. Before we set out, Amelia bestowed a number of different items on Spica as well, but understandably, she couldn't just use holy techniques right away.

Spica's power is not necessarily proportionate to her age. Among mercenaries who show quick wit, there are some her age—twelve or thirteen—who have already made a name for themselves on the battlefield.

Spica will not be one of them. In her current state, it would be dangerous for her to fight against even the lowest-level undead.

"Are you scared?"

"Uh... N-no."

Spica seems flustered and shakes her head back and forth quickly when I ask her.

Silence and darkness await us down the stairwell.

Spica is about level 3. Being so low-level for someone her age is surefire proof she's an orphan. At my level, seeing through the darkness is no problem, but Spica can't see much of anything.

I say a few prayers and cast a ball of light in midair.

Holy techniques include the main four strata of healing, buffs, prisms, and exorcism. Exorcism techniques, also called eradication techniques, stand out for their capacity to destroy demonic and undead foes. The most basic spell among these is *Leading Light*, which I just cast.

The light is strong—not quite as strong as the morning sun, but enough to dispel the darkness. However, we still can't see into the depths of the stairwell.

Spica's line of sight instinctively follows the light source.

"Is that...a holy technique?"

"Yeah. The most basic of them."

I snap my fingers, and the ball of light floats softly down into the stairwell.

"We're going in. Don't leave my side. The monsters here are only low-level undead, but no matter how weak they are...a level three is no match for them."

"O-okay."

Living dead are stronger than the average adult male, and wraiths can inhabit and control the body of a mentally weak specimen. Once you've run into one, you should have a fairly good grasp of them, but you still can't afford to let your guard down.

Perhaps she senses the seriousness in my voice, because Spica cowers closer and closer to me.

We take a step down the steep stairs. I move my arms to adjust my rucksack. The darkness seems deeper... Rather, it *feels* deeper because of the shining orb. I turn up the corners of my mouth slightly.

Fear constricts the human spirit and makes it grow dull. That's why any priest with the Out Crusade must smile—to ensure that they never succumb to the darkness.

Yutith's Tomb is made up of innumerable winding corridors, rooms, and blind spots.

There must have been a grave keeper or someone responsible for the tomb at some time, because there are hardly any traps on the upper levels.

"The overdone sense of justice is a crime."

The presence of unusually powerful followers of darkness emanates from the lower levels. Could the highest level of undead also pervade these ghastly halls? Toudou's party probably can't make it down to the tomb's lower levels, but they should be careful all the same.

I advise Spica, who's huddling next to me, on taking proper precautions as we move forward.

In that moment, I feel the presence of something in front of us.

I snap my fingers. In accordance with the prayer, countless arrows of light float up around us.

The bright white light, representative of the holy techniques, reveals what's coming around the corner.

An otherworldly inhabitant of the dark, a ghastly figure resembling a festering corpse. Its broken fingers brush lightly against the wall with a frightful sound. Its faint guttural groan is filled with resentment. As the follower of darkness approaches with its head down, Spica lets out a small gasp.

"...Ee—"

She begins to shriek but instantly covers her mouth with the palm of her hand.

Spica's eyes are wide with astonishment at what is likely her first sighting of such a being—the image of which is now burned into her mind forever.

These monsters are called the "living dead" because of how they take on a human form when they walk. They're very grotesque but still the weakest among undead beings, and they move so slowly that even a child could escape them.

Spica's face stiffens, but although she's surprised by the monster, she isn't afraid.

It would appear that Spica is less frightened by the undead than Toudou. What the hell do I make of that?!

Undead are weak against magic and physical sword damage, but their noxious bodily fluid will cause incapacitation if it gets on your

skin. Therefore, whether you destroy it from a distance or purify it completely, you should cast a holy technique that increases paralysis resistance beforehand.

Limis should have cast fire from afar or simply completely engulfed the undead and destroyed it.

Spica waits as I identify the monster. I snap my fingers one more time.

The witless living dead wavers slightly at the exorcism's glow.

"*Breaking Arrow.*"

At once, the arrows shoot with incredible speed and pierce the monster's body—truthfully, the chant wasn't necessary, nor were the number of light arrows deployed. Now there's absolutely no chance for the monster to escape.

The battle is over before it begins.

The light bursts and disappears. Only silence remains.

By that time, the living dead remains as neither a shadow nor a physical form. It has been completely purified. It didn't even get a chance to wail in the throes of death. Not that the living dead *can* wail in the throes of death.

Spica looks up at me, visibly more dumbfounded than she had been upon seeing the living dead for the first time.

"This…is divine protection," I say simply.

I move on ahead without waiting for her response. Spica remains frozen stiff for a few seconds but then quickly trots after me.

Affirming miracles, personally experiencing divine protection: These are the first steps toward becoming a priest.

No matter how much it's explained or how much you learn from a book, there is no substitute for a firsthand, vivid experience such as the spectacle that just unfolded.

Although relatively untraversed, the Great Tomb is known as a fantastic battlefield for leveling up.

We continue progressing through the tomb, purifying with a single blast any low-level undead we come across. I don't obliterate them

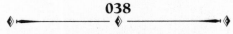

immediately—first, I let Spica behold their form, then purify them the moment before they start encroaching on us.

We arrive at our destination—the location we preselected to which to lure Toudou's party.

Within the holy techniques, there are miracles that prevent the undead from getting close, but we won't use them today. This is to boost Spica's resistance, if only slightly.

Spica was freaked out at first, but she quickly acclimates. By the latter half of our journey, she's only a little bit anxious and no longer afraid. Now, even if she hears a wraith's scream, the mental damage will be minimal, I'm sure.

I recall what Amelia said: *"She needs experience."*

These were drastic measures, but judging by Spica's reactions now, it seems Amelia wasn't entirely wrong.

I single-handedly obliterate every undead in our path, moving through the tomb for approximately an hour before arriving at our destination.

After verifying there are no monsters inside, I open the stone door.

This room is bigger than any of the ones we've seen so far. The ceiling is high, and luxurious ornamental candlesticks line the walls at even intervals—although they're unlit.

A delicate white stone statue about three meters tall stands at the back of the chamber alongside a simple stone altar.

On our map, this room is designated Devil-Faced Knight's Altar.

The statue, wearing a devilish mask twisted in rage, with two razor-sharp horns growing from its head, is clearly the inspiration for the name.

The statue grips the handle of a sword slung from its waist. It feels alive, as if the sword will come flashing out of its scabbard at any moment. Legend states that the statue will come to life if certain conditions are met. The Survey Corps came here on multiple occasions to inspect it, but as of now, it doesn't seem to have ever moved.

The statue's features are distinctive, and it has some connection to ancient religious practices, though its true identity is still unknown. It's not that I have no interest in the statue, but what's more important right now is that this room is perfectly arranged for offering prayers.

This boosts the effectiveness of holy techniques and makes casting miracles easier. This place doesn't compare to a real church, but as it conserves holy energy, it's a well-known training site among priests.

Additionally, it's the ideal place to lure Toudou; barriers are also cast easily here.

The room is expansive, and aside from the statue and altar, there's nothing else to get in the way during battle.

Above all else, the fact that it has only one ingress point is beyond ideal. You can't escape. Given the low-level undead that inhabit this area, even in the worst-case scenario, you wouldn't die. Maybe.

"As planned, we'll make this our base," I say to Spica, who is staring intently at the Devil-Faced Knight.

It's hard to believe this ultrasmooth stone statue was created thousands of years ago.

Should we destroy it, just in case something bad happens? The thought enters my head for a moment, but then I change my mind. I don't know what god is associated with this statue, but we should probably refrain from any unnecessary action. The creed of the God of Order commands us to not show contempt for any other gods.

I doubt it will move anyway...right?

I lay one source of anxiety to rest and turn back to Spica to go over once more the scenario I already explained earlier.

"Spica, as I told you before, you're a budding priest who came here to train but can't use holy techniques yet."

"...Yes."

"You knew the Great Tomb was dangerous but wanted to deepen your faith no matter what, so you came here all alone. The church learned of this through a letter you left behind, and after you didn't

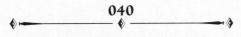

"The overdone sense of justice is a crime."

come back for several hours, they became worried and asked Toudou's party to rescue you."

What sort of budding priest would ever come down into the Great Tomb alone? I pick the scenario apart in my head as I continue explaining.

The logic is full of holes, but even if it comes across as slightly unnatural, the only thing that matters is luring Toudou and his group down here.

"While you pray here, Toudou's party of monster hunters—who are very worried about you—will come save you."

Amelia stayed behind in the village to guide them here as necessary.

Updating me via transmission was too unreliable, so I had her fulfill this role. She didn't seem happy about it, but this was her idea, after all—just get on with it.

"Then, Toudou's party will discover you here in this room... But just as they're relieved to find you, unharmed, there will be an accident."

I recall the words Amelia, stone-faced, had said to Spica.

"You'll get accustomed to the undead as you continue defeating them. At first, I was scared of them, too. But once I eradicated the hundreds surrounding me, I got used to it."

I probe our environs. The undead are swarming, a rotten infestation.

Leveling up in the Great Tomb is accomplished by obliterating the weakest undead by the hundreds.

Even someone queasy at the sight of blood will become accustomed to fear and death after killing enough monsters.

No matter how scared you feel, your enemy is weak. You'll get used to them naturally just from mowing them down. If you still can't get acclimated, then you deal with it as it comes.

"The horde of undead will sense the presence of living beings, and in a stroke of 'bad luck,' they'll flood this room. I'll cast a strong barrier around you. Don't get too close."

"...H-how many are we expecting...?" Spica asks, her voice hoarse.

The answer is obvious.

"They'll keep coming until Toudou gets used to them."

I'll force him to face his fear. If he's a true hero, that much is a given.

Okay, Toudou... Time to begin your fun new training regimen.

§   §   §

"A child in the Great Tomb...?"

The middle-aged father in charge of the Purif church is agog.

The usually majestic worship hall has fallen into a tumultuous flurry.

He looks haggard as he recites the scenario to Toudou.

"Y-yes... Our church also looks after orphans... Somehow, one of them must have overheard you saying you were looking for a priest when you came here yesterday..."

Toudou's gaze turns grim as she listens.

The situation is simple. A young girl who happened to overhear Toudou say she was looking for a priest took it upon herself to aid Toudou's quest and headed to the Great Tomb in hopes of becoming a member of the hero's party. That's all there is to it.

Toudou carefully studies the father's expression but doesn't detect any falsehood.

She herself isn't grasping the gravity of the situation.

"This young girl doesn't have any of the powers of a priest... She left a note saying she was headed to the tomb to deepen her faith..."

"She's got no priestly powers? Will she be okay?"

"..."

The father falls silent, and Toudou realizes the dire circumstances.

She has been down into the Great Tomb only once so far, but she understands just how dangerous it is. The monsters there are relatively weak but would still quickly overpower the average child.

"...Who's going to save her?"

"Well... The church is currently understaffed, so..."

Being qualified as a priest doesn't necessarily mean you can fight. At this church, the priests in service tend to fall in that category.

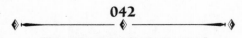

Aria looks toward Toudou, blue in the face.

"Nao."

"Y-yeah…"

Aria's tone prompts terror to flash through Toudou's mind—the terror she felt in the Great Tomb upon encountering the undead.

Toudou's heart feels wrenched in a vise grip simply remembering that sensation.

Yet, she whispers, "We have to go…"

If you can't save even one child, then how can you save the world?

Fear dulls the mind. Every second off the clock decreases this child's chance of survival.

Toudou cannot weigh her terror against this girl's life; even less so if the incident originated with something she'd said.

Naotsugu Toudou is a hero. No matter how fearsome the foe, she must face them in the name of justice.

Without thinking too hard, she looks toward the father. The passing of time would only erode her resolve.

The father's face is white as a sheet and twitching subtly—he looks ready to faint.

"We'll… We will go."

"Oh… Um… But…"

"…It's fine. Leave it to us."

Toudou speaks decisively, quelling her emotions and attempting to calm everyone with a quivering smile.

Toudou's party is also indebted to the church for providing their lodging. They still possess some items given to them for fighting the undead.

We'll go. We have to.

Aria, who put on a similarly shameful display the day before, has no grounds to argue otherwise. Why would she let herself act so pitifully in front of her party members?

Limis, the only one of them able to handle the undead, casts a concerned gaze toward her two companions.

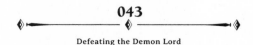

043

*   *   *

After finalizing their gear, the group sets out for the Great Tomb. The girl disappeared the previous evening. There's no time to spare.

It's sunny, not a cloud in the sky—the exact opposite of Toudou's mind. The scorching sun lights up the earth beneath them.

"Are...are you okay, Nao?"

"No...I'm not. But we have to go down there..."

Toudou responds to Limis with an affirmation of resolve.

In a stroke of good fortune, the girl left an exact location behind in her letter: the upper levels of the Great Tomb in a room called the "Devil-Faced Knight's Altar," about an hour's trek from the entrance.

Hordes of undead inhabit the Great Tomb, but they don't appear in such great numbers in the upper levels. Toudou's party hardly met any on their first expedition, and with some luck, they could make it to this specific room without encountering any.

It also meant the girl could still be alive.

Toudou and Aria are silent as they ride in the carriage. Toudou sits expressionless next to the driver as Limis talks her ear off.

"Are you sure you're okay?!"

"I'm fine. Heh-heh... Heh-heh-heh... I can j-just throw holy water at them... Yeah, holy water..."

"You certainly don't sound fine..."

"W-we can just run away if we have to. Let's limit our encounters with them, and if we do run into any, we'll go somewhere we don't have to fight. It'd be a waste of time anyway."

The tomb is massive, and the undead aren't particularly quick, but running away from any that pop up en route is next to impossible. Aria and Toudou are physically strong, so they'd be fine, but Limis is a different story.

"Defeating them would be much quicker, I'm sure..."

"I'll do what I can."

At Toudou's response, Limis resolves to torch every single undead they come across.

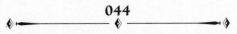

"The overdone sense of justice is a crime."

She'll burn through a ton of magic energy this way, but there is no other choice.

How many mana potions did we have again...?

Mana potions are extremely valuable and rare. They're an ace card for when the stakes are high, but necessity knows no law.

The party is already heavily disadvantaged. Looking in the back of the carriage, Limis sees Aria holding her knees and mumbling to herself, while Glacia is lazing about, yawning and looking entirely bored. Aria will be completely useless, and Glacia is a lost cause to start with.

Quelling the anxiety rising in her chest, Toudou arrives with her party at the Great Tomb without incident.

An air of desolation pervades the aboveground ruins of the tomb.

Compared to the Great Forest of the Vale, it is exceedingly rare to see mercenaries in Purif. Therefore, if you find yourself in need of help, there will be slim pickings.

The group packs away the carriage and heads for the entrance to the tomb. Limis leads the charge in place of Toudou and Aria, who trudge behind. Garnet—the fire spirit Limis contracted—climbs up her arm, coming to rest on her head.

Salamanders are fairly small, and low-level undead cannot sense their power.

Since they're not beings of this world, poison doesn't work on them, and in the worst case, they can even take up the rear guard.

Limis has something to say to her two party members who already look about ready to collapse—something she's been considering for a while.

"...Would you two...like to wait outside?"

"...I'm goin' in."

"...I'll go."

We really don't need any extra baggage, though...

In Limis's eyes, the pair will definitely prove useless here. At most, they'll just be obstacles. But if they say they're coming along, there's no choice but to bring them.

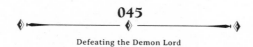

The party anxiously arrives at the underground entrance, where Limis notices the figure of a person.

...A priest?

Limis is dumbstruck. It's a boy roughly the same height as her.

He is clad in a dark-indigo mage robe, and the massive trunk at his side indicated a traveler at first glance. Nobody comes to the Great Tomb on vacation, though.

In the same moment Limis notices him, the young boy turns around.

He has black hair and eyes like Toudou and looks to be a year or two younger. The cross-shaped earring in his right ear is proof of a priest. His face is still quite boyish, and when he sees Limis and the others, he grins.

The boy's hair is neatly cut, and his calm expression is certainly in line with the image of a priest—but conversely, he doesn't look like someone who ought to be in a dangerous place such as this.

Because he looks so out of place, Limis thinks for a moment that he must be the child they're there to save but then quickly remembers they're looking for a girl.

Before Limis can speak, the boy begins to talk. He has a relaxed voice that is pleasant to the ears.

"Imagine that, meeting a friend here..."

"...? Who are you? What are you doing here?"

A friend? But we've...never met.

Limis instinctively responds with a question. The boy gazes skyward and sighs with deep emotion.

His philosophical demeanor clashes with his appearance, leaving Limis unsure just how old he is.

Toudou, still looking white as a sheet, lines up next to her.

"It's...dangerous here. You should leave."

"Dangerous? No, no... I think not. I...was tasked with a job, and I've taken a bit of an unexpected vacation..."

Toudou's party is perplexed by his nonsensical rambling, but he continues.

"The overdone sense of justice is a crime."

"This tomb is quite famous, and I was thinking I might like to visit it. Perhaps it is God's will."

From the way he's talking, he must be completely unaware this is a battleground, but then another possibility occurs to Limis.

"Are you here for training?"

"? Ah, yes... Training... Yes, I am still in training."

The boy squints and stares at the now wide-open stairwell. There's no fear in his eyes. Observing this, Limis comes up with a great idea.

"...Are you high level?"

"No, no... I'm still in training, so I'm nothing special."

"Well, it doesn't matter. You're a priest, right?"

Aria's eyes widen like saucers when she realizes Limis's intent.

Embarrassed, the boy turns the corners of his mouth up slightly.

"No... Well, at least something very close to one."

Limis looks toward Toudou. Toudou hates men but quickly nods vigorously.

It appears the scales have tipped toward the undead and away from men.

"We're heading inside right now, but we don't have a priest with us. If it's not too much trouble, would you join us?"

At Limis's suggestion, the boy taps his chin with his index finger and tilts his head to the side.

At that moment, Limis sees the black ring on his ring finger and is gripped by a fierce jolt of déjà vu.

"I don't mind... But I cannot cast healing spells. Will you still accept me into your party?"

"...What kind of priest can't cast healing spells?"

"It's rather embarrassing, but as you know, I'm still in training..."

He sure doesn't sound embarrassed.

His demeanor is a bit concerning, but it's still better than no priest. After all, Toudou and Aria are going to be completely useless on this quest. Limis sighs deeply and stares at the boy.

He stares back, his eyes so deeply black they might swallow her whole.

"By the way… How far is your destination? I plan on going rather deep myself…"

"We're not planning on going that far. About an hour's journey, one way."

"In that case, would you mind if I part ways in the middle?"

"…Sure."

The boy chuckles at Limis's reply. He extends his hand, smiling.

Transparent veins stick out from his slender wrists, and his fingertips are unblemished.

He certainly doesn't look like he could put up a fight, but beggars can't be choosers.

Limis sighs, switching places with Toudou, and shakes the boy's hand. There's a startling amount of strength in that grip.

"I'm Limis. These two sad sacks are Nao and Aria. Nice to make your acquaintance, however short it'll be."

"Likewise. By the way…"

The boy licks his lips. Another wave of déjà vu washes over Limis when she spots the shape of the golden earring in his left ear.

Before she realizes what that ornament represents, the boy continues.

"My name is Gregorio. Gregorio Legins, my friends. Pleasure to make your acquaintance."

"The overdone sense of justice is a crime."

"Why do you keep saying 'my friends'?"

"In accordance with the God of Order, what else would you call those who you stand beside in order to banish the followers of darkness, if not friends?"

"...How should I know?"

Limis is deeply unsettled by the youth who speaks with such composure.

I don't care how helpful you are—just don't get in my way.

On the Monsters in the Underground Tomb

"Heal."

As I pray, a bright-green light erupts from my palm.

This is the most common healing spell. Any healing spell below this is incredibly weak, so being able to cast this is the first step toward becoming a full-fledged priest.

Spica's eyes are sparkling as she watches the spell unfold. Maybe it's because she's alone with an unfamiliar adult, or maybe it's the way I look at her—either way, she seems to be getting used to me after having cowered around me for so long.

I don't know if she'll be able to use it, but if she can learn how to cast *Heal*, this orphan will be set for life in the future. Even if she's not particularly skilled, if she practices praying every day for a few years, she should be able to cast the lowest level.

"This spell is called Heal. It's enough to cure any kind of injury you might get in your day-to-day life."

"W-will I...be able to cast it, too?"

"You will."

However, in this world, there are some things that just can't be helped for whatever reason.

For example, my devoutly faithful parents aren't able to use holy techniques, but I can. And then there's the fact that Toudou, of all people, has the fate of the world on his shoulders. I can't say for sure whether or not Spica will become an accomplished priest.

Spica looks down at her palm, closing and opening it.

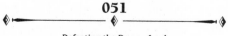

I'm not saying she should be able to do it immediately. She doesn't have the same powerful divine protection that Toudou has. The fact that he was able to cast *Blessing of Ahz Gried* after just *one day* is proof that he's truly something special.

"Spica, you said you were level three, right?"

"..."

Spica looks away and nods in response.

In general, the average person will reach level 5 by age ten, but that applies to those with actual parental figures.

But since Spica might join Toudou's party, she's no good at such a low level. Sighing, I announce, "Spica, we're going to raise your level."

"...Um... But—"

Spica's eyes widen in surprise, and she looks up at me as if gauging my mood.

This isn't the type of monster you would normally defeat at level 3, but luckily for us, it's a perfect match for me. I have to get her level up to the bare minimum before Toudou arrives.

A priest's combat strength is comparatively low in relation to other classes—with the exception of the Mad Eater. However, our battle strength jumps up significantly when fighting the undead.

One of the holy techniques, exorcism, is a miracle given to us to take on the followers of darkness. Any priest who masters it no longer fears low-level undead. Higher-level undead are still a threat, but the ones populating the upper levels of the Great Tomb are unintelligent brutes functioning on instinct alone.

I cast a barrier focused on the room of the Devil-Faced Knight's Altar. This barrier, called a *demon lure prism*, has the quality of attracting undead.

After putting up the barrier, I take the dagger hanging from my belt and hand it, scabbard and all, to Spica.

The hilt is ornamented in gold, and the scabbard is black. It is clearly of high quality, and Spica stares at me, bewildered, as she takes it.

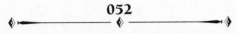

"The overdone sense of justice is a crime."

"It's a mythril dagger. Mythril can ward off darkness. I'll lend it to you."

It's also famous for being incredibly light—enough so that even Spica's slender arm is able to hold it. I've been using the blade for ages but always keep it in perfect shape. It has no issue slicing through bone and sinewy tissue.

It's a rather small dagger for someone my size, but compared to Spica's tiny frame, it looks like a short sword. She unsheathes it slowly, her mouth agape at the silver flash of the razor-sharp blade.

Mythril equipment is very effective against followers of darkness, but it still won't be enough for a level 3.

I put my index and middle fingers on Spica's head and cast a holy technique.

"Full Sacred Protection."

A silver light radiates from her head around her entire body, shimmering with phosphorescence.

This buff turns the human body into a consecrated area for a limited amount of time. It's a high-level holy technique that instantly purifies low-level undead if they touch the person affected. In this state, the person enhanced can defeat the undead with a single stab from a dagger.

Spica twirls in a circle as she tries to look over her shoulder and see how the beads of light are transforming her.

I cast a few other buffs that boost her physical strength for good measure.

Just as I finish the last, some living dead attracted by the barrier appear in the entrance.

There are three of them. Spica stiffens her shoulders and stares directly at the shambling corpses—the same kind she'd seen several times along the way.

Seeing the undead is one thing, but destroying them is a different story. The living dead move very slowly, so defeating them should be easy.

But I want to drive the point home. I cast a fine strand of light from my index finger, twisting the beam around the living dead and tying them up.

This is an exorcism spell that prevents undead movement called *Holy Bind*. The undead are trapped from head to toe by the binding light, face-down on the ground and writhing.

A child could defeat them now. Hell, even a baby.

"Go on, destroy 'em."

"O-okay…"

As I encourage her, Spica approaches the crumpled living dead nervously and pierces one of their skulls with the tip of the mythril dagger. The creature disappears in a flash, as if it exploded. It's been wholly purified, leaving no trace of paralysis or poison behind.

"Now get rid of the rest."

"Got it."

This time she doesn't look scared. She stabs the remaining two undead quickly with the tip of the dagger and purifies them.

A fresh set of undead, including a wraith, are drawn to the barrier, and I waste no time in binding them.

In that moment, I receive a message from Amelia, who's still in the village, having been tasked with luring Toudou's party.

The father of the Purif church is different from Helios Endell of the Great Forest of the Vale—he's stern and unaccommodating. Amelia needed to deceive him in order to lure Toudou and the others this way, and she has somehow succeeded.

"Everything's finished on my end. How about you?"

"We've arrived on-site. I'm helping Spica level up as we speak."

"Huh? What are you doing that for?"

"It's too dangerous for her to stay at her current level."

As I answer Amelia, I watch Spica jump as high as she can to stab a wraith frozen in midair.

"Ares… Haven't you gotten a little sweet on Spica?"

"I'm not trying to spoil her or anything…"

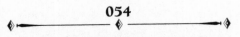

"The overdone sense of justice is a crime."

This is normal. Totally normal.

"You were opposed to using Spica as bait, too… This isn't like the coldhearted Ares I know."

Just what the hell does Amelia think of me? Coldhearted… Pssh.

While talking with Amelia, I continue using Holy Bind to freeze the undead that are now entering the room in droves.

Although she seemed tense at first, Spica quickly relaxes as she finishes off the rest of her foes.

I confirm that she's gained enough life force to attain the maximum of three levels, and I perform the level-up ritual.

Spica is now level 6. She needs an additional 152 life force to reach her next level.

I'm not sure what's bothering Amelia, but she repeats herself indignantly.

"I told you, you're absolutely favoring her."

"I am not favoring her… Although, you could say I'm used to orphans."

Maybe that's why it looks like I'm taking a shine to Spica.

Spica begins breaking out into a wide grin, and I pat her on the head as I point to newly approaching undead foes.

Higher levels become exponentially harder to gain, but she should be able to reach level 10 easily. Even if Spica doesn't make it into Toudou's party, there's no disadvantage to her being at a higher level.

"Used to orphans?"

"Yeah, because my parents ran an orphanage."

I grew up around a lot of orphans like Spica. It was like having a bunch of brothers and sisters.

It's been almost ten years since I last saw any of them. I wonder how they're doing now.

"Ares, were you also an orphan?"

"No, my parents *ran an orphanage*. I'm just used to orphans because I helped out a lot."

They're all old memories now. Somewhere along the way, someone started a lie that I'm unsentimental.

Spica looks my way—maybe she's gained enough life force? I give her a thumbs-up. I'm the positive-reinforcement type.

If she gains enough levels, Spica might be able to use low-level holy techniques. Even now, she ought to be feeling the power of holy techniques resonating within her. When people experience miracles for themselves, their faith deepens.

Amelia, clearly unsatisfied, continues complaining.

"I see... So you are favoring her after all."

"No, I'm not!"

I really wish she would explain to me how this amounts to playing favorites.

The undead just keep coming, and Spica's level continues to rise.

When she reaches level 10, I break down the barrier and keep away the undead. Limis is currently level 17, so I decide to keep Spica relatively low in comparison.

It wasn't exactly the most furious battle, but maybe because she was moving around so much, Spica's breathing is ragged. I pass her some water.

From roughly around the point she passed level 7, the hesitation gradually dissipated from Spica's movements. Watching her fear melt away before my eyes boosted my hopes that Toudou can conquer his fear of the undead.

Toudou's party won't have the advantage of a buff, but their equipment alone should easily prevent the undead from frightening them. Once they see how readily their swords can kill an undead, their fear will dissipate, too.

I check the time. Calculating backward from when Amelia sent notice, it wouldn't be surprising for Toudou's group to show up at any moment.

I turn toward Spica again.

"The overdone sense of justice is a crime."

"Spica, it's almost time for our plan to start. Do exactly as I told you."

"O-okay! Um... What about you, Mr. Ares?"

"I'll lure some more undead here. And, well, worse comes to worst, I'll purify them for you, so don't worry."

I wouldn't be able to bear it if the hero died trying to get over his fear of the undead. I'd be marked a traitor.

There's also a technique that purifies a targeted area. It can pass through thin walls, so purifying this entire room should be easy. I'd have to come up with another excuse, but at the very least, I can keep the undead at bay.

I cast another full round of each holy technique on Spica. Her eyes twinkle as she is once again entranced by the various colors of magical light. A lot of people become priests because they want to learn holy techniques. In that case, Amelia might have been right all along.

"Are you tired?"

"No, I'm fine! Um..."

Spica looks up at me. She pauses, then continues with resolve.

"C-can I...can I become like you, Mr. Ares?"

"No chance."

There's no way she could, and she's got no reason to.

My experience as a priest is unusual. That's how I ended up playing adviser to a hero's party.

Tears spring to Spica's eyes, and I pat her.

"Do whatever you feel you can do. You don't need to be just like me."

Every person has a role, a fate that exists for them. That means there's a possibility that Spica's role in life is to assist a hero's party and, in turn, save the world.

That's why I'm going to keep doing whatever I can.

I leave Spica and generate another demon lure prism from a separate room.

I've lured the undead on many occasions. As a crusader, I did it to

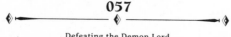

level up my subordinates, and I've helped everyday mercenaries gain levels as part of my general responsibilities.

The undead are attracted to the light, and a number of them enter the room.

I repress the urge to purify them on the spot. Instead, I make sure the exit doesn't get clogged and push them toward the center of the room. Given the difference in level and my divine protection, whenever undead get close, they don't even attempt to touch me.

In this area, aside from living dead and wraiths, there are walking bones and wisps that appear as well. Regardless, they're all low-level undead, and it doesn't matter which you attract first.

After I essentially fill the room to capacity, I lock the exit with a barrier and move on to the next room.

Once I finish filling three whole rooms, my heightened senses detect the presence of some living beings nearby.

Because I'm inside this chamber, and thanks to the swarm of followers of darkness, the presences are hard to detect.

I focus my mind and retrace my steps, hiding myself in a small, empty room along the way. Things come further into focus when I close my eyes.

The presence shining the brightest is Toudou's; the small yet brightly flaming presence is Limis's; the quiet, sharp one is Aria's; and there's Glacia's, a massive, heavy presence belying her size. They're gradually proceeding toward the Devil-Faced Knight's Altar. That's when I realize something:

There's another with them.

It should be four people—Toudou, Limis, Aria, and Glacia—but there are five. What's going on?

This doesn't match what Amelia told me. There wasn't anyone from the church—she said the *four* of them were headed this way.

When did the additional person step in? Should we abandon the plan...?

I shake my head and quash the ideas popping up in my mind. I don't

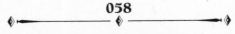

"The overdone sense of justice is a crime."

know who's joined them, but Toudou overcoming his fear must take top priority. If this person managed to make it down into the Great Tomb, they won't die that easily.

Their presences come closer. One hundred meters. Fifty meters. Ten. Five.

Suddenly, I realize I recognize the fifth presence. It's quieter than Aria's and calm as a still water's surface. And yet it completely repulses me. For a second, my head is screaming in agony.

I do know it. I know I've felt this presence before, but...I can't place it.

They pass in front of the room I'm in, and I can hear Limis's voice.

"Looks like we somehow didn't run into any undead this time."

Yeah, that's because of the demon lure prism I cast.

The next voice sounds calm and entirely out of place.

"Yes. Such a disappointment... I was hoping to see droves of them."

"'Hoping'? ...You're a strange one."

"Hoping"...? Maybe it's a mercenary who came to hunt undead and happened to run into Toudou's group?

I spread out my hands. They're covered in a cold sweat. Nothing's wrong, and yet my heart is beating a mile a minute. It's like I'm trying to remember something that I absolutely shouldn't...

"...What's in the suitcase anyway?"

"Oh, this? It's empty. There's nothing inside, my friends."

"Huh? Then what are you lugging it around for?"

Their words are a curse, eating through my brain like maggots.

I crouch and hold my head. *Shit. I feel like I'm gonna throw up.*

My fervent prayers are not to be answered. Soon I'm able to hear their entire conversation.

"It is for the purposes of the faith, my friends. This here is...my mace."

"...Um, are you okay?"

AHHHHHHHHHHHHHHHHHHHHHHHHHHHHHHH!!!

NO, I'M NOTTTTTTTTTTTTTTTTTTTTTTTTTT!!

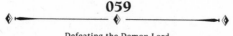

059

I clench my teeth and resist the urge to bash my head against the wall. Instead, I put a call through to Creio, and the second he answers, I ask him one thing.

"Hey… What happened to Gregorio, the guy you called on to handle that demon in Vale Village?"

"Hmm? Oh, him… He said if we didn't need his help, there's a place he wants to visit, so he'd like to take a vacation. He's on leave now… Did you need his help again, or—?"

"N-no… I don't need him…so call him back."

"…Pardon?"

"Please…take him back. I beg of you."

I DON'T NEEEEEEEEEEEEEED HIM!!

That piece of shit… Why is he here? Switch him! Switch!

What kind of fate is this? Who the hell is messing with me? Is it fun, screwing me over?!

I steady my breath and conceal my presence. It feels like I've turned into some sort of small prey.

I search for their presences. No matter where or how many times I look, I can feel Gregorio, who I met so long ago. It's no wonder I didn't notice. I didn't want to remember. *DIE!*

The Mad Eater. Gregorio Legins.

He calls people his friends and his trunk his "faith." He declares the extermination of heresy his holy calling… A mad, twisted crusader.

Law and morality bend before his faith. He's like a crazed machine, exterminating every single enemy of the Church he comes upon. The lowest of the low among the Out Crusade.

This is a man I never want to see, who I never want to introduce to anyone. And now I'm going to run into him, under the absolute worst circumstances.

"Issue the Mad Eater a direct order to return."

"Sorry, but I can't get through to him right now. Gregorio is scheduled to give me his regular report in a few hours. I'll relay the order then."

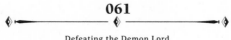

"...Got it."

Our connection cuts out. In the same moment, Toudou's party's presences reach the Devil-Faced Knight's Altar.

My mind is absolutely roiling. I desperately manage to stay calm.

What do I do? What should I do? Does he know Toudou is the Holy Warrior? No, he can't possibly. If anyone found out that an apostle of the God of Order, the Holy Warrior, was afraid of the undead...there'd be hell to pay.

"Oh... There she is!"

Just then, I hear Toudou's ragged voice cry out.

He must have been particularly spooked, but as calm returns to his voice, I hear the footsteps of Limis and the others rushing over to Spica.

Everything is going as planned—aside from the one thorn in our side.

Gregorio takes pride in being one of the most battle-proficient crusaders around. Even the average crusader could purify every undead within reach in an instant. Our plan was to start luring hordes of undead at this juncture, but clearly, it would be pointless.

First and foremost, I absolutely need to separate Toudou and Gregorio.

Gregorio's dangerous. His nickname, the Mad Eater, doesn't refer to those he annihilates—it refers to Gregorio himself.

I want to fill Spica in on a change of plans, but there's no way to contact her. The magical tool that allows me to communicate via transmission will connect only to headquarters, and at this point, I won't even be able to reach Amelia.

"Are you okay?! You're okay, right?! I'm so glad. Let's get outta here!"

"Um... Thank...you?"

Toudou's lilting voice overlaps with Spica's complete bewilderment.

I gave Spica general information on every party member coming to

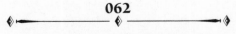

"The overdone sense of justice is a crime."

help her. She's probably confused by the extra person in the rescue team. Seriously, why the hell is he even here?

Everything that's transpired since arriving in Purif has gone completely off the rails. Makes me want to just quit my job.

Just then, Gregorio says quizzically, "...Goodness, little lady. That's quite the powerful prism you've got here, isn't it?"

"?!"

Spica gasps. Toudou won't understand, but Spica will fall for Gregorio's act—he's a fellow priest.

He continues speaking to her with concern in his voice. This is just like Gregorio: get close with a gentle missive and then dive in for the kill.

"Prism...?"

"Yes... A top-level protective prism and a first-rate buff... You aren't a regular caster. The prism barrier holy technique drains massive amounts of holy energy. Heh-heh-heh... A priest who can cast spells of these classes simultaneously must be...at least level seventy, no? For someone like yourself to manage this level of protection is a bit much..."

"Level...seventy? ...Her?!"

"Um... Well..."

Toudou can't hide his bewilderment. Obviously, a child could never employ that kind of magic—*use your head, dammit!*

Gregorio's voice is tinged with glee as he happily shoots down Toudou's remark.

"No. This girl here is level...ten. It can't be her casting. This is the work of a powerful adversary, one with an impressive amount of holy energy... Could it be—?"

The most aggravating thing about Gregorio is that he's not only ridiculously strong. To be a crusader—those tasked with vanquishing the enemies of God hiding in plain sight among humanity—you can't get by as a dumb brute.

Gregorio whispers happily, "Perhaps...I'll be able to meet one of my compatriots."

*I REFUUUUUUUUUUUUUUUUUSE!! Take a good look at yourself,
asshole!*

"Compatriot...?"

"Heh-heh-heh... I'm talking about my fellows who wait for orders
to vanquish demons, my friends. Although, since we're all so busy, we
rarely have the chance to meet one another..."

And thank God for that. Because Gregorio and I are both dispo-
sitioned toward battle, we hold similar roles and are rarely grouped
together.

As I wait for the situation to dissipate and cast a tranquility spell over
myself, Spica suddenly speaks up in response to Gregorio's comment.

"Huh? ...Are you...friends with Mr. Ares...?"

Whoa—don't say my name out loud!

As I freak out elsewhere, Gregorio's voice swells with emotion.

"Oh! Yes, my friend Ares! So he's been here as well... This surely
must also be a sign from the God of Order..."

*AHHHHHHHHHHHHHHHHHHHHHHHHHHHHHH! MY NAAAAAA
AAAAAAAAAME!!*

Shit, I should have locked her mouth shut. But really, who could
have predicted that Gregorio of all people would be here?

I cast a holy technique to soothe my splitting headache. Hurry, Amelia! Hurry up and put me through! Someone stop Spica!

"Young miss, when you say the person who cast this barrier around
you is named Ares... Surely that must be my dear old friend."

The hairs on my neck stand up, and a shiver runs down my spine.
How dare he spread such lies?!

Since when the hell are we dear old friends? Huh? How does a
one-sided relationship count as friendship?!

Toudou and Aria whisper to each other behind the rest's backs.

"Ares? ...You mean *that* Ares?"

"...No, that's highly unlikely. There are many priests named Ares."

"Oh, I see..."

"The overdone sense of justice is a crime."

Well, that much is a blessing in disguise. It looks like I'll get away without Toudou's party finding me out.

Limis has been quiet thus far, but suddenly, she pipes up with a clear sense of boredom, the entire situation having gone over her head. "Well, we found Spica, so let's get out of this depressing place!"

"Y-yeah! Let's get out of here!"

"Well, I hate to take my leave of you now, but I guess this means our travels together end here. There are further enemies of God hanging around this tomb that need eradicating..."

My eyes fly open at Gregorio's unanticipated announcement.

Maybe they did really just meet along the way. If that's true, then everything could still work out once they separate.

It feels as if I stepped on a land mine that turned out to be a dud.

Let's face that fear of the undead somewhere else, shall we? Getting over it as quickly as possible is paramount, but right now, ditching Gregorio is more important.

Just then, I hear Spica say something I would have never expected.

"N-no... Just a bit more."

"Huh...?"

"A bit longer... Um... I just, I want to stay here a little longer..."

AHHHHHHHHHHHHHHHHHHH!! Spica! Are you planning on keeping them here until the undead invade?!

No, no—there's no need. The plan has already failed.

Without any transmission magic, there's no way I can get the message to her. Maybe we do need one more person who can use transmission magic after all. Guess I'll ask Creio about it later.

"H-hey, it's dangerous here, so we should just leave—"

Toudou makes a strange hiccuping noise and goes over to convince Spica. This might be the only time Toudou and I are in agreement.

"Listen... Um..."

I appreciate his efforts, but Spica answers fervently.

"I just...like danger."

"Wh-what?! B-b-but why?!"

His voice is already thin and hoarse.

Really, though, is she serious?! No one would give an answer like that!

"Just the kind of girl I would expect Ares to protect. What bravery! Perhaps we already have all the compatriots we need?"

Gregorio is the only one unbothered by Spica's bizarre reply. He must feel sympathy toward another human who thrives on danger. But he is mistaken.

I've had enough—won't he just leave us alone already?

Fed up, I hear Limis's brusque voice again. I don't think it's going too far to say that breaking out of this deadlock is entirely dependent on her inability to read the room. *Come on, Limis!*

"...Okay, so I'm just gonna ask—how long have you been here?"

"Well... Hmm... An hour...?"

"What?! A whole hour?!"

"Th-that's quite..."

Toudou shrieks like he's seen a ghost. Aria also sounds a bit shaky. *Where did she get that number—one hour?*

"Heh-heh-heh... Well, then, I'll be off to purify some nearby undead."

Gregorio then leaves the room.

His capacity to detect nearby undead is the same as mine.

Gregorio strides over to the room that I painstakingly crammed with fodder and opens the door.

The second he does, any trace of undead writhing inside disappears instantly. He purified every one of them without making a sound. I hear a single ominous suppressed laugh.

Should I engage him now, in this moment? No, it's pointless.

It would be too weird, no matter how I did it. If I interact with him, he won't stop asking what I'm doing here. That might necessitate a negotiation, but now isn't the right time.

I can hear Gregorio talking to himself. His presence passes in front of the room in which I'm hiding.

Happily, it looks like he still doesn't know where I am. I don't wanna see that asshole.

"Heh-heh-heh… Ares, were these undead a present for me? Or perhaps you're apologizing for stealing my kill in the Great Forest of the Vale?"

No damn way. Use your head, dumbass!

He purifies the undead in every room in a matter of minutes before returning to the Devil-Faced Knight's Altar.

"I've finished the purification. Have you made a decision?"

"Yes… We've decided to wait another thirty minutes."

A compromise. I breathe a slight sigh of relief.

Thirty minutes should still guarantee Toudou stays undiscovered. The hero and his party will hide the fact that he's the Holy Warrior, and why would Gregorio ever suspect that someone afraid of the undead could even *be* the Holy Warrior?

I'd like them to split up and Gregorio to take off somewhere alone, but it looks like he plans on waiting, too. As I pray for time to pass even one second faster, Gregorio speaks.

"This is my first time beholding this incredible statue…"

"Oh, right… It's said to have some connection to a god enshrined here, but no one knows its origins."

Gregorio must be staring into the face of the Devil-Faced Knight in front of the altar. Aria contributes yet another piece of worthless trivia.

In response, Gregorio declares frankly, "This statue honors another god. We must destroy it."

"Wha…what?!"

"This is simply another of my responsibilities."

That's not even close to one of our jobs! If anything, the credo states that we must *not* show contempt for other gods!

"Wait—"

067

My voice doesn't reach Gregorio. I hear the slight *ping* of the metal clasp on his trunk opening.

No one can stop him now. His trunk is made of mythril.

Go ahead and smash it—I don't mind. It doesn't matter, but...please, don't let anything drastic happen!

At that moment, contrary to my prayer, I feel the entire room vibrate. It looks like the gods might actually hate me.

"Wh-whoa!"

"Huh?!"

"Wha—?!"

A massive presence. Something is about to betray my expectations. I'm ready to quit my job and go home. Of course, that would never be allowed. But could everything that's happening actually be my fault and not Toudou's?

I hear fragments of the walls falling and shattering.

Next, the entire room echoes with a thunderous roar of hard stones smashing into one another.

Screams from Toudou and his party slowly reverberate. Among their cries, oddly enough, I'm able to hear Gregorio's voice clearly.

"Heh-heh-heh... A false idol... An enemy of God. Our god will not give you the time to regret your sins."

The entire hallway shakes heavily. I can't see anything, but I have a pretty clear idea of what's happening.

The Devil-Faced Knight is moving.

That bastard Gregorio has obviously never heard the age-old adage—let sleeping dogs lie!

Die! You alone, just die! Why the hell is this crazed mercenary meddling in things he shouldn't be?!

Ignorant of my invectives, Gregorio begins introducing himself in a dignified tone.

"It is I, Out Crusader of the third order Gregorio Legins. In the name of my god, I shall be the one to gauge the weight of your sins. Heh-heh... Ha-ha—AH-HA-HA-HA-HA-HA-HA-HA-HA-HA!!"

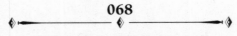

"The overdone sense of justice is a crime."

§ § §

"Eek! The statue moved?!"

Moving statues and ghosts are one and the same for Toudou.

A bitter shriek echoes through the room. Aria, also white as a sheet, takes a step backward.

The devil-masked statue looks ready to attack at any second. Of course, the statue itself is so elaborate that it already seems as if it could move on its own—but having it actually do so is a different story.

Perhaps by some certain providence, the statue's eyes emit a pale-blue light in the darkness. Its gaze is horrifyingly inhuman, filled with palpable malicious intent.

Toudou reflexively draws her sword halfway with a shaky hand, but at that same instant, the devil-faced statue draws its own sword from its hip. Its metal blade flashes brilliantly like the crescent moon in the darkness.

To Toudou's knowledge, this weapon is called a katana. However, the length of its blade is vastly greater than any katana she knows—nearly twice the length of Toudou's holy sword, Ex.

Toudou inhales sharply from nerves. The statue ignores her and turns its neck as if to take in its surroundings.

Until just a few moments ago, it was merely a stone statue. Struck dumb by its bizarre nature, Limis lets her eyes go wide. "A golem?! This presence—" Her voice quavers.

"This is merely the crumbling relic of a pagan god—"

Unlike Toudou, who is trembling with fear, Gregorio takes one step closer to the Devil-Faced Knight without hesitation.

The statue then looks down at Gregorio.

It's more than twice as tall as he is. The crusader must be feeling some intimidation right about now.

Directly in front of Toudou, the pallid, inhuman eyes of the statue and Gregorio's jet-black pupils meet with fearsome intensity.

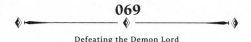

069

Aria comes back to her senses and grips Spica by the hand, pulling her away. In nearly that same instant, the statue's blade strikes.

It's a swift, heavy blow. The two-meter-long blade makes a strange sound as it cuts through the air, the gleaming metal cleaving a massive arc.

Gregorio moves forward even farther, almost as if shielding Toudou, who is already immobilized with fear.

The rush of steel jolts their eardrums, and the entire room shakes. Limis shuts her ears, and Aria opens her eyes.

"Wha—?"

"It's not working... It seems...this statue is not a follower of darkness."

Its blade stops. Having finally come to her senses, Toudou takes a few steps backward and readies her sword once more.

Gregorio is using his massive trunk as a shield.

There's nothing inside, just as he said, and it flashes a dim silver glow in the darkness.

There is the sound of metal clashing as the statue's sword comes slashing down on the trunk. The statue is trying to slice it in half, but the trunk remains completely unscathed.

The statue lifts its sword again and flies down from its pedestal, unleashing a second strike. Wielding his trunk, Gregorio deflects the swipe easily as the blade pierces a hole in the wall.

Toudou's party is completely dumbstruck, but Gregorio just smiles gently.

He isn't even out of breath. Rather, one look in his eyes, and it's clear he is excited.

"Yes, but... Heh-heh... That doesn't matter. Not at all, my friends."

"Are you...okay?"

"Yes. I'm fine. I'm in fine fettle. My faith... There is not a cloud in it."

Just as he stated, although faced with a sword much larger than himself, Gregorio exhibits neither trepidation nor fear.

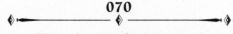

"The overdone sense of justice is a crime."

The statue must have perceived the strength in Gregorio's temperament because it brings its weapon back to eye level and takes a few steps back. There is a definite measure of skill in the way it handles its weapon. With Spica still hidden behind her, Aria murmurs in amazement.

"What on earth...? I've never seen anything like this... A golem that can actually wield a sword?!"

"The techniques of another god are not our concern. This is simply...a test of strength between my own faith and that of the statue."

Gregorio closes the trunk, which he had been holding wide open. Gripping it by the handle, he approaches the Devil-Faced Knight nonchalantly.

He looks utterly defenseless despite having been able to stop the statue's blows with his trunk. Toudou tightly balls her left hand into a fist and takes a step forward.

Her ring—a magical item she keeps tucked away—flashes brightly, and a massive shield she'd stored in another dimension instantly appears in her left hand.

Now aware that this living statue is somehow not an undead, Toudou is able to regain her composure. In response, her holy sword, Ex, shines in her right hand and lights up the room ever so slightly.

"Aria, Limis. Let's go, too."

Limis quickly takes up her staff. Aria inhales deeply and draws her sword.

However, Gregorio already closed the distance between himself and the Devil-Faced Knight and is now standing before it.

The giant sword comes down like a guillotine. Gregorio watches the blade intensely.

He sidesteps the attack and kicks off the ground.

At the same time, he brandishes the trunk again, and with the momentum from his kick, he spins around in midair and smashes the box into the Devil-Faced Knight's torso with the full force of his body.

The corner of the trunk scrapes into the stone, and white fragments scatter down to the floor. The Devil-Faced Knight is blown against the wall, its massive body bent over from the extraordinary power of the mythril trunk.

The air trembles. Toudou is completely dumbfounded by the spectacle, mouth agape as she blinks twice.

"...Huh? What was that?"

"..."

Gregorio is even shorter than Toudou, but he blasted the statue—twice Toudou's height—across the room. The entire scene is surreal. And yet Gregorio, a priest, did it with luggage.

Aria rubs her eyes as if waking from a dream and checks her surroundings again. Gregorio approaches the Devil-Faced Knight. Its body is smashed up against the wall, caved into the stone. Gregorio brandishes the trunk again.

He bashes the blunt instrument mercilessly into the Devil-Faced Knight's face as it attempts to rise.

A crazed laugh resounds throughout the room.

"AH-HA-HA-HA-HA-HA-HA-HA-HA-HA!! May those who encounter my faith be turned to ash!!"

"What... What's...happening?"

Gregorio has transformed. There is no stopping his deranged barrage of attacks.

A fearsome clash of heavy metal against stone reverberates repeatedly, each strike launching chunks of stone into the air. The Devil-Faced Knight's horns are smashed to oblivion, and its face is being whittled away bit by bit. Its body contorts, feebly trying to lift off the ground with its right arm, but without missing a beat, Gregorio immediately stomps on the arm, sending cracks through it. After the second and third stomp, the appendage is smashed to pieces.

Gregorio sneers, and he spits into the quivering remnants of the statue's face.

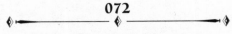

"The overdone sense of justice is a crime."

"Shall that be enough? You are a heretic, after all."

"Sir...Sir Gregorio—"

Gregorio ignores Aria and brings the trunk crashing down on the Devil-Faced Knight's head with all his might. Cracks begin forming on the ground from the impact, and then, he looks back at her, suddenly himself again.

"Is there something the matter, my friend?"

"N-no..."

His voice is still as calm as ever. For a moment, Aria loses her nerve at the disparity in Gregorio's demeanor, but shaking her head, she voices what she is thinking.

"The...the statue is likely a golem. That means it has a core some- where. If you don't destroy it—"

"No, I believe you are mistaken—this is not a golem."

"...Huh?"

Gregorio continues silently looking down at the statue's face. Its eyes are as calm as a lake's surface.

"If this was a golem, we would have sensed the magic energy from its core from the very beginning. Even now, as it twitches on the ground, there's no sign of it. I'm sure Limis has noticed as well..."

Aria turns to Limis, who nods timidly.

"What? Then why—?"

"Perhaps she thought it was the work of an unknown false god? In the end, my friend, the principle behind it doesn't matter... It's purely inconsequential."

Gregorio responds to Aria's confusion matter-of-factly and picks up his trunk by the handle once more.

"Why, you ask? Because regardless, my annihilation of heresy is a given. It doesn't matter if they are followers of darkness or the tricks of another god. Purifying them all is an order handed down to me, a holy decree—who or what guides the enemy doesn't matter to me."

"?!"

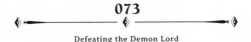

Just then, the Devil-Faced Knight uses what remains of its left arm to swipe at Gregorio, who is standing on its torso. He dodges the attack by swiftly leaping behind the statue. As the Devil-Faced Knight gets to its feet, Gregorio grips his mythril trunk and points it at the statue's arm.

"I-if it doesn't have a core, then how are you going to destroy it?!"

At Limis's words, Gregorio swings his trunk open yet again with a practiced hand and smiles.

"I'm going to completely obliterate it, my friend. This is the only method of salvation for the idols of foreign gods."

With its remaining hand, the Devil-Faced Knight picks its massive katana off the ground. Its head is riddled with cracks from the severe beating, and even though half its right arm is torn off, its movements give not even the slightest hint of hesitation or emotion.

With the same force as before, the statue swings its massive katana sideways toward Gregorio's neck.

The audible slash rips through the air, but Gregorio intercepts it with his trunk and lets the blade slide across its surface before dashing forward.

"Wha—!"

Toudou gasps in surprise.

A fearsome clash of metal against metal. As he approaches the Devil-Faced Knight, Gregorio bends his knees and takes a giant leap. The statue's blade fails to connect with its target and slashes through the air.

Toudou watches the two of them just miss each other without batting an eye.

The open trunk's surface conceals Gregorio from view for a moment, and in the next instant, he brings it down on the Devil-Faced Knight's head once again. Metal on metal again, only this time it isn't a dull *thud*—it is the shrill clanging of weaponry.

Toudou opens her eyes wide.

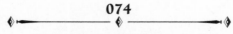

"The overdone sense of justice is a crime."

Gregorio lands next to the statue, and a white chunk of stone crashes beside Toudou: one of its devil horns, an intricately carved fang—and a single colorless eye.

"...Huh?"

For a moment, Toudou is unsure of what has just transpired. She looks up at the Devil-Faced Knight, now dejectedly on its knees. More than half its face is completely caved in. A gaping hole stretches from horn to fang.

Nonetheless, the statue's remaining eye is still emitting a faint light. The Devil-Faced Knight brandishes its sword as if completely unscathed.

Gregorio sneers before flying at the thing once again, laughing maniacally.

"AH-HA-HA-HA-HA-HA-HA-HA-HA-HA-HA-HA-HA-HA-HA-HA-HA-HA-HA-HA-HA-HA-HA-HA-HA-HA-HA-HA-HA-HA!!"

Limis quickly hides behind Aria. She intended to fight alongside Gregorio at first, but now, she just doesn't see an opening.

Because of the frenzied nature of the battle, any magic attacks would likely end up hitting Gregorio. That isn't her excuse, however... If she joined in now, she would quickly become a target.

You can't call this battle well-executed or smart, even if you are being polite. Rather, it looks like two beasts trying to eat each other alive.

However, now that it has lost an entire limb, the Devil-Faced Knight is limited in its offensive capabilities.

Every attack its massive sword launches is easily blocked, and its stone body chips away further with each swing from Gregorio's weapon.

As the Devil-Faced Knight loses its poise, Gregorio conceals himself under its abdomen. Utilizing his small frame, Gregorio kicks its knees and spins in midair, slamming its head into his mythril trunk.

A muffled *thud* like a guillotine dropping reverberates throughout the room. Something tumbles to the ground near Toudou's feet.

"——?!"

She just barely manages to contain a horrified shriek. It is the head of the Devil-Faced Knight.

The entire upper-right portion of it is bashed in. The light fades from its remaining eye. Although it was moving just moments before, it now looks like nothing more than a peculiar chunk of stone.

Even with its head ripped off, the Devil-Faced Knight shows no signs of stopping. But the winner is already clear.

The headless knight lets loose a barrage of slash attacks, clearly on its last legs. Gregorio blocks them all with his trunk.

Perhaps due to the strain of its onslaught, the Devil-Faced Knight's body begins to crumble.

The slight cracks in its body grow larger with each swing. It was only a matter of time before it self-destructed simply due to the force of its own barrage.

Just then, Gregorio furrows his brow for the first time and makes the most unbelievable comment.

"This is bad... It's going to destroy itself. It must be annihilated... by my faith."

"What?!"

Gregorio sets straight at the Devil-Faced Knight's sword. As the blade comes down diagonally from overhead, Gregorio spins and smashes his trunk against it. The statue's right wrist snaps from the force of its blow being intercepted.

This gives Gregorio a gap, and he steps in quickly, ramming the trunk full force into his enemy's solar plexus.

Gregorio laughs as he continues whaling on his opponent twice his size. Flabbergasted, Toudou whispers, "The priests in this world are really...incredible."

"W-well...if that's the standard we're going by, then..."

Aria turns to Toudou, a worried look on her face.

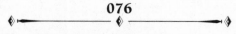

"The overdone sense of justice is a crime."

§ § §

The endlessly echoing noise of destruction and laughter rife with derision.

These sounds invite more bad omens than the followers of darkness themselves. I want to hold my head in my hands and cower in the corner.

The only silver lining is that even if holy techniques have no effect on the enemy, with Gregorio around, that won't be a problem. And maybe the fact that Toudou and his party, now privy to Gregorio's fighting style, will stay away from him entirely.

In general, the monsters that priests are capable of fighting on their own are limited to the undead and demons—anything that exorcism works on.

But crusaders are different. They each possess various skills to deal with an array of foes.

These could include the military arts, or holy techniques other than exorcism, or even sheer bravery or a strong network of allies. But for Gregorio—it's faith.

Gregorio's fanatic zeal for battling followers of darkness has left him without the use of most techniques performed by typical priests—aside from exorcism—including healing, buffs, and prism barriers.

But his combat skills put every other crusader to shame.

The best way to describe the battle prowess of this man—who wields a custom mythril trunk in place of a standard weapon—would be "crazed." Had the Church not given him specific directives over their concern for his spirituality and lack of holy techniques, his level might even be higher than mine.

The sounds bring me back to our current scene in the chamber with the Devil-Faced Knight.

It's very difficult to hear from the other side of the wall, but Toudou and his group seem to be unharmed, and there is no sign of Gregorio struggling. Before long, the sounds of battle become heavily one-sided.

077

Soon, all that remains is the noise of Gregorio's maniacal laughter and his trunk slamming against something, over and over and over.

Gregorio isn't the type to abandon Toudou's party that quickly.

Regardless, was this the work of a foreign god...? I don't understand the reasoning, but perhaps it's better it was destroyed.

At that moment, I finally receive a transmission from Amelia.

"How is everything going?"

"Our plan has failed. Tell Spica to return to the village."

"...Understood."

Perhaps she senses something in my voice, but Amelia asks no further questions and cuts the transmission.

Okay,. what to do now...? In any case, I need to get them separated.

Gregorio's goal appears to be the underground tomb below us. I should get Toudou to another area right away.

...Why must I concern myself with keeping away not only demons but now the Church, too? Gimme a break.

Soon, the roar of battle ceases entirely. Their target has fallen silent, it seems.

It doesn't matter where—just hurry up and leave Toudou's party alone and go as far down into the Great Tomb as you want...

I watch over the situation and pray. Just then, Gregorio speaks up, puzzled.

His tone shifts from crazed laughter to serious ponderance. He isn't speaking to anyone in particular but rather more like he's talking to himself.

"...I see. No, it's not. Yes, I understand. I do. This was...not the reason I came here."

"...Wh-what are you talking about?"

Limis's voice is much higher this time around when she asks.

"My apologies. It appears that...I should be returning to Purif with you all."

His voice is light but somehow self-assured.

My head is pounding.

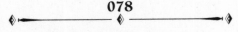

"The overdone sense of justice is a crime."

Dread shoots through me like countless insects writhing beneath my skin.

A loathsome stench. My perception warps. What is this sensation I'm feeling?

The taste of blood spreads through my mouth. A delayed, searing pain. I've bitten straight through my lip without even realizing it.

I can never understand the logic behind this guy's actions.

Third Report

On Dealing with the Mad Eater

Gregorio calls it "a hunch" or, sometimes, "guidance."

It had already been more than ten years since he first stepped onto the battlefield.

The experience he'd built up over time gave him a special breed of perception that he called a "miracle." This intuition of his meshed perfectly with his own mentality, the kind that made him willing to sacrifice himself for his faith.

In fact, it's fair to say that this is the very essence of this man who'd climbed his way to the third rank within the Out Crusade.

For that reason, Gregorio Legins never hesitates in his actions.

The air is cold and heavy. All that illuminates the windowless stone corridor is the sparkling crimson glow of a salamander.

Quiet footsteps echo along the chilly passageway, and aside from Gregorio and company, not a soul is present.

Ever since stepping foot into the underground tomb, he has felt a sinister presence lurking deep within, more nefarious than the monsters present in the upper levels.

Originally, that was his vacation plan—to annihilate those sinister beings in the far reaches of the tomb.

However, that plan is already far from his mind. It's because of the guidance.

For Gregorio, "guidance" must take absolute precedence. Even if others can only see it as pure delusion, he has a thorough logical impetus behind his actions.

Defeating the Demon Lord

Even as he departs the tomb accompanied by the group of youths he met by chance along the way, Gregorio firmly believes that he is following God's guidance, that he is walking the correct path. It's not that he knows everything. He doesn't have the power of foresight. But that doesn't matter to him.

Everything is as God wills it to be.

"Um... Mr. Gregorio?"

Spica, the girl the youngsters set out to rescue, looks up at him with her gray eyes.

Gregorio answers her beckoning with a slight smile.

"Is something the matter, my dear?"

Spica remains under a powerful buff, and in spite of her age, the girl survived the interior of the Great Tomb, albeit not very deep down. It's wholly unnatural, but Gregorio pays it no mind.

Her body is gaunt and her eyes downcast. This introverted young girl is speaking to a crusader who just earlier went on a violent rampage—but Gregorio chooses to ignore this unnatural progression, too.

Spica swallows a lump in her throat and continues nervously.

"Mr. Gregorio... Why did you decide to go back to the village?"

"It was God's guidance. Heh-heh... If you, too, wish to become a priest, then someday, you'll understand."

Gregorio never demands understanding. Priests are different from common folk, crusaders even more so.

Gregorio knows how different he is from everyone else, based on his experiences up until this point.

He knows it well, but he decidedly does not care. The only person who could understand him would be someone of the same ilk—a fellow crusader.

Spica falls silent, perhaps having felt something in the timbre of Gregorio's voice.

In an attempt to ameliorate the uncomfortable silence, Aria, the swordmaster walking beside Spica, asks, still pale in the face, "Sir Gregorio... Is—is that how you always fight?"

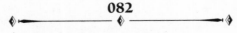

"The overdone sense of justice is a crime."

"No…I am a priest, after all."

Aria goes wide-eyed at Gregorio's reply.

"…Are you perhaps an exorcist?"

"Well, yes…something like one. However, my friend, being able to kill demons is a given for any priest. And that is because it is our God-given decree."

Suddenly, a black mist descends from the ceiling in the direction the group is headed.

It's a type of low-level undead. Gregorio nonchalantly points his index finger at it.

A moment later, their surroundings are engulfed in a white light, including the glow from Limis's fire spirit. Then, the darkness returns, but not a shred of the black mist from a moment ago remains.

Toudou is flabbergasted. Aria's breath catches in her throat, but she quickly regains her composure.

"I see… So that's exorcism, huh…?"

"I swore an oath to exterminate every enemy of God."

Limis opens her mouth to reply, but she glances at Toudou and decides to shut it.

The journey out of Yutith's Tomb takes longer than the way in.

The sun is high in the sky, and rays of light shine down. Toudou, the first to exit the tomb, squints from the sudden brightness.

Spica, Aria, Limis, and Glacia—who hasn't said a word the entire time—stagger up the stone stairs and make their way aboveground. When Gregorio, taking up the rear, appears, he looks at Toudou's party with the same expression as when they first met.

"Thank you very much, my friends. I will be taking my leave now."

"…Where will you go?"

Limis looks as if she wants to ask something more, and Gregorio thinks for a moment before smiling.

"I intend to stay at the church in Purif for some time. Please come by to see me if you need anything. The father of the church will relay you to me if necessary."

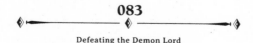

*   *   *

"What did you say?"

Gregorio furrows his brow in the room of the Purif church he borrowed for his stay.

He listens to his superior and leader of the Out Crusade, Creio Amen, over the transmission.

"Sorry, but your vacation is now over. Return to headquarters immediately."

"Why?"

"I have a new job for you."

The only reason Gregorio went into the Great Tomb in the first place was because of this vacation, since his original task of exterminating demons in the Great Forest of the Vale was no longer necessary. Before that, he'd completed all his assignments, and it was rare for jobs to come in succession.

As he listens to His Eminence Creio, Gregorio feels his eyes drift to his mythril trunk in the corner of the room.

Creio's tone of voice seems to indicate that he is trying to avoid further questioning, but Gregorio ignores it and asks in return, "Is it a matter of haste, Your Excellency?"

"Very much so… Is there something going on?"

"Yes. It is God's guidance."

"Is that so? …Regardless, we need you back immediately. This is… God's will," Creio replies without hesitation.

Gregorio is bewildered. *God's will.* His superior doesn't often utter such words.

He sits down on the bed, staring at the ceiling. If only he was relaxing—his eyes blaze with fury.

"God's will… Is the job that important?"

"Indeed it is, Gregorio. We need you."

Gregorio is unmoved by status or money. He is only motivated by God's guidance. There is no mistaking Creio's words. Yet, then, Gregorio's tongue begins forming words as if directly instructed by God.

"The overdone sense of justice is a crime."

"Is it a problem for me to be in this place?"

"I don't understand what you're getting at."

"I humbly refuse your request, Your Excellency."

"...But why? Vanquishing enemies of God is your bread and butter, no?"

Creio is not mistaken. Gregorio has never turned down a request of this nature.

Yet, this is another story altogether. Gregorio calmly replies to Creio, whose expression he cannot see.

"Because that is the way it must be, Your Excellency. I must remain in this land. It is...God's guidance."

"What's your reasoning?"

"God's guidance is my reasoning, Your Excellency. There is no greater motive for my actions."

"So you're ignoring a direct order from God?"

"Your Excellency, I would never do such a thing. Naturally, this is not a request for reprieve, either."

There is no resentment within him. Gregorio respects Creio, and he is in his debt for ordaining him as a crusader in the first place.

However, putting this above God's guidance is impossible. Simple as that.

"Your Excellency, God has bestowed me with a divine message. I must remain here. I must remain in this land. At least...for the time being."

He isn't trying to argue good versus evil, and he certainly can't see the future.

This isn't an issue that can be explained through mere language, nor is it something that Creio will understand.

But Gregorio's voice does not waver. He does not seek a yes or a no—his mind is made up.

For the first time, Creio struggles to find the right words. He asks Gregorio a question, his tone heavy.

"...Just what do you plan on doing?"

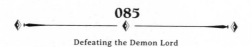

"Everything will be as God guides me, Your Excellency. I will be in contact."

He ends the transmission without waiting for a reply from Creio.

Back in the silent room, Gregorio smiles—the exact same smile he always makes when alone.

§   §   §

Spica felt she'd been through more in the past two days than in her entire twelve years of life.

The town in which she was born was far from wealthy and had very few prospects. Time ebbed slowly there for Spica. Change was an extremely rare occurrence.

Spica knows that she isn't the assertive type. And that she is easily influenced.

As a result, it's not as if she wasn't given any options as an orphan, but rather that she never made any decisions of her own. Thus, for Spica, the current options suddenly laid out before her are too many.

She is at a crossroads in her life. The choices she makes will determine her future.

We'll make you a priest. Amelia's sudden declaration had practically been an order. So Spica had followed along. She lacked the courage to say no.

However, the choices she faced after following Amelia were not requisite. Rather, they were entrusted to her.

And yet, Spica has no idea what she is going to do with those choices.

Having been rescued from the tomb, Spica now restlessly studies her surroundings in a small room of the Purif church.

A simple light hangs from the ceiling against the sun-faded wall. The room was originally constructed for distinguished guests of the church, and given the overarching standards of the village, it isn't exactly luxurious. But compared to what Spica is used to, the difference is night and day.

"The overdone sense of justice is a crime."

The three people Spica was supposed to lure into the Great Tomb are changing in the other room. Only the girl with the dark-green hair, who looks younger than Spica—she heard from Ares that her name is Glacia—is with her. What can Glacia be thinking? She is staring into space with a vapid expression.

As Spica sits still, she is somehow drawn to the weight of the borrowed mythril dagger hanging from her waist.

The brand-new priestly vestment she was made to wear is easily the most luxurious piece of clothing to ever touch her skin. When she was in Yutith's Tomb, she managed to forget how uneasy she felt in it, but now it comes back to her as she fidgets with the hem.

Her body feels heavy from the repeated scenes of tension in the Great Tomb with the group of warriors, but for some reason, she is not sleepy.

As she stares at her palms for lack of anything else to do, the remaining three party members return.

"Sorry about that... We kept you waiting, didn't we?"

"...It's okay."

The young man laughs bashfully, having removed the armor he'd been wearing in the Great Tomb and changed into casual clothes.

Spica has never seen such jet-black hair and eyes—indescribably beautiful.

Naotsugu Toudou. This is the person Spica had been tasked with luring into the tomb, per Ares's command—the leader of the party that Spica *might* still be joining.

Each soldier Spica has seen thus far has had a different aura and disposition.

This group is different than the brawny, muscular types. They're small-framed and gentle in appearance. None of them seem violent, and they definitely don't look like the type to fight monsters.

Spica already received some information about the three of them beforehand.

Next to her stands Limis Al Friedia, a fifteen-year-old elementalist with long golden hair.

Poising straight as an arrow beside Limis is Aria Rizas, a statuesque swordmaster who has her long blue hair tied back in a ponytail.

All three of them give a completely different impression than any of the mercenaries Spica has met prior. She is unable to find the words to express their character, but it certainly isn't anything negative.

Toudou smiles at Spica, who is taking it all in, and sits down at the table across from her.

Spica turns over Ares's words in the back of her mind.

Originally, she'd been asked to help the boy in front of her—Naotsugu Toudou—get over his fear of the undead. That failed spectacularly due to unforeseen circumstances, but she still hasn't decided what to do about the second directive.

Toudou opens his mouth to speak. His husky voice is pleasant to the ears, and Spica doesn't sense any of the condescension or intimidation she is used to.

"Um…Spica? That's what we should call you, right?"

"…Yes. I'm Spica…Spica Royle."

"Gotcha… Um, my name is Naotsugu Toudou. This is Limis and Aria. The green-haired girl is Glacia. So just 'Spica' is fine?"

"…Yes."

Toudou points at the three girls in turn before looking at Spica. Then, he cracks a cheerful smile.

Her first impression of him in the Great Tomb, pale-faced and sickly, had been much different.

Spica is still staring open-mouthed at Toudou, but he just keeps on smiling.

"Spica, I heard that you want to join our party as a priest… Is that right?"

The words seem to grab hold of Spica's heart and squeeze. In the back of her mind's eye, the serious, deep-green eyes of Amelia's superior, Ares Crown, swirl into view.

At that time, after explaining the variety of dangers involved in his plan and briefing her on Toudou's party, he'd given Spica a choice.

"Spica. You can make your final decision once you're face-to-face with

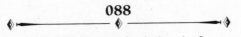

"The overdone sense of justice is a crime."

Toudou himself. I won't interfere, and even if you decide not to join their party, I will still pay you your reward. The most important thing is…whether you feel you want to assist Toudou and his party. Don't worry. If you refuse… no matter what happens, it will all work out."

Spica carefully observes Toudou's expression as she recalls Ares's words once more.

The vast amount of information and differing perceptions flood Spica's mind, tormenting her. As she desperately wavers on how to answer, Limis knits her brow and slaps Toudou on the shoulder.

"…Nao, are you really sure that bringing along a girl this age is a good idea? I mean… She's even tinier than I imagined…"

"Indeed… We didn't even ask her how old she is beforehand, did we? …Leaving on a quest at her age is quite, well…"

Limis is blind to her own short stature. Aria, who sits at the opposite end of the table with her arms crossed, is of the same opinion. She stares at Spica with her mouth twisted into a solemn frown.

True, Spica has also never seen a mercenary her own age.

Toudou's expression grows weary at their back-and-forth, and he asks Spica a question.

"…Spica, how old are you?"

"…I'm twelve."

Limis brushes her bangs from her face and inconspicuously throws her hand to her forehead. Her blue eyes cast a scrutinizing gaze on Spica no less piercing than Toudou's.

"She's still a kid. What was she doing in a place as dangerous as the Great Tomb?"

Spica is miffed by Limis's blunt remark. She glowers at Limis, looking her whole body up and down—especially her head and chest.

"…You're not much older than I am, Miss Limis."

"Grrr… I'll have you know that I am *fifteen* years old!"

"Okay, okay. Settle down, Limis."

Toudou soothes Limis, who is biting her lip, before turning back to Spica.

Spica stares straight ahead into the distance, seemingly dejected.

"Spica. I can't tell you the exact details, but...we're on a quest to vanquish the Demon Lord."

"Demon Lord...?"

This is also something Ares told her. The party is on a quest to defeat the Demon Lord. They were constantly being chased by demons, so they moved around a lot to keep gaining levels.

She was also informed of their lack of prowess for the task at hand and how odds were high they'd fail halfway through.

Even so, hearing the Demon Lord's name out loud doesn't stir much of anything within Spica.

Demon Lord Kranos. The name of the king of demons, whispered far and wide.

The enemy of humankind.

Word had spread throughout Purif, causing fear and trepidation whenever the subject arose, but at the same time, its inhabitants didn't get far outside their gossip circles. There were also rumors of demons proliferating, but as none had actually made it into the village, Purif itself had yet to suffer any direct damage at their hands.

Spica tries mouthing the Demon Lord's name again silently, but it doesn't evoke any real emotions.

It feels the same as whispering the name of a demon from a fairy tale.

Toudou continues speaking with a stern expression.

"This is a dangerous quest. We're gonna keep on fighting because we have to defeat the Demon Lord as quickly as possible, and our levels are still really low. If you join us...you may come face-to-face with death."

"..."

In that moment, hearing Toudou's stifled, fearful voice, Spica comes to a realization.

She finally understands that the young man before her embarked on this quest to vanquish the Demon Lord knowing very well that he could die.

"The overdone sense of justice is a crime."

Spica's mouth shudders open of its own accord. She is speaking before she knows it.

"I—I...I...can't use holy techniques...yet."

"Yeah, we heard all about you from the church. That said, I've been happy to receive your help so far... If you keep up that attitude, you'll be able to learn holy techniques in no time, I'm sure. Actually, I learned them in only ten days!" Toudou adds with a laugh.

Aria raises her eyebrows at hearing this.

"...Nao...that is *you* we're talking about—"

"Even if you can't learn them quickly...I'll protect you with everything I've got. Of course, Aria and Limis will, too—right?"

Aria sighs and holds her tongue. Limis, who was opposed from the beginning, has no intention of contradicting Toudou now. She says nothing, a look of exasperation on her face.

Toudou stands up and addresses Spica resolutely.

"Spica, you were probably just as terrified as we were in the Great Tomb. In all honesty, it'll be even rougher from here on out. But if you still want to aid in our quest...and it'll be a really long one...then I'd like it if you came with us."

"..."

"I'd like it if you came with us."

Spica reflexively begins to say, "Yes!" in response to such a passionate statement, but then she remembers what Ares told her and comes to a sudden stop.

"Um... If I don't go...will you be in trouble?"

Spica speaks as if her life depends on it.

Toudou stares vacantly for a second but soon breaks into a wry smile.

"No. The most important thing is what you want to do. After all this talk, if you decide you don't want to come along, that's fine. I mean, it's true we need a priest, but we'll manage somehow."

Hearing this, Spica is once again able to clear Ares's words from the back of her mind.

Before she realizes, she's gotten to her feet, too. Maybe she had been

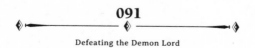

listening too intently, but the strength goes out of her legs, making her wobble unsteadily.

Spica's tiny palm grips the table to steady herself. This must be how it felt when Toudou was given the massive responsibility of vanquishing the Demon Lord.

As Spica shakily rises, Toudou takes one step closer to her.

The young girl glances up at Toudou. He looks gallant and dignified, like a fairy-tale hero. His bangs just brush his forehead, and his black eyes shine behind them like prized jewels.

"I—I..."

She starts mumbling and takes a step toward Toudou, as if being pulled by a string. Just then, Spica loses her balance and trips over her own leg, nearly falling to the ground.

"O-oh—"

Spica stammers, in a daze. Toudou reacts and moves forward, catching her fall.

He feels soft. Toudou's arms wrap around Spica, holding her in an embrace. Spica opens her eyes and looks up at him.

"Careful, now... You okay?"

"...Um..."

Toudou's voice is gentle, and he carefully brushes Spica's long bangs out of her eyes with his index finger. He looks astonishingly beautiful in this moment, but all Spica feels is shock—so much so that the anxiety she was feeling seconds earlier disappears into thin air.

The arms wrapped around her let go, and Spica somehow manages to stand on her own. She takes another look into Toudou's eyes.

"Are you hurt?"

"..."

The words fly right over her head. In her confusion, she reaches out her hands.

Just like that, her tiny palms press right up against Toudou's breasts.

Toudou's smiling face instantly freezes stiff.

"?!"

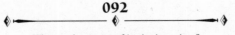

"The overdone sense of justice is a crime."

"…You're…a girl?"

"Uh…"

Spica gapes at Toudou's face, and her eyes widen from the sensation at her fingertips—the same soft, enveloping feeling she experienced just now when Toudou hugged her.

Come to think of it, Toudou is pretty androgynous. Since she dressed in rather masculine clothing, Spica hadn't noticed, but now she could even say that Toudou's features were slightly feminine.

Toudou's face remains frozen as Spica looks her over.

At the same time, Spica's mind races at this unexpected turn of events.

—Mr. Ares…did you tell me he was a she?

Spica desperately sifts through her memory but has no recollection of any explicit mention of Toudou's gender.

Is it just me…who's confused?

Regaining her composure, she once again studies Toudou keenly. Toudou's expression is frozen in place. So are Aria's and Limis's at her side.

Spica quickly hangs her head when she realizes the extent of her mistake.

"I—I'm so sorry… I…I…thought that Toudou was…a boy…"

"Ah-ha…ha-ha-ha-ha… R-right…"

Toudou's eyes and cheeks twitch. Spica fails to even register Toudou's dry laughter and peers up at her with innocent eyes.

Then, she asks Toudou about the very reason for her confusion—something she'd learned from Ares.

"Um… I kinda heard this somewhere, but… Toudou, so you're a girl, but do you also like girls?"

§   §   §

The room of an inn. I can see my ill fortune reflected perfectly in the cheap glass window jammed haphazardly in its frame.

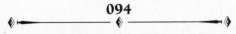

"The overdone sense of justice is a crime."

"Disobeying an order from God, huh?"

My voice is deep and threatening. Amelia, who is sorting papers, looks toward me worriedly.

My gut churns painfully. Creio's blunt tone only spurs it on.

When will peace return to me?

"Yes, well... That's no good, isn't it? Said he received a 'divine message.'"

"...Dammit. There's just no end with this guy, is there?"

A divine message. The motivation behind Gregorio Legins's actions.

What kind of logic is that? His behavior is clearly arbitrary. If you ask me, it's probably more like his intuition.

In any event, this is no regular intuition—this is a fearsome one. Gregorio has laid waste to so many followers of darkness through this fanatical "sense" he can't put into words.

So what is it he's sensing? Sure, even I get a hunch sometimes, but for Gregorio, this is more like a premonition.

—Are you the new crusader?

At first glance, he looked like just some mild-mannered kid.

Black hair, black eyes. He was shorter than me, and if it wasn't for the calmness in his gaze, I would have thought he was younger than I was.

He was the most laid-back-looking man I'd ever met. But I already knew he was much more than what was evident on the surface.

I had been gathering information on crusaders. Well, I didn't even have to gather it—within crusader circles, this guy was already known as a nonconformist. His name struck fear into the hearts of anyone who whispered it.

Mad Eater. A crazed warrior who obliterated every enemy of God in his path.

Even more terrifying was how normal he looked in spite of this. He was my senior. I put my hand out and introduced myself.

—Ares Crown. I just became a crusader recently.

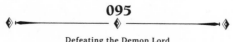

—I'm Gregorio Legins. Nice to meet you, my new compatriot Ares... I welcome any and all new servants of God.

His hands were so soft. You would never imagine that he'd killed so many enemies of God. But his body reeked of blood.

The crusader whose soft exterior concealed a villainous, terrible nickname smiled at me. The trunk he carried rattled.

—Now, Ares. Please show me...your faith.

Immediately after that, I realized just how deeply psychotic he was—more so than I could have ever imagined.

In that moment, he became the most abominable character in my entire life.

There exists a level system among the crusaders.

It is determined by the upper echelons of the Church based on one's skills and accomplishments, and it doesn't always exactly match one's strength.

Gregorio is level three. His track record as a crusader is longer than mine, but aside from his combat skills, not to mention his offense, we are essentially evenly matched.

For example, if Gregorio had been the one to take on Zarpahn in the Great Forest of the Vale instead of me, he probably would have defeated him before the vampire had the chance to self-destruct.

One thing supporting his unsettling combat skills is his weapon—his mythril trunk.

He calls it "Pandora's Coffin," a casket for followers of darkness.

The trunk, unwieldy and cumbersome, has a lot to do with why he became a crusader in the first place. Among those who know him, the rather plausible rumor is that he fills it with the corpses of the undead legions he's annihilated.

I draw a short breath and collect my thoughts.

I already knew it. Ever since I met Gregorio, I knew that no matter how the dice fell, he would be trouble. That means this still isn't the worst-case scenario.

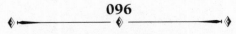

"Did you tell Gregorio about the Holy Warrior?"

"No, I did not. For the time being, information on the Holy Warrior is being withheld. We must also consider the intentions of the Kingdom of Ruxe. Regardless, everyone will find out eventually, yes?"

"But there's still the possibility of certain rumors getting out."

There is precedent—Helios from Vale Village predicted as much. People will talk.

Creio's voice is tinged with a rare pang of anxiety as he asks, "Ares, it'll be fine, won't it? That much is...a foregone conclusion."

He's right. I don't need to say it. Really, I shouldn't even have to ask. It would be inefficient, and even if everyone did find out...there's nothing we can do.

I take a few deep breaths and cast a tranquility spell over myself. My headache subsides, and I feel the calm return to my body.

"If Gregorio finds out that the Holy Warrior is terrified of the undead...he'll destroy him."

The Holy Warrior is a disciple of God. Gregorio would never be able to forgive one of God's disciples for being terrified of the legions of darkness.

"This isn't a joke, and it's not some gloomy delusion. This is...fact."

"Yes, I understand. I understand, Ares."

Creio and Gregorio have known each other longer than I've known them. I'm sure Creio understands the situation perfectly.

I need to get Gregorio far away from Toudou's party...but it's proving extremely difficult.

His actions are inexplicable, and even if I do separate them, there's always the chance he'll turn up. Common sense doesn't apply here.

"I wonder if he'd follow us if we ran off..."

"Ares... You'll be fine, right?"

No, he would follow us, I'm sure of it. Nine times out of ten. Regardless, we shouldn't even be taking "risks" of that nature.

There are those who flee and those who chase. The latter always has the advantage. The highest casualties in war are incurred during retreat.

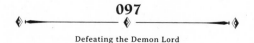

I don't really like Gregorio, but I know him well enough. His abilities, too.

Emotion is hardly a critical component of reason.

I can't avoid facing Gregorio just because I don't like him.

This is...business. I don't want to do it, and it might not work, but I must.

"I will...get in contact with him and persuade him. Please keep trying to pry him away from the group."

"...Understood."

Creio's voice is stern. I think he himself realizes how difficult it will be.

Just then, I remember something I've wanted to ask for some time. In an attempt to change the subject, I say, "By the way, Creio. I was hoping you might have someone to spare who's able to use communication magic..."

If we'd had someone who could use communication magic to direct Spica in the heat of the battle, the entire outcome would've been much different. Amelia and I can't provide all the support necessary by ourselves.

"Communication magic, hmm? ...Operators are valuable these days, you know..."

Creio disapproves. Holy casters, also known as white mages, are some of the elite, so I understand where he's coming from. However, we also need to be fully prepared. I think for a moment before responding.

"...What about the current operator? Stephenne Veronide, was it? She'd be fine."

Stephenne is the operator currently handling my communications. Compared with Amelia, who was my previous operator, Stephenne is inexperienced, and it takes her multiple tens of seconds to connect me to Creio. But she can still handle all the duties of an operator.

I have some concerns, given how flustered she was during our first interaction connecting a call, but I can overlook a few small flaws for the merits of being able to use communication magic.

Going forward with just Amelia and myself would be a struggle, and it wouldn't be a bad idea to train someone on our team—the sooner, the better.

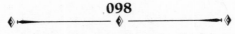

"The overdone sense of justice is a crime."

Creio turned me down once in the past, but I remember he has since offered to assign someone.

Creio's response to my request is unexpected.

"Ares, you must be mistaken… She's, uh, terrible."

"…What?"

Terrible? I've never heard Creio speak like this. I shudder reflexively before asking, "Is it her skill level?"

"No… She's well skilled. But terrible. Really terrible, Ares. Personality and skill level are not always related."

I'm fully aware of that thanks to Toudou.

But it's still better than a terrible personality *and* zero skills, right?

Creio's voice gives no indication that this is a joke. Amelia's qualifications are apparent just from looking at her. Taking that into consideration, I still believe that letting Stephenne into our party would have value. I hem and haw for a moment before answering.

"…I get it. If you put it like that, then she must be truly horrible. Taking that into account, would you assign her to us as an intern for the time being? If she's really that bad, we'll send her back."

With duty come qualifications. If we don't give her a chance, we'll never know if she's any good.

At any rate, I could use all the help I can get. After a few moments of silence, Creio sighs deeply.

"…Understood. If it means that much to you, Ares, I'll dispatch her. But don't come complaining about her to me, okay?"

"I told you, if she's useless, I'll send her back."

"…Right. Send her back if you must. I'll have her head there now. But…you'll regret this."

I have no idea what's coming my way, but it can't be any worse than Gregorio.

The connection cuts out. I heave a deep sigh of my own and turn toward Amelia.

I need to forget about the new member for now and think about

how to persuade Gregorio. This is a test. I also have to continue improving Toudou's battle potential, but this is even more pressing.

Amelia bats her deep-indigo eyes and looks at me. She's my only ally.

...Even so, I can't give her the responsibility of persuading Gregorio.

"Are you finished with your briefing?"

"Yeah. It's not exactly a walk in the park. I've been tasked with persuading Gregorio."

I snuff out the complaints welling up inside me and take a seat. Amelia pours me some black tea with a practiced hand.

The scenery outside is already shrouded in the black veil of night. Compared to Vale Village, Purif is small in scale, and there are few streetlamps. Nighttime is pitch-black.

I kind of miss back when I went on crusade missions alone about two months ago.

I rid myself of these thoughts and face the present. I already know where Gregorio is. He's staying in one of the churches, but not the same one as Toudou.

I should engage him as soon as possible. Maybe first thing tomorrow morning. Right now would be...too soon.

Amelia circles behind me and touches the nape of my neck, causing me to shiver.

"...You're so tense. Your shoulders are stiff."

"That's just the difference in our levels. My defense is higher than your offense."

"...That's absurd."

Yet that's precisely what it is. Amelia and I are vastly different in our total amount of life force.

You could say the same about Toudou and the Demon Lord or Toudou and Gregorio.

"Ares, what are our next instructions for Spica?"

"I'm speaking with Gregorio tomorrow. We'll decide how to instruct Spica based on how that goes and whether or not Spica is going to join Toudou."

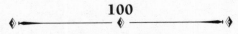

"The overdone sense of justice is a crime."

If I'm able to persuade Gregorio, then we should ideally be able to get Toudou over his fear of the undead, too, as planned.

Above all else, Yutith's Tomb is the perfect location for leveling Spica up. She's level 10 and has zero attack power compared to Limis. There is no better place for her to level up than this area.

However, this is also dependent on what Spica wants—her own desires. I gave her a warning: *"It'll be risky."* Toudou is a womanizer. I didn't tell her he's the Holy Warrior, but that can't be helped.

Spica seems easily won over at first glance, but I want her to make her own decision on this matter.

Amelia is still trying to massage my shoulders as she asks, "Did Spica show signs of talent?"

"None. If she had any, she'd have been able to use holy techniques before she met us."

Among renowned priests, it's not rare to find those who can use holy techniques before they start their priest training. But a priest who doesn't show an affinity can still become one.

Whether Spica can get along as a member of Toudou's party is entirely dependent on her own efforts. She'll be given ample teaching in her apprenticeship, and the proper equipment will be provided to her.

"I spoke with Spica earlier. She asked for a little more time before deciding whether to join Toudou's party."

Disinterested, Amelia continues without any mention of Spica's lack of talent. She really must not like her.

"I see."

We're running out of time, but this is a question of her entire future. If she decides not to come along, her holy techniques will never grow.

I close my eyes and concentrate. Suddenly, Amelia speaks up, attempting to stifle a laugh—a rarity for someone like her.

"By the way, I heard something from Spica..."

"Mm?"

"Apparently, Toudou doesn't like girls. She confirmed it herself."

"Mm...? Mm...?"

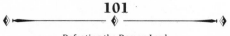

How do you even confirm that? I did tell her to be careful because he's a skirt-chaser, but is that really something you check with the source?

"...What kind of guy says 'Yes' when asked if he's a womanizer?"

I would've said no in a heartbeat. Not to mention, that's a pretty lame excuse for joining a party of two girls and one guy. I can't speak for anyone else, but still...

Then, while rubbing my shoulders, Amelia drops another bomb.

"Either way, it would seem that it's normal for Toudou to like boys."

"..."

A shiver runs down my spine. It's normal to like boys...? What is this? How is that normal? Is this part of his native culture?

I silently ponder the implications for a while, but I reach my conclusion quickly.

"...Toudou and Spica sure cooked up one hell of a story, didn't they?"

"I think you're right."

No matter how difficult a question you're asked...saying that you like boys is simply ridiculous. And to say that it's "normal"... What the hell? What's so normal about that?!

Maybe he was flustered? Did he think about how Limis and Aria might feel when they heard that?

"Anyway, it's a total lie. I don't think Spica is taking Toudou's word as gospel, but regardless, tell her to continue being careful."

"I already reminded her so when she told me this."

Seriously, though... Liking boys? What a bizarre answer.

"It's kinda funny, though."

"I also found it hilarious."

§　§　§

Toudou is standing in the rear yard of the church, completely dark aside from the moonlight.

Only the warm breeze brushes against her skin; she feels the heft of the wooden practice sword in her hand.

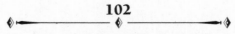

Toudou narrows her eyes in the darkness and stares straight ahead intensely. Three meters away from her stands Aria, sword drawn.

In the month since they left on their quest to vanquish the Demon Lord, there hasn't been a single day that Toudou hasn't had her sword at her side.

She had zero swordsmanship experience until being summoned. Once summoned, she received all applicable training at the castle, but to soften her lack of experience, she has Aria mentoring her on how to use a blade.

Toudou exhales sharply. She focuses her nerves and studies Aria's stance. Despite not having taken even a single step, sweat pours down Toudou's back.

Aria Rizas. Daughter of the Grand Swordmaster. Born into a preeminent house of swordsmanship in the Kingdom of Ruxe. Her stance is quiet and still but full of tremendous power.

Aria is taller than Toudou; their difference in height is about an arm's length. For Toudou's blade to reach her, she would have to make it one full step past Aria's potential attack range.

Toudou's level is a bit higher than Aria's, but it's not enough to overcome their difference in experience.

Aria's wooden sword never wavers. She points it directly between Toudou's eyes.

They shuffle bit by bit toward each other, gauging the distance—then, Toudou steps forward and rushes at her.

"Nao, one of your biggest weaknesses is…your lack of physical strength."

Training is finished. Aria casually lowers her sword and delivers her evaluation.

In the end, Toudou didn't score any hits on Aria. Toudou never won a match against her. Her clumsy feints never went through, and Aria is clearly more skilled and powerful.

Toudou listens to Aria's assessment, trying to calm her ragged breathing.

103

"Your attacks are…light. In the Great Forest of the Vale, you survived due to your holy sword, Ex, but moving forward, there will be monsters that can't be destroyed in one fell swoop… It's going to be hard for you."

"Will I get stronger if I increase my level?"

"Yes. However—only at a slow rate."

Aria sheathes her wooden sword and continues, as if the words pain her.

"In general, female humans…gain strength slower than their male counterparts."

Toudou stares down at her own palm. There's still some numbness in it—a delicate palm.

The holy sword Ex is sharp enough to slice through metal, but that's strictly the power of the sword itself and not Toudou's.

"Males easily gain strength and agility, making them ideal as swordmasters. Conversely, females gain dexterity and magic ability more quickly. That's why we don't need to be swordmasters."

"…I see… That makes sense."

As the daughter of a swordmaster, Aria has a hitch in her tone that she can't wipe away.

Toudou furrows her brow.

"Does that have anything to do with the fact that every Holy Warrior summoned until now has been a man?"

"…If you're summoning a swordmaster, then yes…choosing a male makes sense."

Aria continues with a slightly pained, bitter expression.

"Luckily for you, the holy sword Ex doesn't weigh anything. Neither does the holy armor, and the shield given to you is far lighter than average. Also, it's magical. It would have been difficult for you to fight otherwise."

"What can I do to make up for my lack of physical strength?"

Aria answers without hesitation.

"That won't likely be possible with a sword alone. But you have

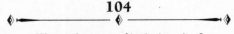

magical power. Combining physical force with spell-casting is the best route, I believe."

"…You're surprisingly pessimistic for the Grand Swordmaster's daughter."

"I know this particularly because I trained for so long in swordsmanship. There's just…no way to hide that gap in physical strength."

Aria heaves a deep sigh. Seeing her sorrowful expression, Toudou refrains from asking any more.

Instead, Toudou brandishes her sword playfully, the sharp sound cutting through the air. The flashing blade would impress the average person, but because Aria is on its receiving end, she knows Toudou's strokes are largely powerless.

Toudou's moves have speed, and she can use the holy sword Ex to rip through the flesh and bone of monsters, but in the end, that's all she is capable of.

"…However, Nao, you have incredible magical aptitude. Conversely, when it comes to mages…there are actually more women than men."

"Magic, huh…?"

Toudou holds her sword aloft and slices downward with all her might. The same sharp sound reverberates. Beads of sweat flit through the air and fall to the ground. As she watches her, Aria recalls her own younger self—how hard she struggled to perfect her swordsmanship.

"…Man, I really wish I could've been a gifted swordmaster…"

"Why is that?"

"'Cause it's so cool, using a sword!"

Toudou smiles wistfully.

She's somewhat baby-faced. Her gentle features and lustrous black hair could easily be seen as male or female.

Aria looks away from Toudou's jet-black eyes hidden behind her long bangs, sighs one more time, and changes the subject.

"Nao, your hair has really grown. You should cut it soon."

At that, Toudou grabs a length of her sweat-drenched bangs between her thumb and forefinger.

"Yeah, I guess it's kinda getting in the way..."

"If I may be blunt... Right now, I wouldn't think you were a boy unless you told me."

"Huh...?"

Her voice is too high and her stature too short to belong to a man. She might just be able to pass, but compared to the average male swordsman or mercenary, she just doesn't have the build. It wouldn't come as a surprise if she said she was a girl.

She looks and acts female. Although it was a shock that Spica realized the truth, at some point, Toudou might no longer be able to conceal her gender.

Aria shakes her head to escape the reality of the situation. Toudou looks at her, blinking wildly.

§　§　§

As I spread my gear out on the table to check it, I remember the dagger I lent Spica.

Dawn has broken, and the moment of truth is near, but I've been in a foul mood since the morning. This is bad luck. A sinister omen. No matter how many deep breaths I take, I'm unable to banish my sense of dread.

A few of my weapons are laid out on the table. I have two mythril knives I can use even with a prism barrier cast. There's also my main weapon, a battle mace, and I have a few vials of holy water that can repel any followers of darkness.

If you include the dagger I lent Spica, I have the arsenal to take on any adversary.

I originally always kept six knives on hand, including spares, but I lost a few to Zarpahn and haven't had the time to replace them.

Today, my adversary is a crusader.

I have no intention of killing him, but I'm not taking any chances by confronting him unarmed.

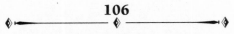

"The overdone sense of justice is a crime."

I look down at my gear and scowl. Amelia asks after me, worried.

"Um... Ares, should I go with you?"

"I'm telling you, he doesn't hold back. Even against women."

Gregorio has only one standard of judgment: Are you an enemy of God or not?

"That's fine. I've met him before."

"...Is he a friend of yours or something?"

Surprisingly, Amelia's expression sours at my question. I don't even have time to act shocked before she says, "Well...he nearly killed me once."

"..."

I instinctively do a double take. Amelia has on her usual poker face. *How on earth did she manage to be nearly killed by him?* ...Never mind that.

"Want to go and speak to him for me?"

"...You really don't want to do this, do you?"

Fighting a high-level demon one-on-one would be hundreds of times more ideal. I just can't stand this guy! He's a pain in my ass.

...Of course, I would never let her go in my stead—that was a joke.

I prop my elbows up on the table and hold my head in my hands. I'm already regretting this.

Even though it was the best route, I should have never called on Gregorio in the Great Forest of the Vale.

If I hadn't, he would have never ended up coming to Yutith's Tomb.

Using him was a mistake. I should have left everything up to Creio, including who to dispatch. This is all my fault. Dammit—even though I fully understood the risks involved...

Despite the sense it made at the time...I should have never used Gregorio.

"Ares, I've never seen you so reluctant to fulfill a task..."

"...Even I have preferences, y'know."

It's not as if I have no grounds for it. My disgust stems from a long association.

Plenty of crusaders have their own quirks, but Gregorio's take the cake. The fact that Gregorio was the only crusader not assigned to a mission with me whenever I requested backup is ample proof.

I hate this. I don't want to see him. I don't want to speak to him. I don't want to go near him. My stomach hurts.

Listen to your superiors, GREGORIOOOOOOOOO!!! AHHHHHH HHHHHHHH!!

I close my eyes for a few seconds, get my ragged breathing under control, and open them.

Finally—my mind is clear. Well, maybe not. It's dicey, so let's just say it is.

"Okay......let's head out."

"I'm not sure how, but thanks to you, Ares, now I have a stomachache, too."

"Recovery."

"...Only once?"

Given the circumstances, I'll cast another one or ten or one hundred—I don't give a damn.

Using the church meant there was a chance we'd run into Toudou, so I chose the dining hall of the inn as our meeting spot.

I asked Creio's permission but kept secret how badly my stomach hurt the second he approved.

It's ten minutes before our scheduled meeting time. I poke my head through the door of the dining hall to investigate.

Sure enough, he's already here.

We hadn't met face-to-face back in the Great Tomb, so I'm just now seeing him for the first time in years. Ugh, my stomach is killing me.

As expected, no matter how many years pass, he still looks like a child. He's wearing a Church-designated deep-indigo robe and has his earring on. He's a model priest from head to toe.

Based on appearance only, he's a far more fitting image of a priest than myself. It makes me miserable to think about.

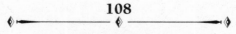

"The overdone sense of justice is a crime."

There's no one else in the dining hall aside from Gregorio. Even though I am holding back severe abdominal pains for this meeting, Gregorio looks completely at ease. My stomach hurts even more. I can't stand him, but it seems he doesn't mind meeting me.

At any rate, I can't stay here peeking through the door forever.

I take a deep breath to prepare myself, but the very second I go to step through the door, Amelia asks me, "...Are you sure you don't need a buff?"

"...If I buff up and he thinks I'm coming after him, that would be bad."

"Would he?"

"He would."

There's no point in complaining. I shift my mind-set to battle mode and take a step inside the dining hall.

A terrible fear grips my entire being.

Malice. An urge to fight. Bloodlust. A similar yet disparate presence causes my level-93 legs to momentarily give way.

"!"

I've prepared myself, so not a sound comes out of my mouth.

Something black cuts through the air and blocks my field of vision. I quickly smash my mace across it.

I feel my mace hit something sturdy and hear the sound of metal against metal. My field of vision is restored. The moment I notice, I'm already making my next move.

He's gotten close. It was his trunk that flew at me—but it's a trap. Suddenly, we collide.

His black hair is disheveled, and his bulging eyes turn a bizarre color. I expect this and am able to respond accordingly. Without a moment's hesitation, I knee him directly in the face.

I hear the sound of smashing flesh and bone. Gregorio's boyish frame flies into the air. Wait, no—he took the blow in his palm and flew back on purpose.

"Ares!"

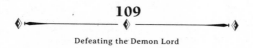

Amelia shouts, nearly in hysterics. I, on the other hand, am completely calm.

Don't worry. This is…the chance of a lifetime. Since he threw the first blow, I can claim self-defense if I kill him, and that's just the way things would be. I'm positive Creio would forgive me if I apologized to him afterward.

Gregorio's trunk that I'd smashed my mace into crashes into a table and tumbles to the ground.

I inspect it out of the corner of my eye before quickly looking back at Gregorio lying on the floor and giving him a kick. I am armed, and Gregorio is empty-handed. He might be able to withstand a few kicks, but he won't last against the razor-sharp metal barbs of my mace.

Bloodlust congeals in my brain. I'll murder him with a single blow.

I'll aim for his head. Even the most ghoulish creature can't survive that.

I pick up speed with my first step, reach full tilt with my second, and fly through the air by my third. I raise my mace above my head with all my strength. My arm muscles clench, and I can somehow clearly hear the blood pulsating through my body.

My target is directly in front of me. Even Gregorio can't evade an attack from midair.

"DIEEEEEEEEEEEEEEEEEEE!"

I scream in an attempt to freeze him in his place. The air around us trembles.

In the exact moment I bring down the mace, I'm able to clearly see the look on his face.

There's no fear. He's smiling. The second I see his expression, I reflexively change the direction of my swing, forcing myself into a tailspin, shifting my attack behind him.

The force with which I brought my mace down is incomparable to my earlier strike. The shock travels up my arm, and the room reverberates with what sounds like a massive ringing gong.

"—Rrgh."

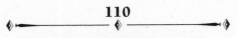

"The overdone sense of justice is a crime."

I land on the floor. Finally, I realize it was the mythril trunk I just hit. I smashed it with all my might, but it didn't even leave a scratch.

This can't be right. He flew through the air. His trunk should have tumbled to the ground.

This unfathomable turn of events races through my mind. But it's already over.

Gregorio, safely on his feet, dusts off his robe. There's no longer a shred of that urge to fight left within him.

Gregorio begins speaking as if nothing happened. A smile appears on his face as though he's giving me a warm welcome.

"Ah, Ares. My compatriot. You look well, I must say."

...*Shit. I missed my chance.*

Gregorio beams as if chatting to an old friend.

"Long time no see, Ares Crown. It seems that your faith has not dwindled in the slightest."

"Tch—"

"I am...overcome with sheer joy. Among my few fellow compatriots, I can't believe you would call upon me here. I attribute this good fortune to God and give Him thanks."

"...Fuck you."

"Now, now, Ares. We are one of the same ilk. Let us fight side by side, until not a single follower of darkness remains."

Amelia, who is hiding behind me, pokes me repeatedly on the shoulder and whispers into my ear.

"Ares, I don't think you're getting through to him."

As if I don't know that! Gregorio and I operate on completely different wavelengths.

"Sister———Amelia! What are you doing here?!"

"Eep?!"

There's no way Gregorio didn't notice her before now, but his eyes still fly wide open at this dramatic exclamation. It is strikingly different

from when he spoke to me—lively and spirited. He practically screams, as opposed to speaking.

This is the first time I've heard Amelia shriek in fear. I totally know how she feels.

Amelia continues hiding behind me as Gregorio stares at her, his eyes ablaze. These are the eyes of a devil targeting its prey. Maybe she wasn't lying about Gregorio nearly killing her once.

Now I kind of regret bringing Amelia along. I'm worried about the ramifications.

I raise my arm slowly, bit by bit, in order to not spark Gregorio's emotions.

I point my finger. Gregorio looks away from Amelia and follows it to the chair to which I'm pointing.

"Sit."

A wide grin spreads across Gregorio's face. I really wish he would stop smiling at damn near everything.

"Certainly, Ares. But first, why don't you explain your relationship to Sister Amelia for me?"

"She works under me. Got a problem?"

I wish he would come at me. That would give me the chance to dispatch him quickly.

Gregorio certainly possesses fiendish power, but without the advantage of surprise attacks, I'm sure my tactics can best him one-on-one. He can't use any holy techniques aside from exorcism, and those don't work on me.

Gregorio surprises me with his reaction to my provocative tone. He opens his eyes wide and joins his hands together in front of him, as if praying. His pupils shrink instantly.

"That is—fantastic!"

"Huh?"

Gregorio brushes off my slight irritation and finally takes a seat.

I simply cannot keep up with his energy level. I push; he pulls. I pull;

he pushes back. Next, he utters softly, "If Sister Amelia works below you, then she definitely still has a chance to clear her name."

Seriously, what the heck did Amelia actually do? I'm curious, but for the time being, it's none of my concern. Amelia is here on the Church's orders, and sure, a lot has happened, but at the end of the day, she's helpful.

I ignore Gregorio's remark and sit down across from him. Amelia follows and takes the seat next to me. She looks as if she wants to say something, but perhaps because I remained silent, so does she.

Even though I just sat in the negotiation hot seat, my body feels languid. I pay it no mind and peer into Gregorio's eyes.

"Gregorio, do you have any idea why I called you here?"

"Why, of course. To reignite an old friendship, no doubt."

He finishes his sentence in the blink of an eye. What the hell is he talking about? Is there any hint of sentimentality in my expression?

I look around for a mirror...but why would there be a mirror in a place like this anyhow?

He's throwing me off my game. I press on my forehead and collect myself. I can't afford to take his words at face value.

I resist the urge to bite my own tongue off, quell my emotions, and speak up.

"Not in the slightest. Gregorio, it appears that you've refused the cardinal's orders—is that right?"

"? Yes, I did. What of it?"

Gregorio blinks. He genuinely seems to not know what I'm getting at.

This bastard ought to be bound and gagged and locked in a dungeon cell.

"Did His Excellency say something to you?"

"Why did you refuse his orders?"

I ignore his query and continue my questioning. Yet his expression does not sour, and he slowly begins pointing directly at my nose.

"It's *fate*, Ares Crown."

"Be more explicit."

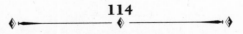

"The overdone sense of justice is a crime."

"Ares. You and I are the same—you should understand."

Confused by his conclusive tone, Amelia shoots me a look as if to say, *Huh? You understand?* I have no goddamn clue!

The corners of Gregorio's mouth turn up as he speaks. "An enemy of God, Ares Crown."

"..."

I respond with silence. A small fire is burning in his eyes.

"There is no other reason for why I am here—it is the guidance of God. This is…fate! A miracle! Our God, the God of Order, Ahz Gried, has bestowed a divine message upon me!"

Gregorio raises both his hands to the sky and screams in fervent prayer.

He arches his back as he stands tall, spasming. His bloodshot eyes sing with adoration.

After basking in his delusion, he suddenly falls silent. How does this make him feel? I don't care if he thinks it's the guidance of God or whatever. I can't be responsible for the delusions of a madman. My biggest problem is whatever the hell he has planned.

His rant suddenly ceases. Then, he completely switches gears, speaking softly, as if scolding a child.

"You see, Ares, it is utterly disrespectful to His Excellency, but I must remain here."

"There's no sign of any followers of darkness here."

"Yes, yes, that's true. However, as you know full well—our enemies are not limited to the followers of darkness."

As crusaders, a majority of the foes whom we strike down are not undead, although they are the most powerful and require the strictest vigilance. Also…they are the simplest to fight.

That is the biggest difference between exorcists, who fight only the undead, and crusaders.

After all, there are enemies of God everywhere.

Priests who serve evil gods. Mages who sell their souls to demons and cultivate the evil arts. Corrupt knights cursed by followers of darkness.

Although the undead can be sensed from far away, human beings who fall into the darkness are undetectable by crusaders.

This is the reason why members of our order require so much more than just mere combat skills.

In reality, crusaders need to gather information on these types of *human foes*, but Gregorio possesses a God-given intuition that allows him to sense them.

I can't read his mind, but if Gregorio was to realize that Toudou is the Holy Warrior and so scared of undead that a wraith's shriek causes him to faint, Gregorio would instantly target Toudou and annihilate him.

Even if I stood in his way, nothing would stop his crusade.

If possible, I want to kill him myself before this gets out of hand. But that's just not in the cards. He may be the greatest thorn in my side, but in the end, Gregorio is an ally. And he also received specific orders not to kill me.

Unaware of what's going through my mind, Gregorio chuckles to himself.

"Heh-heh-heh... In the end, I can't believe a first-rank crusader such as yourself would be in a desolate village such as this. Surely by now, you must have an inkling of why I'm staying here?"

There are only ten crusaders in existence, all scattered across the globe at any given time, hunting down the enemies of God. Wherever there is a crusader, there is also likely an enemy of God.

My current assignment is to support the Holy Warrior, so there aren't any such enemies here.

...Should I tell him that I'm supporting the Holy Warrior? Maybe then he'll leave us alone?

No. Impossible. Absolutely out of the question.

If I give him that information, Gregorio will want to confirm the Holy Warrior with his own eyes. The issue is that Gregorio and Toudou already have a common acquaintance. Gregorio also likely saw how terrified Toudou was in the Great Tomb.

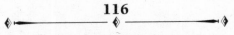

"I was on leave, Ares, until I realized I could help you in whatever way I could."

Please just don't make a big fuss... Your very existence is a liability.

Once again, I promise myself that no matter what happens, I will never call on Gregorio again—that much is certain.

"Let's cut to the chase. The reason I've called you here is simple."

He truly is a man of great prescience. In times like these, I need to keep it plain and simple.

I glance toward Amelia for a moment, then fix my gaze on Gregorio again.

"Get lost."

"...And what do you mean by that?"

"You just don't get it, do you? This is my assignment, and you are not needed here."

Silence fills the room for a moment. I laid out my rejection clearly, but there's no sign of Gregorio's emotions stirring in the slightest. No sadness, no anger, no joy—nothing.

I continue pushing him. He may be legitimately psychotic, but he's intelligent. Above all else, although it makes me sick to my stomach, he feels we're cut from the same cloth. I have to use that against him.

"Ares, I simply don't understand. You do know what I'm capable of, correct?"

"Get it through your head, Gregorio. This is a trial."

"A trial...?"

If this was an average mission, I would have accepted Gregorio's help. In all honesty, it would have been foolish not to.

Just as he said, I truly understand what he's capable of.

Gregorio is like a first-class hunting dog—he can chase down any prey. His divine intuition is extremely valuable when faced with enemies of God undetectable by normal means.

That's why Gregorio can't understand what I'm telling him. Just as I know him so well, he, too, knows me.

I've used every trick in the book to bury my enemies. Why wouldn't I want his help?

"This is...my trial. God is testing my faith. As a disciple of the God of Order, against all odds, I must complete this assignment by my power and my power alone."

I ramble on, my words completely nonsensical. It's entirely unlike me, but I've got no choice.

I am being wholly abstract, without a sliver of concrete reality. Gregorio, the crazed fanatic, is sure to believe me.

Amelia stares at me blankly. Her gaze pains me.

"You get it, right?"

Gregorio falls silent at my inquiry. After a few seconds, he finally nods sincerely, as if it's clear as day. I don't know what struck a chord with him, but the smile fades from his face as he turns utterly solemn.

"Understood. I would never impose on an issue of your faith, my friend."

"Much appreciated."

Hearing him say that, I'm convinced my bet has paid off. I breathe a sigh of relief to myself.

Gregorio knits his brow and looks troubled.

"In that case, I shall be taking my leave of this village. If you are here, there is no longer any reason for me to stay behind... Originally, I planned to delve into the Great Tomb, but it seems I would only be getting in your way."

Leaving the village. That's exactly what I want to hear. I suddenly grow curious and ask, "Where are you headed next?"

"Wherever God guides me. For starters...the north."

"Where exactly in the north?"

"? ...Northwest, perhaps?"

Northwest. To the northwest of Yutith's Tomb lies...Golem Valley.

I can feel my eyelid twitching. Must be from stress.

"...You should avoid going northwest."

"? And why is that?"

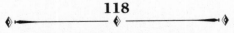

"The overdone sense of justice is a crime."

Gregorio looks perplexed. *I'm* the one dying to know why he has his sights set on the northwest!

This is bad. After finally getting rid of Gregorio, it'll all be for nothing if we run into him again. I can't let him go on ahead.

We planned on Golem Valley for our next round of leveling up. Without that as an option, the level-up process would be dramatically less efficient. Any detriment to Toudou's performance out of fear of Gregorio would amount to putting the cart before the horse.

Perhaps we should get Gregorio to stay here and send Toudou off to Golem Valley in haste? But that also presents a touch of anxiety. Toudou isn't guaranteed to follow my lead. Seems like everyone around me has that propensity.

Just as I thought: The safest solution would be for Gregorio to die right here on the spot.

"What troubles you, Ares?"

"…Nothing."

Shall we have him return to the Church headquarters? No…it would be weird for me to give that order.

Maybe I could ask Creio to give Gregorio return orders. But would he follow them? He's already refused one set of directives.

Before I realize it, my knees are shaking. I glare at Gregorio, wishing I could kill with a single look.

"Is there a problem with my leaving this place?"

"The problem is your very existence."

"Ares, don't worry yourself. I have no intention of impeding your trial."

Maybe so, but if you happen on Toudou and try to kill him, I'm screwed!

I ask my untrustworthy colleague a question.

"Gregorio, which church are you currently staying at?"

"? The third parish. Why?"

Purif is home to three churches. Toudou is staying at the largest, the first parish. The first parish has complete provisions—there's no reason Toudou would ever need to visit the third.

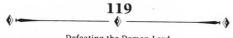

I sigh deeply and address Gregorio.

"Okay. In that case, you're to stay in the third parish until I say otherwise. Don't step a single foot outside!"

If someone told me that this was all Toudou's fault, I would merely shake my head.

I don't even like Toudou—he evicted me from the party in the first place, and his fear of the undead is the cause of this entire debacle. Yet if Gregorio killed him, the blame would fall on the Church.

If the mission to defeat the Demon Lord failed for such a stupid reason, I would no longer be able to show my face in the Church or the Kingdom ever again.

"...I'm sorry I couldn't be of any help to you..."

Back in the room, Amelia's shoulders droop dejectedly.

She didn't say a single word, but I never considered asking her to do anything in the first place. I didn't expect Gregorio to react the way he did, but Amelia is now more of a mystery to me than ever.

"Well, there's nothing you could do. No one is any good at handling Gregorio."

"...Yes, perhaps you're right."

Regardless, I was pleased with how well we persuaded him. He looked suspicious, but he was convinced that my "trial" was legitimate, of his own accord. I take a deep breath and finally feel momentarily relaxed.

...But I still can't let my guard down. That same negligence nearly cost me my life in Vale Village.

I need to play it safe. I walk over to the window and peer down below.

I can see Gregorio's back. Even from a distance, I'm able to identify his trunk and priest's robe instantly.

"Amelia, I'm going to the third parish to make sure he's returned as promised without causing any trouble."

"...Should I go instead?" she asks, her voice a bit more high-pitched

"The overdone sense of justice is a crime."

than usual. I don't even have to see the look on her face to know that would clearly be asking too much.

"No, I'll do it. In the one-in-a-million or one-in-a-trillion chance that Toudou gets attacked, you wouldn't be able to help him."

"...I sincerely doubt that would ever happen."

"I hope it doesn't."

I'm the only one capable. Just me. The one to stop Gregorio has to be of the same level or above, have the same battle experience or more, and be just as merciless.

I put on a hooded brown overcoat and give instructions to Amelia, who still looks crestfallen.

"We're going to clean up this mess, one problem at a time. Amelia, give Cardinal Creio a report on the current situation and keep a close eye on Toudou and his party's movements."

"Understood."

"I will return as soon as I've confirmed that Gregorio has gone back to the church. If something happens in the meantime, contact me immediately."

"Yes. Please take care."

I debate whether or not I should leave my mace here. It would be heavy, but it's far more inconspicuous than the one Amelia wields.

Yet, if I was to get in a fight with Gregorio, doing so without my main weapon would be foolish.

I decide to bring it and make sure I have knives tucked into my chest, too. Gregorio doesn't wear any armor, which means knives might be highly effective against him. He could be wearing chain mail under his priest's robe, but even then, I could aim for his face or hands. A knife straight through the eye to scramble his brain matter would definitely do the trick.

As I check my gear, Amelia addresses me in amazement.

"Ares, you're really going all in..."

"...No, I'm not. This is all in the name of preparedness. He's still

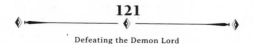

121

valuable. If anything, I'd rather he die in a suicide attack on the Demon Lord."

That would give Toudou's party a slightly improved chance of coming out victorious.

I conceal my presence and put ample space between Gregorio and myself before trailing him.

There are approximately three hundred meters between us. My view is obstructed so that I can't see him. I hear the wind rushing and footsteps, then the sound of someone talking. Within the scattered noise, I use my senses to focus my awareness. Suddenly, I hear Gregorio whispering.

His dispassionate voice is aimed at someone, but there's no sign of anyone around.

"Ah, Ares. You are...strong."

His voice is soft. A low-level commoner would never be able to hear it.

"It's clear you have been selected by God. Your enduring holy energy, your iron will, the way you deliver judgment to your enemies with ease—it is evident that you are worthy of the highest rank. Yes, Ares. When I first met you...I was so surprised. I have met so many priests, but none has ever surprised me, before then or ever since—not a single one."

His quiet voice is full of admiration. It's eerie.

I am an ordinary person. I simply have a high level, and I've been a bit lucky. His words are off target and do not flatter me in the slightest.

He keeps speaking as he walks in the direction of the third parish, as I demanded of him.

"A transcendent being. The Ex Deus of Out Crusade. Anything less is nothing but common riffraff. Any other crusader is worthless. Yes, but you! Only you! I am so genuinely curious—what manner of trial...? What precious fate has our God bestowed upon you?"

He stops in front of the church. In the end, Gregorio never strayed suspiciously from the path at all.

"This is fate."

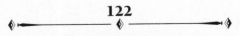

"The overdone sense of justice is a crime."

The only unnatural thing is his voice. Before long, it becomes obvious he is no longer talking to himself.

He's practically singing. His voice is overcome with emotion, and I, too, stop in my tracks.

We're too far apart to see each other, and there's a din surrounding us. If Gregorio and I traded places, I doubt I would be able to notice him. That is...if I wasn't expecting it.

"Ares, you might think it was coincidence that we met today, but this...is fate. Following the guidance of God, I was able to meet you in that predestined place. After all—you and I are simply cogs in the wheel of fate. I won't forget that."

His voice resounds with certainty. Is this a madman's creed?

...Dammit. He definitely knows I'm following him. No, it doesn't matter if he knows—I'm aware of how sharp his senses are.

However, the fact that he knows I'm trailing him means that he's woven a separate plot I'm unaware of. Even though he's a deluded fanatic, he's not completely unhinged, after all.

Within extreme madness is a glimpse of reason.

"Please rest easy, Ares. At this juncture, I have no intention of interfering with your trial. I shall remain within the confines of the church. It has been so long since I was last involved in its day-to-day affairs... I welcome it."

There is no way I can believe that. Amelia once told me suspicion is my vice. Yet, given his track record, how can I not doubt him?

"Farewell, Ares Crown. I pray that we may meet again. May you go—as God wills you."

The door closes behind him with a *thud*. At that, his presence dissipates.

I take a moment to make sure he won't come out again and then finally turn on my heels.

I steady my breathing, which had become ragged before I realized it. A truly terrifying man, that Gregorio.

From our stats alone, there was no way I could lose to him, and yet

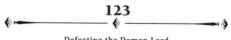

I didn't feel like I could win. It must be due to his faith, the kind that I lack. Those of great volition are formidable opponents, even if they are insane or biased.

"A cog in the wheel of fate, eh?"

I mull over Gregorio's words.

That's the exact reason my faith is shallow. If my current situation is all God's plan, then I want to punch God in the face.

I suddenly receive a transmission from Amelia. I finally switch my mind off Gregorio after having obsessed over him for an entire twenty-four hours. For now, I can only take him at his word.

"It's about Spica—"

Sounds like Spica decided to join Toudou's party. I entrusted the girl with the decision, but in my heart of hearts, I really didn't think it was a good idea.

My personal opinion of Spica is a bit lower now.

She got over her fear of the undead and reached a bare-minimum satisfactory level. Yet, she has zero experience or knowledge, is extremely young, has little aptitude, and lacks any sense of moral cause. There is significant merit to her joining the party, but it's outweighed by the risks. At this stage, she's nothing more than an empty vessel—there are so many things she still lacks.

Nonetheless, if she decided to join and Toudou accepted it, then I can only make the best out of the situation.

In order for her to understand how a priest operates, Spica needs the right equipment. She needs to know how to level up and how to boost her holy energy. Having grown up as a priest, I know these things full well. I've already given her the bare minimum for gear, but if she really is going to follow Toudou's party, then there are still a lot of items she'll need.

"I'll prepare the necessary equipment for her. Contact the Church right away."

"I've already contacted them."

Various types of equipment are available through the Church. Even

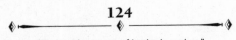

"The overdone sense of justice is a crime."

if Purif doesn't have the required items, I can simply order them from the next village over. That leaves the biggest issue: increasing Spica's abilities.

It doesn't matter that she can't use holy techniques yet. She will, in time.

"Then the issue is what to do about leveling Spica up..."

"You're right..."

Leveling up is difficult for priests. Our creed forbids us from wielding bladed weapons, and we lack the attack magic to combat average monsters. For every party, leveling up their priest is a major concern.

And Spica in particular is still just twelve years old and doesn't have any physical strength, much less the amount required to swing a battle mace.

Priests fill a supportive role within a party. They rarely have the chance to kill monsters themselves, hence the general difficulty in leveling up.

The most effective method would be to cast a powerful buff on Spica and allow her to slay undead—as we did—but that doesn't garner any real battlefield experience, and this is the only place that a low-level priest can easily ascend.

Should I have her level up here for a while...? Would Toudou even approve of the idea?

"Amelia, how did you boost your level?"

"I can use magic, so...I used it until I learned exorcism..."

Wait—can she use attack magic as well...?

I find myself staring fixedly at Amelia.

Well, since she's able to use difficult magic such as detection and communication, it wouldn't be surprising if she could cast low-level attack magic as well... But that's no help. We can't simply teach Spica magic at the drop of a hat.

Amelia averts her face from my gaze and asks, "How about you, Ares?"

"I could cast exorcism from the very beginning, so..."

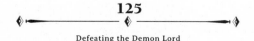

And not just exorcism. I could cast buffs and Heal, and I could swing a mace. Crusaders have special permission to carry blades. I knit my brow as I recall the distant past.

"I joined a party at first to gain battlefield experience, but...I never had any problems."

From the beginning, my background was far different from an average priest. I was scouted by a crusader and entered the Church through that route, so the curriculum given to me mirrored that of a crusader. Again, zero help for Spica's situation.

"If we had around three months to spare, we could get her up to speed..."

"Three months..."

A warrior isn't born in a day. Battlefield experience is crucial for growth, but even that has its limits.

We'd planned on heading to Golem Valley next. The golems that inhabit that region are renowned for their astronomical defensive ability. Even the revolver I gave Limis wouldn't be able to pierce their rugged armored bodies. Monsters of this ilk are susceptible to blunt-force damage, and Spica doesn't stand a chance in her current state. No chance in hell—she has zero strength.

Perhaps we should head to a different location before going to Golem Valley? No—that would just be confusing our priorities.

The most important factor is Toudou. Only the Holy Warrior himself. If his performance was to drop and if his level was too low when it counted the most, we'd be toast. His level is already lagging. In the worst-case scenario...Spica could die.

I take a deep breath in an attempt to calm myself down. Amelia is waiting for my reply. She's strictly here for support. In the end, I need to make the final decision.

I thought as much, but then I realize my grievous error.

I was wrong. The final decision isn't mine to make—it's Toudou's. All I can do is guide him—after all, he's the one who changed course and took us to Yutith's Tomb.

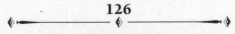

"The overdone sense of justice is a crime."

For a moment, I remember Gregorio's words from earlier.

A cog in the wheel of fate. I lift my head, make up my mind, and meet Amelia's patient gaze.

"I negotiated with Gregorio. He'll stay put, at least for a few days. In the meantime, let's raise Spica's level, get Toudou over his fear of the undead, and head for our next battlefield. That's the ideal plan."

It is an ideal plan, but in this world, things don't tend to go so smoothly. I learned that the hard way in Vale Village. But there's no other option, even if I'm well aware that this could fail.

"Should we...make the preparations during that time?"

"Yeah, we'll continue getting ready. However, what Toudou's party does is up to Toudou."

I can't cover for them entirely, and I can't guide them any more than they want to be guided.

The Holy Warrior's path cannot be forced, and even if I try, Toudou isn't the type to be coerced.

At any rate, things are in motion. Whether that's good or bad or, as Gregorio put it, through the guidance of God—I don't have a clue.

Fourth Report

On the Hero Overcoming His Fear of the Undead

"Make the decision for yourself," said Ares and, in turn, Toudou.

It was a kind yet cruel thing to say. Spica hardly ever made any decisions for herself.

After sleeping on it, Spica opted to join the party not because Toudou had saved her life or because she now knew that Toudou was a girl. In the end, it was because she felt like she was needed for the first time ever.

"Spica... Thank you so much. Your decision is a noble one. Let's do our best together!"

Although Spica was anxious when she announced her choice, Toudou welcomes her warmly. That alone helps her anxiety recede, even just a little.

Because they are staying in a room at the local church, they can't throw a proper welcome party, but there is nevertheless food and drink on the table.

Even Aria and Limis, who'd voiced their disapproval of Spica joining due to her young age, now join Toudou in offering their congratulations. Glacia is the only one disinterested as she nibbles on a piece of jerky.

"Let me introduce myself again. I am Aria Rizas, the swordmaster of this party. We're counting on you."

"I'm Limis Al Friedia, elementalist. I'll be taking up the rear guard alongside you, so...let's do this!"

"My name is Spica Royle, level ten. I'm a priest-in-training, and...I can't use holy techniques yet. Thank you for this opportunity."

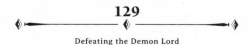

After everyone else finishes their self-introductions, Toudou stands up.

"Naotsugu Toudou. I'm the leader of this party. For the most part, I fight with a sword, but I can also use magic and holy techniques, so...I think I can help teach you."

"Holy...techniques?"

Spica blinks a few times as she stares at Toudou.

Only priests are supposed to be able to use holy techniques. At the very least, Spica never saw anyone outside the clergy use them.

Secretly confused, Spica decides to remain quiet and assume this is just another thing she doesn't understand.

"It's a pleasure...to make your acquaintance."

"Yeah, same here!"

Toudou smiles and sticks out her hand to shake Spica's.

Then, Spica finally asks something that has been on her mind. She turns to look at the reticent girl eating jerky who has remained silent ever since they met.

Spica has interacted with Toudou and her party on multiple occasions now, but she has yet to hear this girl speak a single word.

"Um... What about her?"

"Oh...that's...Glacia. We kinda ran into her...and now she's with us... She doesn't talk much...but she's not a bad kid."

Hearing her name, Glacia peeks at Toudou for a moment but then quickly looks away.

Toudou laughs in resignation and shrugs.

"She's also new to the party. She rarely speaks, but I'd appreciate it if you guys got along."

Limis taps Glacia lightly on the shoulder.

"Glacia. Aren't you going to introduce yourself?"

"..."

Glacia eyes Limis suspiciously, her mouth not budging a bit, and Limis sighs deeply. Having expected this, Toudou smiles wryly.

"She can speak. She's just not very used to it..."

Following Toudou's words, Limis continues to introduce Glacia.

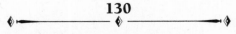

"The overdone sense of justice is a crime."

"Also…she's always hungry—"

"I'm not hungry."

"?!"

Limis goes completely wide-eyed at Glacia's sudden denial.

Everyone's gazes fix on their silent comrade. She stuffs the entire piece of jerky in her mouth and chews it loudly. She bats her eyelashes and looks at each member in the room with her translucent green eyes before saying again, "I'm…not…hungry."

"…So it seems."

Limis glances at Toudou, exasperated, and Toudou looks to Aria with the same expression.

Aria breathes a small sigh.

"…Well, she does speak in small amounts, on rare occasions…"

"I—I see…"

"I'm not…hungry."

The second Glacia finishes saying it, the sound of her gurgling stomach fills the entire room.

Limis gets to her feet and reaches into a bag lying in the corner of the room, retrieves a piece of freshly purchased jerky, and hands it to Glacia.

"Well… At any rate, please be good to her. She doesn't generally join in any battles."

"Okay…I understand."

Spica nods slightly, completely perplexed.

"Okay, here's to our new companion! Cheers!"

""Cheers!""

The table is lined with food that Spica has rarely seen or eaten.

There is only one watering hole in Purif, and maybe it's due to the early hour, but the place is practically empty. Spica and company are the only group sitting at a table.

At Toudou's prompt, they clink their glasses. Spica imitates her peers as she lifts her glass of fruit juice, having never performed a toast.

"Thank you so much… But…you didn't have to throw a welcome party for me…"

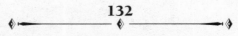

"Heh… Just relax and enjoy yourself. You'll have to work for it from now on."

Limis smiles faintly and gives Spica a pat on the head, then takes a graceful drink from her glass.

Next to her, Glacia is eating meat from the table at a steady, perpetual pace.

Spica realizes she shouldn't protest further and puts her lips to her glass. Her eyes fly open at the sweet, refreshing liquid on her tongue, and she pushes the glass away unconsciously. Toudou beams as she watches her.

"Well, we've still got some funds left over, and sometimes you just need a break. Plus, we're all a party now. I wanna hear more about you, Spica."

"Yeah… Don't, like, blame yourself so much. When I heard you were headed to the Great Tomb by yourself, I was like, whoa…"

Aria had drained her glass immediately. Despite her tone, her eyes are completely calm.

Limis replies to Aria, teasing her.

"Yeah, but you were shaking in your boots even with the four of us!"

"Shaddup! You passed out once, too!"

The party is a more curious collection of individuals the more you look at them. Glacia and Toudou in particular don't give the impression of risking their lives day in and day out on the battlefield—and neither do the others, really.

Most curious of all is how many people try not to be noticed by them.

The conversation soon focuses on Spica, from her upbringing to her life in Purif to her likes and dislikes. It is all the more difficult for her to navigate certain topics since she is forbidden from mentioning anything about Ares.

Toudou's eyes widen with surprise as she asks, "Huh? So you decided to join my party…just 'cause?"

"…Yes. I just sort of, all of a sudden…had a feeling…"

"A feeling? …You're a pretty reckless kid, huh?"

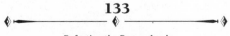

Judging by Limis's astonishment, Spica was too late to realize she had made up the wrong kind of excuse.

"I mean... You hear a lotta stuff about priests receiving revelations from God. Maybe this was that kinda thing?"

"A divine revelation? ...You realize Spica is twelve, right?"

Aria's eyes appear glazed over—maybe from the alcohol—as she slams her fist on the table.

"No, age's got nothin' to do with it! From the very beginning, I swear, I've been convinced Spica's no ordinary human being."

"...Huh?"

Aria stares down at the bewildered Spica and folds her arms across her chest.

Doing so only further emphasizes her breasts, but Aria seems unaware of this as she grabs a bottle of wine and swigs straight from it.

She downs half the bottle in one go before grinning from ear to ear.

"Spica's not even a mercenary, and yet the undead don't scare her... So crazy."

"No, that's not it... You're just weak."

"It's crazy. Totally nuts. Almost as crazy as Nao's fear of the undead."

"...I don't wanna hear that from *you*, Aria..."

Is she drunk or is she sober? In any case, she looks exactly the same.

Spica is flustered, and Toudou forces a smile at her before saying, "But anyway, we'll be fine as long as we've got you, Spica! And who knows, maybe that feeling you had really was a message from God?"

"Ugh! Not you, too, Nao..."

"C'mon, like... There is a God, so why would it be strange if They sent a message?"

Everything's gotten all weird just because I couldn't come up with a good excuse...

Bewildered, Spica hears a voice pop into her head. It isn't divine— it's Amelia.

"Say something to Toudou's party that might rouse them."

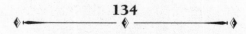

"...Rouse them...?"

Nothing comes to mind. She glances at Toudou and the others, who are chattering excitedly, and replies simply, "...I'll do my best."

It's no lie—this is Spica unmistakably speaking from the heart.

She's just met them, but Spica doesn't hate Toudou and her party, or Ares for that matter.

She doesn't know if she's capable of anything, but she knows she has to try, for the sake of Toudou, who looked so happy when she said she would join her. She also wants to be useful for Ares, who helped her, too, albeit for his own reasons.

It was a single utterance, spoken softly, but her simple expression of commitment sets Toudou's party alight.

"Yeah, that's the spirit! With Spica here, the Demon Lord is...nothing to fear!"

"W-well... Um... I don't know about that..."

"Don't be so impulsive. Make sure to wait for your cue before giving any directives."

"W-well... Um... I don't know about that, either..."

Flustered by being pulled in two confusing directions, Spica resolves once more to do her very best as a priest.

After returning to the church and spending the night, the group discusses what to do next.

The most pressing topic is leveling up their newest and most inexperienced member, Spica.

"Okay... Moving forward, how are we going to approach leveling Spica up?"

"...A level-ten priest, hmm...?"

Aria, the person with the most knowledge on the subject, regards Spica upon hearing Toudou's question.

She stares at Spica in silence for a while before parting her lips with chagrin.

"In all honesty…her options for leveling up are extremely limited."

Spica doesn't know anything more about being a priest than the average person. She watches Aria earnestly, determined to absorb every last word of advice.

"Priests have a very hard time gaining levels to begin with…and Spica is simply too young. Normally, when a child needs to level up, an adult will beat a monster half to death and let the child finish it off."

"Or they put the monster in a cage and let them defeat it with attack magic—right?"

Limis nods, acting the expert.

Humans are weaker than monsters in the first place. Children even more so. Spica already received help to level up, so she understands that well.

Spica peeks toward Limis. They aren't too different in height, but Spica is much thinner. Her strength and stamina are low, even compared to other orphans in the same circumstances.

"She'll fill out more as she grows, but at twelve, her body simply isn't done developing. If she could use magic like Limis, it would be a different story, but both swordsmanship and magic require long training periods. Even if we started now, she wouldn't see results for quite some time, and priests…cannot wield swords, per their creed."

Hearing Aria's words, Spica remembers the weapon that Ares used.

A long staff with a spiked ball at the end—the brutal weapon known as a battle mace. The one in Ares's possession is longer than Spica is tall. There is no way she could wield it.

Toudou pipes up as if recalling something or other. "Ohhh…*that* thing…"

"Yes, that."

Aria must be keyed in to what Toudou is thinking, as she nods solemnly.

"…You're right; it'd be impossible…for Spica…"

"Certainly, it's not a weapon that priests normally use…but Ares is the exception to the rule."

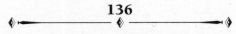

"The overdone sense of justice is a crime."

What are they talking about? Spica tilts her head in confusion, and Aria awkwardly changes the subject.

"We were planning on heading to Golem Valley, but...Spica cannot defeat the enemies there. The golems are infamous for their rock-hard bodies...so even if she did defeat one, it would take a considerable amount of time and effort."

"...Is there another good location?"

"I have a few places in mind, but—"

Aria frowns. Spica keeps her mouth shut, since she has no idea herself. If Amelia was connected via transmission, then she could ask, but the transmission is currently disconnected.

Aria lets out the deepest of deep sighs—as if expelling the weakness inside her. Once she finally finishes, she returns to her normal expression and announces to Toudou, "The best place for raising Spica's level is... well...right here."

"...*Guh?!*"

"This area is renowned for being the prime location when it comes to leveling up priests."

Toudou makes a sound like a squashed frog as the blood drains out of her face.

Spica has heard this before, but she stares at Toudou, floored by the dramatic change in expression.

Unable to tolerate the staring any longer, Toudou averts her gaze.

"Um... I'm a bit reluctant myself...," adds Spica.

"...It's—it's fine. Let's hear her out. We'll decide then."

Aria nods at Toudou. "The undead in these parts are low level and have next to zero defense. With the proper preparations, they're nothing to be afraid of. With *the proper preparations*."

"Preparations... Right. Can fear be erased?"

"...Nao, what are you talking about?"

Limis sounds exasperated. As Toudou looks away from Limis, her eyes meet Spica's. Toudou immediately drops her gaze to the floor reflexively.

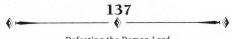

Aria continues. "In particular, the undead's greatest weakness is exorcism. Remember when that masked man blasted a light arrow in the Great Forest of the Vale? It doesn't have to be anything that powerful—even the bare-minimum exorcism will take care of any low-level undead."

"...But she can't use exorcism."

Aria takes a drink of water to refresh herself, then speaks as if she is attempting to reason with a small child.

"That's correct. If she can't...then someone must teach her how. Someone who *can* use exorcism."

"...Ohhh, I get it. And now...we've got Spica, a priest!"

According to the doctrine of holy techniques, only priests are allowed to learn exorcism. Although she is still a priest-in-training, Spica is now a party member.

Toudou and Limis react in agreement with Aria's assessment, and Spica tilts her head to the side, perplexed.

§　§　§

The Church is a hierarchy, and crusaders are at the top of the pile.

My requests for priest equipment and for Spica to be allowed into Toudou's party were given favorable official treatment.

There is an elderly sister who tends to the orphans of Purif. For all intents and purposes, Sister Yolande is the closest thing to a mother that Spica has. There is worry in her eyes as she addresses me in a heavy tone.

"Bishop Ares. That girl Spica... She hasn't received a single minute of training as a priest. Are you sure she will be all right?"

Although not bound by blood to Sister Yolande, Spica is almost like a daughter to her.

Is Spica really going to be okay? Well, that has yet to be seen, but the die has already been cast.

In any case... There's no way for the sister to check on her former ward now; she's joined the quest to vanquish the Demon Lord.

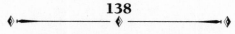

"Sister Yolande. Even if she hasn't received training as a priest, she was brought up in the church...under your pious tutelage. This solid foundation ensures that she will grow into a splendid sister herself."

I feel slightly disgusted with myself for so easily saying something I don't believe at all, but this is an imperative part of the process. Leaving Sister Yolande with even a shred of worry won't end well for anyone.

I rub the black ring on my ring finger—the sign of a crusader.

All my sins will be pardoned in the name of the Church.

"Please, be at peace, Sister Yolande. The God of Order, Ahz Gried, has certainly blessed this child."

"...Yes. Please...take good care of Spica."

Sister Yolande bows deeply. I heave a sigh, still full of ill feelings.

I bid the sister good-bye and retreat to the church's storehouse to search for equipment for the girl.

She needs a priest's robe, and there might be other useful items as well. I turn on the storehouse lights. It looks like it's cleaned regularly, but the place still smells a bit dusty.

I check the supplies quickly, but as is common with most church storehouses in the area, there is little to nothing of value.

I find a basic mace and a church-regulation robe. There are some empty bottles for holy water but no mythril gear—which I'd been hoping for—not to mention anything made of plain silver.

The Purif church fell on hard times, or so I heard. Perhaps church management was handling those more valuable items. If that was true, then applying to headquarters with an equipment request would provide gear of vastly higher quality.

Amelia already made a request, so that's fine as is, but I can't seem to shake my feeling of disappointment. Churches in this region are rumored to store treasure often enough, but perhaps I can't count on being so lucky.

I grab a number of children's priest robes from a shelf and stack

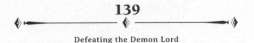

them on a desk. I find a newly bound copy of the scriptures of Ahz Gried in a box and take it out.

The source of spiritual power, holy energy, correlates directly to faith. Reading the scriptures alone grants the reader some measure of holy energy. I'll slip a sheet of paper into the book detailing other specific training methods for Spica—that will be enough to get her started.

I'd like to teach her myself if possible, but it would be suspicious for Spica to be gone that often. The best thing I can do is look for gaps and check on her level of progress.

I keep fishing through the desk and find an accessory in a small box toward the back. It's a necklace of a pair of scales wrought into a cross—the symbol of Ahz Gried. I pick it up by its fine chain.

Normally, accessories worn by priests are made of mythril, which wards off followers of darkness. At the very least, wearing silver is desirable. Priests themselves or those of a significantly higher level can cast a blessing through holy techniques on these items, which adds a slight level of protection from attacks by followers of darkness.

The necklace I found is a cheap gold-copper alloy. It isn't particularly useful, even with a blessing cast on it—probably the reason it was left behind in the storehouse.

It will have to do for now. Besides, any particularly luxurious equipment will only serve to lure the undead toward Spica. Until she learns to evade the undead herself, giving her high-class items would only be a detriment.

I gather everything we'll be borrowing and put them in a box.

I'll get them to Spica through Sister Yolande. I'll just let Amelia know via transmission.

I am just about to gather up the box and head outside when a transmission from Amelia comes in.

I stop walking as I hear her familiar voice but soon start moving again.

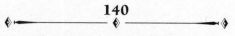

I've become all too used to voices suddenly sounding off in my head...but communication magic is so useful. I'm eager to have Stephenne join our ranks soon.

Amelia says a quick greeting before getting to the point.

"Toudou's party has decided to stay in this area a little longer to level up, it seems."

"I see."

"It was Aria's idea, I'm told."

"That sounds about right."

Aria's family is of genuine warrior stock. Accordingly, she has been handed down a certain knack when it comes to matters of battle.

She still lacks experience, which has led to some grievous errors, and her sense of danger is weak. Yet despite this, she always puts her best foot forward. In my personal estimation, she is the top member of Toudou's party—although she has no future.

She was at a loss when she learned of Toudou's fear of the undead, but she didn't let her personal feelings cloud her judgment.

As far as basic strategy is concerned, the Holy Warrior cannot stay in one town for very long—there's always the chance of monsters detecting his presence and attacking.

We've already been in Purif for a week, so we still have another month at the longest. I should be able to keep Gregorio locked up for that long. No, I *will* keep him locked up for that long.

"Raising Spica's level is a given, but this is convenient. Let's take care of Toudou's and Aria's fear of the undead—what we set out to do in the first place."

Now that I know Toudou's course of action, I recalculate our plans in my head.

I initially intended for Spica to acquire healing and buff holy techniques first, but if she's going to level up, I should really teach her exorcism first. Toudou can cast Heal and buffs, and those techniques can be supplemented to a certain degree with potions.

141

Also, having a priest who can cast exorcisms should help assuage Toudou's fear of the undead, if just a little bit…

"I'll teach her exorcisms first. Put on a display. Make the arrangements for Spica's training schedule."

"Yes…that's just the thing—it appears the whole party will go to the church to ask a priest there for instruction."

I stop in my tracks.

A priest at the church…? Sure, there are a number of priests at the church in Purif, but none of them are mercenaries. Even if they are able to use the most basic holy techniques, they're amateurs when it comes to the battlefield. The only high-level priests dispatched by the Church headquarters are wardens, and they're even lower level than Amelia. They wouldn't make adequate teachers.

It isn't necessarily a mistake to choose a priest to teach holy techniques, but the ones here aren't the most qualified for the task. Helios, who oversees the Vale Village church, would be more apt…

"So who's the priest?"

"I haven't quite… I'll confirm now."

I've met all the sisters and priests here. Just who does the church have in mind to instruct Spica?

Regardless, I'm glad they're trying to solve some problems on their own.

However, not all priests are benevolent. I would need to lay some groundwork. Toudou's party already distrusts the Church because of their inability to dispatch a priest for them. I need their impression of the institution to improve.

Depending on the outcome, we may have to ask the priest Spica learns from to introduce her to a different priest.

Hmm… I could wear a mask and teach her myself… Nah, that won't work. Even Amelia would be too…unnatural.

Our communications, which were cut so Amelia could confirm which priest is available, come back online. Her voice is shockingly dispirited.

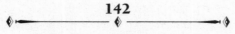

"The overdone sense of justice is a crime."

"It's Gregorio."

"…"

§　§　§

"…Is it okay to just show up all of a sudden?"

"…I'm not sure, but our only option is to try. Above all else…his level is higher than all of ours, at the very least. I'm not sure if he can teach us, but we should speak with him…"

Toudou and Aria concluded that Spica would be best off learning exorcism. Gregorio popped into their heads in part because they had just met him a few days before, but also—and more importantly—because the image of his crazed melee in the Great Tomb was still burned into their memories.

Aria answers the nervous Toudou.

High-level priests are extremely rare; those who can perform exorcism are even more so.

Even though he calls himself "something like an exorcist," selecting him for the job should not be an issue.

"He said he can't use any other techniques, but he ought to know the basics."

"…Yeah, you're right… He's kinda weird, though."

Toudou furrows her brow as she agrees with Aria's insight. She doesn't particularly care for men, but it isn't as if Gregorio is joining the party. It would be narrow-minded of her to hesitate in asking him to instruct Spica.

They learn of Gregorio's whereabouts from the father of the church, who immediately tells them he's staying in the third parish.

All five members of Toudou's party set out in the direction of the third parish. Toudou looks a bit sullen, perhaps because she has yet to summon the courage to delve into Yutith's Tomb again. Aria addresses her in an attempt to lift her spirits.

"We're very fortunate. Exorcists are quite rare."

"Is that so...?"

"When Spica learns how to use exorcism, let's get her leveled up quickly and move on from here."

"Will she really be able to learn that fast?"

"I—I'll do my best."

Spica balls her small hands into two fists.

The third parish is located in a building one size smaller than the first parish, where Toudou and company are staying. It is on the edge of the village where the surrounding area is fairly dull, and the desolate air that wafts through it makes the sanctity of the church all the more evident.

They enter the building to search for Gregorio and find him in the chapel.

Limis is momentarily taken aback by Gregorio's appearance but soon finds her composure before asking, "Um... What are you doing?"

"Mm... Ahhh... Limis and Toudou. We meet again... It is an honor."

He has the exact same expression as when they parted ways.

The chapel is empty. Gregorio turns his head to look at Aria and the others.

He is perched high up toward the ceiling near a stained glass window. There is nothing protruding from the wall for him to grab hold of; he looks like a gecko clinging to the wall.

Disregarding Toudou's dumbfounded look of amazement, Gregorio releases his hands. He falls several meters to the ground in complete silence, stands up, and brushes off his hands as he approaches them. Toudou reflexively takes a step back.

"Please excuse me. I was polishing the stained glass."

"Oh...really... That's very like you..."

Limis is stumped—that's all she can come up with.

"Forgive me for being in such a state."

"N-no... We were the ones who were intruding... Oh, thank you."

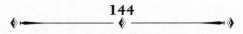

Gregorio pours them all black tea. Toudou accepts the fragrant cup and hesitates, scratching her cheek in embarrassment.

The room Gregorio brought them to is far more austere than their room in the first parish. There aren't any personal items save for his mythril trunk, and it looks as if nobody is living there.

Limis glances around the room, deeply intrigued, and asks Gregorio, "…I'm curious… How were you clinging vertically to the wall like that?"

"Ah, yes. That was nothing at all. It was simply a matter of…faith."

"…You don't say."

That's completely absurd. Limis takes a moment to once again permanently remind herself that the person before her is some kind of madman.

Aria coughs loudly and puts her hand on Spica's shoulder before saying, "We came here today with a request for you, Sir Gregorio. Do you have a moment?"

"Yes. As long as it doesn't require leaving the church building."

Gregorio calmly sighs in assent without a trace of ill will. Aria continues to the issue at hand.

"Actually… We're here to ask you to teach Spica exorcism."

"It would be my pleasure."

"The fact of the matter is that Spica, who we rescued just days ago, has now joined our party, and— Wait… What?"

"It would be my pleasure."

In reality, holy techniques are secret arts of the Church. They aren't something you can simply ask to be taught and expect training right away.

Aria, who was fully prepared to convince Gregorio, is not expecting his ready consent.

Gregorio smiles ear to ear and continues speaking to Aria and company, who are flabbergasted.

"It is a great pleasure to see more people willing to destroy God's enemies. I feel that all of humanity should do the same."

"…I thought holy techniques were secret arts of the Church?"

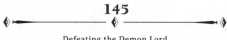

"This…is the will of God, Aria. If you are attempting to learn exorcism, if that is your wish, then it surely must be by the grace of Ahz Gried, and His alone. All I can do is abide," replies Gregorio frankly to Aria's tentative attempt at confirmation.

"I-is that so…?"

Gregorio's words are far beyond Aria's personal impression of a priest. She feels a twitch in her cheek.

At the very least, no such declaration is part of the doctrine of Ahz Gried with which Aria is familiar. Though she is a student of the sacred teachings of Ahz Gried, Aria is not a priest. She does a double take to verify that Gregorio is indeed wearing the sign of a priest affixed to his ear, then forces her cheeks to cease twitching. The sheer capacity for faith of the man in front of her is leagues beyond her own.

Gregorio speaks again, as if he suddenly realized something.

"Oh, I do have one condition. Currently, I am under special request to not leave this parish; therefore, I will have to assist you without defying that request… Will that be permissible?"

"Y-yes. Of course."

Toudou and her group all nod in inevitable agreement. Gregorio nods in return and empties his tea in one gulp.

"For starters…let's find a new location. We need more space."

"Excuse me… Is there anything I need beforehand?"

"Faith."

"Any implements, tools?"

"Unnecessary. So long as you have faith, that is," Gregorio responds to Spica with utmost confidence.

Spica decides to not risk saying anything unnecessary in the presence of a professional priest.

Gregorio leads the party to the inner garden of the church. It's a small patch of about four square meters with stone tiles interlaid throughout. A statue of a goddess holding a pair of scales is tastefully located in the center.

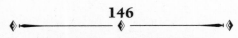

Toudou looks up at the statue casually as Gregorio explains. "This is a statue of a goddess who serves the God of Order, Ahz Gried. The scales are the symbol of Ahz Gried, who, as the God of Order, uses them to weigh sins and determine the fate of the world."

"A scale to weigh…sins."

"You can see the same symbol adorning such things as my earring, yes? In common speech it's called the 'cross scale.' Sister Spica, you—"

Gregorio looks at Spica's ears. Feeling his gaze, Spica quickly turns her eyes downward.

"—don't appear to have yours yet."

"I c-can't use holy techniques yet, so…"

"That cannot be helped. In the same vein…there was a time when I, too, could not use holy techniques."

Gregorio's voice is full of emotion. He then places his mythril trunk on the ground, at which point, he claps his hands together to dust them off and looks Toudou, Aria, Limis, Glacia, and Spica directly in the eyes, one at a time, before quickly licking his lips.

His expression brings to mind a snake closing in on its prey, and Limis's shoulders shudder.

"Now then. What do you think is the first and most important thing necessary for holy techniques?"

"The most…important thing?"

Gregorio's gaze moves over to Spica.

Spica looks up at the statue of the goddess and thinks long and hard.

An image of every priest she's ever met wells up in her mind's eye: the Purif church father casting holy techniques. Ares casting holy techniques in the Great Tomb. Priests who cast holy techniques are truly the embodiments of miracles themselves and receive great respect from anyone who beholds them.

After thinking for a full minute, Spica finally opens her mouth to speak.

There was a hint—something that Gregorio kept repeating.

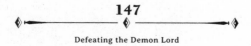

"…Faith?"

"…Excellent! That's precisely correct, Sister Spica."

Spica speaks with trepidation, but Gregorio is elated, raising his eyebrows while he applauds.

Gregorio looks up at the statue of the goddess and starts walking in a circle around it. Toudou's group stares at him as he continues his explanation, almost like he's warning them.

"The weapon of a priest, the mace, is the embodiment of that faith. The same goes for holy techniques. For us priests, our level and physical abilities are of secondary importance. We are disciples of the God of Order, and we use that weapon to rain destruction down on enemies of our god. If you only remember one thing, remember this."

"Hang on a second. Does that mean that even non-priests can cast holy techniques if they have faith?"

Gregorio stops dead in his tracks at Limis's query and declares, "Affirmative. If you, Limis, cannot cast holy techniques at present, it means you simply do not possess an ample amount of faith."

"And having enough faith will allow me to defeat demons?"

"Correct. If you are defeated by the followers of darkness, the only plausible explanation is your lack of faith. That is all."

"That's so stupid…"

Toudou makes a face at Limis's blunt remark. Aria speaks up softly. "In other words… Sir Gregorio, does that mean that the kingdoms that are embroiled in a losing battle against the Demon Lord, some of them wiped off the map completely—is it all due to their lack of faith? Is that what you're telling us?"

"Yes. It is truly heartbreaking."

Gregorio's response is curt. Aria opens her mouth to fire back at the priest's thoughtless comment but quickly thinks better of it and bites her lip.

Had Gregorio's words come from a Kingdom statesman, Aria would have had a thing or two to say in response. But before her stands a father of the Church—someone with an entirely different status.

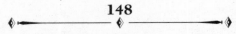

"The overdone sense of justice is a crime."

Toudou likely also understands this. She, too, bites her lip and refrains from speaking.

"That said, there is nothing that can be done about those who are weak of faith. That is the very reason for humanity's existence. In order to protect the weak, to represent their faith as well—that is why we exist."

It's almost as if Gregorio is delivering a sermon. He then raises his hands to the heavens.

"God has given us the power to protect the people. As long as we have faith in God, we shall never know defeat. Under His name, we will be free from every form of disaster. This is the divine order handed down to all priests, Sister Spica. For instance, even if your level is low, even if you cannot use holy techniques...you must never forget this. This...is your obligation. A priest who refuses to face this fact no longer has value in our world."

There is no fervor to Gregorio's words. The harshness he espouses leaves Toudou and company with an even stronger impression of his intrinsic principles.

Limis suddenly glares at Gregorio intensely and breaks her silence.

"Gregorio, if you're going so far as to say all that, then surely you can use all holy techniques, yes?"

"Alas, my faith is still...incomplete."

"Wha—? After all that yapping on about—?"

In that moment, as Limis begins to harangue him, a pillar of light erupts around Gregorio and shoots into the sky.

"?!"

"What the—?!"

Not a single pillar. Countless pillars of light erupt in the inner garden, filling it completely.

Toudou and Aria both gasp aloud. The pillars are easily distinguishable even against the daylight. As the party surrounding him ceases functional thought due to this sudden occurrence, Gregorio sighs.

"This is the extent of my capabilities."

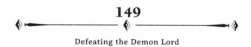

"The...extent?!"

Hearing this, Toudou realizes for the first time that the scene in front of her is all due to the priest in their midst. Limis's mouth is agape and stammering wordlessly. Gregorio does not appear to be particularly proud.

"What is this—?"

"Simply a breaking arrow...more commonly called an arrow of light. The most basic of exorcism techniques."

"The most...basic...?"

Gregorio lifts his right hand and audibly snaps his fingers. At his signal, each pillar aims and fires directly overhead.

The innumerable pillars of light gather together and form a massive ball that shines brilliantly like a small sun. Spica recoils and takes several steps back.

The light is blinding, but Toudou stares intensely into it without blinking once.

It is clearly God's judgment, a name perfectly apt for the holy techniques. Its wielder recites the words:

"Breaking Arrow."

At the sound of his voice, the dazzling orb shoots into the heavens like a bullet. It leaves a trailing afterglow behind as it disappears into thin air. Even after the light vanishes far into space, everyone aside from Gregorio remains rooted to the spot, unable to peel their eyes away.

Gregorio claps his hands together loudly, the sound pulling Toudou back to reality.

She stares at Gregorio in pure awe. Even someone unfamiliar with holy techniques could tell that this was a special performance—an extremely sensational display. Gregorio begins lecturing the party in the exact same tone as before, as if nothing had happened.

"This *magical arrow* that transforms energy into a shaft of light is the most fundamental technique of all magic. Holy techniques are not magic, but you could say they're equally difficult. Against high-level followers

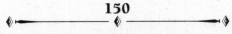

of darkness, they will only prove capable of stopping the enemy in their tracks, but without the holy techniques as a base, one falls short of practical use. In other words, if you cannot conjure arrows of light, you will not be able to cast other holy techniques."

Spica replies timidly. "...Will I really be able to cast something like that?"

Having witnessed such a vivid miracle with her own eyes, she senses dark clouds once again hanging over her head.

Gregorio stares into Spica's face, wrought with worry, and responds with a gentle smile.

"Do not fret. Any priest has the capacity to use this technique. If, by chance, you are not able to use it—"

"I-if I...can't?"

"......"

Gregorio fails to answer her and turns to cast his gaze on the other faces surrounding him. He is already in full control of the situation. Even Limis, who started to complain earlier, awaits his instruction.

"Let's begin by learning how to use the technique I just displayed. Fortunately, it easily has enough power to take on the undead in the lower levels of the Great Tomb. Go and purify them."

"W-w-wait, just wait a second... I really don't think Spica can use this technique yet."

"Only in the face of the followers of darkness does one's faith come to the fore."

Gregorio's response to Toudou contains not an iota of doubt. His voice resounds with confidence. He now turns again to Spica, a girl just shorter than himself, and looks down at her.

Spica realizes for the first time that Gregorio's gentle eyes are not filled with affection or kindness.

Gregorio brushes his fingertip against Spica's cheek, from which the blood has drained. Even though his voice is pleasant to the ear, it leaves her with a sense of impending dread.

"Fear not, Sister Spica. If your faith is truly deep and genuine, rest assured God will answer your prayers."

§ § §

According to the information Amelia relayed to me—Toudou's next move is completely beyond anything I expected.

"Gregorio is insane..."

"..."

I sit down heavily in my chair and cross my legs, my elbows resting on the table as my fingertips absentmindedly play with my knife. I know it's useless saying this to Amelia. But I can't help myself.

"There's no point keeping Gregorio holed up in the church if Toudou and his party go there themselves."

"...Yes, that's true."

"Hmm? What is this? Are they trying to make a fool of me? Is everything I've planned up until now going in one ear and out the other, ultimately working against my intentions? Gah, it's my fault for not properly explaining all the risks to Spica!"

"...No... Please settle down, Ares."

Don't worry. I am calm. I'm listening to everything Amelia is saying to me. I am absolutely calm.

Really, I am. I've always remained calm. One must let anger go. Even if everything happening around you backfires.

I spin my knife in the palm of my hand, following it with my eyes as I continue.

"This isn't the worst-case scenario. We haven't hit rock bottom."

"..."

"But this is no ruse. This isn't a ruse, Amelia. I'm not hoping for them to hit rock bottom. Do you get me? I don't expect everything to go perfectly. I don't expect that, but at the moment—everything is backfiring. It's blowing up right in our faces, Amelia. This is truly...a sight to behold."

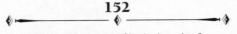

"The overdone sense of justice is a crime."

What is getting in my way? Is it the will of God? Are my methods flawed? From where should I start over? I'm not angry; I just genuinely want to know…

I notice the distance between Amelia and myself growing. Apparently, I've wasted my breath. I stab the knife I was playing with into the table, slap myself on both cheeks, and change course.

I inhale and exhale deeply to center myself. I can't manage to completely relax, but I'm better off than I was.

"This is just between us, but teaching holy techniques isn't exactly my strong suit."

"Nor mine."

"But I'm still better at it than Gregorio."

Gregorio's use of holy techniques is intuitive—and particularly warped compared to a typical priest. He's not right in the head, for certain, but you could call it some form of genius.

"What are we going to do?"

"Among current-day crusaders, there's a custom of showing new recruits the ropes. Gregorio and I both underwent this experience, but here's the kicker: The majority of disciples under Gregorio's tutelage have wound up dead."

Amelia listens to me in silence. This is beyond terrifying—something truly ghastly.

"If you ask why, it's because for him, being able to kill followers of darkness is a given, as is the ability to perform exorcisms. If you have ample faith, these provisions will follow in due course. Therefore, he deemed any priest who died on duty to be of insufficient faith, and for this reason, he had no qualms about their deaths."

"…What are we going to do?"

"Currently, because of the danger involved, no one is studying under Gregorio. The Church no longer has any desire to put disciples under his tutelage. They simply could no longer stand to watch accomplished young priests chosen to become crusaders die idly by the wayside."

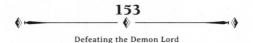

It may be Amelia's first time hearing this—her eyes are bulging out of her head.

The Mad Eater's name is not simply an affectation. Rumors are cause for concern even for the Church. A nickname of such ill repute doesn't come about through normal circumstances.

Shit—why didn't I just impale him on my mace spike in the dining hall? I can't lament this fact enough.

"Shall we contact Cardinal Creio?"

"There's no point now… I mean, of course I'll contact him, but the die has already been cast."

Now that Toudou asked for Gregorio's instruction, any requests for his withdrawal would be denied. We just need Spica to grow. There is no other route for survival than Spica learning enough holy techniques to appease him. Gregorio will never forgive a disciple under his tutelage who cannot acquire the necessary faith.

"Contact Spica for me. I'll come up with a plan."

If Toudou is outed as the Holy Warrior, that changes everything, but in principle, Gregorio does not accept anyone other than priests as disciples. If Spica is able to learn exorcisms, we should be able to fool him.

Spica's face comes to my mind, and I clutch my head. I can't imagine a single scenario in which this will go well. I'm not exactly omnipotent myself. What should I do…?

§ § §

"Can you wrap me up tighter?"

"…Any tighter would surely be uncomfortable, would it not?"

"It's okay… I'm already agonizing here."

At Toudou's command, Aria wrenches the bleached cotton cloth as tight as she can. Toudou screws up her face and lets out a small gasp as it wraps around her breasts over her undershirt, squeezing them down. Her breasts are squashed tight, but she doesn't voice a single

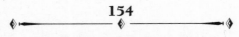

"The overdone sense of justice is a crime."

complaint, despite how uncomfortable she looks. As Aria tightens the inner lining, Toudou takes quick breaths in and out, trying to control her breathing.

Spica blinks, bewildered by this peculiar scene.

She looks toward Limis, who is sitting on the bed and polishing her staff. They're all in the same room. There's no reason why Limis wouldn't notice what's going on, and yet she is paying no attention to it whatsoever.

"...What are you guys doing?"

"...We have to do this, or my breasts stick out and I can't get my armor on."

Noticing that Toudou appears on the verge of tears as she says this, Spica decides not to ask any further questions.

There must be some reason behind it. Why doesn't she just wear different armor? Maybe this is something I shouldn't butt in on since I'm new to the party.

After putting on the slim white-tinted armor, Toudou suddenly looks like an elegant knight. If Spica hadn't seen how shameful Toudou looked just moments ago, she might actually be impressed.

Limis is also putting on her robe and getting herself dressed. Spica's palms are slightly trembling from nerves, and she squeezes them tight. She takes out the copper cross necklace that Ares gave her the night before and hangs it in front of her face, staring.

Limis suddenly takes notice and asks, "...What's that thing for?"

"...A priest I know gave it to me. It's a charm, they said."

It isn't silver, so it's not a very effective charm.

Seemingly sensing Spica's nervousness, Limis claps her hands together in encouragement.

"That's just fine. No matter what monsters appear, Garnet and I will burn them to a crisp for you." Sitting atop her head, Limis's crimson salamander, Garnet, flits out its tongue in agreement. The staff in her hand is topped with a sparkling jewel, the biggest Spica has ever seen, and a small flame burns intensely inside it.

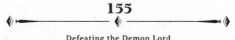

"Also, Spica. You're not afraid of the undead, right?"

Toudou's and Aria's shoulders shudder in horror at the sound of the word.

Spica nods slowly and says with difficulty, "...W-well...not really."

"Then you're fine. Compared with Nao and Aria...you're golden. Those two passed out just from hearing a single wraith's scream."

Am I really going to be fine? Spica is racked with dubiousness as Toudou protests loudly.

"How rude! A wraith scream is a full-on attack! Right, Aria?"

"Yes, that's right. It isn't a physical attack, but a wraith's Scream of Sorrow is unmistakably an attack nonetheless. Don't go spreading lies as if we fainted for no good reason!"

"It's not a lie—you fainted."

Limis obliterates Aria's desperate rebuttal in one fell swoop. She and Toudou look ready to bolt as they avert their gazes from Limis's. Limis shrugs and breathes a haughty sigh.

"It'll be okay. Even if Spica can't learn exorcisms right away, I'll be here to support her. Nao and Aria could even be a wall or something... And hey, I'm sure Glacia could be of some help, too."

"...Okay."

The only one lacking any preparations is the aforementioned Glacia, who shows no concern at all as she sits on a chair swinging her legs.

Spica recalls some of the advice she received from Ares and finally shows a sign of resolve. She grabs the sleeve of her priest's robe, which she finally got used to, and stands up. Her mace handle is smooth to the touch, and she keeps both the weapon and her scriptures in her handbag. Ares's dagger, which he said she didn't need to return yet, still hangs from her waist.

Spica is as prepared as possible now, and suddenly, she remembers something she heard the day before.

"...By the way, that priest I know told me this, but... They said it's extremely difficult to kill a thousand undead on such short notice," she informs Toudou.

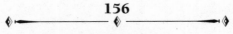

She is referring to the task posed to her by Gregorio: Destroy one thousand undead within three days' time.

Aria's and Toudou's protests had had zero effect; Gregorio's only instructions for Spica, who still hadn't learned any holy techniques, were to accomplish this task that she was in no position to carry out.

Toudou's smile stiffens in response to Spica's statement.

"...Oh yeah... Maybe this priest you know could come along with us? After all, you can't use holy techniques yet, so..."

Spica mumbles her reply in a voice so tiny Toudou can barely hear her.

"...They *will* be accompanying us, it seems."

"...Hmm? Did you say something?"

"No... It's nothing."

Spica smiles bashfully and clenches her fist.

Even if they do accompany the party, learning exorcisms is entirely Spica's problem.

That's the price of making my own choices. No matter what happens, I must follow through with them.

Because even if I can't do this on my own, I now have people here to support me.

§ § §

The only sound in the dim passage is that of Amelia's footsteps and my own.

There are many locations inhabited by monsters, but underground tombs, for starters, are a great example of some of the most dangerous man-made facilities for doing battle.

These also include: abandoned ruins; old, uninhabited castles; and cities that show signs of former prosperity, now laid to waste.

Delving into these places means one must remain conscious of the variety of traps set to repel outside invaders. Even if the previous inhabitants didn't set any traps, there are intelligent monsters that can detect

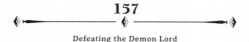

157

traces of previous human activity, and they tend to haunt those locations, possibly laying traps of their own.

Yutith's Tomb is an underground catacomb and no exception.

In particular, tombs used as battlefields expect a certain amount of grave robbing and, as such, generally include a number of highly lethal traps. In Yutith's Tomb, there are a number of dangerous snares of which one must remain wary.

That being said, this area was once filled with Survey Corps officials dispatched from the Kingdom, and humans have set foot inside on many occasions. Nearly all the traps in the lower levels have been disarmed. It's not that dangerous so long as you don't enter any of the unmarked locations on the map.

The Devil-Faced Knight statue that Gregorio destroyed was also likely a trap. However, despite being in the tomb's lower levels, it remained wholly intact—certainly a rare exception.

Before Toudou and his party enter, we've already delved into Yutith's Tomb.

I lead, and Amelia follows. The *Leading Light* that I cast ahead of us serves as a pseudo torch and illuminates the area. We have an ample field of vision.

As I confirm our location on the map ingrained in my mind, I investigate the presences surrounding us. This is in order to limit the chances of a powerful undead creature attacking Toudou and his party. In actuality, there isn't anything to fear in this area, but when it comes to Toudou, every last precaution should be taken.

"Don't you think you're being a bit overprotective?"

"You might be right," I reply to Amelia curtly.

I can't deny it. Hunting monsters is primarily one's own responsibility. This applies to the heroes as well. Thinning out the monster hordes certainly raises the safety level, but at the same time, it will inhibit Toudou's capacity for dealing with them. However...despite this—

"Until the party's average level is thirty, we'll continue with the same policy."

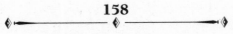

"The overdone sense of justice is a crime."

"May I ask why?"

"Because one's capabilities generally increase at that level."

Mercenaries' mortality rates are starkly different before and after level 30. That's where one of Toudou's party's obstacles lies. And that was precisely why I was so adamant about leveling them all up to that point within the first month.

The passageway twists and turns. A human skeleton holding a sword—a walking bones—appears around the corner and attacks.

The creature is trying to bypass the ball of light floating between us, and as it lunges forward, I casually kick it and send it flying. Its bones smash against the wall, and a shrill sound pierces the air as they scatter across the ground. Every remnant of the walking bones disappears into thin air. Its decrepit sword and decayed armor also vanish.

The only thing left tumbling on the floor is an ominous crystallized chunk of crimson the size of the tip of one's pinkie finger. This is the source of the undead's power, a physical representation of their thoughts—a mass of magic energy. Known as a magic crystal, it's one of the few items the undead drop when they die.

It's tiny and would garner an insignificant sum when sold. I crush it under my boot. Leaving any magic crystal behind allows the miasma of the tomb to absorb it, resulting in the undead reappearing. Their respawn takes up to a week, so we have no use for it.

I brought Amelia along with me so we can contact Spica at any time. I also wanted to ascertain Gregorio's movements, but we're severely lacking in personnel who can use communication magic. *What's going on with Creio's supposed dispatch of Stephenne?*

I promise myself I'll investigate later and turn to Amelia. Even in the dull lighting of the tomb, her expression hasn't changed. If anything, she looks to be in good spirits.

"Where are Spica and the others?"

"They haven't entered the tomb yet."

From a logical perspective, the task assigned to Spica—a priest-in-training who can't even use holy techniques yet—is completely unrealistic.

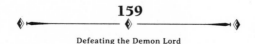

"There are a lot of undead here... Will she manage?"

"An ordinary person wouldn't be able to manage this."

This is impossible...absolutely futile. To kill a thousand undead in three days would entail hunting them down at a pace of more than three hundred per day without stopping. Not to mention, finding that many means going deep into the Great Tomb, where the thick miasma begins to erode human flesh.

Judging from her skill level alone, Spica will need an absolute miracle to complete the task at hand. Gregorio, too, is likely praying for one.

"What are you thinking about?"

"There's no way for me to understand Gregorio's reasoning. However—"

This assignment of his is insane. It is, though, a fact that failure is the foundation of success.

"—if Spica is somehow able to succeed, she'll grow by leaps and bounds."

"...And if she doesn't?"

"Then we'll make her."

We aren't encountering any particularly strong undead, and our journey has gone pretty smoothly thus far.

As we walk, Amelia speaks to me with the same unchanging expression. I really want Toudou and his party to take a page out of her book.

"I do wonder what's buried in this tomb... I can feel a powerful maliciousness."

"No idea. And I'd like to keep it that way."

The year it was constructed remains a mystery. The Kingdom gave up on unraveling the story of this tomb. Judging from the scale of the labyrinth sprawling in all directions, it wasn't built for the ruler of some small nation.

It wouldn't be surprising if it wasn't people buried here but some sort of forgotten evil god or demon. But that's not our concern right now. I must remain focused on keeping Toudou from taking a wrong step and

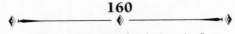

"The overdone sense of justice is a crime."

getting close to anything of that nature. As I consider this, we reach our destination—the Devil-Faced Knight's Altar.

On long-term monster-hunting expeditions, maintaining security is paramount. My intention is to have Toudou and his party stay in the room with the Devil-Faced Knight statue. Of course, there's always their previous experience in this chamber to consider, and we can change locations if necessary. However, this is a suitable space, as holy techniques function well here.

The rusted black door screeches open. I furrow my brow at the scene inside. The room hasn't changed in the slightest since the last time I entered. The spacious hall is complete with the stone altar and, atop it—the Devil-Faced Knight statue.

"Amelia, stand down."

"Huh?"

I stop Amelia from following me in and grip my battle mace fiercely as I approach the relic.

Nothing's out of the ordinary with the statue. It looks like it did before: a fiendish demon from the eastern region with a large sword hanging from its waist. The subtle features make it look like it might swoop down on us at any moment. Unlike the last time, I now know that it actually can swoop down and attack.

Yet there is something fundamentally wrong with the situation. I frown and take another step closer to inspect. There isn't a single scratch on the Devil-Faced Knight.

"...Why is it fixed?"

Gregorio completely laid waste to it. I saw the obliterated remnants with my own eyes after they all left. I saw the scattered rubble—its caved-in head, its arm broken in half. Even if someone who sincerely cherished this idol tried to repair it, there's no way in hell they could make it look this pristine. You can't cast healing spells on a statue, either.

There are traps that perfectly reset themselves automatically, but this is...beyond the pale.

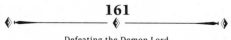

"What's the matter?"

Amelia stands next to me, looking up at the Devil-Faced Knight.

It's common for the founders of relics like this one to have their own lore. This must be that sort of gimmick. It's a respawning trap.

"I'm at a total loss... I can't figure this thing out."

"Oh, I see... So is this the statue you said Gregorio...destroyed?"

Amelia is ever observant, and she carefully puts her hand forward to touch the stone guardian.

I'm ill-suited to this manner of trap. Physical traps are one thing—I can usually figure them out—but at the end of the day, I'm just a high-level human. My knowledge is trivial, and my technical capacity isn't especially high.

I don't have the skills to solve this if it's magic. There's no mistaking that the Devil-Faced Knight statue reappearing in perfect condition is indicative of a magical power.

Amelia is inspecting something with zero expression on her face. Grasping at straws, I ask her in desperation, "Figure anything out?"

"It's a normal stone statue... It doesn't appear to be a golem or anything else."

"I see."

That much I already knew. Both Limis and Gregorio had said the same thing.

Perhaps the reason this room is always spotless isn't due to the respect of mercenaries who entered but, rather, because the room automatically restores itself. At any rate, this place should probably be...avoided.

Amelia suddenly looks toward me and tilts her head.

"Does it move when attacked?"

"No clue. Although, last time, it did appear to activate and move after Gregorio attacked it."

Using this chamber was the best-case scenario, but if we can't, we need a backup plan.

"...As a test, may I attack it?"

"Absolutely not."

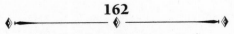

How would I possibly agree to that? Why does she insist on stepping into an obvious trap?

Amelia's at a loss for words. Then, the next moment, as she opens her mouth to speak again—

"...Ohhh... Sorry, my mistake. His attack didn't activate it. It moved before he attacked. More specifically, it must react to the intent to attack and then activate?"

I sigh deeply and cast a buff on myself.

A groaning sound. Minuscule fragments flutter down from the ceiling, and the ground rumbles deeply. Amelia's eyes fly open, and she retreats a few steps. Almost in jest, the Devil-Faced Knight statue stirs and casts its gaze between Amelia and myself before stopping on me.

"So it reacts to the intent to attack, huh? Of all the traps out there, that's a pretty vague mechanism, isn't it? I have a hard time believing Gregorio was the first to set it off... Then again, I had no prior information—"

It doesn't seem like such a complicated mechanism...but this isn't the time for that, I suppose.

"Ares, it's coming."

"Yeah, I know."

The Devil-Faced Knight's hand reaches for its blade. As it flashes out of its sheath, I block the incoming attack with my mace. There's less than a meter between us. The slash attack was affected by our difference in height, and it wasn't full force. Adding in the height of the altar means the Devil-Faced Knight was trying to slice and kill a human who comes up to its knees, and its attack position was extremely unbalanced.

I stop three additional swipes from overhead. When I block the fourth, suddenly the Devil-Faced Knight's massive sword turns over and comes sweeping at me from the right side, going for my neck. As I halt the attack, I quickly retreat a few steps.

The Knight leaps from the altar and raises up to full height. Given our difference in stature, the blows now raining on me are at full force. However, they're not as strong as I would have thought.

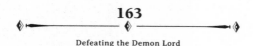

163

The Devil-Faced Knight isn't an undead, so exorcism has no effect. That's all we know.

"Get back!" I instruct Amelia, who's taking cover behind me.

Exchanging blows for a long period of time reveals many things about an opponent. It's particularly easy to do with a golem, mainly because its movements are determined by its primary functions.

The Devil-Faced Knight continues its onslaught, entirely devoid of spirit or emotion. The weight of its steps, the sluggish speed of its blade, the ease with which I'm able to deflect every strike—even though I lack serious battle experience fighting against swordmasters, it's easy for me to handle.

Aria said it was a golem with special techniques, but she was mistaken. It just looks like one.

There's no need for locking sword to sword back and forth. Based off its behavior and basic performance in battle, I estimate it would take someone around level 40 to defeat this Devil-Faced Knight golem enemy.

I repel another strike from the upper right with my mace, and as the Knight swivels around to attack from the left in the same sequence, I step in a few paces to evade the blow. An ingenious scheme isn't necessary when you're winning strictly on basics. I bring my mace down on its torso with the intention of pulverizing the statue to dust.

The stone brute slams against the wall, leaving it massively cracked, and then falls forward, facedown. Amelia applauds and recites apathetically:

"Ares attacks. A satisfactory blow. The Devil-Faced Knight takes one hundred and fifty damage. The Devil-Faced Knight has been defeated."

"...You're certainly stiff, as always."

"The Devil-Faced Knight attempts to get up and looks toward us, wanting to fight."

In tune with Amelia's description, my opponent braces itself with one arm and tries to get up. Just as she said, it really wants to keep fighting. Exactly like her narration.

"The overdone sense of justice is a crime."

What was that about it being defeated? Looks alive to me.

"The Devil-Faced Knight attacks. The Devil-Faced Knight uses its demon-god blade."

What the hell is she talking about? Before I get a chance to ask, the Knight steps in toward me with explosive power and draws its weapon with the speed of a master swordsman. The only thing differentiating it from a traditional swordmaster is that it isn't drawing its blade from a scabbard—it pulls the plate smoothly from the palm of its hand. A human would slice their fingers off; this is definitely a maneuver fit only for a golem.

I gauge its reach and leap backward, dodging the blow.

"The Devil-Faced Knight misses. Ares is unscathed."

The Knight returns to the front of the altar and aims its sword. Its stone body is extremely hard. Normal rock would have cracked under my mace blows.

Compared to the kind of prism Zarpahn received from Lucief Arept, God of Darkness, there's a huge difference, but it appears that a similar sort of barrier has amplified the Devil-Faced Knight's sturdiness. In other words, it's a buffed-up small fry.

Amelia continues to narrate in a whisper. "Ares's attack—"

"Sorry, Amelia—would you shut up?"

"This is my way of supporting you, since there's nothing else for me to do."

Knock it off. It's distracting me, so, seriously—just knock it off.

"I've realized something."

"So have I."

The Devil-Faced Knight is in pieces, having ceased all motor functions. I sit down next to it on the altar.

This enemy isn't just some especially solid golem. I can't be entirely sure, but there's a genuine difference in ability between this thing and a normal golem. In terms of how much of a nuisance this is, Glacia's got it beat.

"The overdone sense of justice is a crime."

Amelia, having just provided a very odd blow-by-blow, now looks up at me seriously. Well...she also had a serious expression while she was playing announcer... I never expected her stoicism to bother me this much. She's either messing with me or maybe she's just ditzy...

I decide to ask for an explanation before laying into her.

"Spit it out."

"It's called *World Heart*."

What is she talking about?

As I furrow my brow, Amelia continues disinterestedly. "It's a spell called World Heart. It's a sort of temporal manipulation magic, I suppose."

"...Are you saying that's the nature of this trap?"

"Yes." Amelia nods as if it's nothing in particular.

Does she mean she picked apart the nature of the snare in this short time? The word *magic* contains a multitude of nuance. Seeing through a spell that isn't even your specialty is a difficult feat.

"It's one of the secret arts, a lost technology. It allows the caster to tear open time and space and create a miniature world that acts according to predetermined laws. It's extremely high level... A very powerful form of magic."

Why does Amelia know so much about it? It is perplexing, but I never asked Creio about her bloodline. As long as she contributes, I'll employ her services. I listen with rapt attention as Amelia continues.

"I'll spare you the details, but the extent of its range is likely this room. The intended effect is clearly to repel any outside invaders who move the statue or perform a certain action. The reason we didn't detect a golem presence is that the spell is cast on the entire room itself."

"And why did it turn back to normal after Gregorio destroyed it?"

"The world therein is being preserved. After a predetermined amount of time, it resets to its original state... That includes the destroyed statue and the damage to the walls and floor. One could say that is the essence of World Heart."

Amelia turns to glance at the massive crack in the wall. It's certainly

true that the damage inflicted to it during Gregorio's battle with the Devil-Faced Knight was completely erased.

Reset. A reset, huh? If what Amelia says is true, then it's truly a terrifying spell. It allows for a perfect trap, and above all else, it makes limitless battle power a reality. It's a good thing this kind of technology was lost.

"The major drawback is the massive amount of magic energy it requires. The quantity is calculated by how complicated the predetermined world's laws are and how often it resets. For this room, the law is fixed to the statue's movements, and the world's reset is...not particularly quick."

The shattered statue certainly doesn't look like it'll return to normal anytime soon. Not to mention, it was still in that shape when I checked it out after Gregorio obliterated it the first time. Something suddenly pops into my mind as I recall this chain of events.

I look toward Amelia. Even in the darkness, I am taken aback at the lack of surprise on her face as she peers down at the stone statue.

"If we had someone with us who could perform this spell, could the reset interval be shortened?"

"Yes. The interval can be shortened, and the laws that regulate it can also be made more complex. For example—"

Amelia looks toward the ceiling in deep rumination.

"Yes, for example... The number of statues that can be animated could be increased to two or three."

"...I see."

At Amelia's last statement, I finally realize something.

This magic—I'm familiar with it. To be more specific, I defeated a user of this magic while on a mission some time ago. My opponent was a man from a storied and prestigious family of magicians, a mage who had conducted intense studies on magic that harmed others and, for that reason, had been banished from his home. One of the spells he used could conjure infinite warriors. They didn't take the form of statues, but

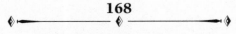

"The overdone sense of justice is a crime."

I recalled with terror their abilities and how they appeared one after the other, without any trace of slowing down.

The Church collected the results of his research, and this is likely why Amelia knows about the World Heart spell. I never thought I would see it again. I look down at the statue, destroyed a second time. Thank God there's just one...

"Lost technology, you say...?"

"...It would be more accurate to call it *former* technology. A mage managed to restore it several decades ago... I don't expect it's gained wide prominence since."

I see now... But whatever. Let's get to the point. I ask Amelia, who has shown surprisingly extensive knowledge on the subject, "Can it be disarmed?"

"It would be difficult... Disarming the World Heart spell would entail getting to the source of the magic energy itself."

"So it's impossible."

"At least in only two or three days' time. Casting World Heart and having it last for a long period requires a semi-permanent source of magic energy—"

"I get it. If it's impossible, that's fine. Thanks for the help."

I stop Amelia halfway through her explanation. If it's pointless, then let it be. I can't understand the fundamental principle behind the spell regardless.

"...You're welcome."

Amelia looks disappointed at having been interrupted in the middle of her explanation.

In reality, even if I did understand the principle behind the spell, since we can't disarm it, there's no possibility of using this room. We don't know how Toudou will muck up the situation, either... At least we now know that the interior of this chamber itself is a trap.

Okay—we need to find a new base somewhere more suitable. I can just set up a barrier and work our way from there. However, a barrier cast so suddenly in this thick miasma won't last long, so I'll likely have to recast it at set intervals...

"Oh, one more thing."

"There's more?"

"...Ares, you're being rather harsh."

Am I? ...I guess that was a bit cruel. But I want her to realize that her valuable information was a means of offsetting my earlier gripe about her narration.

Your helpfulness waxes and wanes from one minute to the next, Amelia.

I remain silent, and Amelia looks toward me and sighs imperceptibly before continuing.

"We know that World Heart was cast here, but we don't know why... The spell consumes an enormous amount of magic energy, and creating a mechanism that maintains the spell over an extended period of time is no simple feat..."

Amelia continues her reportage with worry on her face and a distinct frown. Now I get it... She really is exceptional. I clearly understand why Creio assigned her to me now. The way she's elaborating on the elements I don't understand is truly invaluable.

"...I see."

That was close... I was so caught up listening to her talk that I forgot what I wanted to say. I climb off the altar and walk to Amelia's side.

I stare down into Amelia's transparent eyes at point-blank range. Her voice trembles, a rarity, and given how composed she's been the entire time, I can't help but laugh.

"...Wh-what is it?"

"I forgot to mention it, but there's something I realized, too."

"...Huh?"

I spin around and turn my entire body forcefully, slamming my mace into the altar I'd just been sitting on. The slender, razor-sharp spines of my mace obliterate the stone altar. A thunderous roar shakes the air in the room.

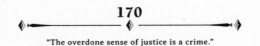

"The overdone sense of justice is a crime."

"?!"

Amelia stares at me in absolute disbelief.

Having finished using it, I pick up my mace and point it where the altar once stood. A hole now gapes in the ground in the same spot.

No—not a hole. It's a man-made *entrance*.

"The Devil-Faced Knight kept circling the altar like he was protecting it. I was positive there was something to it, and it looks like that something was a secret room."

"Wha...? Wha...? What?"

If the switch that activates the Devil-Faced Knight is any intent to destroy the statue, then it should have attacked Amelia, since she was the one who set it off. However, it targeted me instead. This leads me to believe that it goes after whoever is closest to the altar. When the statue was activated, I pushed Amelia to the rear, which made me the one closest.

A number of strange things happened during the fight. First, the statue made its first move on me from atop the altar, even though it was a terrible vantage point for an attack. Then, it got up again to protect the altar after being smashed against the wall. The logical impetus guiding its attacks is clearly quite simple. This is likely related to what Amelia said earlier regarding the connection between a more complex set of laws binding the conditions of the world and the amount of magic energy used.

I summon a ball of light and slowly guide it along the floor and into the hole under the altar. It doesn't appear to be too spacious down there.

I focus my energy to detect any presence but can't sense any followers of darkness. What's more, I don't feel any trace of the thick miasma flooding the rest of the underground tomb.

"The purpose of this spell was likely to keep this underground chamber concealed. For a hidden room, it does seem a bit careless, but the altar was completely seamless with the floor, and there's no way it would open without being destroyed. At any rate, it wouldn't be right to have Toudou and his party stay in the altar room."

"...You're mean, Ares."

Amelia mumbles at me as I poke my head back up and speak to her.

Specially manufactured silver chains hang in all four corners of the hidden antechamber. In the underground tomb, thick with noxious miasma, a mechanism more powerful than a prism is necessary. The silver chains act as a medium for prisms, and they have a greater effect than holy water.

Marking the room with a seal and offering a ritual prayer, I turn this single corner of the tomb into a temporary sanctuary. I confirm that the miasma has been cleansed and address Amelia, who is carefully observing a mythril necklace in the middle of the layout with great interest.

"Did you find anything out from that?"

"...Unfortunately, no. This is...not my specialty."

Amelia shrugs and quickly gives up on it. In the same breath, she hands me the silver-white necklace—the color of real mythril. The accessory is adorned with a small cube at the end of its thin chain. Amelia found it in a box lying in the center of the Devil-Faced Knight's hidden nook beneath the altar.

"Understood. I'll send this to the Church later and have them investigate."

I wrap the trinket in a cloth and stuff it into my pocket. Implements imbued with magical power are sometimes found in historical ruins of this nature. This necklace is that kind of magical tool. I can't be sure of its effects without further investigation, but it doesn't appear to be the type that's detrimental to its owner.

Thinking about it right now does no good, so I chase the thought from my mind.

I take out a map of the first level of the catacombs and spread it out so that Amelia can see, too.

"Let's pick up the pace a bit. We'll set getting Toudou accustomed to the undead as our number one-priority."

High-level undead won't pop up around here, and this go-around is

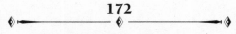

already leagues smoother than our first attempt. One major reason for this is that we can now go through Spica to keep the party's actions in check.

"There are many varieties of undead, and everyone usually has types that either bother them or don't... For example, the vampire we encountered in the Great Forest of the Vale didn't seem to give anyone any problems."

I don't understand how someone doesn't mind vampires but can't handle the living dead... "Amelia, which type of undead scares you the most?"

"...None in particular... But if I had to choose, I'd say the walking bones."

On the verge of contributing nothing, Amelia manages to name a monster at the last second.

A walking bones is a skeleton-type undead. The only thing separating it from the living dead is that its body is constructed completely of bones. Compared with the living dead, it has high agility and low attack power. There are plenty of other characteristics, but none of them are a concern when taking into account Toudou's anxiety.

"And why is that?"

"...Perhaps they're not as scary as the living dead. Those look exactly like corpses, and the aversion I feel toward them is a little different."

"But the living dead *are* corpses, right? They're an example of invisible spirits inhaling the miasma and taking on physical forms. As proof, when they take enough damage and can no longer sustain their bodies, they disappear without a trace."

In response, Amelia blinks a handful of times, then responds, slightly annoyed.

"...Logic aside, they do look like people, don't they?"

"Okay. Let's start with the bones, then."

At the end of the day, Toudou needs to overcome his fear of every type of undead, but whatever Amelia says goes. I trust her sensitivity toward the undead far more than my own.

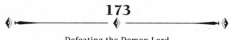

I stand up and breathe deeply, focusing my senses to detect any undead prowling around us.

Time to get down to business.

§ § §

There is no rationality behind fear.

Strength or weakness—these are also inconsequential. There's no reason for it, but Toudou is still terrified.

On the other hand, she can't understand why Limis, Glacia, and Spica aren't afraid of the undead. Toudou's slight hopes that she wouldn't be scared this time were quickly dashed the second she entered the tomb.

Toudou never considered herself timid up until now, but as she watches Limis and Spica stroll through the darkness with only Garnet's meager flame guiding them, she realizes she was wrong the whole time.

"...D-don't you guys think it's cold in here?"

"...Nao, all underground tomb battlefields are...chilly."

Aria and Toudou are at the vanguard. Behind them is the noncombatant Glacia, and Limis and Spica are bringing up the rear.

Despite the pairs of eyes staring at her from behind, Toudou's only saving grace is having Aria, who shares her fear of the undead, at her side. In this moment, Toudou feels more gratitude for her party members than she ever has since embarking on the quest to vanquish the Demon Lord.

Aria's bloodshot eyes fixate on the path ahead, unlikely to miss even a single rat scurrying in the darkness. Garnet's light is weak, and the field of vision it provides doesn't even reach a few meters.

Toudou's breathing is ragged as she focuses her senses. It wasn't very long ago that her level rose to 27, and she has already become accustomed to her heightened physical abilities. Now she is somewhat able to detect the presence of nearby living beings. Not to mention...she can detect other things, too.

"...There're too many of them."

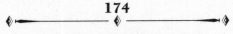

Toudou stares wide-eyed and bites her lip. She can sense so many followers of darkness that she's unable to pinpoint where each one is. Aria taps Toudou on the shoulder as she brushes her bangs from her eyes and stares at the floor.

"...You can do this."

"No, I can't. I feel like puking just imagining them."

The only thing keeping Toudou in this underground sarcophagus is her pride as the Holy Warrior. She also doesn't want to show the newest member of the party, Spica, this pathetic side of herself. Call it stubbornness.

That is all Toudou has prodding her on. Compared to how she and Aria are trudging along in front, the three members behind them are practically skipping. Glacia walks silently, but Limis and Spica are having a boisterous conversation as they take up the rear.

Toudou can't begin to comprehend how the two of them can chat up a storm like that in the dark void of a sunken tomb. Aria must understand the feeling, as she stiffens her cheeks into a bitter smile.

"...As humans, we all have our strengths and weaknesses."

"But still... This is pathetic..."

Garnet makes a slight chirp as if in agreement with Toudou.

As they walk along, Limis can be heard attempting to cheer up Spica, who is still stiff.

"It's going to be fine, Spica. Even if you aren't able to perform any exorcism spells here, Nao will destroy all the enemies for you. People don't usually learn as quickly as she does anyway."

"Um, well..."

"What?!"

Suddenly hearing her name, Toudou turns around and quickly succumbs to Limis's stern gaze. The power dynamic within Yutith's Tomb has already been clearly defined. Toudou laughs pitifully.

"...W-well, Aria *and* me. The both of us. Ha-ha-ha."

"...Don't drag me into this, please."

This time around, Aria is the one objecting, indignant at Toudou's remarks. She is completely serious.

175

"Don't say that... We're in the same party, after all."

"Right now, you're the enemy."

"Both of you, cut it out!!"

Limis's sharp rebuke reverberates throughout the entire passageway, making Toudou and Aria shudder.

Spica is taken aback, and Limis slams the end of her staff into the ground with a piercing sound and reprimands Toudou and Aria.

"You two grown ladies will make Spica anxious if you keep bickering like that! Not to mention, it'll make me anxious, too!"

"...Y-yeah...you're right... I'm sorry."

"Just what are you so afraid of anyway? Didn't I already tell you the undead in this area are super low level? Our equipment is flawless, and we're totally prepared. You've got no reason to be afraid."

"B-but— ...Yes, ma'am."

Toudou attempts a retort, but her expression suddenly turns meek, likely because of the second stern glower Limis gives her. Aria sighs in response.

"Limis. Everyone has their predilections. Some dislike insect-type monsters, and others hate plant-based ones... It's not about whether they can defeat them or not. Surely there are monsters that make you squeamish, too?"

"Nope. I don't care if it's an insect, plant, golem, or demi-human."

The height difference between the two of them is so great that, from the side, it looks like a child lashing out at an adult. In that moment, Limis puts her finger to her lips as if ruminating and says, "Although... if you forced me to answer, then I guess I'd say...I really don't like green peppers."

"..."

Limis ignores Aria, who is totally dumbfounded by her flat response, and instead turns her attention to Toudou. Staring at her intensely, she reaches out and puts her arms around Spica, whose eyes are darting about.

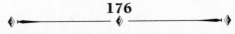

"The overdone sense of justice is a crime."

"But that's not what Aria or I are getting at. Right? We're here because of Gregorio's task to kill one thousand undead... *One thousand!!* And you're sitting here talking about predilections and personal preferences?! Seriously?!"

"...Yes, ma'am."

"And you came prepared for all this, am I wrong?!"

"...Right you are, ma'am."

Toudou can only shake her head dejectedly, and Limis smiles with satisfaction. It's indecipherable whether her next words are intended seriously or as a joke.

"Okay, then let's keep going. If being near the undead scares you, why don't you try throwing your sword at them? Or perhaps casting a spell?"

"...Yeah, you're right."

Toudou idly peers down at her sword on her hip and manages a stifled, dry chuckle.

At any rate, Toudou may not be very strong, but she can use magic and does have a shield. Even if she doesn't chuck her blade at her enemies, she still has options. The one who doesn't is Aria.

Toudou turns toward her friend. She still appears sullen, but she's regained some composure on the heels of Limis's upbraiding. Now is not the time to split hairs over personal preferences. Aria must have remembered what Limis said, as she nods once with conviction and faces forward again.

Just as they are about to set forth, Spica pipes up nervously.

"U-um... Toudou... They're coming."

"...What is?"

Toudou looks back inquisitively. The second Spica opened her mouth, Toudou begins to grasp her meaning.

Aria draws her sword. Limis grips her staff. Glacia yawns. Spica bites her lip and stares into the very depths of the darkness with eyes wide as saucers. And in that moment, Toudou fully senses the incoming presence.

An ominous rattling can be heard from beyond the darkness. The aura of followers of darkness is unique. Under normal circumstances, Toudou should have been capable of detecting them from far away, but the thick miasma and countless undead surging toward them are significantly disrupting her senses. That was why she failed to notice until she could actually hear their approach.

"It's walking bones."

A walking bones appears from the shadows as if to back up Spica's statement.

It's an ivory-colored human skeleton about as tall as Aria, wearing dilapidated armor and holding a rusted sword. A dark-purple light peeks through the eye sockets gaping in its skull. It has neither skin nor flesh. The ominous rattle comes from its bones and shoddy armor banging against each other and the sound of its bony feet hitting the pavestones.

It moves slowly, just as the "walking" part of its name suggests.

Toudou swallows hard and unsheathes the holy sword Ex, a stolid expression on her face.

"...I...got this!"

She observes its behavior as her brain turns to ice. Its movements are sluggish, and from a single glance, its weapon is clearly battered and powerless. The holy blade Ex could easily cleave its dilapidated armor in half, and even if her strike failed to make it through the armor, the walking bones looks like it would crumple to a heap from a single kick.

It has no savage capacity nor special powers. It's a small fry, simply shambling toward her. For all she knows, it might not even mean her any harm; Toudou isn't sure it even notices them. The only thing she can feel is the strange and ghoulish hatred emanating from its orbital sockets.

The majority of undead are not corpses, but rather, they are formed when negative thoughts of the earth's perished souls combine with magic energy. These beings, having the forlorn chagrin of perished souls

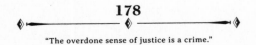

at their core, cannot help but hate all living things. Toudou turns this information she gleaned from Limis and Aria over in her mind.

She raises her shield in her left hand and braces full force. She bites her tongue and lip in order to divert her fear with the resultant sharp pain. To emerge victorious against the hatred, she stares down the being in front of her, full of murderous intent.

Limis sees Toudou's bloodcurdling expression and, worried, calls out to her.

"Nao!"

"!!"

Toudou stomps the ground with all her might. She looks as if she's going to trip over her own feet as she plunges toward the enemy, her large shield upheld in her left hand.

"HAAAAAAAAAAAAAAAAAAAAAAAAAAAAAAAAAAAA!"

Her subsequent shout sounds more like a shriek than a battle cry, and it echoes throughout the tomb. The walking bones takes the full brunt of the attack Toudou has unwittingly imbued with magic energy. It crumbles from the feet up and lands in a jumble.

Toudou smashes her shield down on the pile of bones with gusto. The walking bones's armor is crushed flat, and its splinters scatter everywhere. Its rusted sword smacks against the wall with a dry *clang*.

Toudou looks around the corridor, her eyes bulging.

"*Haaah...haaah...haaah...* I...killed it...?"

"Um...yeah... You sure did. Well done."

The scattered bones ripped from the undead's skeleton body disappear into thin air. Limis's response to Toudou almost sounds put off.

Aria surveys the area as Toudou gasps for breath, and she remarks, "...That was total overkill... It was already dead when you cast *Howl*."

"...Howl...?"

"Howl is a technique that allows you to fortify your voice with magic power and damage the enemy. It's the most common form of magic use for swordmasters."

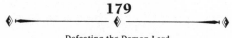

Aria eyes the spot where the undead had just stood. Howl is a very basic spell, but she had not yet shown it to Toudou. Aria had heard of certain spells being cast unconsciously when their users got psyched up. That must have been what just happened—Toudou's rich capacity for magical power allowed her to cast the spell without knowing it.

"...Um... I-in other words, does that mean I can kill undead without getting close to them?"

"Howl deals very little damage. For the average enemy, all it will do is momentarily stop them in their tracks. It's a very inefficient use of magic energy, and I advise you not to..."

Indeed, the intent of Howl is not to defeat the enemy. The reason Toudou destroyed the walking bones with it was due to their vast difference in physical strength.

Toudou's shoulders droop in disappointment. She's fought only a single battle, but her entire body already feels like an anvil. Perhaps she doesn't look so good, because Limis asks anxiously, "...You put too much magic energy into that. Are you feeling okay?"

"Y-yeah, I'm fine."

Using a vast amount of magic energy in a short time can cause a person to faint. At any rate, Toudou's capacity for magical manipulation is not high. As she looks down at her hands, opening and closing them to get a sense of her condition, Aria gives her a further warning.

"Magic gets depleted quickly, so until you can control it and use the smallest possible amount, you probably shouldn't use any at all."

"Yeah, you're right..."

"!!"

Toudou finally looks composed. Spica's eyes are darting in every direction, and she says, as if apologizing, "Toudou...I think a lot more of them are coming."

She is right—another horde of undead appears in no time. It's an innumerable drove of walking bones. In that moment, even Limis, who isn't particularly averse to them, exhibits a huge change in demeanor.

"The overdone sense of justice is a crime."

"WHAAAAAAAAAAAAAAAAAAAAAAAAAAAAAAAAAAAAAAA
AAAAAAAAAAAAAAAAAAA!!"

"What the... Nao?!"

Tears stream from Toudou's eyes as she plunges into the center of the throng. She's put an excess amount of magic energy into Howl this time, and the air around them ripples as the first skeleton falls to the floor, as does the one behind it. However, the third skeleton in line only pauses in its tracks.

By nature, magic energy has no shape or form. As such, a Howl cast from a distance or with something blocking its path will greatly lose attack power. This diminishment is not a formula for comparing this phenomenon with the sacrament of magic expressed in this world.

Toudou frantically swings her sword and shield, smashing the skeletons in her path. Aria also takes up her sword again behind the hero. Aria's magical blade Lightning Howl, forged with the power of fire and earth spirits, is a weapon of ancient and honorable origin bestowed to the Grand Swordmaster by the Kingdom of Ruxe. It has immense spiritual power.

Each and every slash of her superior sword obliterates a walking bones, turning it to dust. However, the surging waves pouring toward them do not recede in the slightest. The skeletons keep appearing one after another like an incoming tide. A terrifying thought passes through Toudou's mind: *What if they keep on coming forever?*

"Nao! Aria! Get out of the way! I can't use magic in a free-for-all like this! Get back!"

Limis's irritated voice can be heard through the din. However, the droves of skeletons filling their field of vision don't exactly promote calm decision-making. Toudou holds her shield strongly against the onslaught, cracking through bone and slashing diagonally through their ribs.

If she stops now, Toudou might not be able to get moving again. She bellows in an attempt to stifle her fear.

"WHAAAAAAAAAAAAAA!! AHHHHHHHHHHHHHHH!"

§   §   §

Spica can't move a muscle in the face of the innumerable skeletons that have suddenly appeared. Although she doesn't fear the undead, the sheer momentum with which they attacked is too much for her to bear.

Shrieks and howls intersperse with the clamor of a sword fight.

In front of Spica, who is frozen stiff, Limis screams at Toudou and Aria.

"WHAAAAAAAAAAAAA!! AHHHHHHHHHHHHHHHH!"

"Nao, shut up!"

Toudou and Aria are in a frenzy, doing everything in their power to fight back the droves of advancing skeletons. Each violent swing of their swords cuts down more and more, but to Spica's eyes, the two of them lack a certain vivacity.

"How many of these things are there?!"

Limis grows impatient. At that very moment, Spica hears Amelia's voice in her head.

"This amount seems to be no problem for you all. I will send a second batch."

"??? Huh? A second batch? No, we can't; that's too much—!"

"? Spica, what are you talking about?"

Hearing Spica's sudden shouting, Limis looks back at her quizzically. Spica shakes her head quickly from side to side in a panic.

"It's n-nothing!"

"Nothing, huh...? So what should we do about this, then?"

Cautioning Spica must have calmed Limis down. She is fully composed again. Because Toudou and Aria are running amok, her magic won't be able to reach the rear ranks of skeletons.

Limis takes a deep breath and gauges the battlefield once more. Spica simply gapes blankly at what's transpiring around her.

"Do you know how many are left? No, scratch that—how many have we killed?"

"...I don't know."

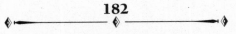

"The overdone sense of justice is a crime."

Spica, flustered by the unexpected assault, certainly doesn't have the wherewithal to count. Limis furrows her brow, and Spica turns her gaze downward to a magic crystal rolling on the ground before continuing hurriedly. "But...if we count the magic crystals later, I think we'll know exactly how many."

"That's true. We need to reshuffle our deck. Nao and Aria have gone completely overboard anyway..."

"But...but how will we—?"

Limis grips her staff and points it toward the ever-surging drove of skeletons—in front of the spot where Toudou and Aria continue fending them off. The jewel atop her staff flickers brightly before Spica's very eyes. Limis chants a brief spell.

"Garnet! **Flame Gust!!**"

The air stirs. The flame magic, now magnified atop Limis's staff, flies to Garnet, who is clinging atop Toudou's head. In the next moment, Garnet begins to swell.

"?!"

Toudou and Aria both reflexively retreat several steps from the intense heat. Garnet leaps forward from Toudou's head, now smoldering a deep crimson. Flames gush forward to fill the tunnel, a veritable firestorm in one direction. The crimson flames engulf the first three walking bones they touch and then fill the entire passageway like a rushing river of fire, leaving not one corner void of their blaze.

"This heat—?!"

Toudou is untouched by the fire itself but can feel the powerful, hot wind across her entire body as she quickly retreats to Limis's side. The firestorm rushes through the area for a few more seconds before disappearing suddenly.

Nothing is left in its wake. The walking bones are gone, their magic crystals along with them. The floor and walls are scorched black, the air is parched, and the only remaining evidence of Limis's powerful magic is the heightened temperature.

Limis fans her chest with her left hand.

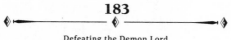

"Whew, it's hot... Guess I shouldn't use it in confined places like this after all... The heat should be more or less gone by now, though..."

"Incredible..."

Limis grins at Spica, who'd barely whispered. Garnet, entirely depleted of power, climbs up Limis's staff to the very top. There isn't any sign of additional skeletons encroaching from beyond the darkness.

"Oh, I've gained a level!"

"Forget levels! That was insanely dangerous!"

Aria explodes at Limis, who was simply staring at the palms of her hands. Despite not being burned herself, her proximity to the flames turned Aria's face bright red. Toudou's face is void of any color from the sudden magic and its immense power.

"It's your own fault for not getting back when I told you! Just be grateful you didn't get totally engulfed."

"No, you're wrong—we *were* engulfed! Flame magic isn't even used indoors—"

"So what should we have done? Kept up whatever you two were doing?"

"No... It's just..."

Aria hesitates, and Limis points a finger at her as she starts to smile.

"If I say get back, you get back immediately. Next time, I'll burn your ass, got it?"

"Uh... Understood."

Aria's face turns pale as she nods. After Limis looks her over satisfactorily, she turns to Toudou.

"Let's reassess our battle plan. At the very least, today we realized we can take down walking bones."

"...Yeah, you're right. Let's find a room to rest in and reassess."

Toudou and Aria down their water like they've been in the desert for weeks.

The room they've moved to after checking the map is largely empty—more than sufficient for taking a rest.

Seeing Toudou's and Aria's expressions, Spica—the only one aware

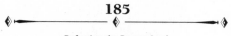

of the real situation—can hardly bear it. Of course, the plan was to get Toudou used to the undead from the beginning, but the only reason they're delving into the Great Tomb at this moment, still racked with fear, is to help complete Spica's task. The hardest thing is that she wasn't even able to help them.

Seemingly recognizing her companion's dismay, Limis calls out to her.

"Come now, Spica, cheer up! We asked you to join the party knowing you can't use holy techniques. This time, you noticed the enemy coming, which is a step in the right direction, isn't it?"

"B-but..."

Spica already knows how good Limis is at looking out for others. It shows in the way she talks to Spica, who is still learning the ropes. But Spica's mood does not brighten. She wasn't the one who realized the enemy was getting closer—she simply passed on the information being fed to her from Amelia.

Spica already knew she wasn't going to be particularly useful, but the image of Limis—who isn't that far off in age from her—casting the epic firestorm is now burned into the back of her mind and will not leave.

"We only just started our quest to defeat the Demon Lord... What good is making that face going to do?"

"Am I...making a face?"

"The same despondent one Nao's making."

Toudou turns her eyes to Spica upon hearing this. She appears exhausted from a single battle but manages a smile before saying, "I'm okay, Spica. I was just...a bit surprised. We're not in a rush, so let's take our time, okay?"

"...Are you sure you're not telling that to yourself?"

While Spica watches Aria and Toudou—who are obviously more than used to each other—she takes a single piece of paper out of the pocket of her inner robe. On it is written the low-level exorcism chant Ares gave her.

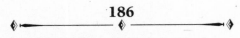

This isn't just a game for Spica. She had been practicing the holy techniques according to the scriptures and training materials Ares gave her, although at this juncture, she still has not succeeded in casting one.

"It's often said that holy techniques require time to be able to use. Don't push yourself too hard just yet," Aria advises Spica, who peers gloomily at the slip of paper.

Spica already knew that. Ares had said as much previously. But it doesn't help her accept her utter inability to help.

"Let's stick to what Gregorio told us. You might be able to use holy techniques as your level rises, and we'll remain by your side until you do."

Spica is very happy to hear such kind words, but they are also bittersweet.

Even in the heart of undead territory, which Toudou and Aria can't stand, they aren't making any attempt to blame Spica.

"That's right. I'm...I'm scared, but I'll give it everything I have. You, too, okay, Spica?"

"We might as well make it a contest to see which comes first: Spica being able to use holy techniques or Toudou and me getting used to this place..."

"...That's a good idea."

Toudou laughs, unsure whether or not Aria is being serious.

Exasperated by the two of them, Limis says, "It doesn't matter how you go about it, but both of you need to get acclimated, and quickly—got it? What happened earlier will only make Spica more nervous! In our next battle, I want you to fight with a bit more composure."

"...Yeah. We get it. I've gotten a little more accustomed to things after the last battle, so... It'll be just fine."

Spica stares intently at Toudou, who still looks a bit blue in the face as she squeezes her hands shut.

Spica can definitely count on Ares, who accompanied her the last time she entered the tomb. However, seeing Toudou and Aria march forward in the face of their fears is truly a brilliant sight.

187

"Once we take a short rest...we'll continue delving deeper. We still have time, but I want to keep stacking our undead body count."

Especially since Spica couldn't do it herself.

Toudou grits her teeth as she swings her sword. Her movements are still a bit clumsy, but the holy sword Ex cleaves the skeletons in her path into pieces. The undead turn to piles of dust without making a sound, and Toudou checks on them, breathing heavily.

"Look at that, you *can* defeat them."

"Of course I can."

Perhaps taking a rest was good for her, or maybe the reduced number of enemies is more manageable, but Toudou is able to finish the first battle of their second plunge into the tomb without screaming even once.

Her face is still blue, and she smiles through stiff cheeks. Aria, who was watching the battle play out from behind, nods solemnly.

"Well, well... It seems the power inherent within you is more than enough to defeat these enemies, so long as you remain calm. Emphasis on the calm."

"...Aria, you'll fight the next ones, too, right?"

"...Understood," Aria responds dejectedly.

The color has more or less returned to her cheeks. She must be just slightly encouraged by Toudou's performance.

Toudou removes her canteen and downs a gulp of water, wiping her mouth with her sleeve.

"I still...haven't leveled up..."

"Maybe that's because you still need to kill another nine hundred ninety-nine skeletons?"

The magic crystals that would serve as proof of vanquishing the skeleton mob from before had been completely incinerated. Thus, the party has nothing to show from that battle.

Toudou picks up a single magic crystal from the floor and sighs.

"If we go deeper into the tomb and fight more powerful undead, we should also gain some levels in the process...," suggests Aria.

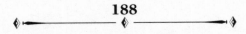

"…How high of a level are we talking, compared with the monsters in the Great Forest of the Vale?"

"…The walking bones we're dealing with now have approximately one-third the strength of an evil treant."

Toudou moans in disgust. In that moment, Spica receives a transmission.

"Please do not let them go any deeper into the tomb, as it's highly dangerous. We'll guide undead to your location."

She has no idea where her guardians are spying from, but they seem to have a full understanding of the situation. Although she has become slightly used to transmission magic, Spica shakes her head back and forth to dispel the weird feeling it gives her. She looks up at Toudou and says, "Um… I don't think it's such a good idea to go deeper."

She stiffens for a moment, worried she'll be pressed for a reason, but Toudou quickly nods in agreement.

"…You're probably right. We need to focus on your task, not leveling up."

"If only I…could use holy techniques…"

"I told you, there's no use feeling sorry about it. Even though I contracted with a spirit—it took me ages to do."

"This evening, we will conduct a special training session. I will contact you again later."

Spica's shoulders twitch in surprise at the sudden voice in her head, and she looks around the room eagerly.

Where in the world are they?

"For now, we'll continue prioritizing Nao's and Aria's capacity to take on the undead. It's common enough for someone to learn spells during battle, even ones they've already practiced. Fire-based elemental magic is only used for attacking, so…I'll use it when necessary. But only as a last resort."

"…Yeah, and it incinerates magic crystals, too."

"Yes, and that's because fire-based elemental magic specializes in the complete destruction of the surrounding area…"

Aria sighs at Toudou, who is glaring at Limis.

"We'll be fine, Spica. Your ability to detect followers of darkness is incredible. You have a true gift."

"Oh... Um... Yes. But I only managed to guess correctly... Next time, I might be wrong."

Since she can't tell them that the information is being relayed to her by transmission, Spica lets her gaze wander in embarrassment.

Compared with their first battle, everything from there on out has gone exceptionally well for the party.

Aria, who clumsily but readily slayed the skeletons she encountered, wipes cold sweat from her face before turning around.

"You've really gotten the hang of it."

"When you're faced with that many...there's really no other choice."

Toudou and Aria took down the skeletons that popped up one after another without a hitch. Their movements were not yet perfected, but compared with how they'd performed just a few days ago on their first excursion to the Great Tomb, it was night and day.

"Still scared?"

"...Yes, but..."

Aria stares deep into the darkness at Limis's question. She sheathes her sword and turns a stern gaze to Limis.

"I'm more used to it now, but all we've fought have been walking bones."

"Ahhh, that's a good point...," agrees Toudou.

They had gone deeper into the Great Tomb since facing the horde of skeletons at the beginning, but no other forms of undead have yet made an appearance.

"If you think hard about the walking bones, they're not that different from the evil treants we faced in the Great Forest of the Vale. They were...eerie in their own way, too," Toudou adds.

"Yes. They're much better than the living dead or wraiths."

Spica is just able to follow what Toudou and Aria are talking about.

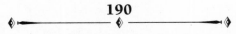

Their appearance is a large part of it, but compared to living dead or wraiths, walking bones really don't conjure up the same kinds of emotions. They don't make much noise, they barely smell, and compared with other undead that attack with deep-seated resentment toward human beings, they're just not on the same level.

Aria suddenly says suspiciously, "Yet, it's odd, isn't it...? According to the map we received from the Church, the majority of enemies in this area are supposed to be living dead and wraiths..."

Hearing this, Spica, the only one among them who knows the reality of the situation, becomes flustered and makes a commotion. In that moment, a coldhearted voice pops into her head.

"Say something clever to deceive them."

Huh? Huh, huh, huh?

Spica racks her brain for a response to this completely vague command. Seeing this, Aria reassures her. "Hey, don't worry about it. It's not that out of the ordinary. We're not trying to make you nervous or anything."

"Oh... N-no... I'm...fine."

But that is not what is weighing on Spica's mind. There is no further talk of the odd distribution of undead in their area, and Toudou sighs.

"I sure hope we can get to one thousand undead with this much ease..."

"...No matter what, be on your guard."

As Toudou and Aria exchange grim glances, Spica uses the opportunity to shift gears.

I can't continue to depend on them for everything. I'm a full-fledged member of this party now.

In that moment, a transmission arrives from Amelia. Spica is again shocked by the sudden intrusion in her mind and turns to Toudou, flustered.

"Toudou... A lot more are coming."

"...Hmm?"

Toudou looks back at Spica. The second she opens her mouth to

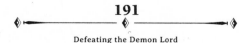

reply, a vile stench rushes to fill the air. Toudou's frozen gaze shifts from Spica to the dark void. A skeleton appears around the corner. The darkness beyond it is deep, and Toudou can't see anything yet, but every one of her remaining senses have alerted her to what is approaching.

§ § §

"How about something like, 'What are we even doing?'"

"Don't say anything that'll take the wind out of their sails."

The underground tomb is airtight, and everything echoes. There are a few air passages, though, and I can hear Toudou's screams from quite a distance.

He's gotten used to skeletons somewhat, but it looks like the living dead are still another issue. However, we've already sent a number of them to his location.

The plan has been going exceedingly well. They've overcome the skeletons, so other forms of undead should be just a matter of time. Amelia was right on the money after all, or so it seems.

Amelia is wearing her standard expression—void of emotion, and she pulls at the light connected to her hand.

"Holy Bind."

This low-level exorcism binds followers of darkness with a chain of light.

On the other end of the braided light chain, innumerable undead are strung up like beads on a rosary, and they shuffle along clumsily as Amelia yanks on the chain.

"WHAAAAAAAAAAAAAAAAAAAAAAAAAAAAAAAAAAAAAAAAAA!!"

A scream much more furious than before echoes through the tomb—one imbued with magic power. Using Howl, a simple technique, to great effect is harder than it sounds. It is not particularly powerful, and it uses a lot of magic energy. It's a good skill to keep on hand, but using it as a weapon requires years of discipline.

The bodies of skeletons, made completely of bones, or those of wraiths,

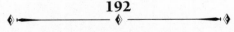

who don't have worldly bodies at all, can easily be blasted to pieces, but the spuriously flesh-based husks of the living dead are more resilient to Howl. It's not entirely useless but largely ineffective against the majority of enemies. Toudou will be in trouble if he abuses it.

Amelia listens to Toudou's scream without moving a muscle before sighing and looking toward me.

"Shall we send more?"

"Let things play out awhile longer."

"How many have they killed?"

"Sixty-two."

"…This is going to be a while."

The goal is one thousand undead. Even if it's just small fry, they're still fighting their least-favorite enemy.

They will become more mentally exhausted than physically, and Toudou still doesn't have any experience in prolonged battle. Taking this into account, Gregorio's task is extremely taxing. In the end, will they be able to overcome this trial without our help…?

At the same time, it is certainly true that Gregorio is no fool. My initial perception of him was perhaps mistaken. There is now ample chance that Toudou and his party can complete the task without our help, and what's more, they just may grow substantially from it. It's also possible that my actions could result in squashing that steadily growing seed. I scowl at the line of undead continually spasming on the chain of holy light.

However… Any assumption at this stage is meaningless. The only thing certain is that Toudou's scream we can hear right now is infinitely more rife with fear than when we first sent the horde of skeletons at him. Amelia sees my expression and says bluntly, "You look most serious."

"I was born this way."

No point in worrying. I will do whatever I can.

I am a strictly logical person. I have felt the strings of fate pulling near me, but I have never reached out to grab them.

I will amend our strategy given the current situation: the status of

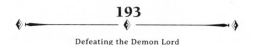

Toudou and Aria overcoming their fear of the undead, their levels, the fruits of their battle. I'll also take Spica's condition into account in order to turn the most predictable future for her into the most desirable one.

As far as Gregorio's speculation goes… He can eat shit.

§   §   §

It has been one and a half days since Sister Spica was given her trial.

The sun has set, and in his room in the third parish, Gregorio raises his head from the scriptures he is reading. Thick clouds fill the sky, and he can hear torrential rain pounding on the roof.

In the middle of the night—especially during heavy rain—the church receives few visitors. It isn't midnight quite yet, but it is deadly still in his room and throughout the parish. The only sound that reaches Gregorio's ears is the rain.

Gregorio speaks out amid the silence. His calm voice resonates through the room, with no ears to fall on. He sounds perplexed, as if he's seen something go awry.

"…God's guidance…is still well within me…"

Gregorio stands, scriptures in hand, and paces throughout the room. His eyes land on the black trunk in the corner of the room.

"If Ares is taking care of things, then I am no longer necessary… Goodness…"

His voice marvels at the circumstances as his black pupils bore into space. A rare sensation smolders in the corner of his mind.

In most situations, Gregorio knows which path he should take. The guidance of God surpasses any individual foresight. That much is a given, and despite the occasional instance of a slight lag, such direction has never failed him.

It was already two days since his encounter with Ares. If this village is no longer the place he should be, then he should know that full well of his own volition. Yet the guidance he received on his first visit to the

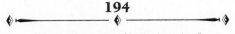

Great Tomb has not subsided in the slightest. In other words, he still has work to do.

Gregorio's nose twitches as if catching a whiff of something foul, and he cocks his neck to the side.

I don't sense any followers of darkness—at least, not here in the village—and if Ares is taking care of things, then my help is not needed.

Crusaders, too, have their predilections, but Ares Crown is well-rounded. He can expertly balance all aspects of a crusader, from support to healing and all the way to battle. He does not have divine protection, yet he emerges victorious against any foe he faces, and even enemies who should be able to crush him will not battle him alone.

Gregorio stares at the ceiling and whispers without a fraction of provocation, as if asking the ceiling to answer him back.

"O God, You say I still have work to be done. Is that so?"

There is no one to answer. Yet, Gregorio is certain he feels a divine message in response to his plea.

If that is Your will, then I will martyr myself to see it through. I will know what I must do when the time comes.

The disciple of God, Gregorio Legins, knows neither apprehension nor vacillation.

§ § §

I wonder just how much time we've spent wandering the depths of Yutith's Tomb...?

This is a first-time experience for Toudou, and her body feels incredibly heavy. *So this is what being riddled with wounds feels like,* Toudou thinks, her mind hazy. Rather, continuing to think is the only way she is able to remain conscious.

Pain intermittently shoots through her head, her breathing is ragged, and her limbs feel like lead from battling undead over and over again. She is both mentally and physically exhausted, the rotten stench of innumerable living dead having left her sense of smell completely numb, and the air chills her sweat-drenched body, draining her stamina. Next to Toudou, Aria stands with exhausted eyes as she scans their surroundings.

Aria braces against the wall with her sword still drawn, breathing slowly. She just slaughtered three living dead seconds ago.

There aren't any monsters converging on them at the moment, yet they don't know if any lurk close by. Even with no enemies in sight, Toudou is unsure whether or not she'll even be able to fight whatever shows up next.

"*Haaah...haaah...* Spica...are there any...monsters close by?"

"...No... There don't seem to be any," replies Spica, who has more color in her face than Toudou and Aria combined.

Toudou is relieved from the bottom of her heart.

Her light metal shield and magical sword feel agonizingly heavy, and her headache is proof that her magic energy supply is low. Toudou can't even remember how many undead she has slain so far.

She was keeping count until halfway through but then gave up on the seemingly impossible target number when the undead kept attacking again and again. Her consciousness had no spare room to count them.

The group didn't meet any particularly powerful undead foes, but the first long, continuous battle alone was enough to push Toudou's stamina to the limit.

"...Aria and Nao look absolutely beat. Perhaps we should call it a day here."

Limis doesn't look particularly well herself as she addresses the pair. It is true that Aria and Toudou have expended the most stamina, but Limis has conjured her magic abilities many times to sear droves of undead to a crisp. Such measures were necessary to defeat the sheer number that appeared.

Although Limis sounds peppy, it is clear from her pallor that she has pushed herself too hard.

Then, Spica timidly offers up a proposal.

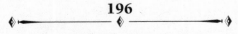

"The overdone sense of justice is a crime."

"There is…a room we can rest in nearby."

"…Let's head that way for now…"

I can hear my heart pounding in my chest. Maybe it's survival instinct… My mind is ready to quit on me, but my body can still move.

The party keeps the same formation as they follow Spica's directions and move forward. They are now very deep within the tomb. If they don't rest, it will be impossible to get back out.

The chamber to which Spica leads them is roughly the same size as the room Toudou and the others stayed in at the first parish. The second they enter, Toudou crumples to the ground in a heap and rests. Her senses, numbed from the chill in her thick cloak, finally return.

"I'm sorry to bother you, Toudou, but…we need to…put up a barrier…"

"…Yeah… You're right."

At Spica's words, Toudou retrieves their enchanted carriage and some holy water from another dimension using her magical ring. She leaves the carriage setup to Limis and sprinkles holy water around the perimeter, crawling on her hands and knees.

There is a strange mark in one corner of their refuge, but Toudou thinks nothing of it and expends the last of her energy to cast a prism.

"Wow, Spica, you've got a good memory…"

"No… It's nothing, really…"

Limis stares at her in amazement and Spica looks away uncomfortably. Spica is being humble, but Aria also joins in to praise her.

"…No, really, it's remarkable. We've been so busy fighting… I had completely forgotten where we were."

Toudou and her party look down at the slightly dingy map spread out before them. They were so busy fighting, they didn't even realize they were lost until they arrived in this room and finally sat down to breathe.

Aimlessly wandering through the infinitely labyrinthine underground tomb is a one-way ticket to death. Even with a compass to tell

the direction, it would be unlikely for one to happen upon the way out among the countless identical passageways.

Surprisingly, the person who lent Toudou and the others a helping hand as their faces grew pale was Spica. Toudou, Aria, and Limis had all forgotten where they were, but Spica recalled the details. She whispers with a hint of self-deprecation, "This is really...the only thing I'm useful for..."

"No, no, no, it's more than enough!"

"Twenty percent of deaths during monster hunts result from becoming stranded, they say..."

Toudou possesses a magical tool that allows her to store items in another dimension. It's chock-full of a large supply of food and water, but it's not unlimited. Above all else, Toudou does not want to think about the possibility of becoming lost in an underground tomb running rampant with undead.

"Okay... Let's confirm the spoils from today's battles."

Limis overturns the bag hanging from her waist. The fruits of their labor—magic crystals—rattle across the stone floor. At first glance, there are too many to count. Toudou counts each with great care and says dejectedly, "Three hundred and...ten... That's it."

"That seems pretty good for just one day's work..."

Toudou felt as if she had slain far more undead than that, but actually counting them, the true number seems paltry. In response to Aria's encouragement, Toudou simply sighs deeply and drops her shoulders.

One thousand undead. If they kept their target number in mind, they would have to slay even more tomorrow and the day after than they had today. Toudou, who was hopeful they'd be able to finish early if anything, is not pleased with this result.

"W-well, there are also those crystals that I incinerated, too."

"...Yeah, but without them, we can't prove we defeated that many, can we?"

Having said that, there is no reason for Toudou to place the blame on

"The overdone sense of justice is a crime."

Limis. Without her magical powers, how many times would Toudou and the others have been swallowed whole by the waves of undead? Even if they somehow survived, there's a very high chance they would have been severely injured.

Garnet is stretched out across the tomb floor, its body serving as the group's source of heat, since they can't light a fire indoors. Toudou and the others make use of Garnet's warmth to replenish some of the stamina they expended.

Aria has nothing to say about their progress but simply slaps her knee before declaring with gumption, "Well, we'll definitely defeat more tomorrow than we did today. Even I...managed to get used to them a little..."

"...Yeah, that's true..."

It's a fact that Aria is finally getting used to the undead. As long as she continues to go in prepared, she shouldn't lose her cool.

That the party has encountered only walking bones and living dead is a source of concern, but nothing can be done about it.

In an attempt to perk up, Toudou slaps herself on both cheeks and lifts her head.

Next, the party initiates their first level-up ritual in ages. Due to the droves of undead they've vanquished today, Limis and Aria have the highest propensity for leveling up.

First, Toudou performs the ritual for Limis, who has a low level. She touches the palm of her hand to Limis's head, shoulders, and arms and makes the sign of the cross—something Toudou is still not used to.

A shining golden light envelops Limis, and she bites her lip before letting loose a rapturous sigh. Toudou's holy energy is depleted to the point where it's obvious, and her entire body is languid. She nevertheless continues to speak briskly, as she was taught.

"Limis is now level eighteen. To reach the next level up, she requires— Sorry, I don't know how much."

"...Whatever, I should just keep vanquishing enemies, right?"

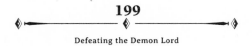

"...That's right."

Although Toudou has been taught the ritual, the number of life-force units needed to reach the next level doesn't simply just pop up in her head. It can be estimated only from having performed the ritual many times.

Toudou then turns to Aria and says with an apologetic expression, "I'm sorry, Aria... I don't think I can perform your ritual right now. Maybe it's from putting up the barrier, but I'm almost out of holy energy..."

"...I understand. If you can do it for me tomorrow morning, when you're replenished..."

The Holy Warrior is the cornerstone of the party. Until Spica can use holy techniques, Toudou running out of holy energy puts everyone else in a tight spot.

Although Aria's entire body is racked with the physical discomfort that accompanies being ready to level up, she does not make it apparent and simply nods. Toudou ruefully bites her lip.

"If only we had *him* with us... He could've done it..."

"...True practitioners are of a different breed, after all."

Toudou recalls Ares back in the Great Forest of the Vale. He was only level 3, yet he completed every task required of a priest without even breaking a sweat. Toudou shakes her head and brushes away the image. *What am I missing? Why can't I do what he can?* Toudou feels completely inferior, but she doesn't have the right to complain at this juncture.

"I'll...do my best, too."

Spica mumbles softly with her hands balled into fists, as though she were able to read Toudou's mind.

That night, while everyone is asleep, Toudou suddenly awakens. The exhaustion still lingers heavily in her entire body. She rubs her eyes in the darkness and looks around the carriage known as Grassland

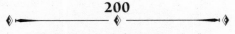

Wind. The cloth canopy is highly airtight, and the interior is much warmer than outside.

Toudou strains her eyes in the pitch darkness. There is a small shadow of a figure with her staff laid by her head, holding her blanket tightly, and another longer shadow sleeping straight as an arrow, breathing quietly. Nothing appears wrong with this scene, not to mention zero detection of murderous intent or an enemy presence. However, Toudou realizes something.

"…Wait… Where's Spica…?"

Spica had been sleeping next to her but is nowhere to be found. Toudou gropes around beside her. There is nothing in the spot Spica had previously occupied except for a carefully folded blanket.

Toudou is still exhausted, and an intense drowsiness threatens to drag her consciousness back into the dark. She fights against it with all her might and shakes her head, still hazy, and searches through her memory.

Spica had definitely been sleeping next to her. She can perfectly recall Spica's face as she nervously whispered, "Good night," to her.

Though half-asleep, Toudou's composure is quickly returning. She shakes her head again and chases the fatigue out of her mind.

Spica is level 10. Even though she claims not to be afraid of the undead, without being able to use holy techniques, even taking on a walking bones is a difficult task.

Did she leave the carriage?

As long as she doesn't leave the room enclosed in the barrier, there is no worry of her getting attacked by undead.

Toudou thinks about waking Limis and Aria but decides against it. Instead, she collects her sword—placed by her pillow side for easy access—and slowly gets up.

Toudou decides to take a look outside, just for peace of mind. But the second she stands—her sight goes completely black.

"?!"

Her heart thumps fiercely in her chest. She reflexively tries to scream, but her voice is muted. A moment too late, she realizes the darkness filling her field of vision is the carriage floor itself.

—*What the…? I just stood up, so why…?*

The void engulfs Toudou's senses. The strength with which it seizes her is far more powerful than the sleepiness she'd overcome mere moments ago.

"Good night, Toudou."

She hears a soft voice—one she's heard before.

Before she has a chance to think about who it belongs to, her entire consciousness is swallowed by the darkness.

§　§　§

"Holy water's not enough for this. I give him thirty points."

The barrier Toudou put up couldn't be called robust, even under flattery. In this place, filled with thick miasma, its strength continues to deteriorate.

The moment I enter the room, Toudou's barrier is already nearly broken. It likely won't last until morning. If the barrier is too weak, then based on the estimated time it will last, it will require repeated recasting.

The barrier I've put up in its place is still there, so it doesn't matter if Toudou's breaks. I make a mental note to have Spica informed of this as well.

Toudou never underwent any rigorous training on the role of the Holy Warrior, so it's not necessarily his fault. Now that he's experienced this place once, as long as he sears it into his memory, he'll never forget it.

Spica's introduction into the party has made our coordination of information so much easier. She's a big help. At Amelia's beckoning, she crawls out from under the carriage's cloth covering. She must be extremely tired—she rubs her eyes and walks on shaky legs.

I cast recovery on Spica without saying a word. *Sorry, but we're on a tight schedule here.*

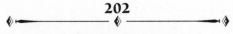

"The overdone sense of justice is a crime."

Spica immediately shakes off her drowsiness and blinks repeatedly, while Amelia, trading places with her, moves toward the carriage with an open palm. She mumbles a few words without thinking twice, and a thin haze envelops the carriage.

I've never seen this spell, but it must be the same *Sleep* spell we used to knock out Limis and the others before.

"Don't dare to wake them, no matter what. In particular...Toudou has resistance to this type of spell."

"Okay."

Spica runs over to my side. Even though she hasn't directly partici-pated in battle, at just level 10, she must have been affected by the strict forced march. It's clear from her expression that she's still exhausted.

Regardless, Spica doesn't seem to mind at all. She should be able to perform another duty without issue.

"Amelia, stand watch here to make sure that Toudou and his party don't awaken."

"Yes, sir."

"...Also, perform a level-up ritual for Aria right away. I want to conserve Toudou's holy energy."

"Understood. I'll do it immediately."

I see Amelia nod in confirmation, and I head for the exit. Spica fol-lows absentmindedly.

"How are you feeling? Tired?"

"N-no. I'm...fine."

Her words are brave, but they're likely half lies. Orphans are well known for their capacity to overcompensate.

"We'll finish up as quickly as possible. I know you're tired, but this is all for tomorrow and beyond. Stay by my side a little longer."

"...No, of course... Um... I mean... Thank you very much."

One, at least. After today, I have two full days to teach her just one holy technique, at the very least.

On the first day, I managed to give her a full impression of Toudou's party's current situation. The fact that she hasn't been able to learn any

203

holy techniques so far is something I was well prepared for. Whether magic, holy techniques, or miracles, the very first spell takes the longest to learn. It's easier to start from scratch than to go from the basics.

I guide Spica to the room I prepared for her. The second we enter, her expression stiffens, and she swallows a lump in her throat. Her eyes turn to the center of the room where a massive skeleton is standing upright atop a stone table. It's about twice as tall as the skeletons that Spica and the others fought all day long. It's the same size as the Devil-Faced Knight statue, and unlike a walking bones, it's clear these bones aren't of human origin.

This is a monster called a giant skeleton. It is multiple times stronger than walking bones, but I currently have it bound to the table by thorns of light stemming from its feet.

The appropriate level for taking one on is around 30. It isn't the most fearsome creature, but this is surely Spica's first time seeing one. She stares up at the behemoth with strained eyes.

I remain silent and move toward the giant skeleton, taking a seat on the stone table. In the cool air of the chamber, Spica's greenish-gray eyes turn to look at me. The gigantic skeleton twists its body.

Its bony frame touches the thorns of light, and a sound like flashing lightning erupts. *Holy Thorns* is a higher-level exorcism technique than Holy Bind. There's no worry of an undead of this level breaking through it.

As Spica's body trembles at the sound, I announce to her in the calmest voice I can muster, "Spica, I'm gonna teach you holy techniques. By the end of tonight...you will learn one of them."

"...Okay!"

Her voice is different now—she's found some fighting spirit.

It must have been hard for her to trail behind Toudou and his party all day long... She was extremely useful for transmitting information, but she likely doesn't consider that of her own merit. The most important element for casting holy techniques is emotion—the stronger, the better.

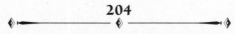

"The overdone sense of justice is a crime."

For example... Rage, mercy, sorrow, courage. Or potentially obligation or conviction, and of course faith and piety.

The reason Spica can't use holy techniques yet is partially because of her low level of holy energy, but more specifically, she simply doesn't have enough faith yet. A priest must go through a long period of apprenticeship and service to attain that skill. Others come from tragic circumstances and are capable of wielding powerful holy techniques from the intense emotions that result from their trauma.

But neither of these applies to Spica. I haven't known her for long, but I can tell she's relatively introverted. People of such temperament often quickly develop inferiority complexes. What's more, she's surrounded by girls like Limis and Aria, who are close to her age and from distinguished bloodlines.

In general, a pessimistic emotional bent doesn't lend itself to a capacity for holy techniques. If Spica were a more confident person, she might be motivated by Limis and the others and end up learning holy techniques just from tagging along. But given her disposition, the chances of that happening are low.

That's why I've taken it upon myself for Spica to master holy techniques through the use of illusions. Human beings by nature have the holy energy for even the lowest-level holy techniques from the moment of birth. Spica is no exception.

"Spica, did you read the scriptures I gave you?"

"Yes. Just the basics, though..."

Her expression is serious. She didn't have that much time to read them, but she obviously made quite the effort.

"As you know, the god Ahz Gried governs the order of our world. As priests, our calling is to follow His teaching to preserve that order and the harmony that serves as its cornerstone. Healing sickness and injury, helping those who are weak, and obliterating the manifestation of disaster that are the followers of darkness are all within our realm of responsibility."

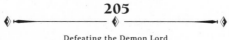

The thorns of light illuminate Spica's hopeful expression. I originally had my doubts about Amelia's reasons for choosing Spica, but it looks like her instincts might not be so bad after all. Although, she did say she picked Spica based entirely on her appearance...

I stick my hand directly into the holy thorns and show them to Spica. Her eyes are wide as saucers.

The physical strength of the undead in front of us is leagues beyond that of the average adult male. The holy thorns, which have completely nullified the enemy's movement, do not adversely affect me, a disciple of God.

"In essence, every priest is the recipient of a miracle. There are no exceptions. Spica, what did that bastard Gregorio show you?"

"Um... Well..."

Spica begins to explain in earnest.

Innumerable pillars of light. A bullet of light that pierced the heavens. Her words accurately describe the rare exorcism powers of the one and only Mad Eater.

I can't help but find my interest piqued by the contents of her tale. The spell he cast in front of Toudou's party was not of this world. Breaking Arrow is only supposed to shoot arrows of light.

Casting them as pillars is tough enough, and combining those into a single shaft of light is extremely difficult. Being able to reach that level isn't a matter of high energy output but rather a highly complex set of processes. Gregorio looks like he's simply running amok, but the level of precision involved in his exorcisms, honed over years of experience, is one of the best of all crusaders.

What he demonstrated is really difficult. Showing her the sheer power of holy techniques is a given, but his method was truly heavy-handed.

I take a deep breath, slightly worried. This level of precise manipulation is extremely difficult even for a high-level priest like me. I drop down from the stone table and back Spica away from the giant skeleton.

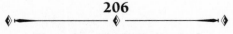

When we're two meters from it, I stand next to her and snap my fingers, chanting the incantation.

"Breaking Arrow."

"Oh—!!"

Before Spica's eyes can widen, a small ball of light hovers in the air. It quickly expands, and when it reaches one meter in diameter, it twists and changes shape. The ball of light has become an arrow. No—it isn't an arrow but a spear of light.

I pour more holy energy into the spear than generally necessary, and it sparks and glows, illuminating the dumbstruck expression on Spica's face.

If we're talking about impression alone, this is surely just as incredible as Gregorio's trick. Although from a technical standpoint, it's not even close...but that's fine. I have to dispel the illusion that Gregorio enraptured her with.

The spear of light fires forth on my silent signal. Within a split second, it pierces the giant skeleton's torso and explodes in a vivid display of fireworks spread in all directions.

Spica hides her eyes behind her arm, and the illumination disappears instantly without a sound. The light is gone, and only darkness remains.

I explain matter-of-factly to Spica, who is still shielding her eyes, "Priests are bestowed miracles in accordance with their faith. Gregorio has pledged his entire being to eradicating the followers of darkness. His rare exorcisms are a manifestation of that resolve. Normal priests are incapable of such techniques."

His oath robbed him of all holy techniques other than exorcisms and gave him powerful attack abilities. Neither most priests nor I can mimic this capacity, let alone Spica. There's no point in even trying.

The monster and the holy thorns that bound it are now gone from the stone table.

Spica finally lowers the arm covering her eyes. She opens them for

a second, and a dull clatter echoes through the darkness—the sound of the giant skeleton's magic crystal hitting the floor. Spica's eyes widen in shock, and she wordlessly turns her gaze to the now-empty stone table. I take a seat on it and continue.

"They won't be nearly as powerful as this, but Spica—you already have the foundation for casting holy techniques."

"Um... Are you...s-sure?"

"Yes, I'm sure. But you couldn't use any when you tried...right?"

Spica seems to wither away and shrink her already tiny frame. This is some sort of hint. Yet, I can't know if she really feels that way.

"You have faith in the God of Order. You've read the scriptures. You pray in the morning and evening. You're prepared to fight Toudou's enemies—the followers of darkness—and you want to be of use to his party."

"Y-yes... Yes, I do."

I tell her this all again in order to permanently etch it into her mind. I aim those emotions, that faith, toward her heart.

Fighting the followers of darkness. Joining a party as a priest. From a humble everyday existence as an orphan in Purif, she is about to embark on the extraordinary journey to defeat the Demon Lord. I infuse my words with strong conviction and encourage her with my gaze. These are some of the things she'll be able to do as her level increases.

Finally, I lick my lips to moisten them and pose a question to Spica, who is hanging on to my every word with bated breath.

"In that case, Spica—do you know what it is you're still missing?"

§   §   §

"Wait...why?"

Toudou blurts out the words before she can stop herself as she takes a long, hard look at Spica's face.

There are dark circles under her eyes. Her hair and eyes are gray. Her tiny frame is wrapped in her priest's robe. She looks the same on the

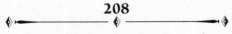

"The overdone sense of justice is a crime."

outside, but her demeanor is more positive than yesterday. Limis and Aria must feel the same way as they gaze at Spica as if they're still dreaming.

There doesn't seem to be anything different about her appearance, save for a small ball of light floating in front of her.

Yes, light. A ball of light a few centimeters in diameter. Its pure luminescence is without a doubt cleansing the surrounding darkness.

"? I thought you couldn't use techniques just yesterday?"

Aria is bewildered and stares raptly at the ball of light floating in space. It's small and faint but unquestionably a holy technique. The light flickers and disappears silently. Spica whispers, sounding almost like she's coming up with an excuse.

"Last night...I practiced..."

"...W-wow! Way to go, Spica!"

Limis's face is joyful as she squeezes Spica's hand. In that moment, Toudou and Aria also finally realize what is happening. Partially encouraged by Limis's enthusiasm, Spica smiles, looking very happy.

"But you still couldn't use any techniques yesterday... So what happened?"

"This is just...the simplest exorcism... Using it's a cinch..."

"It's still amazing!"

Toudou's eyes shine as she praises Spica wholeheartedly.

The light Spica cast is not strong enough to destroy an undead monster, but it is a significant ray of hope—even if it is a low-level holy technique.

Their bodies are heavy. Unlike in a video game, the group didn't heal completely after one night's sleep, and Aria and company's movements are a bit sluggish. Yet their voices are bright and cheerful. Toudou announces vigorously, as if to blow the surrounding darkness into oblivion:

"Okay! Let's get after it today, too!"

"Yeah! Let's do it!"

Spica plays with the cross necklace hanging from her neck and responds, her voice much louder than usual.

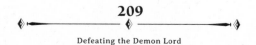

§　§　§

There's no sign of screams mixed into the sound of battle reverberating from deep within the tomb's passageways. While pulling the next group of undead to be sent to battle alongside her like dogs on a leash, Amelia says, "They seem to be doing quite well."

"Yeah, they are."

Amelia's comment was concise but accurate. Leading Light, the holy technique that Spica was finally able to learn overnight, is extremely rudimentary.

It's a technique that effectively pushes away nearby undead. That makes it useful in battle, but even if it touches an undead, it won't kill them. Given Spica's current low level of holy energy, it also won't last long.

However, as a source of mental support for Toudou, it is more than enough.

"How were you able to teach her the technique?"

"Here's a simple hint. I had her return the dagger I lent her. The use of blades is taboo for priests, as you know."

Spica has the specs to use holy techniques. Therefore, all she had to do was make up a reason for not being able to use them and then nullify that reason. The use of illusions is one way to bestow faith. Spica might not have believed Toudou if he'd been the one to tell her that, but when I used a powerful holy technique in front of her—as a bona fide priest—she had no reason to doubt me.

"But…that's just a cheap trick…"

"Sure it is. But that's what got her to actually learn a holy technique."

Timidity and earnestness have their own advantages. As she gains experience as a priest, at some point, she'll likely realize she was deceived, but a holy technique that is learned once will not be forgotten. Amelia seems unconvinced, but she holds her tongue.

This is Toudou's second day in Yutith's Tomb. The speed at which they're slaying undead is leagues beyond day one. If Toudou, as the

leader of the party, can get back on form, Aria's burden will be lightened, and if that happens, Limis will have fewer opportunities to use magic. As for Glacia... I don't even know if she'll gain any levels, and truthfully, I don't care. Yet, if she can manage to kill some monsters while using the lowest level of energy possible, she should be able to conserve plenty while contributing somehow. I'd suspected Spica's development would boost morale, but to be honest, I wasn't expecting these kinds of results.

"How many have they slain?"

"Hmm... The exact number is three hundred twenty-three, but they only have proof of two hundred fifty-one."

"They're getting used to it. It's time to send some wraiths."

At first, we sent walking bones, which aren't particularly scary, and after Toudou and the others got used to them, we moved on to the foul-smelling and grotesque living dead. Now that they're used to those as well, it's finally time to send wraiths, which specialize in mental attacks.

The plan is going well. They should even be able to withstand a Scream of Sorrow at this point.

"...Does he still appear to be fighting through gritted teeth?"

"I dunno. I'm not here to make Toudou's life easier."

"...Understood."

In the end, I decide not to send new undead and remain a spectator for the time being. It might seem effective, but for us to continue meddling in the battle would ultimately have a negative influence. At the end of the day...we're here only for support.

Amelia releases an undead she's been restraining—a wraith, whose voice is only manifest as a scream rife with sorrow and resentment. It swoops down upon us, swaying to and fro, and Amelia skillfully casts Leading Light, which repels undead beings, to send the wraith in Toudou's party's direction. It lets loose a bloodcurdling shriek before turning toward the group, as if it was running away in fear.

"I see. You're finally reaching a solution?"

There's a hint of relief in Creio's voice as he responds to my report.

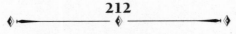

"The overdone sense of justice is a crime."

The second day of the party's quest into the Great Tomb is already coming to a close. At the moment, there are no problems that require special mention. The party has vanquished the wraiths we sent as well, and they are steadily overcoming their fear of the undead.

It's already evening. Tonight, Amelia is taking my place as Spica's holy technique instructor.

The party is gaining levels, and Toudou is now 28, Aria 27, and Limis 19. Spica remains at level 10, still unable to defeat undead monsters, but it looks like they'll be able to complete the task assigned to her.

If that happens, they will break all ties with Gregorio. I will continue teaching Spica holy techniques when the occasion calls for it. As for leveling up... It would be unnatural for her to do so without seemingly doing anything, so I'll have to leave that to Toudou and his party.

"There's no sign of demons in pursuit. At any rate, even if they do attack, I don't foresee any problems. I can handle them, and Gregorio's also around."

I don't understand the method demons use to track the hero's presence, but as we have no intention of staying in Purif for an extended period, I'm not particularly worried about it.

"Will the hero still be a handful?"

"I don't intend to babysit him forever, but let's continue as planned until he reaches a certain level."

There's a limit to what I can do, supporting him from the shadows. Cultivating a hero from square one is no laughing matter. Currently, there's still a high risk of mortal harm, so we remain on their tails. However, once Spica has matured, I plan to quit following them around and put my efforts into other causes. At any rate, I've got a lot to think about.

This comprises the majority of my report, and I ask Creio something that's been on my mind.

"Tell me what Gregorio is up to or if he has any specific aims."

"Ah, yes... Gregorio has informed me that he still has unfinished business in Purif."

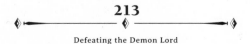

" . . . "

That's exactly what I didn't want to hear. What the hell does he have planned? It's nearly impossible to predict his movements, and really, he shouldn't be there for long—I need him to quickly disappear to somewhere else.

I want to know more, but asking Creio at this juncture would likely prove fruitless. This is all Gregorio's fault, and I don't have the time to keep looking after him. I become lost in sentimentality for a while but then remember something else I need to ask.

"That reminds me—what's going on with Stephenne, that girl you said you'd send?"

It hasn't been long since she was promised, but remembering how Amelia was dispatched in a matter of hours, this is slow. The next time I contacted Creio after making the request, a new operator put me through, so I thought it would be quicker.

Creio sounds uncharacteristically exhausted in his reply.

"She's lost."

". . . Come again?"

"She's running late because she got lost."

?????????????????

I turn my neck and look around. There's no one else nearby to hear this.

. . . She's . . . lost? I don't get it. That doesn't make any sense.

I furrow my brow in deep thought, and Creio continues, almost as if making an excuse.

"I was told she mistakenly got on a carriage that was headed in the wrong direction. I should have sent an attendant with her. Ugh, this is all my fault. Ares, I'm sorry. I'm so sorry . . . but I've sent her again, with an attendant this time, so she should be arriving to you before long."

Isn't it a bit late for apologies? I'm not angry or upset; I'm simply doubtful.

"How old is Stephenne?"

I've spoken to her only enough to guess, but her voice didn't sound particularly young. Perhaps the same age as Amelia?

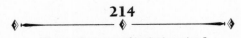

"The overdone sense of justice is a crime."

"She's sixteen. She's still young, Ares...but she is a prodigy."

"A sixteen-year-old is...lost?"

Sixteen. In this kingdom, sixteen is considered an adult. I have a really, really bad feeling about this.

I desperately attempt to convince myself: *It's no big deal. Everyone gets lost sometimes.* But to get on the wrong carriage... It doesn't sound like she's very on top of things...

A prodigy, he says... I wonder what exactly makes her a prodigy...

"...Does she...have a poor sense of direction?"

"Well...not in the strictest sense of the word, but in the loosest sense, you could say so. I dare say she sees things differently from you or I. Ares, she has...a poor sense of direction for life in general. Ha-ha!"

Well, I wasn't asking for such a clever explanation, but..."ha-ha"? *You're not that kinda guy, Creio.* I never would have thought she was such a problem from the few times we spoke...

"Is she a troublemaker?"

"That's what I'm telling you, Ares. You said it yourself: Even if there's a problem, you wanted to give her a chance."

"So the Church doesn't have *any* competent personnel?"

Even Amelia is...a bit of an oddball. Not that I dislike her.

Creio ignores my accidental outburst and, as if totally dodging the issue, says, "May you receive God's blessing today, Ares Crown."

"...That phrase isn't some indulgence!"

He should really stop using it at every last opportunity—it'll traumatize me!

§   §   §

The holy sword Ex boasts an extreme sharpness that leaves the wielder with barely any sensation of hacking through bone or viscera. The skeletons are slashed in half and disappear without making a sound. Toudou fends off a living dead approaching on the left side with the shield gripped in her left hand.

215

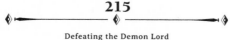

A fetid stench rushes to burn her nostrils, but she's already used to it, along with their grotesque appearance. Her fingers have stopped trembling, and fear no longer shows on her face. She still feels a lingering discomfort in the back of her mind, but it's safe to say it no longer has any effect on her.

Toudou's body is filled with a level of power she previously experienced in the Great Forest of the Vale, and now, she fully realizes just how mentally unstable she was on her first day down in the Great Tomb.

"Nao!"

Limis cries out sharply, and in that exact moment, Toudou completely loses her train of thought. She freezes momentarily from the shock. Her heart pounds wildly in her chest.

A fearsome, earth-shattering shriek. Toudou bites her tongue to prevent her consciousness from clouding any further. The pain brings her back to her senses, and the haze shrouding her mind readily lifts. Her breath comes out ragged. Cold air fills her lungs, and her thoughts become clearer still.

Next to her, Aria battles a wraith, the source of the shriek, and as she cleaves its translucent body in half, it vanishes from this realm with a spiteful look on its face.

Toudou takes a small breath in and swiftly pushes a living dead clinging to her shield away from her before slashing it to death. She exhales deeply.

"Are you okay, Nao?"

"Oh... Yeah..."

Aria had been much closer to the Scream of Sorrow when it hit, and her face is white as a sheet as she runs over to Toudou's side. Toudou's face doesn't look as well as it normally does, but she's still conscious. There's a world of difference between now and her first experience with a wraith, when she was completely incapacitated.

Toudou looks back at Limis, who had been watching over the entire battle with her staff at the ready. If she hadn't warned the party when the Scream of Sorrow was coming, it could have been a lot worse.

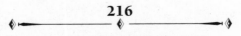

"The overdone sense of justice is a crime."

"Limis... You saved us."

"They're such a nuisance, making that wretched scream every time they die."

Limis sighs in exasperation even though she didn't bat an eye during the attack.

"If you obliterate them in one go with an exorcism or high-level fire spell, they should die without screaming."

"I can't just cast a high-level fire spell every time we come across one. It's super-exhausting!"

"Well, we managed to withstand it this time. If we get even more used to them, maybe their screams won't bother us, just like Limis and Spica."

Limis gives a light shrug and eyes their surroundings.

"...That's true. But whether we'll be here long enough for you to get *that* used to them is a different story."

A stone wall against the pitch-black darkness. They've already become accustomed to the chilly air and formidable pressure of this place that grinds one down psychologically.

The deadline of their task is soon at hand. Aria sheaths her sword and mutters while staring ahead into the darkness.

"This place is terribly inefficient for leveling up..."

"You just don't want to fight any undead."

"But it's also true that it's inefficient."

Limis and Aria argue, but it's not serious. They've been acquainted since before the journey began, and their interactions are generally on this level of back-and-forth.

Toudou forces a smile and butts in.

"Hey, even if we don't completely get used to them here, we'll have a chance to fight them somewhere else, right?"

"...Yes, you're right."

Spica picks up the magic crystal from a freshly slain undead and hands it to Limis, who says, "And this one is...number eight hundred ninety-two."

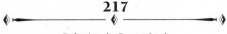

"So that leaves…another one hundred and eight?"

They all thought it was a preposterous number at the beginning, and yet here they are. Everyone is exhausted, but with the end in sight, they feel surprisingly lighthearted.

Toudou basks in the feeling as Limis makes a suggestion.

"Shouldn't Spica get in on some battle action before too long? She must be used to it by now."

"Ohhh… That's a good point."

Toudou, Limis, and Aria all turn to look at Spica in tandem, and her face stiffens slightly.

Toudou and Aria aren't the only ones who have grown during battle. Spica has learned a new holy technique. She raises her voice just barely and says a prayer. A small orb of light floats in the air and slowly begins to morph into a long, thin beam before turning into a single arrow. It's only a single arrow and not a particularly powerful one.

Regardless, it is most definitely an exorcism technique—the most basic one. It's a priest's most fundamental attack skill.

"Breaking Arrow."

The fully formed arrow shoots off in a flash. Toudou shifts her shield nonchalantly to block it.

"I—I'm so sorry… I still can't keep the arrow in midair…"

"No, you're fine. But it's true—when we move to the next place, it'll be harder to get your level up…"

Gregorio's task has taken all their composure, so they forgot the reason they wanted Spica to learn exorcisms in the first place was to help her level up quickly.

"Leveling up aside, we should really test the strength of Spica's exorcisms at least once."

Hearing Aria's words, Limis remembers just how uncouth she'd been only two days ago and pokes fun at her.

"Confirm their strength? That means she'll at least need to stop undead in their tracks, right? You think you can hold them off?"

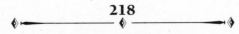

"Of course. Spica, leave stalling the undead to me—you just shoot them down."

Aria thumps her chest proudly as she makes her proclamation. The disgrace that Aria was two days ago is nowhere to be found.

Toudou chuckles to herself, amused by Aria's behavior and Spica's nervous flailing.

§ § §

Amelia opens her eyes and suddenly mumbles.

"I'm bored."

"I'm not sure I'd put it that way."

Toudou's task is now on its last phase. He and his party are still delving into the Great Tomb of their own accord, and we know approximately where they are, but the only thing we have to be careful of is that they don't go too deep down.

As the group continues to succeed, we've become a bit bored. Toudou and Aria have gotten over their fear of the undead, in their own special way. Spica, despite being still very inexperienced, has managed to learn a few holy techniques. They're getting closer to their goal of vanquishing one thousand undead. I welcome the boredom.

Amelia looks toward me, and I have no idea what's on her mind.

"Do you want to play a word game?"

"...No goddamn way."

No matter how much time we have on our hands, why in the name of all that is holy would I play a word game in a tomb crawling with undead?! She needs a sense of TPO—time, place, occasion. Seriously—what is she thinking?

"That's too bad."

Amelia looks genuinely disappointed by my rebuttal.

I sigh and suddenly remember what Creio and I talked about earlier.

No one in Toudou's party has gone missing, and no matter how much spare time we have... A word game? It's not like it would cause

me any physical harm, but I can already feel myself eroding mentally bit by bit just thinking about it.

In that moment, Toudou and the others encounter a larger undead presence than any they've met so far.

"It's a big one."

"Oh, a giant skeleton, yes?"

Even though it's a large monster, they should have no problem defeating it. Judging from level alone, they're actually slightly below where they should be, but they have quality equipment, and the giant skeleton doesn't have any powerful special abilities. I ponder the situation for a moment but ultimately decide to leave them be.

In reality, giant skeletons should appear only on the second-level basement floors of the Great Tomb and below, but as there aren't any barriers cast between the floors, it's entirely feasible that it came up to the first. I ran into a few of them back when I was luring monsters to the area earlier.

A few minutes later, Amelia, who had been spying on the party, gasps in amazement.

"...Toudou defeated it. He was flustered for a moment, but in the end, it came down easily."

"He is the Holy Warrior, after all."

I hear shouts of joy alongside bones falling to the ground, but this really shouldn't be a hard-fought victory. Furthermore, if they can defeat a giant skeleton, then they should be able to defeat anything else on this floor.

They're already close to taking down a thousand undead. Even if we don't check up on them, they'll make their goal in the next hour or two. The situation is under control. It just needs the finishing touches.

"I'm heading back to the village before you. I'll remind Gregorio once again and have a talk with him."

"I'll stay here and make sure nothing happens to Toudou."

"...I'm counting on you."

She promised what I was going to ask of her before I even said it. I

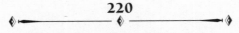

"The overdone sense of justice is a crime."

grab my head out of habit, and Amelia imperceptibly turns up the corners of her mouth in response.

At the beginning, I really wasn't sure, but Toudou and his party have reached the final stages of getting used to the undead and are showing signs of true resolve. Spica has learned holy techniques, and guiding Toudou has become so much easier. They even found a priest for their party, albeit one still in training.

Everything is going so well. Or does it only seem that way?

I must not forget: The future is always uncertain. As an outsider, I don't have complete control over Toudou's actions. And above all else—the responsibility for those actions, actions taken in the name of the Holy Warrior, are not to be taken lightly.

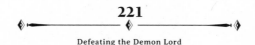

Fifth Report

A Full Account of the Hero's Support in Purif

Toudou and his party pay a visit to the church, having finished their three days of veritable hell. Gregorio greets the weary group with the exact same smile as always.

"Magnificent. This is also most certainly God's will."

Toudou and her party show legitimate signs of exhaustion, but their faces are beaming.

"We defeated one thousand undead. This is the proof."

On Toudou's signal, Limis starts upending the bulging sack. Gregorio gently stops her.

"Please. You don't need to show me."

"Huh...? Why not?"

"Because I know, without seeing anything, that you have all honored my request. There is no need for proof...in a trial of God."

Limis blinks wildly. Gregorio turns to look at Spica, who is behind him. He beckons for the party to sit, and as they do, he places tea in front of each member. Then, he speaks to Toudou, who has been waiting in silence.

"What's most important...is not the number of undead vanquished."

"...What exactly do you mean?"

Toudou looks positively dubious. Gregorio nods once and begins to explain.

"Learning exorcisms and mastering them is not a matter of knowledge or skill... It's a powerful emotion that grips the self in the face of followers of darkness. The task I gave served the purpose of cultivating this emotion in you. Currently…you should all have it, resonating in your bodies."

The tribulations of the past three days well up in Toudou's mind as Gregorio speaks. The miasma flooding the underground tomb and the cold, foul stench. The inexhaustible droves of undead that in the beginning froze her body and soul stiff with palpable fear.

She completely lost her cool and attacked in a frenzy to protect her own life and the lives of her companions. She fought through fatigue and nearly had her spirit crushed. Toudou was completely overwhelmed with joy when Spica finally learned her first holy technique, and Spica's hope gave Toudou the strength to go on.

Before she realized it, the fear she experienced in the first half of their task had been overridden by her will to fight. Compared to how Toudou was only three days ago, she can take pride and say with confidence that she's grown by leaps and bounds.

Toudou looks back at her friends—Aria, Limis, and now Spica. She can see the understanding in their eyes.

"You might not realize it yourself, Toudou, but you have undeniably changed."

Gregorio is a formidable warrior, for a priest, and his words are oddly convincing.

"Contending with the followers of darkness brings the soul of man to the fore. Continuing the fight against demons requires physical prowess and a strong spirit years beyond one's experience. If you lose it, that is when you will fall to the demon hordes. My friends, the task I gave to you—there are those who can fulfill it easily and those who cannot, no matter how hard they struggle."

"…"

"Exorcism is simply a means to an end. If you lack the will to battle the followers of darkness, then those techniques become meaningless—and if you have the will, the means to survive will come to you naturally."

Spica stares intently down at her palms as she listens to Gregorio, as if she's trying to verify the power she's gained over the past three days.

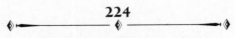

"The overdone sense of justice is a crime."

"Sister Spica, you are especially blessed. The priest who instructed you…is easily a top-five exemplar in the entirety of the Church."

"Top-five…in the Church?"

"However, that is a representation of his power and not your own. Sister Spica, your development from here on is…entirely up to you. And—what you do with your power."

Spica closes her eyes and remains quiet for some time before quickly nodding. Despite her young, innocent looks, the expression on her face is intense to the point of being ghastly.

Spica asks with a shaky voice, "What…should I do?"

Her words are vague and uneasy, but Gregorio does not look the least bit displeased as he replies.

"Sister Spica. I cannot understand exactly what is going on in your mind, but at the very least, you have cleared a very large hurdle through this ordeal. You must never forget that. As long as you don't, every last trial and tribulation that comes your way will be easily tempered by your faith."

Spica simply nods. Now Gregorio casts his gaze evenly on all members of the party. His jet-black pupils are powerful.

"My friends, Ahz Gried will never betray your faith. Therefore, as long as we hold righteous intentions and as long as we oppose the enemies of God with such intentions, we shall never see defeat."

"Does that mean…even in the face of the Demon Lord?"

Before anyone realizes it, Toudou responds to Gregorio's powerful invocation with a question.

Aria and Limis look at her in disbelief. She is entirely serious, and Gregorio shows the first indication of surprise as his eyes subtly flare, before he nods.

"That is correct, Toudou. Even in the face of the Demon Lord, you shall know no fear."

There is not a shred of doubt in Gregorio's voice. Toudou is taken aback by the lack of fervor in his words. She recalls the moment she was summoned by the Kingdom of Ruxe.

225

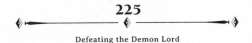

In this society, the unfavorable situation brought about by demons has instilled a sense of fear of the Demon Lord in every person Toudou has met so far. That includes the king, his leaders, and the knights who protect the realm.

However, the man who stands in from of them today shows no trace of this fear. Toudou again recalls the innumerable arrows of light Gregorio cast in front of her just a few days ago—the kind of massive power she still lacks.

Toudou bites her lip hard and speaks in a subdued tone, knowing that voicing her thoughts will be entirely fruitless. But her emotions get the better of her, and she can't stop herself from acting irrationally.

"I have to…become stronger."

"Is that so?"

Toudou really dislikes men.

Her aversion isn't a hindrance in her daily life, but when she has to spend any long amount of time next to one, she becomes unimaginably uncomfortable—to the point where she kicked one out of her party because of it. She also made it a requirement for all her party members to be female in the first place.

She has to triumph. No matter what it takes, she has to come out on top. From the moment she was summoned as the Holy Warrior, she made a pact with herself to use whatever means necessary to carry out justice.

Before Toudou realizes it, she's speaking again.

"Gregorio. I must…triumph. I…have the divine protection of Ahz Gried. Will you please teach me exorcisms?"

Aria's and Limis's faces go slightly pale. Spica also looks at Toudou, dumbfounded.

Many people desire the divine protection of Ahz Gried, but those who actually have it are extremely limited. It's said that even priests rarely receive it and that those who do should never reveal this fact.

However, Toudou is prepared to use whatever means necessary to make herself more powerful.

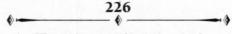

"The overdone sense of justice is a crime."

Gregorio is a devout priest. Just listening to him speak, anyone can see he is nearly fanatical in his faith. So what can one say to gain his cooperation? It's clear what the divine protection of the God of Order would mean to him.

The air in the room shifts. Gregorio wipes the smile from his face for the first time and fixes his gaze directly on Toudou.

"The divine protection of Ahz Gried?" he asks suspiciously.

Gregorio furrows his brow and puts his hand to his chin, his gaze roaming over Toudou's face.

Limis detects the shift in tone and looks between Gregorio and Toudou repeatedly. Aria focuses intently on Gregorio's movements as she anticipates Toudou responding, "Yes," almost immediately.

At that exact moment, Gregorio's pupils dilate, and a dangerous glint appears in his eyes. Aria shudders from the strange chill in the air.

The divine protection of Ahz Gried. In reality, this is not the expected reaction from a priest and follower of the God of Order, who should be welcoming such words.

The glare in Gregorio's eyes could swallow the entire room. He sighs faintly and brushes his hair back with his right hand. Toudou swallows a lump in her throat. She could not have anticipated this sort of response. A chill runs down her spine.

"Ah… Now I see. That I had not yet realized this is…quite alarming…"

"——?!"

Gregorio is now sweeping his hair back obsessively. His gaze remains locked on Toudou.

That's when Toudou realizes—she can't move. It's as if the air around her has solidified. She can't speak. She can't lift a finger. Toudou tries with all her might to look down at herself, but her head won't move. There is no pain—only immobility.

Toudou slightly changes her expression and manages to just barely shift her vision. She blinks. That is the extent of movement of which she is capable, as if her body has renounced her mind's commands.

She works as hard as possible to redirect her gaze to look at Limis

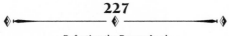

and Aria. The two of them, along with Spica, appear just as stiff as she feels.

This isn't a result of anxiety or pressure. When she was hit with a wraith's Scream of Sorrow, her body literally petrified, but this is different. She is overcome with an unknown sense of dread from her horrifying condition.

On the other hand, Gregorio is suddenly back to his old self. While everyone else remains reposed, he calmly picks up his cup of black tea with a relaxed visage and elegantly takes a sip.

"Less than level thirty... Toudou, my friend—it seems you and I have met far too early."

Gregorio turns toward the corner of the room, leaving Toudou rife with confusion. He picks up his trunk and places it on the table before returning to his seat.

His movements are rough, and he jars his cup of black tea momentarily, spilling a drop onto the table.

"You can't move, can you? Not even a finger. Nor can you speak. Is this a first for you? Toudou... If I must put it this way—this is proof of your ineptitude."

Gregorio opens the gold clasp on his leather-bound black trunk.

Toudou doesn't know what he is talking about, but she does know these aren't normal circumstances.

"It's not a magic spell or a holy technique. This is—a difference in level. Toudou, there are so very many things that I, far above your level, can do that you cannot."

Gregorio opens his trunk with a skilled hand. The lid knocks his teacup underneath the table, and it shatters. Toudou has seen the silvery interior of the trunk once before. Looking at it close up, she can see that the edges of the trunk are dull and dirty, giving an even more ominous impression.

"This is a most adverse fate. Yet, I can only be overjoyed that God has bestowed it unto me."

"—"

The young man in front of Toudou shows no sign of anger or remorse; his face is plastered with that familiar smile.

But then, Toudou notices something.

Just one thing—the spiraling, hazy light clouding his eyes. Toudou's confusion settles, as if someone poured a bucket of ice water over her head. She now understands that she touched upon a subject that should never be mentioned. Nevertheless, the only thing the immobilized Toudou can do is scowl at the man before her.

Limis and Aria are staring at Gregorio with the same stern glare. Gregorio glances toward them for a moment before returning to Toudou.

"The Church and my fellow crusaders call this trunk of mine Pandora's Coffin. A priest's weapon is indicative of their very faith, my friends. As a crusader, I have consecrated my faith in God. This trunk is a sign of my roots, and it functions as a box that contains all manner of transgressions."

Gregorio slowly traces his fingers along the edges of the box. The caked-on filth shows no sign of rubbing off. Caressing it softly, Gregorio whispers:

"Holy Warrior."

Toudou is simply stupefied.

Limis's and Aria's expressions shift at the words that escape his lips. They still can't move their bodies, so that is the only noticeable change. Gregorio nevertheless casts a sharp glance at them. His next utterance brims with confidence.

"The one to defeat the darkness. The one to restore order to the realm. The one who possesses otherworldly knowledge and the protection of myriad divine spirits. I have heard the rumors—the Kingdom of Ruxe used the power of the Saint to bestow a miracle. A being with the divine protection of Ahz Gried, the God of Order, has appeared, they say."

Toudou is unable to respond, and she has no idea what Gregorio is trying to accomplish.

But she knows one thing: Gregorio does not leer like this at his allies.

"In all honesty, although miracles are a gift, I was never that interested... Yet, if it is the will of God, I will not deny it. Toudou—"

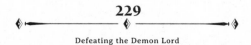

Gregorio lets slip a fiendish sneer, as if looking down at an insect.

"Let us determine your true worth. In God's name, I shall wash away all your sins."

§ §

Gregorio Legins became a crusader twenty-five years ago. Prior to this, he was born to a family of moderate influence and had the same amount of faith as any other adolescent. He wasn't a priest or anything special; he was just a typical boy. That is, until his hometown was razed to the ground by a single demon.

This was before the Demon Lord's name held such renown to the world. The threat of demons was known among men, but circumstances favored humanity. For that reason, their defenses were not properly fortified. What's more, the priests dispatched to their town by the Church were not of high level.

"My hometown no longer exists on the map. The region holds neither military importance, nor is it a valuable swath of land economically. The entire town was in ruins, its people nearly wiped out, and thus, there was zero benefit in reconstructing it."

The demon that attacked the village was extremely powerful. Such an advanced-stage creature capable of devising detailed battle strategy would have required someone more than level 70 to defeat.

When the demon invaded the village, the first thing it did was easily kill all the priests with the capacity to face it. What followed after that was nothing short of a horrific nightmare.

"It was only a matter of hours. In a single night, my village was reduced to a mountain of rubble. My friends and family and everything I knew were gone. The demon, having destroyed an entire village, was not driven out by anyone and didn't receive a single blow of damage. It left at its own leisure."

Gregorio's calm voice is at odds with the content of his story. Yet he is nearly preaching to Toudou and her party, who can still do nothing but remain motionless.

"The fact that I escaped unharmed was pure chance. I just happened to be at home—and at the time, I was small enough that I could just barely fit my entire body inside a large trunk."

Gregorio's parents, who quickly realized the unusual turn of events in the village, hid Gregorio in the trunk to protect him and closed the clasp. In the end, their plan worked—something he only could know now. Had he tried to escape with his family, the demon would have certainly killed him, too.

Gregorio was stuffed inside that box, which wasn't especially sturdy, and he alone survived. Death and despair, sorrow and terror—Gregorio has never forgotten the night he spent inside the pitch-black trunk.

The fact that something so mundane had saved Gregorio from the immensely cunning and perceptive demon, one that had obliterated his entire community, was nothing less than a miracle.

"I became a believer in miracles, a devout follower of our lord Ahz Gried—and one capable of using holy techniques—from that very day. He bestowed a miracle upon me, gave me a divine order. To repay Him, I vowed to vanquish every last one of His enemies. The reason I became a crusader instead of an exorcist is because those enemies are not only limited to demons."

Gregorio speaks gently, but his eyes burn with a black flame that could scorch a person on sight.

Toudou is unable to understand every part of Gregorio's story, yet she, Limis, Aria, and Spica are all listening raptly, as if hypnotized by his voice.

Gregorio scratches his head nervously, an unusual glint in his eyes.

"Toudou, I regret nothing from that day, and I do not wish for your pity. My hometown being wiped from the map was an inevitability, and I believe God had no choice but to make my foolish self see that fact. However—I do also wonder *what if*. What if, at that time, the head priest of my village's church had been strong enough to eradicate that demon?"

232

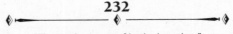

"The overdone sense of justice is a crime."

The emotions pour through his words—another true sign of Gregorio Legins's roots.

Faith and circumstance. The only holy technique he garnered from this tragedy ended up being exorcism. The holy techniques, which are fashioned solely to defeat enemies of God, are of the utmost importance now that the Demon Lord has returned.

Gregorio's disturbingly twisted nature is responsible for his deep faith. Some might even call him the hero of a particular era.

Gregorio stands from his chair and moves his face near Toudou's. Up close, it's as if she's staring into the depths of hell itself. A bead of cold sweat rolls down Toudou's forehead.

"Miracles are not unlimited. To be of shallow faith is sacrilege against God and yields intense tragedy. Yes, my friends, Holy Warrior. It is no mere coincidence that Toudou and I have met here. This is…fate."

"—"

Toudou is terrified, unable to protest. Her fear of the unknown force keeping her immobile vastly outweighs her aversion to being so close to a man. The feeling of being unable to move, no matter how hard she tries, is a special breed of nightmarish torment.

Gregorio's hand reaches toward Toudou. All too naturally, his slender fingers envelop her throat.

"We don't need a weakling as the Holy Warrior. Cowardice in the chosen warrior is…a sin. Countless innocent people will perish due to your frailty."

The atmosphere in the room warps. Toudou is in a trance for a moment, but then she realizes—it is murderous intent, a brand of which Toudou and her party have never experienced thus far.

The thick, stagnant air hinders Toudou's breathing. It isn't just her; Aria's and Limis's pupils dilate as their airways begin to seal shut. If they could speak, they'd be screaming.

This is different from the loathsome resentment they felt at the hands of the undead. It's nowhere near the same as the evil treants and beasts they had encountered in the Great Forest of the Vale.

In response to the distinct malice being aimed at her, Toudou feels unspeakable terror toward another human being for the first time.

Gregorio's fingers begin applying pressure around Toudou's throat. Suddenly, everyone hears a childlike voice.

It's Glacia, who had been sitting quietly the entire time, as if she were another piece of furniture. The dragon-turned-little-girl blinks her eyes as she asks a question.

"So…what happened to the demon?"

Gregorio's grip loosens at the sudden interruption, and in that instant, the force restraining Toudou is broken. Her stiffened body slumps from her chair to the floor, and her sudden movements feel like a foul ruse after being frozen stiff for a prolonged period. She coughs and splutters from the sudden rush of fresh air to the back of her throat.

Gregorio glances at Toudou for a second but then turns quickly again to Glacia and smiles serenely. He points at the open trunk in front of him.

"Ah… Fear not. The demon has already been vanquished. Please take a look—the exterior leather on Pandora's Coffin is the skin removed from its hide."

"*Cough, cough*— N-no…way—"

Toudou's emotions swirl together in the back of her mind. She simply does not understand. Why in the hell…? What does any of this have to do with attacking her?

Gregorio's eyes threaten to force their way out of their sockets as, fraught with emotion, he holds his head in his hands.

"And so… Heh-heh-heh… Ha-ha-ha-ha-ha… My faith deepens further whenever I lay my eyes on it!"

As Gregorio roars, the remaining three girls' restraints disappear completely. Their stances go completely limp from their newfound freedom of movement.

Gregorio upends the table and flies at Toudou, still bent over on the floor. He aims a kick at her face, but Toudou promptly retrieves her shield from her ring. At that same moment, Gregorio's foot collides with it.

"This is…God's will! He has given the Holy Warrior another trial!"

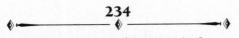

"The overdone sense of justice is a crime."

That Toudou took out her shield in time was nothing short of a miracle. A tremendous force ripples through it.

Unable to brace herself against the blow, Toudou slams into the wall along with her shield. Her bones and insides creak, and the back of her head smashes against the wall, causing her to see stars.

"Garnet!" screams Limis.

Toudou can see Garnet flying from Limis's shoulder toward Gregorio. Garnet's tiny body reacts to Limis's battle cry and cloaks itself in intense heat.

Gregorio is unfazed even as Garnet's sizzling heat warps the air around them. When Garnet lands atop his trunk, Gregorio closes the lid and snaps the clasp shut. Limis stares for a moment at his abrupt reaction but quickly gives Garnet an order:

"Burn it to ash!!"

Her voice projects throughout the room, and Garnet follows her command.

However, the trunk is wholly unaffected. Toudou fully knows Garnet's power. She's heard Limis's stories of his divine flame that can easily melt metal and stone.

As an elementalist, Limis was not unprepared for this result and is astonished.

"—?!"

"Ha-ha-ha…ha-ha-ha-ha…ah-ha-ha-ha-ha-ha-ha-ha! It's useless, absolutely useless. Pandora's Coffin…is crafted from orichalcum and mythril! No form of magic or noxious miasma will ever penetrate it! It has the same composition as your shield, Toudou—the one used by Holy Warriors of epochs past."

Gregorio swings the blunt instrument with ease and smashes it into Limis. She's low on stamina and not wearing any armor, and so she flies into the air, landing in a heap on the ground without a chance to defend herself.

"Oh…"

Spica, who had been sitting flat on the ground near Limis, lets out a muffled cry.

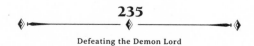

Toudou glances toward Limis, who lies facedown as if dead. Gregorio quickly approaches Toudou as she cowers.

Aria finally comes to her senses and jumps to her feet, drawing her sword in the same instant.

"HAAAAAAAAAAAA!"

She lunges forward with a relentless slash maneuver, but Gregorio brings the trunk down easily to block her. Her blade is sent flying, and Gregorio lands a kick to her wide-open torso. Although armor protects her vital organs, her tall frame is lightly cast aside and smashes into a shelf.

Broken dishes crash down on Aria as she crumples to the floor. Toudou can clearly see her expression, contorted into utter shock. As Aria lies there, her eyes are still open, but due to the severe blow she's taken, there's no sign of her getting up.

"HA-HA-HA-HA-HA-HA-HA-HA-HA-HAAA! So frail...so utterly frail!! ...Is this the Holy Warrior?! Humanity's hope?! Don't be ridiculous! This is too much—even for a complete failure. Heh-heh-heh... But really, if this is God's will—then I will sacrifice myself for the cause."

Aria's and Limis's actions were not in vain; Toudou's severe dizziness slightly subsided after her head had been jostled by Gregorio's attack. She grips her shield and manages to stand up, but Gregorio is already after her.

Her entire body aches. She swallows the pain and raises her shield. Gregorio mercilessly slams into it with his trunk. Attacks from walking bones and giant skeletons had no effect on her shield, but now it creaks and groans. Even though Gregorio is the same height as Toudou, his blows are tempestuous and volatile.

Toudou's hand goes numb from bracing her shield against each strike that sends waves of pain through her body.

Toudou's shield—the Shield of Radiance—is not a supreme item like the holy sword Ex or her holy armor, but it is an ultra-high-class item of the Kingdom of Ruxe. It is made of blue metal, a strong, easily

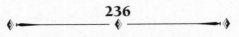

modifiable material highly resistant to blunt damage, slash damage, and magical damage.

But it still can't fully defend against Gregorio's onslaught.

"Come, come, come, Holy Warrior! Show me the power of the will of Ahz Gried!"

"Nngh—"

Even as Gregorio screams through his attacks, his vigorous blows give no indication of faltering.

Toudou resists with all her might. She wants to draw her holy sword, Ex, but she doesn't have the chance as she endures the maelstrom of attacks. If she doesn't hold her shield with both hands, she'll be blown away in the blink of an eye.

Aria summons the fortitude to stand in spite of the pain and moves to slash at Gregorio from behind. She sees an opening to strike his back. An instant before her blade can reach him, Gregorio spins around and pummels Aria in the torso with his trunk, mowing her down. Her sword strike whiffs, and she tumbles through the air.

"Aria!!"

Yet this move has provided a split-second opening. Toudou unsheathes the holy sword Ex. It is entirely reflexive—she's done this more than once now. The blade flashes a mystical ivory-blue in the sunlight coming in from the window. Gregorio pauses for an instant at its glimmering.

Toudou does not miss her slim window of opportunity, and she brings the holy sword Ex down on him using every last ounce of her strength. Gregorio uses his trunk as a shield to block her strike.

The explosive sound of metal on metal. Toudou's blade rocks back in her hand, the sensation completely unexpected, and a stupefied murmur escapes her lips.

"Huh...?"

Her mind goes blank.

Gregorio's box deflects Toudou's blade, and it is thrust back into her unprotected lower body. She hears the horrible sound of broken bones

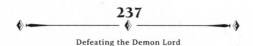

237

and flesh ripping apart. As she collapses in agony, Gregorio says almost in astonishment, "…My, my, Toudou, don't tell me…you've never come up against something you couldn't slice through, have you?"

"…Ugh…"

Toudou cannot breathe. A paltry wisp of breath escapes her mouth.

The holy sword Ex is a supremely sharp blade. She fought beasts with bones as hard as steel in the Great Forest of the Vale and armored, sword-wielding undead in Yutith's Tomb, but she never once had a problem slicing through any of them. This is a blade forged by the gods that can easily cleave through metal without resistance.

Toudou's vision goes dark in a rush of shock, pain, and confusion. Even trying with all her tenacity to remain lucid, she feels her senses begin to fade, as if her very will were ridiculing her. Her consciousness plunges into a deep bog. Toudou hears Spica calling her name, but she cannot find the strength to respond.

However, the moment before she loses consciousness, she hears the sound of a massive explosion and Gregorio's rapturous voice—

"The Wrath of God— Heh-heh-heh, I have been waiting for you, Ex Deus."

§　§　§

I have no intention of griping. I already know exactly what's going on. I knew, and I was fully prepared. Ready for the worst.

Toudou is reckless. I have no idea what he'll do next.

There's a massive hole in the door. I can feel a powerful, searing sensation pulsating in the back of my skull. I've already cast every buff on myself possible. I put on my mask as if it's second nature to me.

"This—is what I was prepared for."

I stomp through the remains of the door and enter the room. I already threw my mace—to stop Gregorio.

"I've taken action. I gave everything I could, tried my very best. Yet,

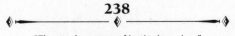

"The overdone sense of justice is a crime."

I can't deny that I've become demented in the process. This must be—a result of my inexperience."

I have no regrets, but if someone asked me if there was a better way, I would still have my doubts. Faced with the same situation again, I would definitely do better.

The room is in rough shape. The shelf is destroyed, there's a gaping hole in the wall, and the table and chairs are overturned, a few of their legs broken off.

Gregorio stands near the wall. A small-framed man lies collapsed at his feet, not moving a muscle. He has black hair, armor I've seen before, and a massive shield. And lying beside him—the holy sword Ex.

I know he's still alive. I barged in before Gregorio could kill him.

"Oh... Mr. Ares—is that you...?"

Spica is nearly paralyzed in the corner, pale-faced, and calls my name. Glacia reacts differently and steps back as if she's seen a demon. Limis and Aria are lying facedown just like Toudou. They're unconscious but alive. That means that Gregorio went easy on them.

I glare at Gregorio. Looking him in the eyes inevitably entails looking far down to meet his gaze. His breath is calm.

"This is a little something called—*fate*, Mad Eater. I anticipated this scene. No matter how hard I tried to sneak around here, there was always the possibility of you detecting me and of Toudou's cover getting blown as well. I mean, you've been waiting for an altercation between us. That's the kind of man you are. Isn't that right, Gregorio? That's why, right now—I'm exceedingly calm."

Even experienced mercenaries balk at my gaze, but Gregorio looks completely aloof. He lifts the trunk next to him with ease and shrugs. Then he begins yammering like a detective cracking a case, without so much as a mention of my mask.

"I thought that something was amiss. There was no good reason for Ex Deus, a first-rank member of Out Crusade, to be tasked with a trial in a place such as this."

True. But what the hell do you even know about my job, Gregorio?

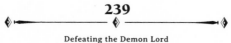

239

My mace destroyed the wall Gregorio stands next to and is sticking out of it.

"I always consider the worst-case scenario. Toudou and Aria and Limis are down, and you're the only one standing. But this isn't the worst-case scenario. Because the three of them are...still alive."

The Holy Warrior, the daughters of the Grand Swordmaster and the Mage King—none of that matters. Gregorio is on a completely different plane from the three of them. Their relative experiences are like night and day.

A difference in level entails a difference in experience, and Gregorio is leagues above them in every regard. They couldn't take him down, even three to one. If Gregorio really wanted to, he could've killed Toudou with his very first strike. Just like when I immobilized Glacia that one time, he could have sucked Toudou's will from him and splattered him against the wall.

Gregorio's expression still hasn't changed. Is it our difference in level or experience? No, this is...preparedness. Just as I anticipated this very scene, Gregorio probably anticipated my smashing the door and breaking in here.

"The only thing that gave away Toudou's true identity...was you, Ares. The rare divine protection of the God of Order and the Church's strongest crusader. It is simply too perfect to be a coincidence. Heh-heh, Ares... This is no divine message. This is—simple deduction."

Divine protection from Ahz Gried isn't something that can be seen with the naked eye—unless you possess a very particular type of eyes.

Toudou should have seen this plainly. He should have understood Gregorio's character thoroughly before deciding what to say or not to say... But who can understand the thoughts of a madman anyway?

A hero is destined to face endless trials. Perhaps I could call this fate. I should, shouldn't I?

I assess my surroundings in an instant. The cracked floor, the remnants of the table and chairs, the location of my mace, the condition of the injured, Gregorio's behavior, Spica's and Glacia's positions. And

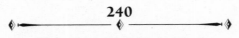

above all else—my own demeanor. I sweep my bangs out of my eyes and lord over Gregorio. My performance is immaculate.

I could kill him—anytime.

"This is a warning. Fall back, Gregorio. This is my trial. I already told you not to get in my way. Right?"

Maybe he doesn't understand our difference in level or battle prowess. No, there's no way he doesn't get it. He knows, and he's still standing in my way. That's what makes him genuinely terrifying.

No matter how much experience he acquires, there will always be a gap between us. This is nothing like beating down three low-level warriors. Not to mention, Gregorio can't even cast Heal.

Gregorio smiles as if he's chatting with an old friend.

"Ares, my countryman. Just this morning, you inquired of me and demanded Sister Spica remain safe. I respected your command. Sister Spica does not have a scratch on her."

Spica shudders upon being pointed at.

Not even close! That's not what I was trying to say at all, goddammit!

It's true I met with Gregorio before everyone returned and demanded Spica stay safe, but that was with the understanding he should refrain from going overboard with Toudou and his party. It was absolutely not a suggestion to create this mayhem.

In a literal sense, the only noncombatant, Spica, is unharmed. *But is being literal all you know how to do, you dumbass?!*

I want to shout all of this at him but swallow the urge. Losing your cool is equivalent to falling into your opponent's trap.

"Gregorio, you understand, yes? This is my trial."

"I do understand. And—it is also mine."

I'm not...getting through to him.

I figured it would go this way. I was sure it would. That's why I didn't give him the details. He's guaranteed to pretend to listen to orders, but at the end of the day, he'll scrap them all in the name of his precious faith. You can never take him at his word—ever.

Gregorio turns his face to the heavens. With that exaggerated gesture, he shouts as if delivering a prophecy:

"Yes, Ares. This is a conflict of faith. Your will and mine are—in competition. Do you know what this is called?"

I don't wanna know.

"This is most definitely—the will of God. It is without a doubt—fate. Ares, God says unto thee: 'Show me your faith, for if you do—victory will be thine.' This is tragedy and comedy! Ares Crown, my countryman—I am nearly crushed by the sensations of sorrow and delight!"

A tear begins falling from Gregorio's left eye—only his left. Terror runs through me at the sound of his overly emotional voice. Madman. A fanatic. There's no other word for what this man is. You hear me, Toudou? There are a finite number of people in this world who you simply can't get through to.

Gregorio turns his eyes downward as they take on a new hint of danger.

"Ares. A crude sense of justice can be toxic. An incompetent ally can sometimes pose a bigger threat than an enemy. We, as crusaders, have killed countless people with this in mind— Am I mistaken?"

"I didn't come here to debate you, Gregorio. I'm on the orders of His Eminence Cardinal Creio."

I already contacted Creio and told him there would likely be a battle. I've also already given Amelia instructions.

I take a deep breath and center myself. Then, I spit out Creio's orders to Gregorio, except in my own special phrasing:

"Get out of my goddamn sight."

"Isn't it presumptuous for a mere mortal to give orders to his fellow man?"

Gregorio responds blankly as he lifts his trunk, a peaceful, somehow saintly expression on his face.

Although we haven't exchanged any blows, the air around us starts to feel like a battlefield. Gregorio licks his lips casually.

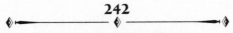

"Ah, Ares, I remember the time we first met!"

"I have no desire to do the same!"

Gregorio Legins and I are the same breed of crusader, but that doesn't mean we're equally matched. There's our difference in experience, the kinds of holy techniques we can cast, our levels, body size, physical strength, our thoughts and faith, our acquaintances—the list goes on.

Thinking of all these things makes me not want to fight him. I wanted to resolve this diplomatically, but...at the end of the day, I am a warrior, and my skill in persuasion isn't particularly high.

"Gregorio, my level is—ninety-three."

I tap my foot on the ground and get my bearings. Level 93 is the ultimate class among all human beings. Taking into account the fact that level 100 is the maximum for the typical human being should impart a decent impression of just how high that is.

Reaching this level through typical monster hunting is extremely difficult in the first place.

Most warriors would and should assume they're out of their league. But Gregorio's expression still hasn't changed. He even looks joyful.

"Ares, my level is—eighty-three. Heh-heh-heh... That makes us just ten levels apart."

I can tell from Gregorio's voice that he never had any intention of retreating.

Level 83 is among the highest of all. I wonder how many priests have managed to reach that height? Yet, it's as I expected. Well within my estimation. It is high but still lower than mine.

...*Ugh, I don't wanna deal with this guy.*

"Gregorio, this is my final warning. Do yourself a favor and get lost. Any dispute between two compatriots would be...inefficient."

I let loose all my emotion, yet Gregorio responds by looking perplexed and blinking.

"Ares, you are quite strong. Even among all priests who have received God's blessing, those who could defeat you are surely few and far between. And among those priests, your capacity to vanquish followers of darkness is unparalleled. That is why you have been nicknamed Ex Deus. However—this is not enough of a reason to abandon our conflict of faith."

Gregorio rips my mace from where it's stuck in the wall.

My battle mace is riddled with spikes. Gregorio generally wields his trunk with both hands. He's not used to dual wielding, so I should be able to exploit an opening.

Even if I lose my mace, I have a dagger and am highly versed in unarmed combat.

However, Gregorio lobs my mace toward me, and I catch it in midair with my right hand.

"Ares. If you want to prove to me the legitimacy of your faith, you should do so using Wrath of God."

Wrath of God—the name given to my long-handled battle mace. It's not the name I gave it. Before I realized, those around me had begun calling it that.

It's an over-the-top nickname I'm used to by now. I swing the weapon lightly through the air, creating a thunderous rushing sound. Bring on every calamity known to man. This will crush them.

Gregorio turns his gaze to Toudou, still collapsed at his feet.

"Ares. I respect you. The fact that Toudou is still alive is proof of that. If a crusader other than yourself had been responsible for this trial…I would have eliminated him already. For the sake of people from all walks of life—and for the sake of my faith in God!"

Gregorio's trunk clatters unnaturally in his hands, almost as if it's communicating his emotions. His expression is one of drunken ecstasy.

"God always smiles upon the righteous."

He sounds so convinced of his own righteousness, his own faith.

"I may be crude. I may not be able to persuade my fellow man. But there is one thing I do understand."

Gregorio. Even though I've been terrified of you up to this very moment…I have never once thought I would lose to you.

"Victory does not go to the righteous but to the strong."

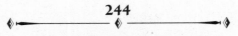

"Heh-heh... On the contrary, my friend."

Gregorio's cheeks turn up slightly as he smiles. This isn't his usual smile. It's the twisted grin of a demon that strikes despair into the hearts of men.

"Righteousness is power. Triumph is the Lord's will. Righteousness that lacks power is poison. And a righteousness that cannot save even the weak means—"

Gregorio's form instantly disappears. No—my enhanced senses allow me to just barely see his movements.

He has a peculiar way of moving. He's quite fast due to his high level, and his techniques are polished. Splinters ripple from the floor as his feet pass over it. Gregorio brandishes his trunk and aims for my blind spot, but I meet his blow with my mace.

"—nothing!"

"!!"

Sparks fly from the explosive impact. My mace hand, which wasn't even affected when it blocked Zarpahn's attacks, goes numb. His strike is so powerful, I can't believe he doesn't have a buff cast. Yet I'm able to block it.

My breath is hot. Gregorio's nebulous pupils are threatening to swallow me whole, and due to my enhanced senses, I can see our surroundings flowing smoothly within them.

I catch my reflection in his pupils. My expression is the same as his.

"Guh— You really oughtta quit this priest business and become a mercenary instead!"

"AH-HA-HA-HA-HA-HA-HA-HA-HA-HA-HA-HA-HA-HA-HA-HA!!!"

My stance holds him off. The trunk is deflected and flies into the air, along with Gregorio's slim frame.

I chase after him. Between the two of us, the fact that I know more holy techniques than he does makes me the stronger one. I know the true nature of Gregorio's abnormal strength. That's why I am neither afraid of it nor am I unprepared.

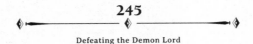

245

I crush the remnants of the furniture as I rush to engage him. Pandora's Coffin is sturdy, but strictly speaking, it's not even a real weapon.

My reach is far superior. If I lose to him now, I suppose that would qualify as the Lord's will.

I swing my mace diagonally from the upper right, and Gregorio blocks with his trunk. I repeat my attacks again and again, and Gregorio continues blocking them.

The floor is wooden. Even if Gregorio can withstand my blows, it will eventually give out, and the resulting fissure will swallow up Gregorio's legs.

This time, I swing my mace from the side. I can observe Gregorio's movements, but I wonder if he can see mine...

My mace and his trunk collide, and the piercing sound of metal on metal reverberates in my eardrums. The floor splits from the impact and Gregorio is sent flying—

—through the window, smashing it. He lands outside on the ground. Just as I planned. Even if Gregorio didn't intend it, fighting here leaves the possibility of Toudou getting dragged into the fray.

Spica is trembling nearby, and she speaks as if clinging to dear life.

"Mister...Ares?"

"Spica, stay calm. I'll clean up this mess."

Spica looks around the disheveled room and then up at me, asking, "Um... Uh... Are you going to...k-kill him?"

"...It's a damn shame, but Creio didn't give me permission."

This is business. I'm not like Gregorio.

"DIEEEEEEEEEEEEEEEEEEEEEEEEEEEEEEEEEEEE!"

"AH-HA-HA-HA-HA-HA-HA! The heavens—they are granting me their blessing!"

I roar, and Gregorio rejoices. Thankfully, there aren't any people below Gregorio's room, in the back of the church. Two priests fighting to the death—if someone happened to catch this scene unfolding, they would likely lose all faith.

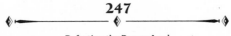

Defeating the Demon Lord

I leap through the window and use the force of gravity to slam down my mace. Gregorio has already prepared himself. His trunk is less of a weapon than a shield—an extremely hard shield that's resistant to every kind of attack.

The ground is wet from last night's rain. My steps are encumbered, and Gregorio slips on the ground when he receives my strike. I continually hit Gregorio without giving him a chance to counter, and he blocks each volley with an experienced hand. Every single one of my attacks is countered with precision. I clearly have the upper hand. My physical strength is obviously overpowering him, if just by a margin.

I fire an arrow of light between my melee attacks. It shoots out of the opposite side of my mace and pierces Gregorio in the neck—but he doesn't seem the least bit perturbed. I already knew it, but I scream anyway:

"Shit! Are you even human?!"

"I owe all the glory to God."

What the hell does that even mean?!

I put my entire being into each and every mace strike. The attacks are heavy enough to blast a dragon off its feet, but Gregorio takes each one in stride. This isn't a competition of strength—he's eluding my every move. How is he even human? Exorcisms don't work on him, either. Something is wrong with this world.

As I continue to rain down blows on him, Gregorio's stance falters. *Did he slip on the mud?!* Not letting this opportunity go to waste, I bash the side of his trunk full force.

"Ngh—"

Pandora's Coffin is blasted from Gregorio's hands by the impact, flying away a few meters and rolling on the ground. This is Gregorio's main weapon, the very root of his faith—he doesn't have another.

I quickly change positions and put myself between the trunk and Gregorio. I steady my breath and get low, looking down at Gregorio, his eyes still like those of a crazed beast.

"Surrender, Gregorio. The match has been decided."

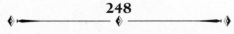

"Heh-heh-heh… AH-HA-HA-HA-HA-HA-HA— Ex Deus, my body is still whole, so how can you tell who the victor is?"

Gregorio raises both hands and leaps toward me, nearly flying. I see his nails, teeth, fists, and feet—I guess he is still whole. At level 83, even his body can become a lethal weapon.

That said, the gap between us is still a factor, and I sincerely doubt he can inflict mortal harm on me with his bare hands. Not to mention, I'm stronger than he is—and armed.

"If we continue any further, I'll end up killing you."

"If that is the Lord's will, let it be so!"

He just doesn't get it. I click my tongue and take one step back. I can clearly see his profile as he flies at me again. I wind up, feigning to strike him in the head from the side and flip my mace over in my hand, piercing his stomach.

Gregorio brings up his knees to defend the blow, but I'm positive I managed to damage his hand. It's not broken, but it'll do. I can't tell whether he's in pain as he takes a step back. I waste no time and immediately advance on him. Gregorio erupts, as if enjoying every second.

"AH-HA-HA-HA-HA-HA-HA-HA! Ares! You are so—magnanimous! You're not trying to destroy me… You want to gain complete control!"

"Shut your damn trap! If I'd aimed for your head, you'd have evaded me, you little shit!"

I lift my mace and feign a strike, instead delivering a step kick. I manage to move in deep and aim for the top of Gregorio's foot with my stomp. I then bring my mace down with my right hand and make a fist with my left, striking him on the chin. For Gregorio, being dealt a mortal blow is equivalent to defeat.

I continue to set on him, combining bluff attacks, but I can't generate enough power. I'm not sure if it's his intuition or actual capability, but I can't get a feint to work. But even defending will eventually take its physical toll.

As a specialist in exorcism, that is Gregorio Legins's greatest weakness.

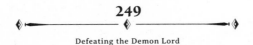

Fatigue and damage are guaranteed to dull his movements. Also, he should be able to clearly see the green light enveloping my body. I've cast *Regen* on myself—I won't amass any physical fatigue or damage at all.

"Heh-heh... Ha-ha-ha-ha— So strong! Ares—your faith is emanating from your very being!"

As long as Gregorio is focused on defense, it'll be very tough to incapacitate him with a single blow. I remove my dagger from my waist with my left hand. During the exchange, I confirm that Gregorio definitely noticed while I drew it.

Okay, Gregorio, blunt attack or slash attack—what's your preference?

I thrust the blade from below, aiming for his chin. It's fine. It'll be fine, as long as he doesn't die. Wounds can be healed. If I can get him to bleed, his stamina will fade more quickly.

Gregorio must have balked at the prospect of getting cut. He quickly snaps his head back and dodges the thrust. As a consolation, when his stance becomes completely exposed, I aim for the obvious opening and swing my mace toward his torso.

Yet—I'm not after Gregorio. I take a hard leap off the ground and spin in the air.

Gregorio is flabbergasted. My mace smashes into Gregorio's trunk as I swing it behind the back of my head. Pandora's Coffin bounds along the ground a few times and finally stops, now another few meters away.

A revolting sensation crawls up my spine. This is the second time. I saw it before when I met Gregorio in the dining hall. I'd been prepared for this since our battle began, which is why I was able to counterattack.

Gregorio's no fool. He understands our difference in combat strength. Had I not been on the lookout for it, I wouldn't have been able to evade. My heart is pounding out of my chest.

Mud flies and covers my face. I stare down Gregorio without wiping it off.

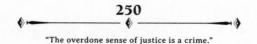

"The overdone sense of justice is a crime."

"What the hell...is this?!"

"Incredible... Truly unbelievable, Ares Crown. There is ample reason for your first-rank status."

Gregorio has already realigned his stance as he whispers in admiration.

His voice is low, yet it sounds young. Pandora's Coffin rattles, despite being several meters away from him.

Is this a spell? No—there's no indication it is. Gregorio hasn't moved a muscle. There isn't even a breeze. I can't see any factor that would cause the trunk to move.

"No one has ever detected my little friend before."

"Your little...*friend*?!"

As if reacting to Gregorio's words, his "friend" launches into the air. I can't help but be amazed. The trunk flies a few meters and soars in a circle before barreling toward the ground in an aerial assault. I swing at it with my mace.

The trunk flies into the sky from the impact, but it doesn't land. It whirls through the air and lands at Gregorio's feet. Gregorio strokes the box with great affection.

I have no idea what this thing is. I ready myself and take a step back, returning my dagger to my hip and hoisting my mace. It's not a spell, and there isn't any special privilege that could enable this trick through leveling up.

"What the hell is that?!"

"Heh-heh-heh. Ares, have you—never seen one before?"

Gregorio puts his hand on the clasp of the trunk and releases it carefully like he's unbuttoning a shirt. The lid opens. A dimly glowing salamander falls out and stealthily crawls away. But that's it—there's nothing else inside. It's just a regular trunk.

"Let me introduce you, Ares, to my friend Pandora."

Gregorio releases his friend, and it flies into the sky once again. It circles around Gregorio three times at intense speed, then veers intimidatingly toward me, snapping open and shut.

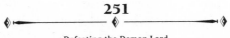

251

Defeating the Demon Lord

Based on appearance alone, it looks like some type of monster, almost identical to the ones that dwell in labyrinths and mimic treasure chests. But as it hovers in front of me, I don't get any sense it's alive. It's just—luggage.

I raise my guard. Just what is this moving block, if not a monster? It's something akin to the Devil-Faced Knight we fought in the Great Tomb, but Gregorio can't use such powerful spells as he lacks magic energy.

Pandora comes flying at me without any signal from Gregorio—a possessed hunk of metal that even blocked the holy sword Ex. I swing at it from head-on with my mace. In the same moment, I can see Gregorio lowered to the ground and charging at me.

"Ares, this is—a miracle."

I've always had my doubts about him.

Level 83. The higher your level, the more difficult it becomes to level up. Gregorio's level is representative of his experience and also of his faith. At level 83, one's battle prowess is comparable to high-level monsters, but in general, no matter how high one's level becomes, as a human being, one will never be as physically strong as the highest-level monsters. That's why we have to make up for it with techniques and experience.

However, Gregorio had the biggest gap to bridge during his long career of service as a crusader. Among a priest's abilities, holy techniques that restore wounds or fatigue—healing spells—are the most important. Such techniques are particularly indispensable in order to take on monsters with high stamina.

It was always odd to me. Even with a fanatical level of faith and exorcism powers, how has Gregorio, who generally acts solo, managed to survive for so very long? How is Gregorio—who can't even heal his own wounds—not dead yet?

"This—this is the reason why!!!"

Pandora (or whatever this thing is) flies at me from behind, and I beat it back with my mace. The trunk bites down on my weapon, nearly

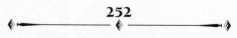

devouring it, so I bring both down on Gregorio, but he sidesteps my attack.

My nerves are fried. This is like fighting two opponents at once. Human peripheral vision is approximately 120 degrees; no matter how one turns, there's always a blind spot. Focusing the senses allows one to react to attacks from behind, but that leaves your front vulnerable.

This is simply beyond the pale. A hackneyed word like *miracle* isn't convincing me at this point. Someone has to be pulling the strings here. I stop and shift my priorities.

Gregorio digs his heels into the ground, scattering mud as he leaps at me with a low kick. His physical abilities are still a threat, but in the end, he just has his bare hands and feet. I block his kick with my knee. The numbness that spreads through my leg is nullified in a split second by a Regen spell.

—*This is getting old.*

There is no sign of Gregorio's will to fight dwindling. He's had the same fiery look in his eyes since we started.

My mace is heavy in my hand. Pandora is still chomped down on one end, making a rattling noise. Unbelievable.

I brandish the mace with Pandora stuck to it and bring it down toward Gregorio's shoulder, but the trunk forces me off track. I miss.

This causes an opening, and Gregorio kicks at me. I have no time to evade, so I block the blow with my arm. My flesh and bones cry out in agony.

I take a step back. I'm not really damaged, but I get the sense the rhythm I'd established earlier is now on Gregorio's side. This is bad.

The second I step away from Gregorio, Pandora releases my mace and snaps its metal maw open and shut, guffawing. It's not a monster. It's not a demon or some variety of spirit that's possessed a material object. Otherwise, Gregorio, a priest, would never lay a hand on it.

Pandora returns to Gregorio's side. He grabs it by the handle and sneers.

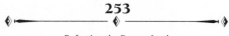

I calm my breath, then cast Heal on my numb arm to restore it instantly. I planned on overcoming him in one fell swoop, but…this has become a war of attrition.

"What kind of unearthly spell…? Seriously, are you even human?"

"Heh-heh… Ares, you can do this, too."

Pandora swoops down toward me in an arc, and I cast my mace aside to catch it with both hands. It tries to bite my arm off, and I use all my strength to stop it.

There is nothing more terrifying than an undecipherable attack. I should have…done my research.

I keep Pandora from moving and observe it while stepping back. Its leather upholstery is made from the hide of a high-level demon. It is composed of the metals orichalcum and mythril. Aside from the demon skin covering it, the trunk itself—as a weapon—was gifted by the Church.

As Pandora struggles to escape my grasp, I use it to block all of Gregorio's incoming punches and kicks. There's nothing unnatural about it, neither inside nor out. It's just a…trunk.

I brandish Pandora and smash it toward Gregorio, letting go simultaneously. He dodges it, and at the same time, I remove a knife from my chest pocket and throw it at him.

Gregorio isn't necessarily caught off guard, but he stiffens for a moment and evades the knife at the last second.

Something doesn't feel right. Pandora swivels around behind Gregorio, targeting me again. As it aims directly for my face, I bash it with my fist. The trunk is blasted into the air, spinning frantically. I may have broken a bone, because my fist is searing with tingling pain.

As I heal it with holy techniques, I run toward my mace before Pandora can return. Hand-to-hand combat is utterly banal. As long as this remains two versus one, I'll always be left open.

Gregorio stands in my way, blocking my weapon. After being blasted out of sight by my fist, Pandora falls back to earth.

I've made up my mind. I know I can intercept Pandora. It's not as

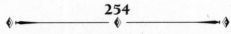

"The overdone sense of justice is a crime."

strong as when Gregorio wields it directly. I throw another knife to keep Gregorio on his toes. His reaction is dull yet again, but he still manages to avoid it.

In that second, as I was just a step away from my mace, I feel a tremendous impact strike my back and surge through my body.

"Remarkable, Ares. Even among the Out Crusade, your prowess is... unmatched. I'm sure that before long, you will surpass me and become a supreme crusader capable of wreaking havoc on all of God's enemies."

Pain evokes terror, they say. However, the impact I feel doesn't fill my mind with terror. Rather, it's filled with the memory of when I first met Gregorio immediately after becoming a crusader.

That memory instantly flashes through my mind. It's been many years already. I can still see Gregorio, attacking me under the pretext of confirming my faith. The lengthy trial felt like an eternity. I still remember the psychosis dwelling in his eyes and that fanatical laugh of his.

Until another crusader intervened, there was no sign of a clear victor between Gregorio and me. It's one of the single most bitter memories I've accumulated since becoming a crusader.

—But had that trial kept going, I would've won.

My breathing stops for a moment, and my internal organs feel compressed. Even wearing mythril chain mail that's resistant to impact, I am shaken to the core by the force of Pandora rocking into my body.

But it's not gonna stop me. Using the force of impact to my advantage, I quickly advance a step and retrieve my mace.

As I pitch my body forward, I quickly cast Heal on myself. I don't have to wait for Regen to take effect—my wounds and fatigue instantly vanish. I turned my back for only a second, but Gregorio didn't pursue me and attack. He's just gazing down at me in wonderment.

"Just as I would expect from you…Ex Deus. How many buffs did you cast on yourself?"

"…"

"You've cast Heal repeatedly on yourself, too, which takes a lot of magic energy, but your expression remains the same. You truly have infinite holy energy—an unbelievable capacity for prolonged battle. You are most certainly—different."

"You expect me to revel in your acknowledgment?"

I stand and brush the dirt from my priest's robe. My reserve of holy energy is still ample.

You will lose, Gregorio. There's a reason behind that—something I've known from the start. Earlier, Gregorio said he knows why I'm first rank, but there's a stark difference between this man and myself.

Ever since I was old enough to be aware of my surroundings—I have never connected pain with fear. The reason for that is I've been able to heal my own wounds since before I became a priest.

That's the difference between Gregorio and me. If Gregorio's special characteristics are his fanaticism and intuition, then mine are the variation of holy techniques I can cast and my supremely high level of holy energy. But it's not like I have only two or three times as much as he does.

For support and restoration, even high-level priests are wary of spam-casting Heal, given the high amount of holy energy it consumes. But I can cast it repeatedly.

From Gregorio's perspective, I'm a terrible matchup. His exorcisms have zero effect on me, and I have extremely high resistance. I'm high level, and above all else, I know nearly everything about Gregorio. Since he can't even use Heal, his capacity for prolonged battle is leagues below mine.

Gregorio doesn't seem tired or damaged. Yet, no human is immune to fatigue.

He knows this full well. That's why he tried to end our showdown with a sneak attack.

Despite this, he's entirely unfazed. His lips twist into a wicked smile,

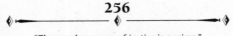

and he comes at me even harder. This must be the sheer power of his will… Fair enough. Rather than threaten, he smiles at me.

I've asked Amelia to look after Toudou, so I'm not worried that he'll get in the way. It might not be so bad to tidy up a few loose ends. I'll have Amelia stay with him for a day or two—until I'm satisfied.

Time to change tactics. I'll focus on piling on Gregorio's overall damage. He's taken every hit so far, aside from mortal blows.

"May you be rendered whole by the LORD'S WILLLLLLLLLL LLLLLLLL!"

Gregorio screams with bloodshot eyes—infinitely more terrifying than any undead's gaze. Pandora flies at me again, along with an unforeseen kick from Gregorio, which I block while bashing Pandora back with my mace.

My thoughts race as we continue battling without respite. At last, I have enough strength to spare for thinking. This is proof the conflict is slowly but surely turning in my favor. Gregorio is lightning quick and strong. But…I'm handling it.

Gregorio's limited combat abilities lean prominently on his exorcisms. His physical strength is also high, but at the end of the day, his body is only a supporting factor in the equation. Without exorcisms, his attack power is negligible. This is the same reason we never settled our battle as youths, when I was still inexperienced.

Pandora is clearly compensation for this shortcoming, but its movements are simplistic. It has only two modes of attack: biting and striking. It's just a trunk, and that makes it a lot easier than fighting against two human opponents. It's an incredulous, ridiculous foe, which put me on my heels at first, but once I got used to its attack patterns, it turned out to be not such a big deal.

I parry Gregorio's fist with my own, then block his kick and Pandora's swooping attack with my mace handle.

"Truly outstanding! Your faith—is giving you power!"

Gregorio roars. I see his former self superimposed over the man in front of me now. But there's no need to rush. All I have to do is calmly sustain his attacks. Exploiting my enemies' weak spots is my specialty.

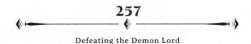

I gather my knowledge of him, gradually accumulating a detailed analysis of his go-to tactics. Gregorio is a fanatic; people call him the Mad Eater, but at the end of the day, his style is completely rational. Pandora's only real worth lies in a sudden victory from a surprise attack.

The only win Gregorio's scored against me is the sneak attack from behind at the start of our battle. That's it. The fact that he didn't send the trunk flying at me from the very beginning is proof he knows surprise is his only opening.

He made just one mistake—showing me Pandora when we first met in the dining hall.

I smash the trunk out of the air. As I rush at Gregorio, I kick the knife lying on the ground in his direction. He manages to twist half his body out of the way, but the blade grazes his cheek, leaving a thin, bloody red line. He wipes it with his finger, and with a smile on his face, he licks it off.

Gregorio calls Pandora a miracle, but I don't believe in miracles. I've been studying him painstakingly. I've taken his hits on purpose. I've knocked Pandora back into the sky and even taken the risky move of discarding my weapon just to further investigate the trunk's behavior.

There are merits to intuition, and there are merits to logic. As a result, I've realized something.

I stop Gregorio's kick with my hand and block Pandora, zeroing in on my flank, with my elbow. I can keep this up all day as long as I'm prepared. Then, I whisper into Gregorio's ear.

"This Pandora thing—there's no way it's attacking of its own volition."

"!"

Gregorio's eyes widen in response.

Pandora is completely different from a golem. In that case, how does it attack? Its strikes have become more severe, now coming in as pincer attacks, and I fend them off with my mace's handle and spiked head. Gregorio's reaction is dulled, and as I flip my mace in my hand, the handle

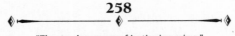

"The overdone sense of justice is a crime."

scrapes his chin. Pandora smashes into my knees in compensation, but I can handle the damage.

"Can't you tell? You maggot—ever since Pandora started flying around, you've gotten weaker."

It's a fractional decrease. At first, he was blocking or evading everything. Now, I'm starting to land small, inconsequential blows. In reality, even a knife thrown from his blind spot should be easy for Gregorio to dodge.

It's just a scratch, yet for Gregorio, who can't cast Heal, evading or blocking every attack is paramount. He's a level-83 crusader; his techniques are clearly highly advanced.

So why has he gotten weaker? He doesn't appear out of breath or hurt, so why is he slowing down? He just introduced it as his "friend," as if it moves of its own will, but maybe Pandora is—

"You're obviously controlling it somehow."

"..."

Part of his consciousness is controlling Pandora. That's why he's becoming careless. The drop-off in his remarks since the start of our battle is also clearly because he's focused on manipulating the trunk.

At my words, Gregorio's smile disappears for a moment before being replaced by a greater sense of jubilation. I catch a glimpse of his white teeth shining behind his lips.

If I trace back from the end result, I can deduce the principle behind this and the fact that Pandora is the mechanism lying at the core.

It's not magic, let alone a supposed miracle. I already know the answer. The hint was in the difference between my weapon, Wrath of God, and Gregorio's, Pandora's Coffin. Not to mention Gregorio's own words:

"You can do this, too.

"This is—a miracle."

These aren't the ravings of a fanatic. Neither is it a joke. It is pure, unadulterated truth.

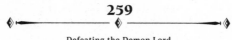

It's a truly horrific technique. A magnificent idea. This technique will surely...work to my advantage.

Pandora attacks with increased vigor. It strikes from the sky like a tempest and tries to chomp down on me with its mythril maw, but I thrust my mace directly into it.

It's so heavy and so quick. I'm using all my energy, but that won't last long—I need to conserve for defense as well.

Above all else, I have to avoid taking a direct bite. It could easily remove a whole limb or two. Even if it's ultimately healable, losing an appendage will definitely leave me wide open. As long as I'm prepared for its bite, I can block it.

Gregorio lands a kick to my arm, and it bends under the force. I swallow the pain.

Gregorio is truly a terrifying foe. He's using everything he has to take me down—all to prove his faith. But a madman's sneak attacks mixed with lies won't work on this foolish, headstrong warrior.

"I knew it! There was no madness in my eyes!"

Gregorio screams with glee. *So what is that look in your eyes anyway?*

His power is not of magical origin. It's not from a magical tool, and it's not the kind of telekinesis possessed by certain demons. If he did have that kind of power, it would be more effective for him to simply steal my weapon.

In that case, there's only one answer. It's something both Gregorio and I have.

I inhale deeply and brace my abdomen. Pandora, which clearly hasn't learned anything, tries to chomp down on my neck, and I launch it heavenward with my mace. I offer up a simpleminded prayer.

Gregorio's knee strikes the pit of my stomach, and my consciousness shakes violently for a moment.

His attacks are sharp, and I still can't detect fatigue in him. But I can bear up. Gregorio's face contorts suspiciously.

Gregorio. You should watch your mouth on the battlefield.

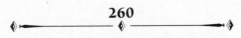

260

"The overdone sense of justice is a crime."

Pandora—Gregorio's faith incarnate—plummets from the sky with terrific velocity. It flashes brilliantly in the sunlight, appearing to fall directly from the heavens.

I quell the nausea rising from deep within and simply laugh. Gregorio's eyes lose their fanatical gleam and, for a moment, he blinks in confusion. Pandora aims to land directly on my head—

—and in the instant before it does, I reroute its trajectory to Gregorio's own skull.

§ § §

"You are a disciple of God. As the flesh of man, you transcend His will."

It was several years ago, on the day of that trial. Gregorio had been pushed down to the ground and pinned by other crusaders. Yet his eyes didn't lose one iota of their shine. They showed absolutely no sign of regret or exhaustion.

He rolled his shoulders back and lifted his face, whispering to me as I breathed raggedly.

"Ares Crown. I pray that someday we shall fight alongside each other."

I stood there, my breathing becoming still more ragged, and even though he was restrained, Gregorio never lost his determination.

Ultimately, our battle was never decided, and if we'd kept fighting, I'd have come out on top. However—

In the end, who can really be called the victor? Even now I have no way of knowing.

"Ares, are you okay?"

"...Yeah..."

She must have followed us. She didn't come through the window but ran out through the front entrance of the church.

Amelia is in complete shock at the sight of me, covered in mud, and

Gregorio, splayed out on the ground. Cloudy blood oozes from his head, but he's not dead, just unconscious. At Gregorio's level, even without using Heal, he'll come to in no time flat.

Next to him lies Pandora, the cause of his incapacitation. Ever since he was knocked out, his precious "friend" hasn't budged an inch.

"How are Toudou and everyone?"

"They're safe. I've healed them and put them to sleep."

I'm finally awash with relief at this news. My shoulders relax, and my entire body shakes violently. Amelia rushes to support me, but I manage to stay standing on my own. I'm not injured or even particularly tired. This is purely mental. Amelia makes a face and grumbles.

"Hmph..."

That was a hell of a fight. It was way more exhausting than when I battled Zarpahn. I'd been prepared for the worst, but even so, did I really imagine—that I'd go head-to-head with the Mad Eater?

The idea of joining forces with him repulses me, but being stuck as his adversary was...way too intense. Not to mention, he hasn't changed one bit from how I remembered him. I wish I could at least just stick with fighting followers of darkness.

"Did you kill him?"

"He's alive. He's just passed out from being hit on the head with his own weapon."

"? ...What on earth...?"

Amelia cocks her head to the side. I silently point to the trunk and chant.

"Holy Bind."

A pale light extends from my hand and adheres to the front of the trunk. I manipulate the binding light without moving my hand and pull on it hard. The trunk flies into the sky at a high velocity, and Amelia's eyes follow its progress.

This is the true nature of Gregorio's Pandora's Coffin. Knowing how it works, I couldn't care less.

My weapon and Gregorio's are made from the same metal. Aside from their shape, there's only one other major difference.

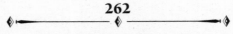

Holy Bind works only on followers of darkness. Naturally, it's ineffective against metal, but an object covered in demon skin is another story. Attaching two threads of binding light to both sides of the trunk, one from each hand, it's completely possible to open and close it.

Gregorio, you're unquestionably an ingenious fellow, but this isn't a street performance, you little shit.

No one would expect the man called the Mad Eater to stoop to such pathetic—excuse me, *unique*—battle tactics in a million years. But even taking this into account, there's no doubt that he and I are completely incompatible.

Followers of darkness cannot cast Holy Bind, but I can. Gregorio is more skilled at precise manipulation than I am, but maximum output is determined by holy energy—where I am far superior. The fact that I took control of Pandora is an unimaginable outcome.

Regardless, Gregorio knew that using Pandora's Coffin would ultimately pit me against a follower of darkness, which is precisely the kind of battle tactic I would expect from him.

"Looking back, once the trunk started flying at me, Gregorio mainly attacked with kicks, and he opened the metal clasp with his hands. There were hints... Or perhaps he was giving me hints on purpose..."

At this juncture, I can't be sure that Gregorio really intended to defeat me at all. He used a sneak attack, but I have vastly superior fundamentals, and defeating me head-on, on even ground without any obstacles, would prove difficult. If he really wanted to win, he would've fought me indoors, where he could take cover.

Also, if Gregorio had just kept his mouth shut, it would have taken me a lot longer to realize how his mechanism functioned. I still don't know what he was thinking and am truly not interested, but what he said could be true—perhaps he attacked me just to assess the extent of my faith.

Amelia nods in response, clearly disinterested, and looks down at Gregorio again.

"...Can't we just slit his throat right now while he's lying there?"

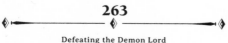

"...No, we can't."

Her proposal is highly appealing.

But even Gregorio would admit defeat at this point. And Creio has ordered him to stop.

I look toward the heavens. The sun had gone down before I realized it, and the sky is bloodred.

I sigh deeply and stretch my back before reaching down to Gregorio, face in the mud, and hoisting him up by the arm. Even with a disturbing nickname like the Mad Eater, he's unbelievably light.

"We're going home. Time for a new plan."

"Yes, I agree. A new plan— Um... Can we take a little time off?"

"Don't worry. I can use holy techniques to heal my fatigue."

"...That's not what I'm getting at—"

I leave Amelia griping to herself and get to walking.

"The overdone sense of justice is a crime."

Epilogue
The Melancholy of Ex Deus

"I see. Well done, Ares."

It has been a full day since my beatdown—or perhaps persuasion—of Gregorio, and this is all Creio has to say after hearing the full account.

It was an awful fight. I'd anticipated a skirmish and was appropriately prepared—the only reason it finished without worse consequences. Had I not had ample preparation, the result would have been far more severe.

Truthfully, Amelia and I had already been on standby in the next room when Toudou met with Gregorio. We were there to respond...no matter what happened.

The reason we didn't rush into the room until Toudou had lost consciousness was because...I thought Toudou needed to be taught a lesson first.

Amelia finishes getting herself ready and packs the supplies she's purchased into a rucksack. We're making ready to move on to our next location. I glance over at her before continuing my conversation with Creio cautiously.

"I'd prefer not to fight another member of our order—ever again."

It wasn't close, but going in cold, I could easily have lost. If Gregorio had taken me more seriously, it could have been anyone's match.

Creio contemplates the meaning of my words and replies dryly.

"Relax, Ares. The only crusader who would attack you or the Holy Warrior—is Gregorio."

"How the hell could there be anyone else?!"

I can't help shouting. But the worst is over now. I need to think positively. *Positively.*

Aside from the few oddballs, pretty much every crusader follows the orders of a cardinal. At least, most of them do. That's why the worst is now over.

"How is the Holy Warrior's level coming along?"

"It's gone up a bit. He hasn't reached his goal, but aside from that, the fact that he's been able to mitigate his fear of the undead is a big achievement."

"So he hasn't entirely overcome it, then...?"

"It should no longer prove a major obstacle in battle. His problem seems to stem from an aversion to the grotesque, which means high-level undead won't be an issue."

Almost all high-level undead take on a human form, like Zarpahn. It's a bit of a letdown if Toudou's issue stems from the enemy's appearance, but...there's no longer any worry of him withering in the face of high-level demons.

Toudou and his party's wounds have healed completely. Gregorio also regained consciousness and has obediently followed my orders. I also made him apologize to Toudou and the others for having attacked them. I've taken every measure necessary.

There were some complications, but judging solely from the results, Toudou's party has acquired a priest, and every potential latent issue has been squashed. One could say that the challenges this region poses have all been cleared.

"It's up to Toudou, but we should head to Golem Valley next. Before long, we need to truly invest in raising his level to appropriate standards."

These are, however, merely my own wishes. If they decide to stay here awhile longer to raise Spica's level, then we will accompany them on that task. At the very longest, we'll be here for another month.

If they conclude that moving on without leveling Spica up further is best, then I'll have to come up with a quality plan for raising Spica's level in Golem Valley.

"The overdone sense of justice is a crime."

If a priest is a party's only low-level member, the balance is immediately thrown out of whack. In some cases, intelligent undead enemies will go straight for a party's priest—the source of healing. There's a limit to how well we can protect Spica.

I've come up with a plan. I haven't been there in years, but I used to level up in Golem Valley myself. I'm more familiar with it than the Great Tomb. Before the battle with the Demon Lord intensifies any further, it would be ideal to increase Amelia's level as well.

"Understood. Let me know if anything comes up."

Creio makes his final remarks before the transmission is cut. I stretch lightly.

The problem occupying my mind for the past few days has vanished, and I'm in a good mood. But I must remain vigilant. There's sure to be a new obstacle waiting around the next corner. Now is the best time to level Toudou's party up before something else rears its ugly head.

Amelia has finished packing and looks at me suddenly, asking, "By the way, was Gregorio…strong?"

"He's a monster."

Gregorio came at me full strength when I figured out Pandora's mechanism, but focusing his attention on offense left his defense lacking. If that hadn't happened, our fight would have gone on much longer. At any rate, he's not an enemy—yet.

Gregorio wasn't being serious. At the very least, he had no intention of killing me. Or…that's what I want to believe.

Remembering the incident puts me back in a foul mood, and I furrow my brow.

"I never want to fight him again…"

"But Gregorio can't cast buffs, right?"

She's correct. Gregorio can't cast buffs, and the buffs I can cast are incredibly powerful. Plus, my level is higher than his, and he wouldn't be able to compete with me no matter how high his combat skills are.

Yet Gregorio has something I don't. I shrug and stare out the window far into the horizon.

"...Yeah, that's right. He can't cast buffs—but he has divine protection."

"Divine protection? ...The divine protection of Ahz Gried?"

Of course not. If he did, I would renounce my title as a disciple of the God of Order!

"No...of the God of Militarism."

It's not on the same level as Toudou's divine protection from the God of War, but it still vastly raises physical strength and one's capacity to shatter barriers.

It's a divine protection often received by those who stake their lives on battle. Of course, the physical strength is a sought-after benefit, but many powerful enemies or items have defensive barriers cast on them, for example—the Devil-Faced Knight and Toudou's shield and armor.

Any capacity to impede these barriers, especially when fighting against the undead, is extremely advantageous.

Amelia's cheeks twitch lightly at my response.

"...If he's a priest, then why does he have divine protection from the God of Militarism?"

"Probably because it's better than divine protection from the God of Order."

"W-well... If you put it that way, I suppose."

Amelia tilts her head to the side, seemingly unsatisfied. It's a good thing he has divine protection. If he was that strong without it, that would qualify as fraud. It's not even an issue of talent.

In that moment, I hear a knock at the door. The only people in this village who know where I'm staying are Spica, Gregorio, and members of the Church. I unlock the door to see Spica standing there. She clutches the sleeves of her priest's robe, now looking proper on her, and appears uncomfortable. She's wearing the pendant I gave her.

Looking back, she was the one who suffered the most during this whole ordeal, having been shuffled around from beginning to end without receiving any proper information.

That said, it's all in the past. Moving forward, she'll need to constantly be at the center of the fray. Her powers are still very raw, but

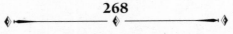

since she proved her ability to properly relay the status of Toudou and his party, she's already far more useful than Glacia.

"What's up, Spica? Is something the matter?"

I've summoned her before, but this is the first time she's come to see me on her own volition. I look toward Amelia, but she says nothing and turns away. I lead Spica into the room and sit her down in a chair.

"Did something happen with Toudou and the others?"

"No…"

Spica shakes her head.

She must have something hard to say, as she drops her head and remains silent. I don't say anything, giving her the chance to speak first. After waiting a full few minutes, Spica finally takes a deep breath and looks up. The hesitation that filled her eyes just a few minutes ago has vanished completely.

"There's just one thing I wanted to talk about."

She speaks with conviction. Looking back, Spica has changed considerably from my first impression of her. Given that it's been only a few days, the difference is almost too great.

The person in front of me isn't some timid little girl. She's still inexperienced but clearly bears the full responsibility of a human being. I remain silent and listen for Spica to continue. Suddenly, she announces:

"I will not be joining Toudou's party."

"…What?"

Spica bows deeply…deep enough that her head nearly touches her stomach, and then leaves the room. I glance at Amelia, who'd been listening absentmindedly, and shake my head.

I am mentally depleted, my mind heavy. Perhaps I should really take some time off.

After several moments pass, Amelia mumbles, "…Are you okay with this?"

There's no rhyme or reason for it, and yet—

I look to the ceiling and remember Spica's gaze, cast directly at me.

They were the eyes of someone who came totally prepared. It was a dim light of conviction, but it was absolutely there. Even if I tried to talk her down, she wouldn't have lost her resolve.

"For better or worse… There's nothing we can do. It's Spica's choice."

"…I suppose you're right. But your dagger…"

Amelia mutters, still seemingly unconvinced. I force a smile and shake my head again.

"We need to restock on weapons anyway. I mean, it was an expensive dagger, but it's not a particularly unique one. I can get as many as I want later. At the absolute worst, I'll fight empty-handed until then."

The dagger I used as my sub-weapon is still hanging from Spica's waist. It will likely come in very handy for her. Not to mention, it's a simple token of atonement for taking Spica's life—which would have likely played out without incident—and throwing it into chaos for my own selfish reasons.

"Amelia, don't look so irritated. We'll modify our plan accordingly."

"…Understood."

I'll need to contact Creio again…

I catch a glimpse of my harrowed expression in the window and heave another deep sigh.

They might call me Ex Deus, but as a priest, when things like this happen—all I can do is pray.

For a glorious future for Spica. And may she find good fortune.

§ § §

In that moment, Spica was undoubtedly scared to death. She'd seen Gregorio Legins turn into a monster before her very eyes, and then the pandemonium that ensued.

She was terrified. Terrified of the fact that she couldn't do a single thing.

Even though the bind that had immobilized her had been broken and Gregorio was already gone, she couldn't move from the spot where

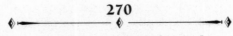

she sat on the floor. She could barely feel her legs and couldn't put any strength into them. Her hands would not stop shaking, and her thoughts were in tatters.

She had gotten a little bit used to fighting monsters, but she'd never seen two humans trying to kill each other before.

There was Gregorio, laughing maniacally. Then Toudou and the rest of her party collapsed on the floor. And finally, Ares, rushing in to stop him.

Her heart ached. Her strength dissipated with each ragged breath she exhaled. Only after running her hand along the splintered floorboards did she finally come back to herself—a result of the sudden, sharp pain.

There was no one else in the room. She could see only Toudou, who lay there immobile.

Spica felt completely empty—and powerless. Even when Limis was tossed through the air like a shred of confetti, she could only stare in dumb amazement.

"I have to...heal them..."

Spurred on by impulse, she crawled along the floor toward Limis, who was facedown closest to her. Spica used all her strength to flip her over—not an easy task, given her unconscious dead weight. She squeezed Limis's cold, limp hand.

Spica had read the scriptures and even practiced a little. But she'd still never been able to cast Heal. She tried frantically to cull information from her memory; Heal is generally cast and applied through physical contact.

"Her head...? Shoulder?"

Spica fumbled over Limis's body. Her heart was beating, but Spica didn't know where to apply Heal, especially in a situation like this. Limis wasn't bleeding. Her face was bruised and black and blue. She had lost consciousness.

—*I...I can't do anything.*

The insanity around her left her dizzy, and in that same moment, she heard a familiar voice.

"Not this again... So over-the-top..."

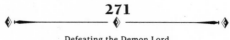

"...A-Amelia?"

Amelia was surveying the chamber after entering unnoticed, and she turned toward Spica at the sound of her voice. Belying her initial statement, her expression was completed nonplussed.

"Why...are you here...?"

"Because I have been assigned to heal everyone. A second too late, and it would all be in vain."

Amelia approached Toudou, who lay unconscious near the wall, and expertly flipped her over. She took her pulse and checked her pupils before gently placing her hand on Toudou's head.

The bright, soft green light that emanated from Amelia's palm was exactly what Spica had been after earlier—Heal.

"Um... Amelia... What should I...do...?"

"You're fine as you are, doing nothing."

"B-but..."

Amelia turned her gaze to Spica, who stuttered a response.

Her eyes were indigo blue. She didn't seem disappointed in Spica, neither was she looking down on her. Spica knew the true nature of this expression full well—it was apathy.

"Sister Spica, you simply aren't capable of anything yet. At the least, please do not get in my way."

"!"

Spica's breath momentarily caught in her throat at Amelia's blunt command. Casting her aside, Amelia continued attending to the party members in turn. Finally, she approached Spica and took her hand, which was bleeding slightly.

"Um... Don't worry about me... Please, just see to Mr. Ares..."

Spica's cut wasn't deep and hadn't received a direct hit. She couldn't think of anything but Ares and Gregorio, who had flown out the window. Yet Amelia's reply was curt.

"That won't be necessary."

"Huh—? B-but...why?"

"Because—Ares would never lose to a fellow priest."

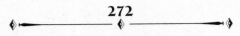

Amelia's assertion was filled with something far greater than confidence.

I hate how useless I was.

The reason she feels this way is the massive contrast between what she is capable of now and what she was capable of before. Therefore, this was no longer an instance of *I couldn't do anything* but rather, *I didn't do anything*.

Previously, the church assigned Spica's duties. All she needed to do was complete the tasks at hand, but currently, she couldn't do the jobs that needed attending. Well—in complete honesty, she still would. But the fact of the matter is, such work would no longer satisfy her.

She has gained levels and physical strength. She has learned holy techniques, albeit only the most rudimentary of them. Yet with each new accomplishment, a feeling of restlessness grows inside her. She can feel herself maturing. But at the same time, that only reinforces how power-less she feels.

In Yutith's Tomb, she had to be protected. On the first day, her com-patriots, whom she had just met, faced injury due to a task that had been assigned to her and only her.

On the second and third days, Spica learned how to use holy techniques but was still completely useless. And then, Ares's battle with Gregorio happened. When Spica saw Toudou, bashed and beaten, facedown on the ground, she quickly understood the difference between herself, capable only of cowering and shaking in fear, and those who could stand up to the fight.

Age. Gender. Birthplace. Experience. Many factors influenced her, but Spica was overcome with emotion in that moment—a miserable sense of self-hatred. She held deep-seated regret at being unable to do more than just silently watch her companions, who had delved deep into the vile and dangerous Great Tomb for her sake, over the course of multiple days.

She should have taken action. Even if she lost, even if she couldn't do anything, she should have faced the fight head-on. Most people would probably tell her she was wrong or there was no point. There was noth-ing she could do about it.

Yet even if they were right, she should have stood in the face of her enemies. If not for her party—then for her sake and hers alone. Why? Because righteousness that lacks power holds no meaning at all.

Then again, if Spica didn't have anyone to compare herself to, she likely would have stuck with Toudou's group. However, quite "fortunately," it turns out Spica has a particular example to follow. She finally acknowledges the change she's gone through and the emotions she never realized hid under the surface until now.

To put it simply, now that she is aware of a world previously hidden to her—Spica has become just a little bit *greedy*.

"Oh-ho. So you want to work below me... You really are a strange one, Sister Spica."

Just as Spica had requested, a man appears before her.

Gregorio Legins. The most relentless priest Spica knows. He looks at Spica with a gentility that contradicts his behavior just a few days earlier.

Spica rests her quivering hand on her knee but remains raptly focused on the man sitting in front of her. Although he looks to be more or less the same age as Spica, and though he may be a priest, this man had laid a severe beatdown on Toudou and her party members, the three of whom were able to defeat scores of undead.

Not sensing an iota of the crashing wave of emotions storming Spica's mind, Gregorio tries calmly persuading her.

"Please allow me to pay respects to your courage. Furthermore, I have a duty to answer it. Sister Spica—if you are asking for tutelage, you should really be asking Ares Crown, not me."

"But...why?"

Gregorio puts his hand on his chin and smiles mildly in response to her question.

"Because it's safer, Sister Spica. If you cannot pass a trial of mine, you shall die. This...is no manner of jest. There is a heavy price to pay for such power."

Gregorio's voice possesses the particular awe-inspiring tone that

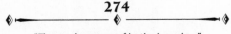

"The overdone sense of justice is a crime."

comes with relaying the truth. Spica shudders in response, but she answers quickly.

"...Ares can't teach me."

"I see. And why is that?"

"Because Ares is...too nice."

He prepared equipment for her. He helped her level up. He helped her wipe away her fear of the undead. He taught her a holy technique. He gave her so many things—so much that mere thanks could never repay.

Gregorio's expression changes subtly upon seeing Spica's shift in demeanor and tone. His eyes are distorted from sheer joy.

"That is truly fantastic, Sister Spica. There is no substitute for the will to face a trial on one's own. You evaluated Ares and myself and chose me. How many priests could do the same—?"

"It's...not that grand a gesture, Mr. Gregorio."

"...?"

Spica caresses the minute craftsmanship of the cross-scale necklace hanging at her chest.

It's the only evidence of her priesthood; she hasn't passed any examination and lacks what even the lowest-level clerics carry as proof of their faith. The necklace is all she has to show for her will to join the fold.

Spica drops her head to her chest but quickly looks up. She stares at Gregorio with her translucent gray eyes.

"Mr. Gregorio. This has nothing to do with my resolve. This is simply my—desire."

Desire manifest from a restlessness burning in her heart. Something she never had in her innocuous, directionless former life. Something she has never known.

And now that she does, there's no going back.

"I'm just—jealous. Of the people who can fight, of those who can face their enemies, of those who can protect and those who have something *to* protect."

She doesn't want to simply receive—she wants to give. That's the desire she feels.

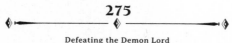

Defeating the Demon Lord

It's a luxurious craving, and she is still unsuited for it. Spica under-stands this. That's why she is reaching out and willing to pay any sacrifice—she truly believes.

Spica is aware of how self-serving this is. She was given the chance to become a priest out of pure necessity. Taking that chance and then throwing it to the wind would be far too selfish, no different from kick-ing sand in everyone's faces.

Nonetheless—there is no other way forward. Her desire has already become palpable instinct.

She's sure to have regrets unless she takes action. That much is crys-tal clear, which is why she says once more, with conviction:

"Please, Mr. Gregorio—make me your disciple."

Her voice is timid but flooded with emotion. Gregorio's smile fades, and he reaches his hand out to stroke his trunk lying beside him.

"Sister Spica. Do you know how old I am?"

"...Huh?"

His answer has nothing to do with Spica's request. She looks Grego-rio up and down again in bewilderment.

She has no clue as to his age. He has black hair and black eyes, and his small stature makes him look relatively young. He comes off quite mature, but based on appearance alone, Spica doesn't think he's much older than herself.

But that can't be right. No such human being exists.

Gregorio chuckles. He's busy observing Spica excitedly.

"The destruction of my hometown, the very thing that drove me to become a crusader—was already twenty-five years ago. At the time, I was fourteen years old—thirteen years and ten months, to be precise."

"Twenty-five...years ago?"

"I shall never forget, nor can I. It was a fateful day. As my hometown was enveloped in flames, the corpses of my friends and family and the innocent townspeople were piled up high as a mountain, their precious blood watering the soil. On that day, I became a crusader. Sister Spica,

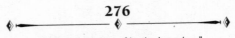

from that day forward, I have not aged a single day…in order to drive out all the darkness of our world."

It is an absurd tale, the likes of which Spica has never heard before. But Gregorio is serious. He speaks so earnestly that Spica herself doesn't find his story strange at all.

Gregorio continues imparting his wisdom to Spica in a near whisper, his expression not unlike that of a demon.

"Sister Spica, allow me to teach you one lesson. You are greedy. Indeed, very greedy. But there are a few things I understand. Powerlessness. Impatience. Despair that engulfs your entire being. Spica, what you need above all else is—"

He truly is a demon; this is the whisper of one. But Spica is confident she's getting the right answer. She can't imagine a more effective means to get what she wants.

"—*the resolve to kill everything in your path.* You certainly have a nice item there, Sister Spica."

Gregorio looks to Spica's waist, where her dagger hangs. She just received the mythril blade from Ares earlier, when she went to tell him that she would be studying under Gregorio. She removes it silently and places it on the table.

"Ares is truly overprotective. I can understand why you trust me. Sister Spica, this blade—will keep you safe. It has been blessed for your well-being and future."

Gregorio continues musingly, yet there is fire in his voice. Ares didn't say anything of the sort when he gave Spica the dagger, but she knows it's true.

Just then, Gregorio declares gleefully, "However, now is the time—for you to commit yourself to slaughter, in order to obtain what it is you desire."

"…"

Spica swallows a lump in her throat. These are bold words; there is no sign of any jest.

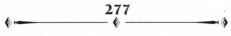

277

She has reached an understanding: Gregorio himself is a result of the same path. Even if they come from different circumstances, their final destination is the same. Gregorio is a man who has thrown away everything for what he wants. It's a fact, no matter how much one tries to deny it.

Gregorio doesn't wait for Spica to reply. He simply takes note of the expression on her face and nods in approval.

"You resemble me in so many ways, Sister Spica. Very well—I shall give you my blessing. I promise to turn you into a splendid crusader."

Of all the myriad stars that shine in the night sky, only one of them is the origin of Spica's name—though she doesn't know which. But there is no doubt it's a lucky star.

Spica has gained the privilege of knowing what it is she seeks, something that a great number of people in this world do not even know for themselves. What greater fortune is there?

Spica reaffirms her resolve and determination before looking up at Gregorio.

It's high noon. The stars have yet to rise in the sky, but Spica knows they are there.

§ § §

Yutith's Tomb, first floor.

Toudou was gripped with terror the first time she came down here. But now, she is completely used to the dark void and how the damp, cold air prickles her skin.

She walks briskly along the underground passageways, and her shoulders are no longer stiff. Facing forward, she addresses Aria in her usual cadence.

"Maaan, I didn't see that coming at all... I can't believe the choice Spica made."

"You're telling me. But...if that's her decision, then there's nothing we can do about it."

Aria answers Toudou from behind, walking just as calmly as the hero.

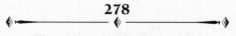

"The overdone sense of justice is a crime."

"I'm worried about her, though… I wonder if she'll be okay?"

The moment Limis speaks, a wraith glides toward them along the ceiling. It instantly vaults at Toudou, having noticed her, and begins attacking from above. As it moves to strike her in complete silence, Toudou jokes—

"This is Spica we're talking about. She'll be totally fine."

—and expertly draws the holy sword Ex before nonchalantly cleaving the wraith in two. It must have been a critical hit, because the creature disappears into thin air without unleashing a single scream. Limis blinks in amazement.

"…Not bad, Nao. Were wraiths always that easy for you to kill?"

"? …Ohhh… Now that you mention it…"

In response to Limis's remark, Toudou realizes something for the first time. Her body just…moves. Ever since finishing that three-day slog, her movements work in complete harmony.

After vanquishing one thousand undead, the fear smoldering in the back of her mind has suddenly vanished into vapor. Toudou opens and closes her fists, furrows her brow, and cocks her head to the side.

"…Come to think of it, I feel pretty good, too."

Aria mumbles a response with the same curious look on her face as Toudou before drawing her sword. She plants her foot lightly on the ground. A single living dead is approaching them sluggishly from the direction they are headed. She rushes toward it and bisects it from shoulder to pelvis with a quick, fluid motion. The living dead vanishes a split second later, leaving only a magic crystal behind, rolling on the ground. Aria stares at the blade of her sword.

"It's strange… My body feels so light. Did something happen? I haven't even leveled up recently…"

"Hmm… Well, at any rate, it looks like we'll be fine without Spica."

Spica told Toudou only yesterday that she'd be temporarily leaving the party. There is no real reason for them to be back down in the Great Tomb, but the group wants to make sure they can take on undead without Spica.

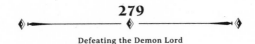

But they already know the answer by now. Things are going swimmingly, even more so than when they had Spica with them.

"? I'm not...scared at all..."

"...Nao, did you eat something weird?"

Limis looks suspicious as she makes her rather rude comment.

A peculiar set of rattling footsteps echoes throughout the passageway. Toudou puts her sword away and raises her palm in the direction of the sound. Her mind is filled with recurring images of the numerous undead she has faced. She stifles this memory and recites a small prayer for a miraculous arrow of light to pierce the darkness.

"Breaking Arrow."

An arrow of light appears. This is Toudou's first successful exorcism, yet she isn't thrilled—only mildly satisfied. The arrow's brilliant holy light tears through the darkness and impales the walking bones, still hidden from view, in the skull. It vanishes without a sound.

"Nao... When did you...learn how to—?"

"Just now..."

This is even more unbelievable after having watched how Spica toiled during their three-day trial. Toudou cast an exorcism without so much as a second thought. Aria and Limis gaze in wonder at her extraordinary accomplishment.

Toudou claps her hands together, oblivious to the situation.

"Ohhh... Now I get it."

"...What do you get?" asks Limis, still astounded.

Toudou's bangs have grown quite long compared with the beginning of their journey, and she sweeps them out of her eyes before telling Limis what she just realized.

"I'm not scared of living dead or wraiths anymore because...Gregorio was way more terrifying."

"Yeah..."

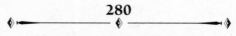

Aria pipes up in agreement. She has a complicated expression on her face, and it's hard to tell if she's happy or sad.

"Ugh... Honestly, the both of you..."

"I—I mean—Gregorio said he was just testing us and had no intention of killing anyone."

"...Looking back on it, though, I think he really wanted to kill us. But that's just me."

Toudou truly thought she was going to die. The second before she lost consciousness, she was prepared to never awaken. But awaken she did, and there to meet her was Gregorio, completely aloof. Her wounds were fully healed.

Toudou will never forget the words he said to her when she woke up, bewildered by the strange turn of events.

"'Righteousness that lacks power holds no meaning at all,' huh...?"

"I suppose roughing him up a bit might be overkill..."

Aria groans, her expression stern.

To add insult to injury, all three of them had been knocked unconscious, and therefore none of them had any idea what more had happened. They tried asking Glacia, but she wouldn't say anything.

Toudou sighs lightly and mutters with conviction, "...Whatever. What doesn't kill us makes us stronger. We've learned so much on this journey."

"Yeah, you're right..."

Limis and Aria agree with Toudou.

Strong enough to save the world. Strong enough to defeat the Demon Lord. The gods of this vast universe have given Naotsugu Toudou their divine protection for that very purpose.

No matter what kinds of trials and tribulations await her in the future, Toudou must get through every single one.

Aria grips the hilt of her sword tightly as she recalls that brutal scene and how easily Gregorio wiped the floor with them. Limis breathes a light sigh and looks to Garnet resting on her shoulder.

"...Let's give it our all so that we don't lose to Spica."

"Agreed... But will she really be okay?"

Limis looks worried as she stares into the depths of Yutith's Tomb.

Toudou recalls the sincerity in Spica's eyes and how downcast yet serious she looked as she gathered all the party members together. They couldn't say no to her—especially Toudou.

"'I'll be apprenticing under Gregorio so that I can be useful to the party.' ...Can you believe that?"

Toudou smiles bitterly as she thinks of Spica.

"...All we can do is pray for her."

"She seems so timid, but she's actually pretty reckless... That girl."

"She sure is."

"I'm hungry."

The party turns back, cutting through the miasma and incessant undead attacks as they head for the surface. Tasked with dispelling darkness from the world, the Holy Warrior doesn't have time to stand around.

But there is one thing Toudou is sure of.

No matter how far along the path they travel, Spica is certain to catch up.

"The overdone sense of justice is a crime."

Part Three

Still Continues

Mankind Yet Strives for Hope

The view on the horizon is unparalleled in scope.

Atop a steep cliff at the edge of town, the blue sky stretches infinitely in all directions unlike anything Toudou has ever seen, and the golden yellow of the valley is majestic and beautiful.

It's summertime, but due to the altitude, the temperature is relatively low. Yet, the cool air and breeze make them feel as if their hearts and minds are somehow being cleansed.

"So this is...Golem Valley..."

"It's...breathtaking..."

Toudou sighs in wonderment, and Limis concurs in a hushed tone as she holds her head to keep her hat from flying away.

Golem Valley is among the foremost dangerous locations in all of the Kingdom of Ruxe. The rugged natural features of this land make it an unsuitable place for humans to gather. The returns from fighting golems, which are an effective source for leveling up and which drop a number of valuable materials, are large. But to properly hunt them requires a certain level of competency.

Mercenaries and monster hunters who gather in the nearby town to level up are all fairly high level themselves, and the mercenaries the group has seen on the road have a sharper glint in their eyes than the ones they met in Vale Village. The atmosphere here is completely different.

This is Limis's and Aria's first time, and their eyes are on stalks as they take in the surroundings. Aria remembers something she heard previously and says, "The royal knights all come here for training after reaching a certain level…and I've heard that the views are the most memorable in the entire kingdom."

"Is that so…? It really is gorgeous. I wish Spica could've seen it, too…"

Aria smiles softly in response to Toudou's whisper and continues.

"Let's find an inn. The day grows late. We need to formulate a plan."

"Yeah, I agree… Oh… Look there, is that a golem?"

Toudou suddenly spots something moving below them and leans against the guardrail, extending her arm. Limis gasps in shock and pulls on Toudou's collar.

"Okay, we get it, so let's hurry up and get a move on. We've got plenty of nasty battles ahead of us."

"All right, all right…"

Toudou takes one last look up at the sky as Limis tugs on the back of her hair, then inhales deeply, acclimating herself to their new surroundings.

§ § §

We're a half day behind Toudou when we arrive in First Town at dusk. It's been a few years since my last visit, yet everything seems the same.

I hear the sounds of wagon wheels screeching and a multitude of footsteps reverberating. Strong-willed merchants have made their way to this extremely remote region to sell their wares alongside powerful mercenaries aiming to advance their levels. Mages also settle here to study the golems, and priests reside in the local church to provide them divine protection.

Compared with the plains, this is an oppressive environment, yet seeing the tumultuous nature of this place with one's own eyes gives an intense feeling of the sheer power of life itself.

Originally, Golem Valley was known as a gateway to success for first-rate mercenaries. Golems are solid and quick, and they don't feel pain or exhaustion. This is definitely a top-class leveling area, but for

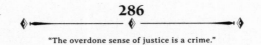

Toudou and his party, it will be an uphill climb. If Toudou can overcome the obstacles ahead of him here, he will definitely become that much better a warrior.

Limis and Aria have their flaws, and I'm really not sure they'll be able to handle this place. But if they can't make it past Golem Valley, there's no hope for them moving forward. If that happens, the party will have to swap out one of their members. And the formerly orphaned Spica is off to study under Gregorio.

I'm counting on you guys. That's all I can say.

As I stew in my own intense feelings, recalling the look on Spica's face when she made that choice for herself, Amelia returns from the church.

She has indigo-blue eyes, and her hair—the same color—is blown by the strong wind, flowing beautifully.

Cooperation with the Church is our lifeline. It's our source of supplies and information on Toudou.

I've already contacted the local church through Creio's good graces, but Amelia went there to ask them to take care of our runner lizard—our transportation for the journey—and to provide instructions to our new recruit who will serve as backup in this area.

"Sorry to keep you waiting, Ares."

I refrain from answering and look behind Amelia with strained eyes.

She's not there. The new recruit Amelia was supposed to bring with her is nowhere to be seen. I have a splitting headache. I grasp my forehead and ask Amelia a question.

"Hey... Where's Stephenne?"

"...Hmm?"

Amelia turns around in confusion, her eyes darting left and right over her surroundings. There are lots of people on the street but not enough for someone to easily wander off. Not under *normal* circumstances.

Stephenne is quite short, but her black hair is extremely rare for these parts and makes her stand out considerably. But she's not there. She's not anywhere.

Amelia bites her lip and looks up at me sheepishly.

"...Um... She was just here... She was following me; I'm sure of it."

"Are you serious?"

"I told her to make sure to stay behind me..."

How can she go missing during her very first task—just following Amelia?!

"What should we do...? She could have...fallen off the cliff."

"Not a chance in hell. There's fencing set up wherever it's really steep. She wouldn't fall from there unless she was a complete moron."

"You must not know Stey, Ares."

Amelia whispers with utmost seriousness, and I can't find it in me to laugh it off.

"...Find her."

Amelia murmurs an incantation and casts a detection spell. As I watch her out of the corner of my eye, I ponder what I'm going to tell Creio.

Shit... I was too quick to request backup...

"The overdone sense of justice is a crime."

Special Story

Amelia's Activity Report Journal Vol.②

Surprisingly, the room is empty when I return to the inn.

Amelia's support in Purif has wrapped up its first stage, and she's gathered together most of her belongings for her departure. So where has she gone…? Not that I have anything special to talk to her about…

Looking around, I notice a leather-bound notebook on the nightstand. She should be all packed, but…

I pick up the notebook nonchalantly, and my eyes pass over the round characters written on the front in blue ink:

Amelia's Activity Report Journal Vol.②

"…What happened to volume one?!"

No—that's not the point. That's not what matters, Ares Crown.

I nearly choke and stop to steady my breathing. What in God's name has Amelia written in here? We've been working together for quite some time, but I still can't read her. I just get wrapped up in her occasional wacky behavior.

"…An activity report journal, huh?"

It'd normally be problematic for me to read her journal, but if this is an activity report, then it's fair game. Besides, I'm her boss.

It might even help me understand her a little better. I forcibly convince myself and open the cover.

○-!-XXXX

I've followed Toudou to Purif and sneaked in after him. This place is more of a dump than I thought. The scenery isn't too great, either. Thirty points.

"Man, that's a harsh review..."

This must be a log from Purif. I'm not sure it qualifies as an activity report, though...

〇-@-XXXX

I went to the church to find a sister, per Ares's orders. It's a hassle, but this is my chance to score points with him. If there aren't any full-fledged sisters, we can always make one. I chose the best-looking girl who might be able to hack it in Toudou's party. She looks pretty miserable, but once she joins the party...who cares? Ares, who is heartless, should be fine with it.

"...That's just mean."

Her assessment of me is awful, but she looks and acts so serious all the time. She's going too far. I turn to the next page.

〇-#-XXXX

I thought I could take it easy today. Toudou was a piece of shit, though, and Ares looked positively hopeless. I don't know how something so adorable like the undead could be frightening. For now, I've decided to say that I used to be scared of them, too. That should score me more points with Ares. Undead were the staple of my diet—morning, afternoon, and night.

"...No extra points for this... No way."

But really—the staple of your diet? I mean, undead are a great level-up resource for priests, but your phrasing needs work...

〇-$-XXXX

Ares is really nice to Spica for some reason. I wish he'd be nicer to me, not her. Does he have a Lolita fetish?

"..."

"The overdone sense of justice is a crime."

*　　*　　*

○-%-XXXX

Gregorio was here. Gregorio was here. I wish he wouldn't say my name. Actually, he should just die.

"She really hates him..."

○-&-XXXX

Spica decided to join the party. Toudou is very nice, apparently. He's a piece of shit, but maybe he has some redeeming qualities. Ares needs to take a page out of Toudou's book and treat me better. There is a chronic communication deficiency between us. If he gets any worse, I might just disappear!

"What do you mean, 'any worse'?"

Anyway, I'll work on my communication for next time.

○-*-XXXX

Providing support for Toudou. We're stuck in the dark together, but Ares won't come help··· That spineless coward.

"I COULDN'T HAVE HELPED EVEN IF I TRIED, DAMMIT!!"

Who does she think I am?!

You call this an activity report journal? Just who the hell are you report- ing to?! I turn to the next page, but it's blank. Nothing in here even counts as a report...

I feel a headache coming on as I reach the last page, where especially large letters greet me: THIS IS A WORK OF FICTION. ANY RESEM-BLANCE TO ACTUAL ORGANIZATIONS OR PERSONS IS PURELY COINCIDENTAL.

...Amelia, the hell's with this?

I instantly feel exhausted and drained of strength. I have so much shit to give Amelia now. But the first thing I wanna know is...

"...Where the hell is volume one?"

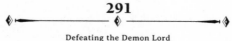

CHARACTER DATA

<table>
<tr><td>NAME</td><td>Gregorio Legins</td></tr>
</table>

【Level】: 83

【Occupation】: Crusader

【Gender】: Male

ABILITIES

Physical Strength: High

Endurance: Moderate

Agility: Very High

Magical Energy: Moderate

Holy Energy: Very High

Will: Very High

Luck: High

EQUIPMENT

Weapon: Pandora's Coffin (a lightweight yet sturdy trunk—bound in demon leather)
Clothing: Robes of the God of Militarism (equipment granted to those who have the divine protection of the God of Militarism—a light, firm priest's robe)

EXPERIENCE UNTIL NEXT LEVEL   96,618,222

A priest affiliated with the Out Crusade. A third-rank crusader nicknamed the Mad Eater. He holds an intense abhorrence of followers of darkness, and his personality hinges on a balance of fanaticism and reason. A veteran of the Out Crusade and feared by many, allies and foes alike. His hobbies include DIY projects and cleaning up garbage.

<table>
<tr><td>NAME</td><td>Spica Royle</td></tr>
</table>

【Level】: 12

【Occupation】: Priest-in-training

【Gender】: Female

ABILITIES

Physical Strength: None

Endurance: None

Agility: None

Magical Energy: None

Holy Energy: A Little

Will: Doing Her Best

Luck: Very High

EQUIPMENT

Weapon: Ares's mythril dagger (able to wield it if she tries hard; can be sold for a large sum)
Clothing: Child's priest robes (soft to the touch)
Accessory: Cross scale pendant (repels miasma—limited effect)

EXPERIENCE UNTIL NEXT LEVEL   1,256

A girl born and raised in Purif. Twelve years old. Her parents were mercenaries, but they passed away when she was very small, and she was then taken in by the Purif church. Highly introverted and easily influenced. Lately she is worried about her weight gain from eating proper meals for the first time. Chores are her specialty, since she had been taught the basics by the church.

AFTERWORD

TSUKIKAGE

Thank you so much for picking up the book in your hands. This is the author, Tsukikage.

Expanding on Volume 1, which was originally published on the website Kakuyomu, this is the edited and revised second volume of *Defeating the Demon Lord's a Cinch (If You've Got a Ringer)*.

In summation of the events of this book, our hero's party has finished their adventure in the Great Forest of the Vale and has traveled to the next village in order to find a priest—and, if circumstances permit, to learn how to cast exorcisms to purify the followers of darkness that inhabit this area. But there's a catch: Our Holy Warrior isn't exactly fond of undead enemies. Will Toudou, our brave protagonist who can't stand the icky undead, live to see tomorrow?! Looks like it. Please enjoy the latest installment in this journey as the group continues to be at the mercy of fate while Ares and company are undoubtedly there to right their path.

Regarding the aforementioned edits and revisions, many were made regarding the two new characters in this volume, who I couldn't fully write about in the original web content. They're two of my favorite characters, so I'd be happy if you came to love them, too. Also, this volume includes newly written text for Amelia's Activity Report Journal Vol. 2. Now just where did the first volume go…?

Lastly, some acknowledgments to wrap things up. To everyone who has supported this series since its beginnings on the web and everyone who started with the published book—thank you so very much. Also, thank you to bob, who has continued to provide beautiful illustrations since Volume 1. I'll do my best to write a story that's on the same level as his wonderful artwork. Last but not least, thank you to my editor, Shukutani, who continues to put so much effort into preparing this book for publication and to everyone in the editing department. I express my deepest gratitude to you all.

"The overdone sense of justice is a crime."

bob Limis really stood out in this volume!

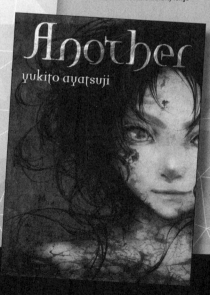

PRESS "SNOOZE" TO BEGIN.

DEATH MARCH TO THE PARALLEL WORLD RHAPSODY

MANGA

LIGHT NOVEL

After a long night, programmer Suzuki nods off and finds himself having a surprisingly vivid dream about the RPG he's working on…only thing is, he can't seem to wake up.

YEN ON

www.yenpress.com

Death March to the Parallel World Rhapsody (novel) © Hiro Ainana, shri 2014 / KADOKAWA CORPORATION
Death March to the Parallel World Rhapsody (manga) © AYAMEGUMI 2015 © HIRO AINANA, shri 2015/KADOKAWA CORPORATION